I0818290

KINGDOMS

OF

BLOOD

For More of Cassie's Works, visit
CassieMorrisonBooks.com

Kingdoms of Blood

Cassie Morrison

Edited by: Charlie Knight
Cover Art by: Elliot Williams
Map and Layout by: Cassie Morrison

Hardcover ISBN: 978-1-7351447-0-2
Ebook ISBN: 978-1-7351447-1-9
Library of Congress Control Number: 2020911486

First Editions May 2021

Published and Printed by
IngramSpark
INGRAM Content Group
One Ingram Blvd.,
La Vergne, TN 37086

IngramSpark.com

*For my Grandma, who made
me fall in love with Norway
over and over again.*

Norwegian Sea

NORDØYA

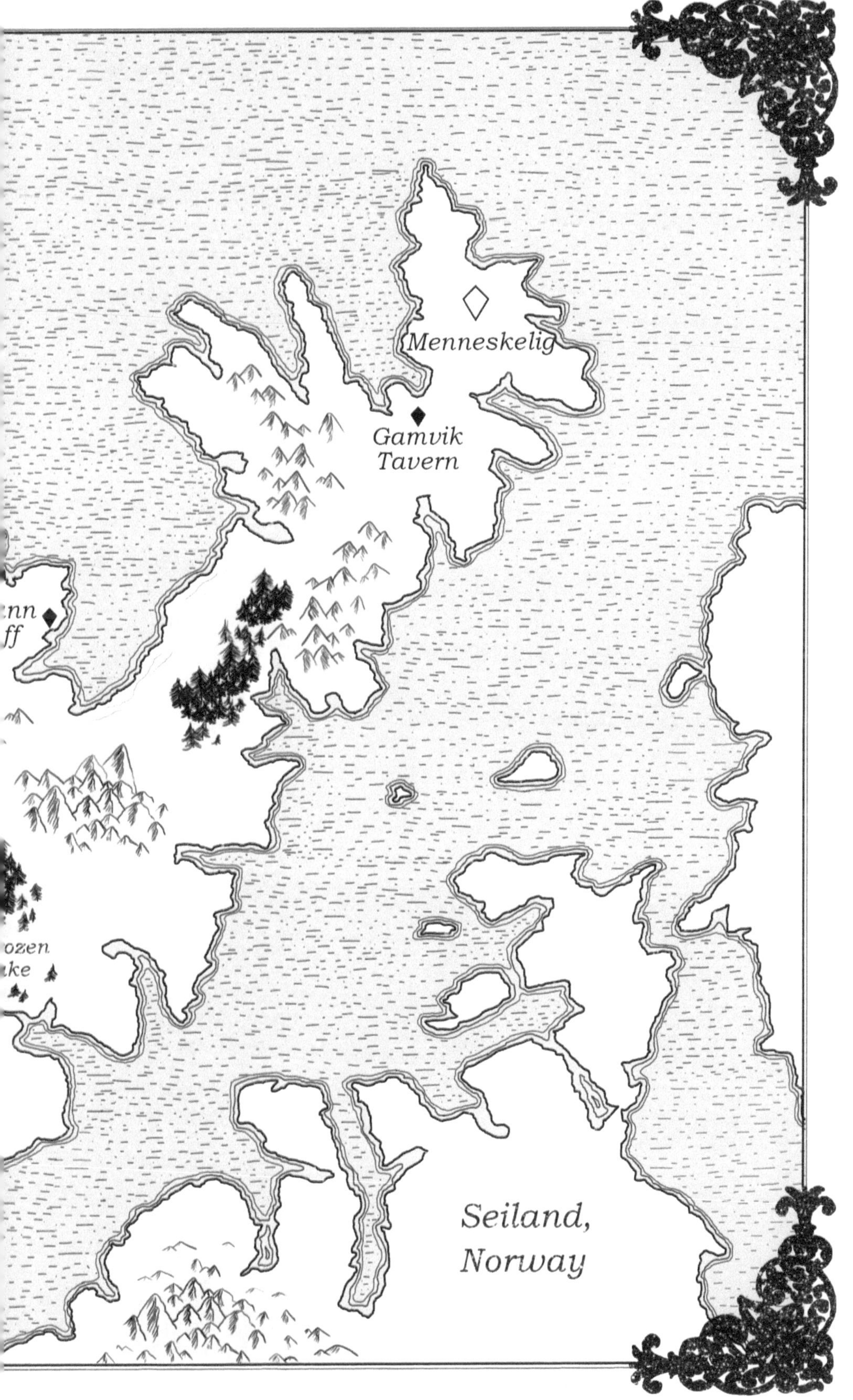
Menneskelig
Gamvik
Tavern
Seiland,
Norway

Kingdoms of Blood

Blod Er Makt

\- Feilfri Crest

LIVSNERVEN

PROLOGUE

KAI

1592

All I see is red.

The color of blood. The color of life.

As a brand-new vampire, you come into the world screeching and thirsty. I can almost remember how it felt to have acid bite through my mouth and throat. It's the same burning I'm feeling now. Through the red, I can see pulses of humans around me. It's like looking through a tangle of arteries and veins, thick with blood just waiting for me.

I snarl, letting my senses lead me. Caden is right on my tail, but I am faster. I dig my feet deeper as we sprint across the island. Snow and ice rip my skin, but it's only small pricks. The skin heals even before I can look down. Despite the arctic weather, I feel hot under my skin. There are humans nearby.

As we close the distance between us and the small group of hunters, I can already taste their blood on my tongue. The thought of ripping into their throats and draining their life away sends shivers down my spine.

My eyes focus now, but I can't see their faces. Only the rapid, red, *hot* pulse of their blood thudding throughout their bodies. I can barely even hear their screams over the sound of their drumming hearts. These are moments that I savor. As a predator, half of the fun is in the chase, the anticipation of the reward. Ripping into their throats now would only result in a quick kill. I want to revel in it.

Is that a sign of maturity? I wonder idly. I don't care. I just take hold of the human's hair and wrench their head to the side, pinning them down with my legs. This human fights back, slapping me and screaming. She's female. I barely notice. I watch in amazement as her blood whips like fire across my eyes. It's incredible, how adrenaline spikes their heart rates. I smile wickedly as I watch the dance of yellow and red in her veins. Humans produce adrenaline when they are afraid. How stupid. They have no idea that it's like a drug to vampires, practically lighting them up like a giant target.

I don't wait any longer. Quick as lightning, I rip into the girl's throat, feeling warm liquid splash across my face. I move quickly to try to catch as much as I can, relishing in the feeling of the feed. The acidic stinging the back of my throat is alleviated, but just barely.

I'm finished with the girl all too soon, and in my search to savor the taste of her blood, Caden has finished the rest of the tribe.

I launch myself at him, growling and snarling like an animal.

"You didn't leave me *anything*." I wrestle him to the ground, and he yelps out, but he's only half-afraid of me.

"You're too slow, big brother," he taunts. I smash his face into the ground. "You shouldn't have wasted so much time on that tiny little girl."

I frown and survey her corpse, just barely feeling a twinge of guilt. She was small, barely old enough to be out in a hunting party. But she had been feisty. She tried to fight me.

I hop off of Caden, and he smirks at me.

"Well, I'm still hungry," I mutter.

"Let's go back home. Maybe we can play with some of the *thralls*," he says.

It's good enough for me. Before I can say anything, he's sprinting off into the distance again. I huff and launch after him, feeling the snow crunch underneath my bare feet.

Before I can blink, we've reached the castle, looming darkly over the rest of Livsnerven. I slow to a quick walk as we pass by nobles. They all turn to bow towards us as we pass. I roll my eyes. It's so annoying to have to pretend to care about politics. Even though, one day, I'll be king. I guess I'll have to care then.

The red returns to my vision as soon as we're past the gates. I can smell the dungeons from here, the sweet smell of the *thralls* living quarters. I smile wickedly at Caden and break into a jog again. He laughs, and I feel him follow me closely. We slow as we move through the human wing of the castle. It's darker here. *Good.*

Thirst bites wildly at my throat like my mouth is being exposed to open flame. I dry-gag at the feeling. I *need* to feed. I move more quickly now, feeling something more than fun dictate my actions. Need and desire intertwine indistinguishably, and by the time we walk through the metal gates, I seize the first woman that I find, seeing nothing more of her than her red hair. Almost as red as the fire singing from her veins.

I sink my teeth into her throat, wallowing in the pleasure that comes from her blood.

"Kai, slow down," Caden grips my shoulders and starts wrenching me away from the lovely woman. I swat him away like he's an annoying fly. "You can't *kill* her, Kai."

I continue drinking, feeling the woman's life drain slowly from her body. Her heartbeat slows and stutters. I can feel my strength returning as her blood seeps into my veins.

"Kai!" Caden shouted.

I rip away from the woman, dropping her on the ground to face my brother. I snarl savagely at him, watching his face contort with fear. Real fear this time. I throw daggers at him with my eyes before settling down to finish the feed.

Slowly, I feel her last drop of life bleed from her neck. Her heart stops. The room stills audibly. Silence pierces my ears.

"Kai," Caden whispers.

I look up at my brother. His face is expectant. Waiting.

Then, several things happen at once. I hear a clanging all around me and a vibrating that pulses throughout my head and body. It's only then that I can see through the red to notice that I'm not alone. There are more people in the room than I'd originally noticed. There are two young girls hunched in the corner watching me, one with skin as dark as midnight and one with snow-like skin. They are clutching one another, shivering and shaking, tears streaking their cheeks.

I look around for Caden, wanting to ask what's happening, when suddenly my vision gives out, and there's a blinding pain tearing across my head and chest. Stars blind my eyes, and a flash of heat across my back makes me sweat. I frantically search my body for the cause of the injury. I can't see anything but the red-haired woman's blood drip from my mouth and stain my hands. In an attempt to stave off the panic, I lose control of my extremities. I press my hands against my temples, trying to soothe the pain, but all I can feel is blistering agony ripping at my eyes. The pain feels like it's coming from *inside* me.

I look down at the red-haired woman in torment, realizing what I've done.

You can't kill a human in Feilfri Castle. It is forbidden.

"Kai, what's happening?" Caden yells as I grip my stomach and gag.

"Moroya," I beg. "Get Moroya."

"What? I don't know what you're saying!"

"The witch, Caden! The witch!" I shriek through the pain and move to grab him by his neck.

"Why? What business is this to the witch?"

"The pain," I choke. "It's unbearable. I need her to heal me."

"That's ridiculous. Nothing can hurt a Pureblood vampire," Caden scoffs at me. I tighten my grip on his neck. "Let go of me!"

"Caden, go get the witch. *Now*," I growl.

He gives me a dark glare before shoving me brusquely away and saying, "Do it yourself."

As he walks away from me, through the far door of the *thrall's* dungeons, the pain tears through me again, like a surge of death radiating through my bones. I fall to my hands and knees, heaving and shuddering from the anguish. Without Caden's help, I won't survive this. I can barely walk to try and find the witch myself. If I scream, I'll just alert the entire castle of my great sin.

Regardless, my eyes pointlessly search for help, pleading with the gods to lift the curse that is slowly crushing me. For the first time in my life, my vision darkens, a wavering black tunnel encroaching on the edges of my sight. There is no red left. Nothing but darkness and torment. Tears roll down my face, and I can't fathom the unbearable betrayal that my own brother would leave me here to die. To him, I am nothing more than a hunting partner.

The pain slowly turns to numbing torture as I grip the stone like I could dig myself a shallow grave and perish. Death would surely be better company compared to this purgatory.

"What is going on?" a voice, like an angel, comes from the doorway.

I turn to face the castle witch, Moroya, standing radiantly above me. She quickly surveys the situation, her expression turning from curious to horrified to grief in a matter of seconds.

"Please," I beg, my voice a haphazard mix of slathering

whispers and savage cries.

"I cannot prevent your fate, *Nikolaj*. I can simply watch. What you will experience next will haunt you for the rest of your life," she says with a voice that's low and full of harsh wisdom. She walks towards me, her skirts dragging across the stone floor. She lays a comforting hand on my shoulder, meaning to console me, but it leaves unseen scorch marks on my skin. "You knew that to kill a human, you would experience that pain seven times over. Or did you forget, Prince?"

I can't answer her. Yes, I had forgotten. I didn't know what that pain would be. I didn't know that it would be worse than death. Instead, I stifle a whimper.

I turn to meet the eyes of the young girls, cradling one another in the corner, trying to find a distraction. I want to take away my mistake. I want to take away the pain. Instead, I feel the blood vessels burst all over my body. The red-haired woman's life slips away, again and again, the pain manifesting in my blood.

I look at the woman below me and cradle her lifeless head. I feel tears stream seamlessly out of my bloodshot eyes. The woman's face is fair and beautiful. How had I not seen it before? I stroke her red hair, soft as silk. Boiling pain sears across my fingertips and up my arms as I keel over the woman. I wretch up all the blood I took from her, tarnishing her beauty with her own blood.

I can feel death as a surety now. It waits for me, just beyond my reach.

I look at the woman's face again, slicked over with bile and blood, and it changes. Before my very eyes, the woman's face turns into my mother's. I watch as the blood eats away at my mother's skin, my mother's hair until her own blood and muscle show through the skin. Acid tears through her flesh and down into the bones, and I shriek, trying my best to wipe away the boiling blood off her face.

This is all my fault. This is *my* fault.

I grip and grapple at the body in front of me until two small hands take mine, pulling me away. My eyes meet the gaze of one of the young girls from before. Her face is round and full of life with eyes as blue as the ocean on sunny days, as brilliant as a cloudless sky. Her hair is red like the dead woman in front of me, and a new wave of anguish rolls over me. This must have been her mother. I killed her mother.

The red-haired woman no longer resembles my dead mother, and her face is intact, though still frozen in death. The young girl's hands are cold against mine, which is shocking for a human. They generally radiate warmth. I must have been blazing in my torment. She pulls at me, tugging me away from her mother, with soundless tears still pouring from her eyes. I follow obediently. I couldn't harm this girl any further.

I stand, feeling the weight of the world on my shoulders, and meet her eyes with mine. Her hands wrap around mine as she pulls me into a tight embrace. She sobs gently against my chest and squeezes her arms around my waist. I cannot resist the warmth of the gesture. Hot, wet tears pour from my eyes, over my lips, and into the girl's hair. She just watched me kill her mother, but without anger or violence, she holds me. I feel my physical pain morph into something wholly different as the young girl cries, staining my shirt.

I wrap my arms around the girl, and my chest explodes with grief. Somehow, this girl watched me experience my pain and somehow declared it penance. She has accepted payment for my sins and forgiven me. I feel my lungs heave with heavy air as I struggle to remain upright in the presence of such grace, such empathy. How can I continue on as I have existed after this? Knowing that I've experienced something worse than death and come out the other side greeted by an angel's forgiveness?

"I'm so sorry," I say over and over again, feeling this girl's grief radiate through me. I look up to meet the witch's gaze where she stands next to the other young girl. "I won't do it again. I will never feed on a human again. I promise."

My words are hardly audible in my sobbing, but the witch nods and stroke's the young girl's brilliantly unkempt hair. I close my eyes and rest my cheek on the red-haired girl's head, holding her in my arms as we cry over our lost youth together. I remain in the grasp of her embrace until she can physically stand no longer. When she collapses in my arms, I follow the dark-skinned witch towards her bed, where I lay the small girl, vowing to never return to the dungeons again.

1
ASTRID

1602

The room is sideways. I'm lying on my left side on a wide wooden table, like the many other humans serving as a meal in the room. I feel a set of cold fingers on my skin, brushing through my hair and touching my neck and shoulders lightly. I smile and close my eyes, feeling small shivers run over my skin. I feel a pair of cool lips underneath my ear and brace myself for the sharp sting of teeth breaking through my skin. The vampire's breath tickles my ear as he drinks, but I don't mind. I like it. I like the way my fingers begin to tingle as he sips on my blood.

When he's finished, he touches my hair again and presses a soft linen cloth to my neck. I open my eyes and look around the room at the other *thralls*. Some of them are wincing and wiggling with pain, something I truly don't understand. Living as a *thrall* to serve in Feilfri Castle is one of the highest honors a human can receive. I've lived here my entire life and have always loved it here.

Still, there are humans, disgusted and confused, hurting from serving their masters. I frown in confusion.

"I'm finished. You can go," the vampire says to me. I clamp down on the cloth and use my free arm to push myself up, slowly, so that I don't become faint. The room spins as I move to sit, my feet dangling lightly over the edge. I turn and bow to him, not meeting his eyes. With my hand still pressed against the cloth, I hop down and start walking towards my chambers in the lowest level of the castle. Some call them dungeons, but we are not prisoners. *Thralls* are simply servants. My feet feel like numb stumps, but I keep going, bowing to other nobles in the hall.

The hallways are lit with large lanterns that flicker as I pass, the dark passages teeming with life as humans and lesser vampires walk to and from the dining hall. I walk by the kitchens, smelling the wonderful food they are cooking as I turn toward the human wing of the castle. The other side of the hall is home to the lesser vampires, those of non-pureblood heritage, such as Halvblods and Dhampyrs, that have chosen to serve the vampire nobility in the kingdom. They seek to please the Pureblood royalty, just like I do. Though they are not very friendly toward us.

I walk into the hall lined with rooms separated by thick iron bars. I turn into my room that I share with my best friend, Alheri. She's a human as well, but she doesn't serve as a *thrall.* She's the kingdom's resident witch. She takes one look at me, and her eyes widen.

"Astrid, let me see." She's on her feet and reaching out to the rag I have pressed to my neck. The blood hasn't stopped flowing since I left the dining hall, and my eyes are starting to blur.

Still, I respond lightly, "I'm fine, Alheri. Please stop worrying about me."

"Nonsense, let me see," she replies curtly, removing the rag from my hand and placing her fingers on my neck. She whispers a chant, and I feel a pinch and small sharp stabbing pains that flicker over the wound as the skin knits back together. She exhales loudly and steps back.

"Thank you," I say. "But when will you realize that I'm perfectly safe? The king wouldn't let any harm come to us."

Alheri scoffs loudly but sits back on her cot, wiping off my blood from her fingers. I rub my hand over the healed wound, constantly impressed with her power. Feeling the sore tendrils, my heartbeat quickens under my fingers, its strength returning.

"Have they brought dinner down yet?" I ask. "I'm starving."

"Not yet," she says. "I'm not sure they will bring it down. We might have to figure it out for ourselves tonight."

"Okay! Do you want to come with me?"

"Sure, I could use a break," she agrees, setting down her tattered notebook.

I listen to her prattle on about the various spells she's working on as we walk. One is hopefully going to speed up the water heating process in the boiler room. It will make everyone's lives a little easier. I smile contentedly as she talks. Her whole face shines brilliantly when she talks about her spells. It's her passion.

My fingers and legs are no longer numb, thankfully, and I practically skip towards the hearth when I catch a hint of freshly baked bread. Stepping into the kitchen, the warmth of the ovens surrounds me like a hug. The room is ablaze with multiple fires, some open and some closed for baking. I step around the giant brick fire pit in the middle of the room. Alheri moves towards the fire instantly.

"Hello!" I call. "How can I help?"

The baker, an older man with tan, leathery skin, looks me up and down.

"We just finished and sent out the last order. Have you two eaten?" he says with a thick accent. "Come sit."

I hop over to the small table, and he brings me a small bowl of soup. I smile widely at him, then take the wooden spoon and dip it into the broth. I sip, careful not to burn my tongue. It's *delicious.* I quickly spoon the contents into my mouth, feeling my stomach growl thankfully. Alheri sits next to me and ladles spoonfuls into her mouth as well.

"Wow! This is exquisite," I say, swallowing a piece of potato. The baker nods at me and continues preparing his dough. As soon as I finish, I get up and ask, "Can I help? Are there dishes?"

"Over by the oven," he says, pointing to the large water basin next to the giant covered ovens.

I move quickly, seeing a hefty stack of dishes soaking in the water. I feel the warmth of the fire color my cheeks. The kitchen is my favorite room in the entire castle. It is the warmest part of the castle as well, though the cold never really bothers me. I love the smells of the rising dough, the tea leaves brewing, the smoky charcoal. I often find myself jealous of the baker and the chef, spending all day near the wonderful smells, but *thralls* are only ordered to a specific post when they prove themselves worthy enough. Though I suppose if the king wanted the baker to do something else, he would, of course, oblige, and someone would need to replace him in the kitchen. Since both the baker and the chef were ordered here specifically by Baldassare, the king, no one but him could order them away from this post. I shake my head. The intricacies of the noble hierarchy are complicated and often leave me confused. I simply do as I'm told.

I fall into the task of washing the dishes, letting my mind wander, humming tunelessly. I pass a damp rag over the various dishes, bowls, plates, and goblets before placing them in the water. Before I know it, the job is finished. Living in a castle filled with vampires, I wonder if most of the food is wasted. It's a shame, really, because the chef here is the very best. His food is always so delicious. I'm often surprised when the king orders feasts, though I suppose the lesser vampires have to eat as well. I wonder if the chef sends the uneaten food across the river to the rest of Livsnerven.

As I dry my hands, my eye catches movement at the doorway. I peek at the door and find an unfamiliar man. I smile and face him, setting the rag down.

"Hello," I say.

"Why hello dear," the man says. His eyes seem unfocused, but he looks at me with a large smile on his face.

"Can I help you with something, sir?" I ask, walking over towards him. I feel the baker watch us, but I pay him no mind.

"I'll say," he says. "Would you mind accompanying me to my room?"

"I don't think that's a very good idea," the baker says, his voice colored with worry. Just like Alheri. I give him a look, then notice that Alheri is looking away from us like she's trying to hide her face. Of course, I will say yes to the man. He's clearly a vampire of nobility. Even if he's just a visiting Pureblood, it is punishable by death to refuse him.

"Nonsense," I say, politely offering my hand to the gentleman. "I would be glad to."

He takes my hand and lifts it to his nose, breathing in loudly. I smile at him when he looks back up.

"Very good, yes. *Very* good," he says and holds my hand tightly. As we make our way out of the kitchen, I smile and wave to the baker with my free hand, paying no credence to the man's wrinkled expression. The noble shows me away from the warmth of the kitchen and back into the dining hall, where I see several of the ruling members of the kingdom. Queen Eileen sits in the corner with that novel she always seems to always carry. King Baldassare and his son Caden are feasting on two ladies, their names I have forgotten. They seem to be enjoying themselves. I bow, but they don't notice me as we pass.

The king laughs at something his son says, his voice booming through the halls. I smile to myself. I've always liked his laugh. As a young girl, I would sneak up to the throne room and watch the king meet with the court. He is so handsome and strong. I would love to meet him someday. I'm sure he doesn't have time for the likes of me, though. I'm just a servant.

"This way," the man holding my hand says, his voice calm and low. He looks me up and down as we walk. "What's your name?"

"Astrid, sir," I say.

"Astrid," he repeats, with a tone of appreciation. "You're very beautiful, Astrid," he says, his eyes searching me for something.

"You are too kind, sir," I reply, looking down at my feet. I've always had a hard time with compliments. I've never thought I looked particularly beautiful. My hair is always tangled, and my dresses are far from elegant. I watch my plain white dress move with my feet. There's no sheen to it, just plain wool. The special materials are saved for nobles like Queen Eileen. I had the privilege to embroider a section of her court gown once; it was the most nerve-wracking day of my life. When she tried it on, though, she beamed and held my hand, saying she loved my work. I was so speechless. I smile, remembering the reassuring, cool touch of her hands. Like soft satin.

The man pulls on my hand and thrusts me into a dark room with a fireplace that has not been tended to. Most of the rooms in the castle have fireplaces, and the servants must keep the fires burning unless specified otherwise. I frown, wondering who had missed taking care of this man.

"Your fire has died out," I say. "Would you like me to tend to it?"

"No," he says, slamming the door shut. I turn to face him, awaiting instructions. Instead, he looks at me with hunger in his eyes. "Yes, you are very beautiful, Astrid. Take off your dress."

I smile, understanding that this wasn't simply a service call.

This man wants to be pleased. I look at him while unlacing my dress, watching his eyes widen as the white dress falls off of my shoulders. I never thought my body was anything worth looking at, but many of the visiting nobility have called upon me. It's not an uncommon occurrence that they seek me out after dinner. This man is no different. His face is almost slack as my dress falls to the floor.

I move towards him, unashamed of my nakedness, and lift my face to meet his gaze as I was taught by my older friend, Annette. She was sought after many times, and we often wondered if she would be chosen as a *kvinne* for one of the princes, Prince Caden or Prince Kai. They are both so handsome. Being assigned as a personal servant to either would be a tremendous honor.

Returning to the task at hand, I eye the man and sidle up close to him. I try to remember what Annette taught me about how to be seductive and flirtatious, the kind of woman a man wanted in the bedroom. It always felt slightly awkward to me, but I did as she advised anyway.

I look at the man, and he lightly touches my body, twisting his hands into my hair and breathing against my skin. His skin is cold against mine, enough to make me shiver, but he seems to like that response. I let out a small gasp, and suddenly, he is upon me, kissing me, biting me, and the events of the evening unfold. He says my name loudly throughout the process, like he's reminding himself of who I am. He stops only to drink portions of my blood, from my neck, my wrist. At one point, he bites into my thigh, which is different. When he's finished and asleep, I smile, happy that I am leaving him content and relaxed. Feeling lightheaded, the tingling sensation returns to my fingertips. I slip on my dress.

Before leaving, I clean the fireplace and prep it for use, the man still sleeping, still naked from our encounter. I walk out of the room without a sound, moving back down to my chambers. Annette always told me to leave immediately after to avoid any unpleasantries.

It was another rule that didn't make much sense to me, but I had to remember that I was not a *kvinne.* Only women chosen to serve one master could stay in a man's room overnight. Annette told me that vampires are often possessive of their *kvinne.* What a wonderful sentiment, to be taken care of in such a way. I often wonder if I will be chosen.

I walk back to my room, smiling and humming softly, entering the wing quietly. I don't want to wake any of my friends. I sneak into my room and find Alheri still awake, writing something down in her journal.

"You're up late," I say, watching her through the candlelight.

"I wanted to make sure you got back safely," is all she says.

"You work so hard, Al. You should be resting."

Alheri works harder than any of us. Though she's not a *thrall* in the same way as the rest of us, she serves the kingdom as healer and protector. Not to mention, she does anything that the king requires that might need a magical touch. As the only witch in the castle, she plays an extremely important role.

"I will when you will." She smiles warmly at me then, sliding her tattered notebook under her hay mattress.

I smile and nod soundlessly as I unlace my dress again, sliding into the thin nightgown that was once worn by my mother. I climb into my cot and pull the thick wool blanket over me, tired from the day's events. Before I can blink, a thick stupor washes over me, and I fall asleep smiling, listening to Alheri chanting lightly like a lullaby.

2
KAI

I open my eyes to the ceiling of my poorly lit bedroom. The fire died out during the night, and the room feels stale with frozen air. The ceiling looks like the top of a dungeon, and frankly, that's what it's starting to feel like. I roll onto my side and look at the glass door that leads out onto the balcony. Grey light filters through the window, illuminating the dust that swirls ever-present in the air. The glass is distorted like it wasn't properly smoothed out and finished, but I don't mind. It never really bothers me that this place feels like a cage. Not until yesterday.

My eighteenth birthday is next week, and that means I'll be of age to take the throne. Not that I *ever* wanted it. My father took me into his parlor last night and told me about the political climate of the kingdom. Dhampyrs and Halvblods want more rights, more of a place in the kingdom, even though they were born with part human blood. It was almost funny how ridiculous he acted as he said it. Father never liked the idea of Feilfri Castle being home to anyone other than the Purebloods. He chastised me over and over about it, demeaning any vampire that comingled with a human. Apparently, *I* needed to be a strong leader and not let the bloodline be tainted by lessers.

I roll my eyes and push off of the bed. I'm still wearing the clothes I had on last night, and my shirt is starting to itch. I stand up, and my feet are as cold as the stone underneath them. I shirk off my pants and shirt and move over to the washbowl. Someone has come in this morning and refreshed the water in the bowl. I scowl; I never asked anyone to do that.

I can only imagine that father had sent in a *thrall* to see to my needs. Ugh. I hate that. Humans shouldn't be used as slaves and servants. Nevertheless, I wash my face and body quickly with a small white rag. I dip it in the water and rub the remnants of dirt off my face and arms. The white rag comes back brown and rust-colored. I throw the rag on the floor. Maybe the rats will come in the middle of the night and eat it. Maybe they'll eat everything they see. Maybe they'll eat me while I'm asleep.

I look down at my body, skin as white as the cloudy skies, fingers with grey nails, dark blue veins running through my whole body. I look back to the balcony doors, the soft light still playing amongst the dancing dust. I open the door, letting in the wintry air. The clouds are low and dark, sunlight barely making its way through. It's not raining, though, so I guess that's a plus. I wrap a large towel around my waist and step outside.

The wind is brisk and cold as it cuts through the stone railing. The air is fresh and calming, without the taste of blood attached to it as it is everywhere in the castle. No, outside, the air is new, untainted by treachery and lust. I like to think I belong out in the wild, with fresh air around me all the time. Maybe that would make me forget what I am, what I crave.

I slump over the railing and let the icy wind blow over my skin, the chill shivering up my arms and caressing my chest, a brief cool flurry between my legs. The air tugs at my long, wet hair and throws it into my eyes. Below the balcony is the ocean, another welcome presence. I often like to jump off of the ledge and plunge into the icy waters below, even though I know there are many jagged rocks, and at any moment, I might tear off a limb.

I watch the waves crash against the base of the castle, trying not to think about what goes on down there. I try not to think about the humans that live on the bottom floor, in an actual dungeon, where they heal and rest from feedings. I try not to think of the dining table where humans come to serve their masters by offering up their veins. I try my hardest, my absolute hardest, not to think about the warm, aromatic sustenance that springs from their necks.

"Fuck," I say aloud, feeling my body turn rigid as I fight the urge to sprint down to the dungeons. My entire body is poised like a cat, ready to spring. My gums itch, and my fingers cramp as I grip the balcony's railing.

I quickly inhale a large gulp of air, washing my senses clean with the frozen wind. Slowly, the urges subside, and I can breathe normally again. I straighten my stiff back and step back into my room, closing the door to the balcony with a click of the latch and a rattle from the glass against the iron fittings. I dress quickly and pull my fingers through my dark hair, loosening the tangles into straight, long strands. After sipping a small glass of water on my nightstand, I realize it's probably time to eat.

As I walk through the rest of the castle, I can't help but shiver and hold my breath. Vampires big and small strut past me, half bowing as I pass. I don't meet their eyes. I don't want to see what they are all screaming on the inside: Prince Kai, Master, Oh great one! It's pathetic. I've never liked being a Pureblood. Snooty, entitled pieces of trash. All of them.

I wish that I could flee from this place. I know that the rest of the world wouldn't care about my blood type or that I'm a monster. Outside of Feilfri Castle, outside of Nordøya, humans and vampires live peacefully, at the crux of coexistence. I envy that. It's something I could never have. I already have a hard time being around humans as it is. If I lived alongside them? I'd never be able to abstain, and no one understands.

Except for my mom. I walk through the doors of the study and find her sitting by the fire with rosy cheeks and a book in her hands. She has small reading glasses perched on her nose, and her eyes light up when I enter the room.

The grey and black stones that make up the entire castle always seem warmer here. The walls are lined from floor to ceiling with bookshelves and small display cases for castle artifacts. In the case closest to the door, there's a small telescope I used to look at and imagine stargazing through as a boy. There are sheathed golden daggers and the original Feilfri crest. I run my hand over the smooth wood of the bookcase and breath in the scent of old paper, rust, and salt.

My mom sets her book down on the small end table by her chair and smiles warmly at me. Almost instantly, I feel at peace, the anxieties and shame withering away.

"Kai, what a nice surprise," she says, removing the dainty glasses and setting them atop the book. "What can I do for you, son?"

I don't respond at first. I'm still looking at the large bookcases. Stories filled with such fantastical ideas. Dragons and knights and princesses and battles. I run my hands across the aged leather spines and sigh. Stories are safe. Stories help me forget.

I shake off the memories and face her, not looking at her eyes.

"Do you have anything to drink?" I say, almost in a whisper.

I don't need to tell her the meaning behind my words. *I don't want to go downstairs and feed on a human. Do you have something, anything, that will satiate my hunger?*

She smiles sadly and goes up a small set of stairs to her desk, sitting in a fenced-off section where she does her writings and sketches. She moves over to the side of the desk, where she keeps a small stash of blood in a stone ice chest. The chest is attached to a small opening that allows the ice and rain to catch and keep the temperature low almost all the time. She pours a small amount of blood into a silver goblet, and immediately, the scent hits me like a punch in the face. I feel my mouth constrict, and I have to restrain myself to act courteously rather than sprinting to her and ripping the leather blood bag out of her hands.

She waltzes down the steps, and her long dress elegantly splays out on the ground. She holds the goblet out to me with a soft smile that lets me know she heard my words and wants to help. She always helps me.

For a brief moment, I meet her gaze and look at her young face. Her eyes are like garnet-colored leaves on an autumn day, sunlight beaming through red stained glass. My eyes flick away and zero in on the cool drink she just poured for me. I nod in thanks and slowly bring the cup to my lips. I feel my teeth sting my gums, and my gut wrenches as I hold my breath. I drink the liquid carefully and quickly, feeling my entire body tighten. The only thing that holds me together is my mother's ever-present support. She lays a comforting hand on my shoulder.

I lost track of the touch when accidentally, I inhale, and the delicious, heavenly scent of the blood assaults me. My stomach knots and I hunch forward, trying my best to keep my cool, but it's too late. I drop the cup, and it clatters against the floor so loudly that both of us jump. The blood makes its way through my body and away from my tongue and olfactory nerves, and I regain control of myself.

I step back from my mother, who is watching me now with a worried look. God, I hate that she worries about me.

"My son, watching you struggle hurts me more than you know," she says, and her voice is like water on a wound. I hiccup a large breath through my mouth. As she speaks, she collects the goblet and returns it to her desk. "How long have you abstained this time?"

I shoot her a look. She shouldn't know that. She shouldn't be able to see through me like that. Her face is still soft, kind, and gentle. How the *fuck* can she be a vampire and not want to rip through everyone and everything all the time?

I look up to the ceiling and find the same grey, rotted stone that's in my bedroom.

"Two weeks," I whisper in a low voice, my throat thickly lined with bloodlust.

She floats back over to me soundlessly and takes my hand in hers. The fire shines behind her black hair, creating a slight halo of light around her face.

"You shouldn't wait so long, Kai," she says quietly. At this moment, both of us know my father, Baldassare, King of Feilfri Castle, is walking towards us. Her hearing is probably better than mine, but nevertheless, we both hear him. He's down the hall, and he's coming this way.

My mother knows better than anyone that betraying your nature, especially as a Pureblood, is punishable by exile. If my father knew how much I detest being a vampire, he would banish me, maybe even kill me.

"Small cups, now and then," she continues in a whisper, prescribing a treatment for what ails me. But I know that the more I consume, the more I want. I have to abstain. I *have* to. The pain I feel otherwise haunts me.

"Kai!" my father booms as he enters the study. My mother

smiles at him and moves aside as he comes in. "Just the man I wanted to see. Let's take a walk."

"One moment, dear," my mother says, touching his arm lightly. "Kai and I were discussing this novel. May he join you in a moment?"

Father looks at me, at my mother, then back at me. He doesn't say anything but simply nods. I know where to meet him: the throne room. We are to discuss more politics, more kingly duties. I roll my eyes at him when he turns away. Luckily, my body feels more alive now that I've had some sort of sustenance. I look down at my hands, less grey than before.

"Kai, listen to me," Mother breathes quietly, urgently. "You *must* not abstain for so long. You will not survive your rule if you take such lengthy gaps between feeding. You don't have to survive on human blood. You're inventive. Find some other way. But you must heed my advice, dear."

She holds my hands as she speaks, and it's hard not to look in her eyes. I look down at my feet instead and watch the skirts of her dress sway as she shifts her weight. She squeezes my hands, and let's go. I nod at her, still not looking. I know that I'm not going to change. I just can't.

I walk out of the study, holding my breath once more, knowing that I have to pass by the dining hall on my way to the throne room. I walk quickly and quietly, not meeting the eyes of anyone I pass. Once outside the doors that lead to the dining hall, I pause momentarily.

I will not engage in conversation with anyone on the other side of this door. I will not accept any offer of food or drink. I will not breathe. I will not open my mouth. I will *not* feed.

Opening the door, I feel strong enough to abstain. With my mother's help, I feel confident I will make it across the floor without any mistakes. The only thing I don't account for is the beautiful rose-golden-haired human lying across the table with a smile on her face and closed eyes.

I pause.

Don't pause. What are you doing?

I look at the human with a vampire feeding on her neck. My whole body is stiff, unmoving. I watch as the human winces in pain but continues to smile. I don't understand. Does she *like* being fed on?

Her hair is like silk that was dipped in sunlight and blood. The fire and candlelight flicker all around, casting shadows against her delicate features. She opens her eyes, finds my gaze, and she smiles wider. Her skin is pale and light, and she's wearing a beautiful white dress. Is she an angel? I haven't seen anything more beautiful. And that *demon* is feeding on her.

My eyebrows furrow and I feel something inside of me boil up. I want to tear that guy apart. I want to take this girl, this human, in my arms and run away with her.

"Kai," my father says curtly from the top of the stairs, breaking me from my trance. I tear my eyes away from the human and continue through the dining hall, up the right set of stairs to the hallway that leads to the throne room.

Who is that? And how have I never seen her before?

I follow my father through the giant double doors, the iron door handles thumping against the dark wood as they close behind us. I take a seat at the right hand of the throne as my father speaks softly to a servant vampire. He's a Halvblod, part human, part Dhampyr. My father looks down upon all Halvblods. He says they're lesser-vampires. They can only reside in the castle as servants or slaves.

I look away, trying not to think of that woman's face as the servant leaves the room, and my father walks towards me.

"No, son," he says in a deep voice. "You'll sit on the throne today."

I watch him with an inquisitive expression but move to the throne as instructed. The chair is large and feels too big for my lanky body, like the back of the chair is back too far. I shift uncomfortably.

"Today, you will get a glimpse of what being a king is. You will taste the power, and, in a few weeks, the kingdom will celebrate your coronation. You will be the crowned prince, and you will rule in my stead until I die. Now, I know this is a hard transition, son. But you need to step up and assume this awesome responsibility. This is a defining moment for you!"

My father is good at monologuing; I consider idly as my mind wanders. He goes on and on for several minutes about the deep responsibility of accepting the crown, but I know he never once had to deal with those responsibilities. In most monarchies, the king at least cares about his subjects. My father feels nothing for his inferiors. He uses them, and that's all. They are a means to an end. His end. Whatever he wants, they are there for that purpose.

I can't say my father doesn't care about my mother, though. He does. He loves her dearly. I would say she's his only weakness. She is the entire kingdom's weakness. Everyone adores her. But my father? He hates everyone else. Even other Purebloods.

Our monarchy isn't any different than others. We have a line of succession, starting with me, and followed by the males in order of birth. Next in line after me is my brother, Caden. I scowl at the mental image of his cropped black hair and rage red eyes. In the past ten years, Caden has gone from annoying to ruthless in his hunting. Shivering, I move on. After Caden would be my cousins, who don't even live in the castle. They live in Livsnerven with the rest of the vampire kingdom. Feilfri Castle stands on the other side of a large section of water that separates the castle from the rest of the kingdom. I suppose that's how my father gets away with not caring about the other vampires. They pretty much rule themselves.

"Son, we need to talk about continuing our bloodline," Father says, bringing me out of my reverie.

"Bloodline?" I echo hoarsely.

"Yes, Kai. You need a wife."

I did *not* expect this. I don't even know how to respond. I just blink at him.

"Have you forgotten your studies? You need to marry a Pureblood vampire and produce an heir so that our bloodline may continue," he continues. "I don't care what you and your brother do on your own time, but you must have a wife of proper lineage. I have several candidates you may choose from."

My eyes are wide, and I just stare at him. What we do on our own time? Does that mean he has sex with women other than Mother? What does that mean? Does he have other children? Offspring from women who aren't Purebloods?

"I…I don't know if I understand."

"Marriage, son. You need to pick a wife."

"A wife? I haven't even dated—"

"Dated? No, Kai, this isn't about love. This is a part of being a king. You will provide a son for the kingdom so that it may continue," Father says. "But now that I think of it…have you lain with a woman?"

"What?" I say, shocked. In no way was I prepared to have *this* conversation with my father.

He pauses, looking me up and down. "A man, then?"

"Dad, stop. No, I haven't had sex. With a woman or a man. But what would be wrong with that if I had?"

"Nothing, nothing. I didn't mean any offense. But love and lust have no place for a king. It doesn't matter. What does matter, for the kingdom's sake, is that you find a woman of pure heritage that you can marry and produce an heir with," my father says calmly. He's obviously feeling just as awkward as I am.

There's a knock on the door, and I sigh, thankful for a distraction.

"My King?" The servant from before returns, and Baldassare gestures him inside, standing up to greet him.

"Son, I want you to have this as a gift for your birthday," he says, and the words fall flat as the red-haired woman from the dining hall glides into the hall behind the servant. She smiles up at me, and I stand as well, my fists clench behind my back. They stop in the middle of the throne room, and I struggle hard not to breathe. I have to remain calm; I chastise myself and my heart as it lodges itself in my throat.

"Sir, this is Astrid," the servant says, his eyes on the ground.

"Very good. Leave us," Father says, walking up to the girl. My heart throbs against the veins in my neck, and my stomach feels as though it's fallen right out of me. He reaches out and cups her chin, tilting her head in different ways so he can take a look at her. I want to throw up.

"Astrid," Father says to her.

"Your highness," she replies with a curtsy as soon as he releases her chin. I want to faint. Her voice is like wind chimes, a breath on icy wind. I can barely blink for fear that she will just disappear into thin air. She looks so delicate, like a flower petal.

"You are a very beautiful woman, dear," he continues. My thoughts churn in my brain like butter. I feel like I'm molded to the stone beneath me. "You're to be my son's personal *kvinne*. I want you to take my boy and turn him into a man. I want you to meet his every need so he can be an effective ruler."

"My King, you are too kind," Astrid says.

My heart is cracking because I know the words my father isn't saying. He wants me to embrace my nature as a vampire. He wants me to have a personal blood bag. He wants me to have sex and be a man, whatever the hell that means.

"Son, come see your *kvinne*," the king says.

I force my limbs to move. In a daze, I walk over to Astrid, and she looks at me with childlike innocence. I look at her eyes, and it's like the entire ocean is captured in her soul. Wide and crystalline blue, they are like nothing I've ever seen. She offers me her hand, and I gulp, feeling my throat constrict. I take it and quickly kiss it before I can do anything else. I shut out all thoughts other than the stones beneath my feet and the distant sounds of the ocean waves crashing against the rocks.

"Very good," Father says in a gruff, approving voice. I turn away from the girl and look at him, waiting for dismissal. "Serve him well, Astrid."

"Yes, Your Highness. Thank you," Astrid says.

I release her hand and turn away from both of them, focusing only on my legs, one in front of the other, all the way until I reach my room. Somewhere along the way, Astrid told me that she was going to retire to her quarters so she can pack. I don't even remember if I replied to her. I must have nodded or something because, by the time I get back to my room, I'm alone. I look around and unthinkingly begin to tidy up the place. My brain feels like mush, and I can't help but look out to the balcony. I haven't taken a breath since before I left my mother. The grey light has faded now, and it looks more and more gloomy.

Frustrated and conflicted, I throw open the glass doors and lean over the ledge. Icy wind whips wildly against me and burns my face. The waves thrash against the slick castle stones, and I imagine myself swimming against the current, the undertow threatening to pull me apart. I can almost feel the frozen water surrounding me. The water would burn my eyes and choke my lungs. Standing here, looking at the unkempt waters below, I'm almost tempted to make the dive like I have so many times before.

I feel powerless against my father just as I would be powerless against the savage ocean. I wish I could cry. It feels as though my chest was going to rip apart. At least my thoughts can come clearly now, with the fresh salty air lashing around me. I hike in a large breath.

A *kvinne*?! What the hell is he trying to do to me? Having a personal servant, a human servant, means I will never be able to abstain successfully. Sooner or later, I will succumb. It's the fate of every fucking vampire.

I push my hands and legs against the ledge. I can't succumb. I don't want to *ever* lose that battle again. But inviting a human into my personal world means incredible temptation that I don't know if I'm strong enough to resist.

Phantom agony rips across my chest as I remember the last time I fed. I know I'm not strong enough. It's the reason I've stayed away from all humans. I can't win in this situation. There is no way out. If I face my father and tell him the truth, he'll exile me to the wastelands or kill me. Maybe that would be better.

I suck in a large breath of fresh air and yell loudly, knowing my turmoil will be swallowed up by the crashing waves and ripping winds.

I have to face my father or face myself. I don't know if I'm strong enough to do either. I don't know if I can make it through this. I'll just end up killing her. My brain turns against me, and I think of her smile, her innocent face, her hair.

"God *damn* it," I whisper against the wind. I breathe the fresh air deeply, taking a sideways look at the castle. It stands tall against the sky, with dark stones that have stood for ages. The jagged rocks jut out of the sides of the castle, and it almost looks like blood has seeped through the stone and into the water. I watch as the waves crash against the castle walls, cleaning away the rust and dirt.

After a few moments of listening to the waves and catching my breath, my ears start to tune into the castle activities. One of the horrifying things about drinking blood after abstaining for so long is that when my powers return, I can't turn them off. So, no matter how badly I don't want to hear what comes next, I hear it anyway. Somewhere in the *thrall* dungeons, a drunken vampire staggers, looking for blood. I hear their screams, their cries for help. No one will help them. Vampires can take whatever they want from the humans, save for their life.

I close my eyes tightly and focus on the ocean, trying my hardest not to hear the vampire rip into a human's throat. I drag in a shaky breath and try not to imagine Astrid's beautifully torn skin against the bloody dining room table. Instead, I replay the moment I met her to distract myself from the sounds of the feed. As I picture Astrid's chime-like voice and sky-blue eyes, my body shifts subtly beneath me, my eyes tinging with red, and my gut clenching inside me.

Now that I've met her, I can smell her *everywhere.* Her scent carries notes of summer honeysuckles and frozen rosebushes. How had I missed this decadent aroma before now? It's so strong, I know exactly where she is in the castle. It's like something's awakened inside of me. I take a deep breath, focusing intently on the sap from the pine trees and salt from the ocean. But unlike before, Astrid's aroma still floats around me, calling to me. Who is this woman that has bewitched me so quickly? And how will I ever keep from killing her?

3
ASTRID

My hands are shaking, and my legs feel like jelly as I follow Prince Kai out of the throne room. The hallways blur around me, and I focus on his long dark hair, the black strands wrapping around his neck. His body is lean, and he's much taller than I thought. His clothes are plain, just simple trousers and a white linen shirt that ties at the base of his throat. I watch as his body moves. His entire back seems clenched like his muscles are all wound too tight.

I look away from his chiseled muscles, feeling my cheeks flush. Instead, I pay closer attention to the stones that make up the walls and the lanterns that hazily light our path. I bow my head, trying to hide my ridiculous smile.

I can't believe this is happening. I can't believe I have been chosen. On top of feeling euphoria wash over me, my fingers and toes are numb from the dining hall. I feel lighter than air, like a bird flying in the sunlight. I'm shaking so hard that I can't find my voice.

I'm not sure what the protocol is now, but I know that I have to pack my belongings and move to his room.

Oh my God, my heart sings. I can't believe I'm going to live with him! How intimate. How exciting.

Prince Kai is even more beautiful than I remember. He was always so elusive. I remember sneaking to watch the king in the throne room, and he would be there, sitting next to the throne, his eyes always looking to the window.

My brain feels like it's on fire, thoughts racing away from me. I have to tell him I need to pack. He just keeps walking. Is he going to give me any instructions? I thought that being *kvinne* would include certain duties. I stare at his back, trying to focus on walking in a straight line. I watch his hands clench and unclench. Does he know that he does that?

I take a deep breath and try and speak up, but only patchy air comes out of my throat. I cough softly, trying to regain my senses.

"Your Highness," I whisper, barely audible. I clear my throat and try again. "I must go pack my belongings. Is that alright?"

Kai doesn't turn or say anything, but his head bobs up and down. I guess that's a yes?

"Thank you, sir," I say, turning away from him to head back to my chambers. I know where his room is, so I suppose I'll just go there next? Maybe Alheri will have advice for me.

I walk swiftly back the way we came, turning to look over my shoulders to see Prince Kai stuffing his hands in his pockets and turning the corner. I smile to myself, my chest swelling with pride and joy. I practically skip all the way back to my room.

The castle is, thankfully, simply laid out. As you enter from the main entrance, the *only* entrance, you walk through a small foyer. Past that, the place opens up into a wide dome-shaped room, where all the nobles feed on their *thralls*. That's the dining room. It's equipped with a large candlelit chandelier and decorative chains and iron gargoyles in the corners. On the far side of the dining room from the foyer, there is a half set of stairs that lines both sides of the walls, curving up towards the extravagant throne room. I suppose I will have to become familiar with that room, now that I'm working for Prince Kai.

I suppress another wave of giddiness. Instead of picturing myself in the throne room, I head down the east hallway, which is cramped and small. It leads to the kitchens and boiler room, and then towards the *thrall's* living quarters. The west side of the castle is made up of large winding spires and staircases that lead to the upper levels, where the royal family and other nobles live. I'm not sure what's past that, if anything. I've never been called upon to work higher than the second floor.

The moment I enter my room, I'm surrounded by all my friends. They had already heard the gossip and wanted the full story. I look around for my best friend, but sadly, Alheri isn't here, so instead, I tell everyone that I can find that I've been chosen to be Prince Kai's *kvinne*! How magical! All of the girls in the room are excited for me, some a little jealous, and some sad to see me go. Annette and Alheri are the only ones missing.

I wish I could talk to Annette. She was the most called upon, and by Prince Caden more importantly. I have so many questions, but ever since she started serving Prince Caden regularly, we haven't seen her. Maybe I'll be able to find her after I move in.

I start to fold my belongings into my small chest. I quickly grab the small pillow that I embroidered with leftover thread. I pack my thin nightgown and my dresses – especially my light blue dress. It's the most beautiful one I own. I also have a pink dress and a patchy orange dress that I don't wear unless I'm working in the kitchens. Since I have to hand-dye all my dresses with scraps of leftover dye, I have a lot of garments that are failed attempts and not visually appealing. I've worked at perfecting my skill at dyeing, sneaking different fruits and vegetable scraps to practice with, and I'm slowly getting better. It's hard work, and I'm certainly not the best, but I love working with fabrics.

I run my hands over the cloth, thinking about my progress and failures as a seamstress. My orange dress was a failed attempt at using onion peels to dye the wool. My pink dress used the tannins in various barks and fruit pits to leech out the pretty pale color, and finally, my blue dress. The best one yet. It was made using a combination of red cabbage scraps and blueberries. I learned a much better technique for that one. I found that a certain quality in urine helped process the dye on the fabric, so as much as I hated working with that particularly disgusting technique, it quickly became a favorite because of how beautifully my work turned out. As time passed on, I embroidered small designs on the sleeves and the hem of the blue dress, and now, it's the most beautiful garment I own.

I wonder if I'll be able to continue practicing my seamstress skills now that I'll have other duties to attend to. The thought nips at my mind as I fiddle with a loose thread.

Shaking off my tangle of thoughts, I gently fold the dresses into the wooden chest, looking around for anything I might have missed. I don't own any books or writing utensils of my own. I barely learned how to write before I was carted off to work with the other women in the gardens and kitchens. Alheri tried to continue my education, but sadly, I was always needed for other tasks. Soon enough, she gave up. It didn't matter now. Whatever Prince Kai needed, I would be there to serve him.

A big smile is stuck on my face like a pin, and I suck in a sharp breath, my heart racing. There's nothing left for me here. I'm moving up in the world. I just wish Alheri was here so I could say goodbye.

Regardless, I pick up the chest by the small handle and start making my way out.

"Astrid!" Alheri's voice calls out to me from the other side of the room.

"Alheri! I'm so glad I caught you! Did you hear the news?" I ask, feeling more excitement wash over me.

"Yes, I did. I was attending to the king, and I overheard him," she says. She looks tired and out of breath.

"Isn't it amazing? I'm so overwhelmed," I say.

"Yeah, just…be careful, okay?"

"Oh, you're always so worried. Don't be! This is a good thing!"

"Is it? I don't want you to get hurt. I know Prince Kai is different, but still," she says.

"I don't understand your confusion here. This is the best day of my life. I can't believe you aren't more excited for me."

"Astrid, you have a gentle soul, and you're a very beautiful woman. I just want your safety and happiness." Alheri's voice is soft, and she reaches out to touch my shoulder. "If you are ever hurt, you know where to find me. I'm always here for you."

"You've been like a sister to me, Al. I'm going to miss living with you, but I'm not going away. I'm just moving upstairs," I assure her.

She doesn't smile at me, and her eyes look glassy and tired. But she grabs me into a big hug. I chuckle at her dramatics, pressing my free arm against her back.

"Okay, okay," I giggle, a little breathless from all the squeezing. She let's go of me, and I give her a small nod before whirling around and leaving our chambers for the last time, stopping just at the threshold to take one last look.

I'm honestly so happy to leave even if it's a little bittersweet my friends are staying behind. I gaze around the room, remembering all the laughs and good times that were had within these four walls. This has been my home for eighteen years; I don't know what

I'm going to do without Alheri's soft chanting to lull me to sleep or chatting about castle gossip with Annette. Everything seems so cozy and warm here. With one last glance around the room, I whisper my goodbyes to my tiny burlap cot, the rusted iron bars, and the dusty, dingy floor that always required extra sweeping. With an excited but heavy heart, I leave the room.

I move quickly through the castle, anxious to get back to Prince Kai. I'm not sure what's going to happen next, but I quickly shove aside my nervousness. I'm sure he will let me know what he needs when I arrive. The thought thrills me, and suddenly I'm smiling and practically sprinting through the dimly lit hallways again.

I move across the dining hall once again, bowing to nobles as I pass through the opposite doorway. Inside the west tower, I take the steps quickly, stopping only once to look through a tiny hole in the wall to see outside. It's hardly a window, and I have to press my head to the stone wall just to see, but when I do, a picture of mountainous terrain and steaming rain clouds sprawls out before my eyes. It's so lovely here. I sigh contentedly before moving quickly again.

The upper floors are glorious and well decorated with wall hangings, swords on plaques, and beautiful iron lantern fittings. I have to close my jaw as I move through all the extravagance. Once I get to Prince Kai's door—his wide, double-sided, dark stained door—I pause and take a deep breath, smelling hints of cedar and moss. Should I knock on the door? Should I just go in?

I look around, and no one is in the hall. I've never been this far up in the castle. These rooms are reserved for the royal family. Prince Caden and Prince Kai's rooms are next to one another, and down the hall is the master bedroom for the king and queen. I wonder if I will ever see that room, if Prince Kai will keep me as his *kvinne* when he becomes king. The thought fills me with glee and dread at the same time.

I inhale deeply and knock on the door. I wait a few moments, but there is no answer. I gently open the heavy door to an absolutely magnificent room. It's probably four times as large as the room Alheri and I shared. Instead of large metal pillars, the walls are stone and covered in paintings and maps. I stare at the map of Nordøya for a moment, tracing the mountains and river lines, finding the gap between the Norway mainland and our little island. I take a deep breath and quickly move on, squashing my roaming thoughts of geography.

There is a large fireplace that's unkempt, an attached balcony, and a small vanity with a washbowl. There's a bed next to that seems too small for the room. The pillows and blankets are in a jumble, with piled laundry underneath the frame. I suppose this is how Prince Kai likes to sleep. A hysterical laugh bubbles up, and I giggle loudly. I clap my hand over my mouth and look around, glad to see that Prince Kai is not in the room.

Okay, I need to pull myself together before he comes back. I need to be proper, not a giggling mess of a girl. I straighten my back and walk through a large opening in the wall into a smaller room, the parlor. There's a small table and bed that looks completely unused. I guess that's where I'll sleep. I shove the small chest underneath the wooden bed frame and start working.

There's leftover food on the table, dirty goblets, and used rags all over the floor. I pick up the used laundry and toss it into a cloth hamper that looks like it's hardly been used. Before long, the hamper is completely filled, and I frown down at it. I'll have to take down the laundry later, maybe after Prince Kai has gone to sleep. Speaking of which. I walk over to his bed, take the crumpled sheets and pillows, and fold them gently over the mattress. I'll have to clean the sheets another time, I suppose. A simple making-of-the-bed shall have to do for now. I run my hand over the mattress, gawking at how *soft* it is. I wonder what the thick linen is stuffed with. Feathers? Hay? Wool? I fold the blanket over the thin sheets and set the pillows down after a good fluffing.

Next, the washbasin is a complete mess. I can't believe Prince Kai doesn't have his room regularly serviced. Surely a servant would do a better job of keeping our crowned prince's room tidy and clean. I pinch my lips into a tight line and take the bowl of dirty water to the adjoined balcony, pouring it over the edge. I stare out for a moment, breathing in the frigid, salty air and smiling. The wind is so cold that it hurts my cheeks, but I stay in place for a moment longer, simply staring at the intricate landscape. The world looks so much more beautiful from all the way up here. I quickly close the balcony doors behind me as I walk back inside.

With the washbasin in such distress, I wonder what the bathroom looks like. I open the door, and the room is dark. I hunt around for some matches and find some on the mantle. I walk back to the bathroom and light the lanterns, seeing that the room looks hardly used. The bathtub is clean, with untouched rags hanging over the sides. My brows knit together in confusion. What odd living habits. Does he not bathe properly? We will have to change that. I cross my arms, thinking of ways to coerce the prince into a bath.

I grab the washbowl and move out of the room and back into the hallway. Almost every floor of the castle has access to the boiler room. I wonder if this floor does too. I walk down, past Prince Caden's room and the stairs, and sure enough, there's a large room with a hole and a series of pulleys and buckets. I lower a bucket slowly, passing the second floor on its way down to the main boiler room. Alheri told me once that one of her duties is to ensure the boiler room is equipped with hot water. She prattled on one day about how all that worked, but I didn't pay much attention. I suppose she keeps the fires burning down in the basement, and we can bring up hot water when we want.

I have heard of newer plumbing techniques from some of the girls that serviced some of the out-of-town nobles. Livsnerven was more of a melting pot society, where many different people and ideas and methods came together. Some of those techniques made their way back to the castle, others didn't. Sadly for me, I'll have to carry the bucket of hot water back to the tub multiple times to get it filled. But I suppose I don't mind. I just want to show Prince Kai what I'm worth. I can imagine the smile on his face when he sees all the hard work I've done. It will all be worth it just to see him smiling at me.

I hoist up the water bucket and carry it back to his room, careful not to touch the hot water. My fingers twitch as I remember the countless blisters from accidentally pouring boiling water on my hands. When I get back to the tub, I dump the water quickly, noticing that Prince Kai has still not returned. I huff in exhaustion and fidget with nervousness but continue on. After several trips back and forth from the boiler room, the bathtub is filled. I light some candles underneath the tub to keep the water warm. Hopefully, Prince Kai will return soon and take advantage of the bath while it's still hot.

I dip the washbowl in the bathwater, filling it up before returning it to the washbasin. I wipe down all the surfaces in the bathroom and look in the side table's wooden drawers, finding untouched goat milk soap. I take out two bars and place one by the bathtub and one on his vanity. Looking at the room now, I'm much more pleased. The last thing to take care of is the fireplace.

My heart is beating quickly from all the physical exertion, but I take a deep breath and lower myself to my knees. I begin to empty out the ashes from the fireplace, sweeping them into the metal pan and dumping them over the balcony edge. Once it is cleared out, I place new logs onto the fire grate and light the fire, watching the smoke billow quickly. I smile, happy with my success. I'm not the best at making fires, but my has grown a lot in the past few months while working in the kitchens. The first thing we did each morning was light the oven fires, and it was my job to keep them burning all day long. I guess that's another thing that has suddenly changed.

I stand up, my bones creaking slightly, and look at the gold sigil on the mantlepiece. I use my dress to polish the crest a bit before noticing that my skirts are absolutely filthy from all the soot. I quickly move over to my chest and pull out another dress, wanting to make sure that Prince Kai doesn't see me covered in dirt. I pull out my blue dress and walk over to look at my appearance in the tall bathroom mirror, noticing how much I've changed since the last time I saw my reflection. Mirrors are a precious commodity, and I've never owned one or even knew someone who did before now. The last time I looked at my reflection was when I looked into a still bucket of water.

I brush my fingers through my hair, noting that it looks darker and redder than before. The thin strands are mostly golden with hints of strawberry tint, but in the dim light, my hair looks warm and rich as it surrounds my face. The flickering lantern makes my face looks older. I smile at the reflection, the skin crinkling just slightly by my eyes. I quickly change out of my soiled dress and into the blue one, smoothing my hands over the fabric before moving away from the mirror.

I look around the room and feel uneasy at the lack of instruction. When will Prince Kai return? The world is dark and quiet outside the glass window, making my body feel tired and heavy. I guess it's time to sleep. I walk over to my new bed and sit down, my jaw gaping at the softness of the blankets and mattress. Almost immediately, sleep hits me like a wall, and my eyelids droop as I sink gladly into a dreamless sleep.

4

KAI

By the time I return to my room, Astrid has unpacked her small collection of clothes into the parlor of my bedroom. I look around, and nothing looks the same. Everything feels tainted by her touch. She's cleaned the fireplace, moved my books into a neat stack on the mantle, made my bed, refreshed the water in my bowl, and picked up the laundry off the floor. The place looks clean, and I feel uneasy.

My room is extravagant. Too extravagant, in my opinion. Most of the items in the room I never touch. The main chamber has my bed, which I insisted be a small wooden bed, room enough for only one person. It's honestly too small for me. My feet dangle off the ends, and my arms stretch past the headboard, but I like it. It doesn't make me feel like I'm some high-horsed royal. The bed sits squarely on the wall opposite the door, and the fireplace is on the adjacent wall between the balcony doors and another door that leads to a small bathroom where I have a personal bathtub and a mirror, a luxury most people don't have. The fireplace is embossed with a golden crest that represents my family's lineage, dating back hundreds of years. It has a large twisted tree and moon with the words *Blod Er Makt* underneath it. Blood is power.

And finally, the parlor. My bedroom, like the rest of my family, has a parlor equipped with a table or desk, a small bookshelf, and now a small bed. I walk to the wide doorway and look across to the bed where Astrid is sleeping soundly. She must not have heard me come in. I stand there for a moment, just watching her sleep. She is breathing so softly, so slowly. Her hair is folded at the base of her neck, and she's facing towards the wall, so I can't see her face. The blanket rises and falls slowly with her breaths.

I look down at my feet and try something. With determination, I take a small breath.

I have to look away quickly and clutch at the wooden doorway, gripping it so that I won't do anything rash. Taking a breath was a bad idea. Now all I can taste is her smell on my tongue, sweet and floral, like honeysuckle.

You have to get used to it. She's not going away, I tell myself. I walk all the way over to the bathroom and close the door silently behind me. I take a seat on the edge of the bathtub and grip the iron tub like it's a lifeline. I close my eyes and lick my lips, tasting remnants of dusty, salty air. I listen to the waves just on the other side of the wall and try again. I slowly, slowly, breathe in through my mouth. In and out. In and out.

I feel like I'm a starving man with a bouquet of poison food just out of reach. I could take a bite, sure. But at what cost? Astrid's scent lingers in the air, and my chest feels tight. In the mirror, I see the contorted face of an animal looking back at me. I've never been afraid of my powers, but now, I don't know. If I stay here tonight, I'm not sure what I will do.

With dragging feet and stiff limbs, I wash my face, then grab my cloak and shoes. Holding my breath, I walk out of my bedroom, up the stairs, and out onto the terrace that resides at the very top of the castle. Night finally settled on today, which seemed to go on forever. The trees are black ink against the swirling purple clouds. I look out on the sky, still dense and dark. It feels like the natural world is anxious, just like me. But up here, it feels like I'm a normal person, not caged by desire. I take a deep breath, savoring the way the icy wind smells. It's all mountains and oceans and freedom.

"Knock knock," my mother's voice chimes from the floor entryway. I extend my hand and pull her up from the ladder. When she's standing soundly, I release her hand and look back out across the water towards the rest of the kingdom. "I heard that you've been given a gift."

I scoff loudly.

"Kai, why do you torture yourself?" My mother asks me gently, returning quickly to our previous conversation in the study. I turn to face her, not meeting her eyes. With all the cloud cover, I can barely see her. The only light is a lantern that looks like it's struggling to stay lit through the rough wind.

"I don't want to be like this," I say. I'm not afraid of saying it. Not when it's almost impossible to eavesdrop on a conversation on the terrace. No one can hear us over the sounds of the wind and water. "I don't want humans to suffer."

"Neither do I," she admits. I look up at her, and she's looking out over the edge. Her brown hair swirls gently in the wind. Somehow, she always looks elegant, even with raging winds whipping past us.

"How do you survive then? How do you do it?" I don't even know how to phrase what I want to ask her.

"How do I not kill?" She meets my eyes and smiles. I drop my head, ashamed. "I haven't taken a human life in very a long time. I'm not sure when I gathered the strength. I suppose along the way,

I just got very tired of treating humans as livestock."

I've never heard my mother talk like this. I'm still as I listen to her words, feeling wisdom seep out of each syllable.

"I think it must have been when you're father gave me Venn as a present, as my own *herre*," she says. She has her own slave? Just as Astrid is my *kvinne*? "Venn was a kind man. One of my greatest friends."

Sadness looms over her as she speaks.

"What happened to him?" I gulp. She must have killed him.

"He died, but not by the hands of a vampire," She clarifies. "He was almost sixty years old by the time he passed."

I blink.

"He was my *herre* for most of his life, and I loved him," she says. I watch her face for a long time, trying to process the words. Her alabaster skin shone lightly in the torchlight, the stone gleaming like black crystals behind her. "Venn provided for me in ways that your father could not, son. Please don't misunderstand me. I love Baldassare very much, but I was always his queen, his wife. I was never his love."

My father's words radiate in the back of my mind. I must find a wife as part of my kingly duties. I realize my mother is that for him. He'd married her simply to fulfill an expectation of the crown.

"When your father gave me Venn, I hated him at first. I didn't want a human as a piece of property. I found the entire notion absolutely revolting. A walking blood bag," she scoffs. "But then I started to enjoy Venn's company more and more. He would offer his blood when I was faint, and I found the strength to stop when I had enough. My friendship with Venn allowed me the strength to resist."

I hadn't thought of that. Could I try to befriend Astrid?

"You can look at your gift in one of two ways: your saving grace or your downfall. For your brother, he has abandoned his sense of sobriety and opted to enjoy his nature to the full extent," she says.

"That's just a fancy way of saying he enjoys feeding and fucking," I say, forgetting my manners. I eye my mother, and her mouth forms a tight line, but she doesn't reprimand me. I bow my head in apology.

"Astrid is very special, Kai. Somehow, I believe you were meant to be with her," she says, but before I can air my multitude of questions, she continues, "You have the chance to be a perfect ruler, Kai. I hope that you will make the right choice for yourself.

I nod and look at my shoes. She opens the hatch again and begins to lower herself down. When she's gone, I close the hatch behind her and sigh.

Contemplating my own mother's relationship with a human somehow doesn't make me feel any better. I feel as though the barriers between adult and child have been torn down, and both my parents are telling me they have had relations with people other than their spouse. I guess I shouldn't be surprised. I just never thought about it. I barely even think about my own relationships. I hardly have any friends.

The only thing that I think about is blood. And I hate it.

I lower myself to the floor, feeling the rough stone against my skin and clothes. Sleeping on the terrace is a risky move since, at any moment, the clouds might part, and sunlight might take me away in a blaze of fire, but I can't go back to my room tonight.

"Stay cloudy, okay?" I say to the sky.

I tuck my arm underneath my head and close my eyes, seeing Astrid's smile behind my eyes, the way she looked on the table, blood staining her skin and dress, tangling into her hair. I take a deep breath of salty air and open my eyes again, willing myself to fall asleep, staring at the sky.

The shrouded morning light almost blinds me when I open

my eyes. Thankfully, the clouds are still thick and low, dancing among the light breeze. I push myself up and stand to lean over the edge of the wall to watch the restless tides. The ocean is as active as ever, the grey waters thrusting against the stone. Greenish foam forms all around the bottom of the castle.

For a moment, I think about jumping into the waters, but I decide that it's time I test myself with Astrid. I can't avoid her any longer. I need to talk with her, see how I react to her if I'm going to work at being around her. I huff, realizing I haven't even had a proper conversation with her yet.

I stretch my arms up high above my head and feel my loose shirt rise above my pants so that the wind tickles the skin on my stomach. In the distance, a patch of sunlight peers through the clouds in a long misty beam of light that touches the far stretch of land. I watch it for a moment before sighing and lifting the hatch, dropping to the ground without touching the ladder. I walk swiftly back to my room, thankfully not meeting anyone on the way there. They must all be downstairs for "breakfast." I scowl and stuff my hands into my pockets.

Once I reach the door to my bedroom, I pause, gathering as much strength as I can. The dark wooden door creaks loudly as I open it. Before I can even fully step into the room, Astrid is there, her entire being surrounding me. I gulp and look her directly in the eyes, feeling trapped like a mouse caught in a snake's gaze.

"Your highness," Astrid's soprano voice chirps, and I jump at the sound.

"No, don't," I respond, in a clipped voice, my heart pumping wildly.

"As you wish. What shall I call you then?" Astrid asks as I walk over to the washbowl. The fireplace is lit and warm. I sit down in the chair and slip off my shoes.

"I don't know, my name?" I say, washing my hands in the

water, feeling more and more uncomfortable. I haven't looked at her since entering the room. I wonder if she feels as weird as I do.

"Oh, no, sir. That's far too informal," she replies, moving towards me. She takes my shoes and kneels at my feet. I jump out of the chair and gape at her, confused at what she's doing. She stares at me with those wide eyes, and I have to turn away.

I grab new clothes and practically bound into the bathroom. I need to be away from her. She stands, and it looks like she's about to follow me. What is *happening*?

"Um, do you mind?" I ask.

"Oh, I'm sorry, sir. I didn't mean to crowd you. I'll be in the parlor when you've finished changing," she says with a small bow and turns away. I stare after her momentarily, wondering how in the world I was assigned the most proper person I've ever met. Sir? God, that makes me feel like I'm my father.

I close the door and quickly undress, seeing the remnants of scars on my torso. I touch over the skin. I must have gotten cut, though I don't remember the wound. Frowning, I trace my fingers over the scars. If I drank blood regularly, the scars would have already faded. I didn't even notice that I had gotten hurt. If I hadn't had the blood my mother gave me yesterday, I wouldn't have healed. I'm sure of that.

I sigh and look at the ceiling. Another reason I shouldn't abstain for so long. My strength is severely diminished every time I turn blood away.

I turn to the bathtub and notice that it's filled with water. I touch the water, and it's warm. I look back at the door. Did she really fill up my bathtub with hot water? By herself? I close my dropped jaw and look back at the bathtub. Taking a bath would be very nice. I haven't cleaned myself in quite some time, and my hair is starting to matte together.

Letting out a loud breath, I tiptoe into the tub and feel the warm water encase my limbs and body, swirling through my creases, warmly everything thoroughly. I sink gratefully into the water and let my head go under the water.

The sensation is completely different than swimming in the ocean. In this warm water, nothing is threatening to pull me apart. It isn't frozen water, cutting into my skin so cold it burns. Instead, I feel like I'm a real person again. I feel like the water is thawing me from the inside out. I bring my head out of the water and take a deep breath, noticing how the steam and humidity make Astrid's smell so strong. Blossoms of honeysuckle and rose swirl in the air around me, making my gums itch. My stomach grumbles, and I feel my eyes tinge red, but I grip the tub and take another breath.

I'm okay. I'm actually okay.

I breathe in through my nose, savoring the scent of the woman instead of turning away from it. Slowly, my stomach unclenches, and I can release the breath. Smirking internally, I begin to wash with the soap and wash rag she laid out for me. I spend probably closer to half an hour moving the soap all over my body. When I lift myself out of the tub, I feel like a new person.

I dry myself off and get dressed, unsure of what to do with the leftover water. I suppose I could just empty it over the ledge of the balcony. I step out of the bathroom, and Astrid is boiling water over the fire. I didn't even know I had a cast-iron kettle.

"Would you like some tea? It's made of pine needles and herbs." Astrid peers up at me while I'm still drying out my hair with a thin woven towel. She smiles widely at me, her lips pale as they stretch across her teeth.

"Uh, no," I say. "No thank you," I amend. "And thank you for the bath. How did you get water all the way up here?"

"We have a boiler just down the corridor. I kept the candles burning so that it would keep warm for you. It was no trouble," she says, stirring the kettle. She's humming slightly as she works, and I'm so confused. I always imagined that humans hated working for us. They always screamed whenever we came near. This woman, though. She flusters me. "Are you excited about your coronation, sir?"

"No, please, don't call me sir," I say, disgusted. "Kai is fine."

"If it pleases you. I will call you…Kai." She smiles, almost giddy. "But only in private. In public, I will address you as the court does."

"Fine," I hedge. I don't even want to think about the court. "To answer your question, no. I'm not looking forward to it."

"Why not? Isn't it a tremendous occasion?"

"Yeah, I guess," I say. "It's a big party for no reason. I don't really care about all the drama."

"I would imagine all the drama would be in your favor."

"I guess, but I don't want it," I say, wondering if I should be sharing this with her.

"I don't see how that's possible," she says, sitting by the kettle and sipping on her tea. "It all seems so glamorous, with all the beautiful gowns and music and dancing—"

"You could never understand."

She looks straight ahead, expressionless. I bite my tongue. I shouldn't lash out at her for my misfortunes. She looks down at her hands like I hurt her feelings.

"You're absolutely right. My apologies, Prince," she says.

"No, I didn't mean…" I stop. What could I even say? I've never stumbled over my words so badly before in my life. "I just mean that it's not all that it's cracked up to be. The coronation will mostly be politics and boring conversations."

"What would you rather do instead?" Her eyes meet mine for a moment, and I'm tempted to stare at her blue eyes, those delicate icicle eyes that are such a refreshing change from the constant blood-red eyes I see everywhere in this damn castle.

"Read," I blurt out. Her eyes are hypnotic. "I would rather be reading or discussing fiction. Or painting. I'm not very good, and we don't have many supplies, but I like to try to capture the mountains around us on a canvas."

"That's lovely, Kai," she says, quirking her head to the side. Her blonde hair falls off the side of her shoulder as she smiles up at me. "I wish I knew how to read."

"You were never taught?"

"Alheri tried, but I was always called away. She gave up after a while. I know only enough to work with numbers and sewing patterns. But I do love stories. My mother used to tell me such wonderful stories."

"Maybe I'll read to you then," I say before my brain can catch up to my mouth. What am I saying?

"I'd like that," she whispers and flicks her eyes to mine again. I swallow an anxious breath before looking away.

My cheeks feel hot, and now I don't know where to look. I opt to look out the glass doors. The sunlight has spread, and the glass glitters as the sun passes through it. Astrid hasn't stopped moving since I came back to the room. I catch myself sneaking glances at her, and she catches my eyes, smiling softly. Her eyes are wide, but as I look at her face longer, I see that she looks tired. The skin under her eyes is a shade darker, closer to blue than pink.

"I'm going to go to the study," I say suddenly, and Astrid blinks in surprise. "Please, no more cleaning for today. Get some rest."

"As you wish," she says, standing to face me. "Kai."

~

The castle feels alight with the buzz about the coronation, plans, and visions coming together to celebrate my birthday. My dread is almost palpable. The parade of vampires, pretending to be a functioning court where the ladies will dress up and try to woo me. Shouldn't it be the other way around? I'm to be dressed up in the finest clothing, dance with the ladies of the court, and by the end of the night, I'm supposed to know which of them I want to take as a wife. To be my queen.

I shake my head as I walk aimlessly. I try to picture the various girls I've met before. Caden was the one they all fawned over. I never paid much attention. Of course, I did have friends. Most of whom were gone now. As we grew older, I found that the people I connected with best were less-than-noble vampires, so as soon as possible, Baldassare found a way to kick them out of the castle and back to Livsnerven. He had made it perfectly clear that I should only be keeping company with proper people of pure lineage. It felt like I was being punished back then. Why else would my father send away all my friends?

I reach the main foyer, and at the front doors to the castle, and in a moment of pure astonishment, my jaw drops. I have to blink twice to make sure I'm not dreaming.

Sure enough, one of my old friends is standing at the precipice of the castle, arguing with one of the guards in her fiery manner. I stare, preoccupied with how *different* she looks. Her brown hair flows easily down her back, stopping at her waist. Instead of remembering the wild young girl with pixie-like hair, I'm looking at a beautiful woman. Her face is more defined, less round than before. Her body has filled out, her muscles leanly hugging the curves of her hips and shoulders. But the most startling change is her eyes. When I knew her, she had bright red eyes. Now, they are a dull, muddy brown. Not silver to indicate an animal diet, nor bright red to show a human-blood diet either. I cock my head curiously, but then I have to stop myself from chuckling as I watch her face contort in shallow anger towards the guard that has stopped her.

"Lilith," I say, smiling, still beside myself that she's here. She's really here. I turn toward the guard. "Please, Garrett. This is a friend of mine. Let her through."

With a demeaning grunt towards Lilith, he stands back, and Lilith's face turns from anger to glee in an instant. I smile widely back at her before she jumps into my arms, embracing me tightly.

I laugh easily, forgetting all of my troubles as I breathe in my long lost friend. I squeeze her for a second, then she jolts backward to gawk at me.

"Wow, Kai," Lilith says, looking me over. I rub the back of my neck sheepishly, hating the scrutiny. "You've grown up! What are you, an adult now? What the hell? Here I thought I'd be able to just pick up where we left off."

"Look who's talking! You're like a totally different person," I say, unable to help my wide smile.

"Hah, duly noted. Well, all that aside, you look great. You've grown your hair," she says.

"So have you," I reply, picking up a strand of her long hair and then making a disgusted face at her.

She scoffs at me, hitting me playfully in the chest.

Aware of prying eyes, I lightly grab her hand and place it in my arm, towing her away from the archway. She doesn't question and lets me lead.

"Let's get out of here," I say quietly, feeling light from her presence. "What brings you to Feilfri? I thought you'd never come back."

"And miss your coronation? Forget it! I'd hate to miss all the drama from the court ladies. Too fun to pass up," she says, with a tinge of something in her voice. I know the words are playful, but she's never liked the court or anything having to do with royalty.

"Yeah, it'll be a hoot," is all I can think of to say.

Before long, we're upstairs, away from the drawing commotion of dinnertime. Once upon a time, Lilith would drink straight from a human, using a method that would allow her to feed without hurting them. She called it "blood sharing." She would feed on a human whilst they fed on her, and her blood would replace that which she was drinking.

I'd often considered trying it, but it's a slow process. Vampire blood can work its way to any part of a human's body, but it takes time. Lilith always said she would have to be careful not to take too much from her end, or else she would kill the human. High risk, high reward, she had said. Though, it wasn't like the human had a choice in the matter.

Either way, she knows my tolerance for human blood is thin, and she's never pressured me in the past, so it feels only natural for her to go without dinner to hang out with me. The warm feeling in my stomach spreads across my chest at the thought. It really is nice to have a friend. I'd forgotten how it feels.

When we reach my bedroom door, chatting lightly about the ridiculous decorations that my brother and father have put up, Lilith freezes. I turn towards her, confused by her sudden change. "What's wrong?"

"A *human*, Kai?" Lilith hisses through her teeth.

Astrid. I'd almost completely forgotten about her.

For a second, my eyes grow wide at the unspoken accusation. I look at the door, hearing Astrid's movements behind it, then I hang my head in defeat. There isn't a way around it. I'd have to explain myself. It's not like I was courting her.

"Yeah, that's Astrid. Father assigned her as my *kvinne*," I say, the words burning the back of my throat.

"*Kvinne*? God," she says, an astounded look on her face. "How do you manage?"

"I haven't," I respond, plainly. "She was assigned to me only days ago, and I've basically avoided her ever since. I've really only spoken with her once."

Lilith nods, her eyes drawing to something far away. For a moment, she's quiet, like she's thinking very hard about something.

"Can I meet her?" she says after a while.

"I guess," I reply, not knowing how Astrid will respond. Lilith's eyes watch me tightly as I reach towards my bedroom door and open it.

"Hello, Astrid," I say as we breach the threshold. Astrid's face is smiling, and she opens her mouth to speak, but then catches the gaze of Lilith standing next to me. Astrid almost drops her belongings in shock, but then with wide eyes, she breaks into a low bow.

"Prince Kai, my apologies, I did not know you would be bringing a guest," she says, her voice light and breathy.

I chuckle softly. "I didn't either. This is my good friend, Lilith. She surprised me only moments ago. She wanted to meet you," I explain, not really understanding most of it myself.

"Mistress," Astrid says, still looking to the floor.

"No no—" Lilith tries to start.

"It's okay, Astrid. She's a lot like me—"

"Yeah, just call me Lilith," Lilith says on top of my words.

I look at her and smile.

Astrid peaks up from her bow and sees our casual stance, clearly measuring the sincerity of our words, before straightening up. She doesn't meet our eyes, but at least she's not bowing anymore. I sigh.

"If you'd prefer privacy, I will excuse myself to the kitchens," she says.

"Sure," I reply, confused at her implication.

In a flurry, she grabs a few articles of clothing, hurries out the door, and closes it behind her. Lilith bursts into laughter after a moment of silence. I look at her, bemused by her expression.

"Oh *please*," she says, plopping down on my bed, still shaking with laughter.

"What?!" I take in the chair in front of the fireplace. "What's so funny?"

"Did you see her face? She thinks—"

Lilith breaks off in another wave of laughter. She grips her torso for support as she chuckles loudly.

"Oh my God, Lilith," I scold, but she holds out her hand to stop me.

"Wow," she says after the laughter wave passes. "My God, Kai. What have you done to that poor girl?"

"What!?" I demand, shocked at the accusation. "What did I say?"

"Oh nothing, I'm just teasing you."

"For *what*?!"

"She is so into you! It's so obvious!" she says, eyeing me again. "And here I thought you'd just be having trouble keeping your hands away from her *blood*!"

My jaw must be on the floor because the shock that's coursing through me is incredible.

"What in the world are you talking about?!" My voice sounds high and squeaky.

"She thinks I'm your girlfriend and that we want privacy to, ya know, be *together*," she explains carefully, enunciating all the syllables equally, using her hands to further clarify.

"What?!" I say for the third time.

"You couldn't tell? She thinks we're going to be all kissing and sexing each other up in here," she says, patting the bed suggestively.

"Oh, God!" I exclaim, not hiding the grimace on my face.

"Oh please, you know you liked it the first time," Lilith says, winking at me.

I shake my head promptly. How in the world had this come up so quickly?

"Re*lax*, Kai," Lilith drawls. "It's not like it's an unheard of suggestion. We did try, you know."

"Yeah, yeah, yeah. That was a long time ago. And—"

"Yeah, I know, Kai. Please chill. We gave it a shot back then, just to say we did. It didn't work, so that's that. It's just funny as hell," she says, wiping away a fake tear of laughter. She's acting like a caricature. "Don't be uncomfortable, Kai. I'm sorry I brought it up."

If I had been better fed, I'm sure my blood would have rushed to my face and turned my cheeks flaming red.

"No, it's fine," I rush to correct her. "It's just a weird time all around right now. You know my father gave me a sex talk the other day? It was so weird. He was saying I need to be a man and all that like it's a fuckin' disgrace if I don't have sex before marriage. How twisted is that?"

Lilith's joking demeanor shifts subtly.

"And then he tells me about how I need a *wife*? And get this, it has to be a pureblood. Like that shit matters," I finish my tangent in a rush.

She sits upright on the bed, then, not meeting my eye. Her smile fading into a slight wince.

"Oh, hey, I didn't—"

"No, don't, Kai. It's fine. It's not your fault I'm a half-blooded vampire, unworthy of a place at Feilfri. I don't want to live here anyway," she says quickly, gritting her teeth at the end. "It's your father who's the messed up one anyway. I didn't come here to guilt you into anything. I just wanted to see my friend."

The warmth in my stomach flares at the words. I'm so glad that our friendship is as strong as always. Seeing her forlorn expression, I stand up and cross the room in one step before sitting next to her and pulling her into my arms. The bond between us has never really been sexual. We've been the closest of friends since I could remember. The one time we'd kissed was a test for us both. Memory serves that it only lasted a few seconds, then we'd broken it off, each of us understanding that it wasn't the right path for us.

"What's wrong, Lilith? Why did you come back here?" I whisper into her hair, feeling nothing inside me but warmth and tenderness for this girl who's been my friend for so long.

"I don't even know if I can explain it right," she says softly. I release her and meet her eyes expectantly. "Well, when I left Feilfri, I left Livsnerven as well. I traveled through the wastelands. I didn't really know where I was going until I found Menneskelig."

My body freezes involuntarily. Menneskelig is the human capital of the island. The place Feilfri Castle had warred with for decades.

"I've been living there, Kai," Lilith continues, ignoring my silent response. "I've been able to mingle easily with humans. I even attend their school, though I don't really speak to anyone. They all have a sense that something's off with me.

"It's easier than I'd thought, though, living with the humans. I was worried that their food wouldn't be enough. That I'd have to feed as well and to be honest, I'm not sure I would have survived if I tried. One drop of blood while living near hundreds of heartbeats...I'd never be able to resist," she says. "Luckily, I've been able to get away with eating human food most of the time and feeding on animals or willing humans outside the city when I need it."

That explains the eye color, I think to myself. A purely human *food* diet.

"Still, most of the humans pretend I'm not there. They don't like how different I look from them. It's just close enough not to draw questions, though," she says like she's explaining it to herself more than me. "Of course, I don't push it. It's safer for everyone if they ignore me. I don't have to worry about bloodlust or feeding, breaking my abstinence. I'm just lucky that I'm only half-vampire, I guess."

"So, what changed?" I ask solemnly. If things were going

well, she would still be there.

She stares into the fireplace, hesitating momentarily.

"Someone approached me," she whispers.

I frown, confused. "So?"

She flicks her eyes to mine. "What do you *mean*? He came right up to me during the school lunch hour and introduced himself!"

I try to hide my smile. Had she always been prone to overreaction?

"What?!" she says this time. Her eyes are wide.

"I'm sorry. You seem so upset, but I don't really see how this is a bad thing?" I confess.

"It…its…well, I don't know," she stutters. "He wanted to sit and *talk*!"

I mockingly open my eyes wide in shock. "The audacity!"

"Seriously, Kai! I literally ran away from him!"

"You ran away? Seriously?" I shake my head, changing direction quickly. "Listen, if you were truly trying to stay away from humans, you wouldn't be living in their city. Aren't you trying to blend in? What's the harm in talking to a random person?"

Lilith ponders this for a moment.

"I guess you're right," she says hesitantly.

"Do you feel you're a danger to them?"

"No, not at all. It's just so strange. The way he approached me, away from his own friends. Like I was just any other person," she says, her eyes far away again.

"Sounds like he likes you," I say, offhandedly, releasing her and reaching for a glass.

"What a thing to say," she replies, visibly less upset than before.

"I'm sorry about what I said," I say, not meeting her eyes as I pour myself some water from the basin. It's chilled, just like I liked it.

I wonder if Astrid left this for me. "About Baldassare and my 'kingly' duties. That was insensitive."

"All is forgiven, friend," she says. "You know it sucks being away from you, right?"

I smile and say, "Right back at you. I can't tell you how lonely it's been."

The seriousness of the moment sits thickly in the room. I gulp down a swish of water, noting how bitter my mouth tastes.

"Are you really going to stay for the coronation?" I ask, still facing away from her.

"Do you think I could?"

"Honestly? Probably not." I hang my head at the words. It isn't fair that my father is the most rotten bastard on the planet. Lilith is silent, and I face her, setting the glass down and taking her hands in mine.

"I'd fight for you to stay," I whisper, her eyes just as intense as mine. "You know I would."

She smirks. "Yeah, I know. You better not push your luck, though."

For a moment, I want her to ask me to fight for her to stay. I want an excuse, any excuse, to go against my father. For my sake, for Astrid's sake. It doesn't seem that it will be that easy, however.

I settle for a defeated smile.

"What about Alheri? Does she still work at the castle?" Lilith asks after a while. "I'd love to see her."

Her tone is expectant. Most humans don't live very long in the capital of the vampire kingdom, often dying at the ripe age of twenty. Even someone as protected and necessary as the witch of Feiflri Castle, even if no vampire can touch the witch's blood, the physical stress of living under duress can snap a frail human body. Luckily, the last time I saw Alheri, she'd been a whirlwind of energy. I smile widely at her.

"She's doing just fine," I say quickly, and the relief on her face is plain. "She's been serving my father as the castle *heks*. She's becoming quite a powerful witch."

"What is the word in her language? I can't remember," Lilith asks.

"*Aje*. It's almost a direct translation from the Sollys language," I say, thinking back to my book on the history of Freyja and the witches in Sollys.

"You're a nerd, you know that, right?" Lilith teases.

I smile but pull on her arm again. We walk all the way down to the boiler room, where I know Alheri spends most of her days. When we enter, the room isn't hot like you'd expect. The air is stale and almost cool, though there are billowing plummets of steam coming off the giant pool in the middle of the room. I see Alheri in her thick leather robes, whispering in a foreign language, her hands skimming across the water. She looks flushed and tired but otherwise pristine. Not a hair out of place.

"Al?" Lilith calls out, breaking Alheri's deep reverie.

The witch jerks up. She's clearly exhausted, with haunted eyes and a sagging smile, but as soon as she hears Lilith's voice, a look of bright curiosity shines on her face. Her black hair billows like unruly pin curls around her head. I smile, seeing her expression brighten up immensely at the sight of Lilith.

The girls break out into a multitude of squeals and jumping hugs. I fight the urge to put my hands over my ears to protect myself from their shouts of joy. Instead, I find myself laughing, watching the two of them talk at a rapid pace. Lilith gives her the same explanation of her presence. She is here for my coronation. Alheri eyes me with an amused and content expression.

"Will you both join me for dinner?" Alheri asks. "I'm finished here for the night. I was just speaking with the water."

"That sounds ominous," I say, chuckling. "What's for dinner?"

"Well, seeing as Jonnas got a fresh cut of lamb in the kitchen, why don't I grab a basket of it? We can have a picnic. After all, you are the crowned prince." Alheri smiles at me.

I shake my head at all the insinuations of grandeur but smile back at her. We make our way through the castle, laughing and chatting lightly about various things, and my heart feels light. I had forgotten how close Lilith and Alheri were. I feel like an ass for never seeking friendship from the woman. She and I were around one another for many years, and I had never noticed her.

"Can we eat outside, Al? Please?" Lilith asks, tugging on Alheri's arm.

"We can't today, Lilith. It's sunny out now," I say, peering through a small window. "It might set in a few hours if you both want to wait—"

"Nonsense!" Alheri chimes in. "We are perfectly capable of eating outside. As long as you're with me, the sun cannot hurt you."

"Whatever that means," Lilith says, the glee pure on her face.

"Lead the way," I say, trying to suppress my shock, and hold out the basket of freshly cooked lamb and vegetables toward them.

Alheri shows us to the front doors, the guards no longer present since most vampires cannot come through during daylight. Alheri opens the doors confidently, and I can't help but jerk away from the light. The bright reflections of the stones hurt my eyes, and I throw my hands to my face to shield myself. Alheri lays her hands on mine, pulling my hands away from my eyes.

"My prince," her low alto voice purrs. "You are safe with me."

Alheri speaks vibrantly, her voice resounding with power and ancient earthly things. Her hands are soft, tugging on mine gently, reassuring me that I'm safe. As I step into the light, I feel nothing but a slight warmth on my cool skin. I look around, and suddenly

I'm a child again with brand new eyes. I'd always imagined sitting, basking, in the sun. Now, I am completely bathed in sunlight, and it doesn't hurt. I gape at the feeling of the sun on my skin, like a brush of down feathers or a kiss from a raindrop. Even the light has ceased hurting my eyes. I can stare for miles, seeing things anew, like I'd been blind up until this moment.

I look at Alheri, her hands still on mine, pulling me out of the castle. Lilith watches my face with a crooked-smile. This is obviously not her first time.

"How..." I try to ask, an overwhelming joy blooming inside my chest. "How is this possible? Do I have to keep hold of your hands?"

"No, Kai," Alheri says, releasing my hands to prove her point. She reaches up and touches a light film-like substance that acts as a barrier around the three of us. It looks like oil on water, with the sun casting rainbows everywhere as it cuts through the film. "This dome protects us from the sun."

"Amazing," I breathe. "You're amazing."

"Thank you, my Prince." She smiles and curtsies. I look at her with brand new eyes. In the sun, her wide brown eyes look like deep golden waters filled with warmth and comfort.

I gape at the sunlit branches of the trees and how the snow looks *alive*. The light bounces off each snowflake like a crystal glittering light in every direction. The grass looks greener, and the trees look browner like they are drawing in the sun's warmth. Even the skin on my hands looks less dead than before as I turn them over, studying the way the sun's rays shimmer across my skin, a highlight of life brightening even the dullest of cells.

I look back toward the castle, seeing it with new eyes, too. I've never seen stone look so beautiful. There are countless colors in the walls, all brought to life by the sun. Smoke comes out the sides of the walls, from each individual fireplace, and wraps up the castle walls, dancing in the sunlight. I turn back towards my friends, feeling a sort of awe in my chest.

Lilith leads us quickly to a patch of ground by the edge of the shore before the drawbridge that separates the castle from the rest of the kingdom.

"I don't understand," I say as the ladies begin to dig into the picnic basket. "How is this possible? It's certainly magic."

"Have you ever wondered why my skin and your skin are so drastically different, Prince?" Alheri asks, with sudden severity.

I gulp, shaking my head.

"When a Sollyan leaves our land, we leave the sun. Our sun. It is the source of life for my people. When we are removed from its nurturing presence, we undergo a process known in your tongue as *blekne*. It means we are bleached of our life."

Lilith looks down at her skirts, nibbling softly on a piece of bread.

"When we are stripped bare of the things that make us unique, such as our rich dark skin, we go mad. I know," Alheri says with a thick voice. "I have seen it happen. When my family left Sollys to come here, my brother did not heed my father's wisdom. He was ravaged by the harsh winters and lack of nourishing sunlight. His skin turned a sickly shade of white like he had lost his entire life force. He slowly lost his mind, and his magic turned to darkness. When we thought all was lost, my father took him into the wastelands and killed him."

I gasp, despite myself. I've never read about this in my history books.

Alheri looks at me with a soft smile. "No amount of reading could prepare you for the truth, Prince Kai."

"So this," I tear my eyes away from her all-knowing eyes and run my fingers along the thin barrier surrounding us. "This is your protection."

"I am refueled by the heat, you see," Alheri explains. "That's why I work in the boiler room so often. It's not that I cannot do other duties or that I've been ordered there. I prefer the heat of the room. I generate most of the fires that keep the waters hot, and they return their heat back to me."

I nod slowly, remembering how the room itself had felt cool, despite the bubbling, boiling waters in the pool.

"But this is not a time for sadness or stories," Alheri turns her attention to Lilith. "You must tell me why you've come back. And no more nonsense about Kai's coronation. I know you better."

"Ah, I've been had!" Lilith says dramatically. She unravels her tale about Menneskelig and her desire to mingle with the humans, to which Alheri is a much better listener than I had been. My thoughts still tangled with Alheri's story, I try to focus on Lilith. As I listen to them, I cannot help but notice the immense timelessness in Alheri's voice. She must have the voice of a thousand-year-old human instead of a seventeen-year-old.

"Well? Are you going to keep me in suspense?! What is the boy's name?" Alheri says.

Lilith blushes, playing idly with the food in her lap. "His name is William."

"And you say he approached you out of nowhere? You'd never spoken to him before?" Alheri asks.

"Yeah. I'm not sure what drove him to say hello," she says with a very distant expression.

"I'm telling you, he likes you," I mutter.

"Why do you say that?" Alheri starts but then sees Lilith's somewhat horrified look. "Why would that be a bad thing?"

"I'm a vampire!"

"You're not really a risk, though, Lil," I say.

"I don't understand," Alheri chirps. "Is there some level of risk that I am misunderstanding?"

I half-frown. "I suppose you've not really been around anyone other than nobles and Purebloods. Not since my father sent away the dhampyrs and other lesser vampires."

"You say lesser as if that is supposed to mean something," Alheri says, clearly confused.

"It doesn't," I say. "But Baldassare thinks that anyone with 'tainted' blood is a lesser-vampire."

"Is the terminology the only difference?" she asks.

Lilith chimes in, "No, not necessarily. There are Purebloods, dhampyrs, halvblods, sølvblod, and the wild ones in the wastelands. Those are halvblods that have starved and gone insane."

"Purebloods are one-hundred percent vampire. We have been bred to keep our bloodline. A dhampyr is the product of a pureblood and human coupling. A halvblod is half dhampyr, half-human," I continue.

"Wouldn't the intermingling result in an indistinguishable product eventually?"

"Yes," I say. "That's why it doesn't matter. We're all on this planet together. It shouldn't matter what's in our blood and what's not."

"But that's not what she asked originally, Kai," Lilith says. "She's not interested in politics—"

"Well—" Alheri starts.

"Regardless, being a pure vampire means you *must* feed on humans to survive. To be a vampire is to require the lifeblood of another to sustain your own life. When a pure vampire and a human produces offspring, they require half as much blood. Like me," Lilith says. "I can survive mostly on actual human food and hunt animal blood as a supplement."

Lilith's expression is almost proud.

"So that's what Kai meant when he said you weren't really a threat," Alheri says. "But that means for you…" she says, looking at me. "You must struggle, my Prince."

"Yes," I whisper, playing with a stick. Alheri grabs my hand, and I look up into her deep almond eyes. I share a sad smile with her, flaring my nostrils at the smell of the witch's cedar-like blood. After a moment, I look back at Lilith. "Whats a sølvblod? I've never seen one before."

Lilith smiles. "A Silver-Blood."

Alheri tears her gaze away from me and looks back over to her friend.

"Silver blood?" I ask.

"We started calling them that. When a vampire lives off of only animal blood, their eyes turn a bright silver."

"Okay, I definitely don't understand that," Alheri said.

"How have you lived your whole life at Feilfri and never noticed our eye color?"

Lilith interrupts before Alheri can respond. "You can tell a vampire's appetite by their eye color. The darker it is, almost black, the hungrier they are. Or rather, thirstier. When they have bright red eyes, that means they have recently fed on a human. Mine are brown because I eat human food. I like to imagine it's the eye color I would have had if I'd been born a human."

"And silver-eyed vampires are those that survive on animal blood," Alheri says.

"That would explain why I would have never seen one," I say. "Everyone in the castle drinks human blood. Even me." The last words are barely a whisper.

"You have to do what you can to survive," Lilith says, rehashing an age-old argument.

"That doesn't mean I don't like it," I say.

"I see your heart, my Prince. You do not need to explain your intentions."

"But you don't understand, Alheri," I say, almost angrily.

"I'm a *Pureblood.* That means no matter what I do, I'll never be able to get rid of my thirst for human blood. I don't know if it's even possible for a Pureblood to survive on animal blood alone."

Lilith and Alheri sigh, almost in tandem.

"It doesn't matter," I murmur. I won't spoil the time I have with Lilith. "Please, let's go back inside. We can sneak some of my father's spirits and drink on the rooftop."

Lilith smiles at me, my heart tugging at the sight. As we make our way back inside, I take one last look at the sunlight, watching the golden rays pierce the sides of the large pine trees and glint off the white snow. The choppy ocean waves look a little bit calmer in the sunset, casting bright ruby reflections every which way. I feel at peace, breathing in the salt spray and watching the sun hide behind the horizon. I will have to take advantage of Alheri's power and presence again. Maybe I can convince Astrid to have dinner out with us one day.

"Hey, leave me alone!" Lilith's voice breaking me out of my daydream. "Get your hands off me," she hisses.

"What is this?" I sprint to her side, seeing a vampire grip Lilith's wrists. His eyes are bright, blood red, screaming of lust and treachery. "Release her now!"

"I'm sorry, Prince Kai, but this *bitch* was trying to enter Feilfri—"

A low growl rips from my lips, and I push the man off of Lilith, hearing her yelp behind me. I take the monster's shirt in my hands and thrust him against the wall. He cries out.

"Never let me see you again," I snarl, red tainting the edges of my vision.

"Sir, you cannot be protecting this half-blood—"

I throw my right arm as hard as I can, my fist meeting his jaw in a sickening crunch of bones. He looks up at me with a disgusted expression. Blood pours from his nose, and he scurries away, but not before he spits in our direction. Rage flares inside of me, and I can vaguely feel Lilith's arms around me, shushing me and pulling me out of sight.

"Don't bother, Kai," Lilith yells. "Kai, *stop*!"

"I can't fucking stand it," I snarl, a vicious hatred pushing me to run after that guy and keep pummeling him into dirt and dust. When he's out of sight, I turn back to Lilith, cupping her jaw in my hands, looking over her quickly. "Are you alright? Did he hurt you?"

"No, no. I'm fine," Lilith says, pulling out of my grasp. She shows me her wrists. "See? Already healed. I *am* a vampire, after all." I hang my head in defeat. I would never be away from the blood. I would never be away from prejudice. Then, I remember Alheri.

"Where's Alheri?" I ask, looking around frantically.

"She's gone, Kai. She will not fight," Lilith says, her voice telling me that this isn't the first time this has happened to them.

"I'm so sorry, Lil. I'm so sorry," I say, my head falling onto her shoulder.

"Don't be, Kai. This is why I made a life elsewhere," she says, unfazed like she expected this to happen. "I shouldn't have come back here—"

"Don't say that!" I say, hearing the panic in my voice. I stare into her eyes and grip her shoulders. I feel like a child who has lost his favorite toy. "I love seeing you. You know that. I miss you so much when you aren't here."

"Then come with me!"

Shock courses through me as I listen to her repeat the same words she said to me so many years ago. I look in her eyes and see that she is remembering the same thing. She wanted me to run away with her, and at that time, when I loved her the most, I almost did. I had almost run away from everything just to be with her. But I couldn't then. And I can't now.

"Lilith…"

She smiles sadly, and my chest tightens. In her eyes, I see that she knows exactly why. I can't abandon Alheri or Astrid. I can't leave Astrid to be reassigned to another vampire, not when that would make me personally responsible. Even if the rest of the world is this beautiful, shining place, I could never survive. I'd perish in the wild, or I'd ravage some poor human town, my thirst growing every time I killed. Anxiety grips my stomach at the thought of Astrid, broken and bloody, as my next victim. And if I don't kill her…someone else will.

"You can't leave her," Lilith says. It's not a question. "And you shouldn't."

"I want to come with you," I say desperately.

"I do too, Kai-Kai," she says, using my childhood nickname. "*Jeg elsker deg så mye, Nikolaj.*"

My heart feels like it's in shambles. Hearing the words of affection come from her mouth now makes me feel so low. I can hear how much she wants to leave. My heart throbs heavily in my chest.

"*Liljen min,*" I say back. After a moment, I continue, "Do you have to leave now? Couldn't you stay? Just for a little while longer?"

Despite the horrible desperation in my voice, Lilith simply responds, "Just a little while longer."

5

ASTRID

I swiftly leave the room, walking briskly away from the idea of Kai spending time with that beautiful, brown-haired girl. Did she have to be so *pretty*? I scold myself wildly. Obviously, I am a no-one to Kai. He is a secretive person and keeps his personal life away from prying eyes, and I am no different. Just because I serve him on a more personal level than other *thralls*, I am just a servant, even if it's to the highest family in all of Livsnerven.

I walk quickly to the kitchens, set on throwing myself into my tasks. I spend the rest of the evening cooking large meals for the royal family, *not* thinking about Kai and Lilith. I work with the baker to knead dough and prepare more wheat for grinding after the loaves are scored and put in the ovens. I clean the dishes in the sink, rubbing them pristinely clean and not thinking about Kai's long black hair mixing with that woman's soft, silky, brown hair.

"Ugh," I hiss at my internal thoughts. The baker eyes me

curiously, but I ignore him. I will not let my petty thoughts about my master taint my work.

But the more I try not to think about it, the harder it is to put them out of my mind. How do I even know there is anything more than what meets the eye? Maybe Kai isn't that sort of man. He's never paraded around women like his brother. He never even dances with any of the women at court gatherings. Not in the glimpses I've caught, anyway.

I huff and dry my hands on my apron before setting myself to another task. I walk down to the boiler rooms, hoping to practice more fabric dyeing with the leftover food scraps. I recently received a portion of dried berries that I wanted to test.

I open the large oak door, hoping to see Alheri at her station. Usually, she keeps me company in the large room while I do my work. Now, the air feels sticky and hot, and the dye pots are all in use. It seems as though I'm not in luck. Though, maybe I can go back to Kai's room?

I shake my head quickly. No, I can't go back up there. Not until he summons me. I will not interrupt him and his guest.

After walking back towards the throne room and hoping to be called upon for something to do, I end up pacing back and forth aimlessly. It's well after dinner, so there's no chance to help there. I know there's probably no use in standing around like this. I can't go back to my old room. I suppose—

"Astrid?" a slight feminine voice calls me out of my frantic pacing. I twirl around to see Queen Eileen in a luxurious dressing gown made of beautiful purple silk.

"My Queen," I say, bowing low to the ground.

"Rise, my child," she says, in a very pretty voice. I briefly wonder what it must have been like to have her as a mother, whispering fairy tales in her lilting soprano speech. "I was hoping I would find you."

"What can I do for you, my Queen?" I say, keeping my eyes lowered towards her waist. She is so slight that one would guess she was made of a bird's feathers, but she holds herself with such confidence and poise, showcasing her obvious strength.

"Astrid, you are one of the most talented seamstresses and embroiders here at Feilfri," Eileen says. "I was hoping you would help me assemble my family's coronation dress?"

"My Queen, you are too kind. I would be most pleased to assist you in any way you desire," I say, bowing low again. My heart flutters in my chest, and my ears ring from disbelief. She wants *me* to help her?!

"Wonderful. Do you have a moment to follow me to my study?"

"Absolutely, my Queen."

"Please call me Eileen, Astrid," she says. Now, I understand more closely Kai's tendency to be on a first-name basis. "For you and I are to become good friends."

"As you wish, Eileen," I say, feeling that the words are inadequate for her regality.

She hooks my arm in hers and leads me down the dark corridor, lit only by torchlight now. As we walk, I try to match my stride to her long, soundless steps. She floats like an angel, and I'm just a stumbling fool.

"How are you fairing with my son?" she asks after a moment.

"Prince Kai is a wonderful host, my Queen," I say.

"That's great to hear," she responds. "And you feel that you are taken care of?"

"Of course, your Highness! I want for nothing."

"Excellent, Astrid," she says, patting my hand slightly. "Ah, here we are."

I have seen the study before, but now it has been transformed into a fashion parlor, equipped with many bolts of fabric in different colors and types. There are four mannequins, each styled with garments of high couture. There are three suits, one for each of the royal men, and a stunningly exquisite gown, obviously for Queen Eileen. I feel my jaw gape at the clothing.

"I see you are impressed with the work I've already done," Eileen says, smiling widely.

"Oh, yes," I breathe. "You made these yourself, my Queen?"

"Yes. I have a deep passion for clothing design," she says, with a wistful tone as she strokes the long, pleated skirts of the dress.

"You've done an amazing job, Eileen," I say, still feeling uncomfortable using her first name.

"Not as good as the work we will do together, Astrid."

"I'm not sure how I could be of use. These garments already look so beautiful," I say.

"Well, these are all from Kai's last birthday. You know how we vampires only celebrate a birthday every few years," she says.

"I'm sorry, I did not know that," I admit. "Do you not follow the new Gregorian calendar?"

"I must be so confusing. We do follow the idea that there are 365 days in the year, split into four seasons and 12 months. I did not mean to confuse your education, dear," Eileen said. "I simply meant that we, as noble vampires, do not age as humans do. You grow at a rate over each year, celebrating another year of life after only one year."

"Vampires do not age in the same way?" I ask, my curiosity peaked.

"Correct, *kjære*," Eileen says in a perfect Norwegian accent. The word is a pet name for so many families, including my own mother. It makes me feel like a child again. "Kai is turning eighteen this year, but he has been growing into his manhood for about four of your years."

This shocks me.

"You mean to say that if he was a human, he would be..." I say, trying to do the math in my head. "No, he couldn't be over 70 years in human time."

Eileen laughs breezily. "You are quite intelligent, Astrid! Yes, he would be turning 72 this year if he were a human."

I feel cool shocks of astonishment course through my body, sending slight sparks across my fingertips. Are Kai and I *that* different?

"I can see this is a shock to you, but do not despair," Eileen says. "Vampires and humans do not age in the same ways. We spend most of our childhood in a blind thirst. Kai did not reach the age of adolescence until he was fifteen or sixteen. Still, he would have been on this earth for over sixty years, but he did not have a conscience. Not like he does now."

"I'm sorry, my Queen. I did not mean to go into such a state of unrest," I say. "I simply did not realize Kai and I were so different."

"In truth, I think you are more similar than you know," she says with a slight smile. "There are not many humans that can converse with me so easily."

"I simply wish to serve, Eileen," I reply.

"Yes," the queen says, with a glint in her eyes. "Now, enough talk of mathematics and science. Let us discuss a plan for my family's dress. I would like to have us wrapped in similar patterns or at least similar fabrics. What do you think about gold silk fabric with black embroidery?"

Before I can hold my tongue, to observe civility and respect, I throw myself into a deep conversation about robes, tunics, trousers, and cloaks. Eileen is easily amused by my thoughts, bouncing off ideas with me, expecting me to counter her thoughts with my own, and before I realize, I'm speaking to her as casually as I would with Alheri or even my own mother, were she still alive. I see now why she insisted on such informal greetings when we first began. Had I continued speaking with formality, I would have stumbled over my words, and we would have gotten nowhere with our discussion.

"And I would be happy to come up with a design that you could use on Prince Kai's tunic that could represent his upcoming coronation," I say, jotting down several concept drawings on the parchment Eileen gave me.

"That would be wonderful, Astrid," she replies. "You are to come here at dusk every day this week. We will work on the gowns and ensembles to have everything finished before Kai's coronation."

"Absolutely. I don't see why we shouldn't be able to accomplish it. I could also have Annette and Alheri join me. They are just as talented as I am. That is, if you are worried we might not finish the task," I say, worried that I've overstepped my bounds.

"Nonsense, I am sure we are up to the task. But just you. I'd like to get to know the woman that will be taking care of my Kai," Eileen says, with a happy if distant expression.

"As you wish," I say, blinking in astonishment. Does that mean she thinks I am going to be with Kai when he becomes king? My chest tightens when I even consider serving Kai so closely.

The next day, I come to the study immediately after finishing my tasks. Queen Eileen is already there, sketching and drawing out patterns on old parchment paper. As soon as she sees me, she bursts into motion, thrusting bolts of fabric at me to unravel and cut to precise measurements. By the time the sun has completely gone down, we've measured and cut out pieces for her entire gown, plus most of Kai's trousers and shirtwaist. I'm so pleased with how everything is coming together so smoothly that I almost forget I'm working with royalty. Eileen has an aptitude and skill with fabrics unlike anyone I'd ever worked with.

"So, tell me, Astrid, how did you learn such fine skills?" she asks me. "Your work is very efficient and tidy."

"My mother taught me most of what I know," I start. "But after she passed, it was mostly practice and need-based. Once my sewing became essential to my job performance, I took it upon myself to become as good as I could be."

"That's very admirable of you," she says, running her hand over the gold satin. "I would venture to guess that your mother would be very proud."

I bow my head at the unexpected show of parental affection. She didn't need to waste her words on the likes of me.

"Thank you, my Queen," I whisper, my voice caught.

"Now, tell me, what does my son have to say about all this?" she asks, fluttering her hands around, gesturing to the various decorations.

"I'm not sure. He mentioned he wasn't much looking forward to the coronation, but I'm not sure how that can be. It all seems so lovely."

"Kai is a delicate soul with much empathy. He feels the suffering around him and cannot turn off his brain long enough to let himself relax," she says, somewhat frustrated. "To him, this day signifies a dark continuation of our long history."

"I'm not quite sure I understand," I said.

"My coronation marks another king in a succession of pious murderers," Kai says, appearing in the doorway of the study.

I whirl, my heart flying up into my throat, and accidentally drop my needle and thread. He's leaning against the wooden doorframe, his eyes cast downward, and his arms crossed tightly over his chest. His long hair shrouds most of his face in darkness, but his crimson eyes find mine, and suddenly, I'm breathless. I try to swallow, but my throat has suddenly gone dry.

"Kai, you know that's not true," Eileen reprimands. I blush, averting my eyes quickly.

"Are you going to keep the truth from her, Mother? Or shall I explain how we've been leading a treacherous kingdom based on blood and depravity?"

I glance up at Eileen, just to see her reaction to Kai's strong words. Instead of finding her angry, she's quiet with a hint of a smile on her lips.

"Astrid, dear, I have suddenly found myself quite tired. I feel the need to retire early tonight. Will I see you tomorrow?" she asks.

"Of course, my Queen." I offer a deep bow.

"Thank you. And dear son, please don't be too rough with my new friend. She's special." She gives me a chilling smile as her eyes flick over my face. "Plus, she's such a wonderful conversationalist," she says with a slight giggle as she sways past him and out of the room.

I only need a moment to see Kai's face go from dark and scowling to uncomfortable as his mother leaves. In an instant, I'm turning to face him, hoping he won't leave.

"Please tell me more," I say, and he turns a curious eye to me. With a hint of a smile, he strolls over to one of the chairs by the fireplace and gestures for me to join him. I sit quietly as he begins to speak.

6

KAI

"I shouldn't have said anything," I say, dropping my head into my hand as I sit by the fireplace. Astrid lowers herself into the other chair with an inquisitive expression.

"No, please. I would love to learn more about your family's history or the kingdom's history, for that matter."

"No, really, I'm too cynical, and it's not my place—"

"I don't believe that's true," she says quickly, and I'm impressed with her lack of diplomacy. Most servants wouldn't dare to cut me off. "I believe it is your place, and you are to be king. I don't think anyone would oppose you."

I feel my lips twitch. Fighting a small smile, I look across the room, trying my best to think of a way to explain our history that doesn't sound so dreadfully boring. Truth is, most of our history is just politics and tedious conversation. It really isn't as bad as I made it out to be. I just let my feelings about human liberties cloud my tone. I honestly don't even know why I bothered Astrid and my mother in the first place.

"Alright then," I say after a moment. "I guess it all started a few hundred years ago when vampires were first coming to Nordøya. The first group was only made up of five or six people, two couples, and maybe a third. They were traveling across Norway, moving from place to place, evangelizing the Christian gospel."

"Vampires as religious practitioners?" she asks, her face open and bright.

"Yes." As I continue, she sits back in her chair with a needle and thread, continuing her embroidery work from before. I smile, wondering for a moment what it would be like to live like this, talking with Astrid as she works and I debrief her on the political topics of the court. That thought alone made the idea of being king somewhat bearable. I shake away the daydream and return to her question. "They fled to Nordøya after several months. They were in Seiland when they were set upon by the great wolves that almost hunted them to extinction."

"Wolves?"

"White Wolves," I amend. "The strongest animal in Scandinavia. The only reason any of them survived was that they could swim across the great river that separates our island from the Norway mainland. They could hold their breath and move with great speeds, and the wolves could not follow.

"But by the time they got to the shore, they were weak and dying. Two of the remaining members were my great grandparents. They almost didn't survive the ordeal," I say, briefly wondering what would have happened if they hadn't.

"What happened to them?" she asks, her eyes wide and crystalline blue. Even in the dark, with only the fire to light the room, her eyes look bright.

"They came across a tribe of indigenous humans," I say, trying to hide the bitterness in my tone. For Astrid, this is a simple history lesson. For me, it's a grim reminder of what I am. "When the humans first came across the vampire group, they tried to revive them and heal them with their own medicine. It wasn't until one of them hurt themselves that they found out what they really were.

"After that, it was practically a slaughter. Once the humans realized the vampires could only survive on blood, they offered their own to heal them, not understanding the power that vampires have when properly fed."

"What happened to the humans?" she asks quietly.

For some reason, her curiosity and understanding make me hopeful. Maybe if she knows how badly vampires can hurt humans, she'll work to protect herself. Maybe.

"Well, luckily for the humans, they were protected by a family of witches that lived alongside their tribe. These are the witches that Alheri descended from," I clarify. Astrid nods in appreciation, her mouth gaping just slightly. She's all but stopped her work, focusing only on my story. "Amongst the killing, one of the vampires fed on a witch. I'm not sure if you know, but most witch blood cannot be ingested by vampires. It can drive the vampire mad. Of course, those vampires didn't know that until that moment.

"The vampire that fed on the witch went insane; he eventually fled and died. Seeing him descend into madness slowed the slaughtering of the humans just long enough for the remaining vampires to realize that they *had* to keep the humans alive if they wanted to survive in the long run. So, one by one, the vampires enslaved the humans and witches. By this point, the vampires had returned to their full strength, so it was easy to compel the humans into submission."

Silence fills the hall around us. Astrid looks into the fire while I wait for her to say something.

"I told you it was horrific," I whisper. "Vampires are a

plague."

"Surely, you don't mean that every vampire is bad," she says, fiddling with her thread.

"No, of course not. But that's not what matters. Even if every one of those original vampires were pure-hearted and kind, they still would have succumbed to the necessity, and then the greed, of drinking human blood. It's in our nature to kill," I say, mumbling the final words.

"But you don't kill," she says. She doesn't ask.

"No," I say quietly. "Not in a very long time."

She nods and is quiet for several moments. After a long breath, she smiles and turns back to me. "Just because our history is brutal and horrific does not mean we are bound to that version of ourselves. As species, we grow and learn, unraveling all the previous pitfalls and wrong behavior of our ancestors," she says, speaking slowly as though each word is important to her to get right. "I don't believe you are the same kind of vampire that your ancestors were."

"Perhaps not," I say. "But that does not mean the temptation and instinct isn't there."

"Of course," she admits. "I just mean that it's how we react to our instincts that define us."

I frown, thinking of all the times I've faltered.

"Would you cast aside your friend, Lilith, simply because she is a vampire?"

"No, I guess not."

"See? Then you should not be so hard on yourself," she says, smiling.

She stands, and I immediately rise and follow her. She continues as she moves over to the worktable. She fans out the fabric she was embroidering, and I let my eyes wander over her beautiful work. Her stitching flawlessly depicts a bouquet of golden roses and feathers amid a deep black velvet. She runs her delicate hands over the material, her lips tight as she tugs on the pattern.

"And I'm sure Lilith does not think of you as a monster either," she whispers.

"No, I suppose she doesn't." I watch as Astrid nods, her jaw tense as she avoids my eyes. "Lilith is my oldest friend, Astrid. She knows me better than anyone. She knows my faults and flaws. And I suppose that validates your point, seeing as she still thinks me worthy enough to be her friend."

"And you? Do you find her a worthy friend?" she asks, looking up into my eyes with an almost expectant expression.

I sigh, still half-smiling. "She's my best friend," I admit. "And every day that she's not around, I feel it in my heart."

Astrid bites down on her lips and looks aside, but I can tell she's frowning.

"Astrid," I whisper. She hesitantly looks up at me, and I feel a subtle shift inside my body. My palms begin to sweat, and I feel nervous in my stomach, but unlike my fear of being around Astrid's blood, this feels different. Like I'm nervous for myself.

"Yes?" she breathes, her sweet scent brushing past my face.

"Lilith is my friend," I say, not really knowing why I'm saying it. "Nothing more."

Astrid's face doesn't change. In fact, she looks completely frozen, like she's been trapped in a paralysis spell. Her eyes are glimmering in the firelight, and her breathing is shallow. Her face flushes a brilliant golden red, and I feel myself lean toward her unconsciously.

After a moment, she blinks and gives me a hesitant smile. I hear a small clattering as she drops her parchment and charcoal on the table. I watch as it rolls away from her and quickly move to pick it up for her. At the same time, she leans over, and for the briefest moment, our hands touch, trying to pick up the graphite stick. As her hand brushes mine, a tremor of electricity jolts up my arm, and

I have to flinch backward, seeing that she does as well. I huff a brief laugh, smiling widely at seeing her just as flustered as I am.

"Sorry," I mutter, rubbing my hand from the phantom shock.

"No, no," she says, her words stumbling over mine.

I clear my throat and look back toward the fire, consciously taking a step back from Astrid. I can hear the faint sounds of the dining room, and I realize how much time we've spent simply talking. And the weirdest part is how much I don't want to *stop* talking.

"I should probably get back to the task at hand," she says, not meeting my eye.

"Okay," I whisper. "Will you be finished soon?"

"Soon," she says with a smile.

"Good. Please don't work too hard."

I have a hard time finding the words or desire to say goodbye, but she's starting to fan out fabrics again, so I turn to leave. With a frown, I turn back toward her, feeling indecision radiate through me.

"Why don't you meet me for your dinner?" I ask suddenly.

"Of course," she says politely. "Shall I meet you…"

"Oh, Lilith's gone back to Livsnerven," I say quickly, understanding her hesitation much better now. She didn't know she could come back to my room. Or is it *our* room? I shake my head and say, "Come to the room whenever you're finished."

Her face is brighter and happier now. I smile back at her, feeling my heart swell ever so slightly.

"As you wish, Kai," she whispers.

It's nighttime again, and I find myself wandering the castle aimless, biding my time until it's late enough to return to my room for the night. I think about Astrid's hesitation about coming back with me. When Lilith was here, Astrid stayed in her old quarters, leaving me alone to socialize with my friend. Lilith's words rang in my ears, about Astrid's feelings, her conclusion about Lilith, and I. I hadn't even bothered to correct her at the time. She thought that Lilith was my...*girlfriend.*

I shake my head, touching the stone walls as I walk. What kind of prince could be afforded the luxury of dating or even having a girlfriend? I think back over the past day with a sense of longing, heightened now by my impatience, waiting for Astrid to finish her tasks.

The few days I had with Lilith were full of life and friendship as I showed her around the castle, eating the chef's divine cooking in my room and drinking until she got wasted. But ultimately, we talked. We talked and talked until we both passed out each night. Then, she was gone. It had all moved way too fast, and now I find myself alone, again, fighting the temptation to leave this all behind just to follow after my friend. After talking with her so long, I'm positive she lives a better life than I do.

But instead of wallowing in my loneliness, I spent time with my mother, discussing the latest novel she's reading, the brand-new Don Quixote, a well-known human novel that she picked up in Livsnerven on our last trip outside the castle. I've always wondered how a vampire came into possession of a novel, but I won't press the issue. Mother says she finds it particularly riveting to see how similar humans act and feel. Honestly, I wasn't paying much attention to the details, but I listened patiently. I'm sure she knew I was looking for a distraction.

In the end, I asked her for another portion of blood, and looking back, it went just as badly as the last time. But I figure my mother has been right about so many things. I should take her prescription of small doses rather than abstaining.

I think about how, when I passed my mother's study, I saw Astrid there, working with my mother. She looked studious and preoccupied, carrying several bolts of cloth and a basket of different threads. I watched her curiously. My mother was chatting away about something, but I wasn't paying attention. I just watched Astrid move about, conversing back with her easily. She looked flushed with sweat and color in her cheeks, breathing loudly as she dumped her handful of items on the rug. She knelt down, scattering the different fabrics in front of her. I remember smiling, feeling like I was invisible, seeing Astrid in her own world.

She flitted her hands about the various fashion fabrics, talking about the weights and draping, amongst other things that I know nothing about. She pulled various threads and held them against the cloth, scribbling down notes in a small notebook. It looked like a tattered gathering of folded parchment, filled with graphite and ink stains. I watched, mesmerized by Astrid's sheer determination.

Of course, I couldn't resist when they started talking about my coronation. It was a dismal reminder of why Astrid was working so diligently in the first place. I found myself drawn into the parlor, without my brain's consent, and suddenly, I was thrusting myself into their conversation. I honestly don't know why I interrupted their work. Maybe because I truly am angry about my coronation, or maybe at the moment, I simply wanted to talk to Astrid. I remember how my eyes lingered on Astrid as I explained our history, almost beside myself when she looked back up to meet my gaze.

I smile as I walk slowly back to my room. Even after all the distractions that Lilith provided, all the confusion and fear that comes from possessing a *kvinne*, I still find myself enraptured by Astrid's very presence. With a sobering breath, I pinch my lips into a tight line as I enter the top floor of the castle.

I've successfully avoided most of the castle's inhabitants all day, and now everyone is missing again. I listen closely and hear conversations, laughing, and feeding down in the dining hall. I suck in a sharp breath and force my legs to keep walking in the opposite direction. Everything is so much harder when I'm alone.

I sigh. I know I'm just biding my time until I have to go back to my room, my brain spinning in circles at the thought of being with Astrid in such tight quarters. As much as I enjoyed talking with her, I'm still terrified of hurting her. I run my hand through my hair and slow to a stop just outside my door. Maybe I could just sleep outside again.

I open a nearby window and peer up at the sky. I huff loudly and snap the window shut. It's almost a cloudless sky. Though my experience with Alheri in the sun was pleasant, I find myself wishing for overcast and stormy skies. Sunlight and good weather don't mix well with vampires. I guess that means sleeping outside isn't an option tonight. I look at the ceiling and pace in the hallway for a few moments before giving up and heading into my room.

As I walk, I hear Caden in his room next to mine, taunting me with sounds of lust, blood, and poison pounding like a drum into my brain. I move to my room quickly and quietly, exhaling my held breath.

Sitting on my bed, I wonder how long Astrid will be occupied with my mother's tasks. I suppose I could take this time to actually be alone. I poke at the dying fire, waking the red-hot embers, and sit down in the chair next to it. Slipping off my shoes, I wiggle my toes in front of the flames, listening to the fresh wood crackle and spark, taking my time to replace the sounds from Caden's nightmare-inducing room with the sounds of the fire.

I lean my head back against the chair and rest my arms comfortably, thinking about Alheri's magical dome, sitting in the sun, the sound of Lilith's laugh, and the beautiful pink color of Astrid's cheeks. Before I know it, my eyes are heavy, and my breathing falls into a peaceful rhythm.

I'm awakened by a loud thud from outside my door. I open my eyes and rise to my feet, opening the door to find Astrid lying on the ground. She's whimpering softly but not crying. She looks faint, and her skin is more translucent than before. I start to bend down to lift her up when her smell wafts up from her hair and into my nose. I cringe and bare my teeth at her, putting my hands over my mouth quickly. I sprint to the balcony, throwing open the doors, and breathe in a gulp of fresh air, holding it tightly in my lungs before returning to the passed out girl outside my door.

I lock my arms under her legs and neck and lift her easily, moving quickly to lay her down on the bed. She stirs in my arms and starts gasping, her hot breath billowing against the skin on my chest. I set her down quickly and move away from her. She tries to sit upright but fails, falling back against her pillow.

A thousand different scenarios run through my brain as to why she's sick, but only one is believable. A brisk wind blows into the room through the balcony doors, breathing fresh air into the stale room. I run out into the hallway and grab the first servant I can find.

"Hey! Bring up some food—*actual* food," I clarify quickly, beating myself up for forgetting to get food. Hadn't I asked her to eat with me? I curse myself for getting distracted. "Bring it straight to my room. Food, drink, water, anything you can carry," I order, and he nods before moving briskly down to the kitchens.

Before I can blink, I've sprinted back in the room, and Astrid is trying to steady herself and stand back up.

"I'm so sorry, sir," she says weakly.

"No, sit back down, Astrid. You're not well," I say quickly. I want to force her in bed, but I keep my distance. She struggles to stand, holding the bed frame with white knuckles. "What happened?" I ask, knowing full well what her answer was going to be.

"Well, when I finished working for your mother, I ventured to the dining hall, thinking you would need me to bring up my own food. I thought you might have been waiting for me there since pretty much everyone feeds in the dining hall. But when I didn't see you,

I went to find you." Her eyes are dropping. "I didn't know if you wanted me to come with someone else or just me to provide for you."

I grimace, hearing her unspoken words. She didn't know if I wanted to feed on her or if I wanted to feed on someone *else* in front of her. She thought I was going to plump her up with food then bite into her to feed myself. The thought made me gag.

"What happened in the dining room?" I ask through my teeth. "Did someone feed on you?"

"Yes," she whispered. "I didn't know what to do. I told him I was your kvinne and that you were expecting me, but the man didn't listen. I tried to tell him to stop, but he forced my hand. I hope you do not mind."

"I do mind! I do!" I'm shouting, and I know how this looks. She thinks I want her all to myself. I growl, picturing Astrid's attacker as torn up shreds that I cast into flame, the smell of incinerating flesh burning my nose. "I could kill him for touching you!"

"I'm so sorry, sir," Astrid's face is tormented. She thinks she did something wrong, but it's not her fault. None of this is her fault.

I rake both of my hands through my hair, trying to steady my rage without taking a breath. "This is not your fault, Astrid," I hiss.

"But it is. I should have come straight to your room. I could have summoned food for myself then. I am so selfish," she whispers, struggling to get the words out. "Of course, you would want to eat in private."

"No, no, —" I don't even know what to say. "Ugh! Are you kidding? You really think it's *your* fault that you were attacked by some self-righteous vampire?"

"Well—"

"Don't even think it," I demand.

"Yes, of course," Astrid says urgently. "I'm so sorry, sir."

"God, stop saying that!" I can barely even look at her, hatred flowing restlessly off of my arms. She winces as she tries to stand, and I can see how much it pains her. I hate that she's hurt. I *hate* it.

Thankfully, there's a knock on the door, and I open it quickly, servants flowing in with food and drink. I point them to the table, and they set down trays of fruit and cooked vegetables, lamb shanks, and a loaf of bread. A pitcher of ale, presumably, and a large basin of water. I thank them as they work, praying I have enough strength to help Astrid.

I step out to the balcony as they set the table. I hike in a deep breath, trying to steady my thoughts and slow my anger, but I just keep picturing a nightmarish portrayal of a young woman's attack. I slam my fist against the stone, feeling my bones snap as I hiss a steady string of profanities. Before I finish swearing, I can already feel my bones knitting back together. When I feel somewhat subdued, I walk back inside.

"Okay, you need to eat. You need to restore your strength," I say, hissing the words through clenched teeth. I move to her side and offer her my arm. At first, she flinches away from my touch, but then she sits up, and I wrap my arm around her waist, holding her up and practically dragging her over the table.

I sit her down and then move away from the table.

"Oh please, will you stay?" Astrid asks, her voice hoarse. I give her a sidelong glance before biting down and sitting in the chair opposite her. I tear into the loaf of bread and place it on my plate before pouring the ale into two goblets and handing her one. She looks confused as I tear off a piece of lamb and grab several pieces of fruit. I start to pop food into my mouth when her eyes widen, and her jaw opens slightly.

"What?" I snap.

"You're eating human food," she says, completely bewildered.

"Yeah? Food that you should be eating too," I reply, pushing the tray of lamb towards her.

"I didn't realize that you could," she says softly, piling her plate with minimal amounts of each dish. I push the plate again, gesturing for her to take more as I chew on a chunk of bread.

"We can eat whatever we want," I say back, taking the lamb shank by the bone and tearing off a chunk of it with my front teeth. Her eyes are still wide, staring at me. "Eat, Astrid."

She slowly pulls off pieces of bread and chews on them slowly. I drink the ale, trying to replace the bitterness in my mouth. My eyes wander over Astrid's face. Usually, she looks bright and buzzing with energy. Tonight, she looks different. Tired. Her face is sallow and grey, and it takes her great effort to swallow each bite. Her eyes are glassy, with tiny beads of water pooling at the corners. She winces as she moves like it takes her a tremendous amount of energy just to move.

I can't help it. I look to her neck, where a large pinkish bruise gleams under her ear. I blink and look away quickly before I see the bite marks. My body trembles with rage. I clamp my arms across my chest, my nails biting into the skin on my ribs.

"Who did that to you?" I whisper through clenched teeth, a rabid sense of violation grabbing hold of me. Never before had I felt such avarice come over me so aggressively. It makes my blood boil underneath my skin.

Astrid looks up at me with a child's gaze. Her eyes are wide and frightened. She reaches up and puts her hand over the marks and says, "I'm not sure. I don't know his name."

There's a silence between us. I don't know why I feel such a strong connection to her. I barely just met her. Even still, my chest is quaking, and my ears are ringing.

"Why?" she whispers. "What are you thinking?"

"I want to hunt him down and tear him to shreds for touching you," I whisper back, barely even shocked at the hostility in my voice. Caden once told me that vampires are possessive creatures. I just never believed him until now. She flinches away from my words, her lower lip trembling.

"Please don't," she says. "Don't hurt him because of me."

I shake my head with a cynical smile. "He doesn't deserve your sympathy, Astrid. None of them do. This is precisely what I mean. Vampires are poison."

I pour myself another glass of ale and swallow it almost in one gulp before pouring another. The alcohol doesn't phase me, but I have to try to get rid of the horrible taste in my mouth. Suddenly, I wish I had Lilith's capability for intoxication.

Seeing Astrid's remorseful expression is too much. I turn to her and say, "Finish eating. I'll be back."

Then I stand and walk out the door, unsure of what I'm going to do. I could try to hunt down this guy, make him pay for hurting Astrid. But as I walk past Caden's doorway, I hear sounds of anger and brutality. I pause, thinking about busting in and saving whatever human he has trapped inside with him, but within seconds, I don't have to.

Caden's door opens, and Annette, a beautiful, brown-haired human, steps out from his door, closing it behind her. I'm frozen, watching her leave my brother's room. Her body is turned away from me, but I can tell she's been hurt. Hurt in the same way that Astrid was.

With anger brewing more and more fierce in my chest, my vision is painted red, and my hands shake, but as I start to walk towards Annette, she turns to me, and I take my first look at her. Her eyes meet mine, and ice slithers through my veins. My fury dies flat as I rake my eyes up and down the small girl's body.

Annette is usually tall with lovely ivory colored skin and silky brown hair that flows easily down her back. Her cheeks are usually rosy, and her green eyes bright and youthful. But today, she looks sick. Her shiny hair has turned dull. Her skin has turned shallow and grey, and her eyes droop to the floor. Caden has her dressed in robes of silk that fall off her shoulders and should suggest seductive charm but instead show dark purple bruises on her neck, collar bone, and breasts.

She looks into my eyes for a moment. Those green eyes that I often looked at with fondness have turned dark and colorless. My demon brother is sucking the life out of her. I clench my fists tightly and watch her leave, her eyes cast down to the ground.

I close my eyes and try to clear my head, my hand resting on the wooden door. Staring at the stone flooring underneath my feet, I try to unclench my body, my fist, my muscles when I realize that I'm tired. I'm so tired. It's only been a few days of this, and I can hardly bear it.

I walk back into my room and look at Astrid. Her eyes are closed, and her head is resting lightly on the back of the chair. Her breaths are shallow, and I listen to her heartbeat for a moment, racing with quick short beats as her body tries to heal itself.

I exhale my held breath, feeling the air move through the open balcony doors. I focus on the ocean below and take a slow breath in, tasting the notes of Annette and Caden in the air but noticing that Astrid's scent is weak. Earlier, her aroma danced in the air like a child playing in a meadow. Now, it's a ribbon that floats aimlessly in the breeze, just barely afloat.

I walk over to Astrid and scoop her up in my arms, my teeth clenched together for good measure. I place her on her bed and cover her up with a blanket before collapsing on my own.

7
ASTRID

I wake up with a blistering headache. My stomach is in knots, and my body feels stiff and achy all over. The blankets are heavy, weighing me down. My eyes flutter open, feeling sandy and dry. I run my hands over my dress, realizing I'm in the same clothes as the night before. *Oh, God.*

Memories of last night flood my brain. Images of working in the study, listening to Kai's story, then being attacked by that man. I wince, feeling bruised and battered all over. I sit up, trying to stay quiet. Did Kai put me to bed? Did I faint in front of him? I run my hands over my face, massaging my eyes and cheeks. I can't believe I let all this happen. Kai had finally started to open up to me, and now I've ruined everything. I blink away tears as I remember how afraid and ashamed I felt in front of him. He couldn't even look at me.

I move slowly, feeling my body ache, and a wave of dizziness swirls in my head. Nausea rolls over me as I try to stand. I grip the side of the bed and let my body settle. I take several deep breaths, and after a few seconds, I feel okay. I finally stand all the way up and take a look around the room. The table is still piled with random bits of food, the candles burned down to nubs. The fire has died out again. I sigh. These are pure signs of failure, that I'm worthless. I have to fix this quickly.

I peek over to Kai's side of the room, and luckily, he's still sleeping, his limbs falling off of his too-small bed. My heart does a small flop at the sight. I feel so privileged to be able to see him like this, with his hair covering the front of his face, his arms sprawled above his head, and his legs tangled in the thin white sheets. My stomach flutters as I ponder what will happen between us when he wakes. Will he send me away? Clearly, I've ruined whatever rapport we had. After seeing his reaction and with his complete inability to even stay in the same room with me, I know I won't be able to recover from this. I sigh softly. I must move quickly before he sees the evidence of the mess I made.

First things first: light the fire. The room is like walking around in an ice bath. I notice the balcony doors open and quickly close them. I wrap a blanket around myself and grab several pieces of wood. Once the fire catches, I thaw slightly, and my skin feels less like stone. I ditch the blanket and move more quickly.

I clear the table of the old food, feeling my stomach grumble softly. I ignore it. Now is not the time to be focusing on myself.

I tiptoe passed Kai, who is breathing so softly, I can't help but take a closer look. His face is relaxed and expressionless. I've never seen him like this. Even in the small amount of time I've been here, his face is always scrunched up, like he's really uncomfortable. In his slumber, he looks very peaceful. The planes of his face are smooth and soft, without a hint of the fury I saw last night.

I move to the bathroom to tidy up and clean out the washbowl. As I work, my mind wanders. I try my best not to think about the man in the dining hall who pulled me away from the crowd to press me up against the stone wall. I shake my head, putting away the feeling of terror as his breath licked my ears before he bit into my neck. Never before had a feeding frightened me. Why was this any different? I pinch my nose, trying not to hear ringing in my ears when I remember how I had whimpered and cried out for someone to stop him. I quickly wipe away a stray tear as I start rubbing the bathtub down with soap and water.

I stand and look in the mirror, shaking off the weirdness that comes along with seeing my reflection. My hair is tangled from sleeping, my dress is wrinkled, and there are blood and food stains on it. I quickly run my fingers through my hair, wishing I had a hair tie to plait it at night to avoid tangles like this. I move the hair away from my neck and see bruises starting to bloom under my skin. The teeth marks are still visible, and blood is caked around the small scabs. My hand shakes as I quickly use a rag to rub away the stains.

I quiver as the marks start to sting beneath the rag. I pull it away, seeing fresh blood surface from the open scab. I press the rag to my neck, hoping the bleeding will stop quickly. I look up at the ceiling, willing gravity to repress the tears that threaten to break me down.

Feeling worthless, I sit on the edge of the tub and start to heave my breathing in and out. I can't let Kai see me like this. He was so angry with me last night; his face was set in a disturbing grimace the entire night, and his dark red eyes glared daggers at me. His jaw was continuously flexed, his neck contracted so that I could see his tendons. I've never seen anyone look more upset.

I hear a small stirring outside the bathroom door, and I close my eyes, desperately trying to still my chattering teeth. I suppose it's time that I face my master and hope that he doesn't want to throw me out. I'm not pleasing to look at, my dress is stained and tattered, and the room isn't clean. I've failed him. I'm a failure.

I take a deep breath and open the door. Kai is standing on the other side, focusing directly on my neck. His face is twisted into a glare, a look even more dismal than the night before.

"Your Highness," I say, averting my eyes to the floor. "I want to apologize for the state of your room and my appearance. I have not had the time to prepare myself for you, and—"

"Shut the fuck up," he seethes, and the words splinter through my heart. My head hangs, and I drop my arm away from my neck. "Are you bleeding?"

He's rigid with anger. His hands are behind his back, and his lips are retracted away from his teeth. I've never seen anyone wear this expression. A shudder runs up and down my spine like pricks of ice scraping my bones, and my heart beats like a hummingbird in my chest.

"I'm so sorry, sir. The wound reopened as I was cleaning myself," I say, brushing my hair back so that he can see. His eyes widen, and he steps backward away from me. He grabs onto the doorframe, the wood splintering loudly underneath his finger. "Prince, I am so sorry for the trouble I caused you last night. Please forgive me."

Kai doesn't reply, but it looks like a million emotions pass over his face in the span of just a few seconds. I hedge a step towards him, and he growls loudly at me, frightening me so much that I jump backward. My heart pounds in my chest, and I can feel a little bead of blood dripping down my neck. I hastily put the rag back to the cut.

Kai's teeth are completely exposed, his eyes black and angry, and his entire body poised. My brain rings with terror and fear, the same emotions that gripped me last night. I try to swallow, but my throat is parched. Even if I tried to scream, I know no sound will come.

Dark, black veins slither out from Kai's pupils, darkness overtaking even the white parts of his eyes. His teeth are exposed and deadly, screaming of viciousness and ferocity. His body is arched like an animal. His black hair falls in front of his face, but he doesn't push it away. He simply glares at me, his black eyes locked on my neck. I feel like a deer trapped in the gaze of a mountain lion, waiting for him to make the first move.

"Kai?" I ask, quivering, my voice barely a whisper. I know he hears me.

The words trigger another million emotions. His glare turns into a look of unbearable pain, then back to anger and dejection. I breathe in shallow gasps, just waiting for him to take a step toward me. I wish he would just feed on me. He clearly wants to. I know I shouldn't be so scared of him, but the feeling of hysteria and dread from the night before seeps into my bones.

"If you wish to feed on me…" I remove the rag again and step towards him, showing him the wound. "I am yours."

The moment my foot hits the floor, he's sprinted out of the room with an excruciatingly loud roar, and before I can blink or even register the movements, he's flung open the balcony doors, shattering the glass, and jumped over the ledge.

My heart beats so hard that I gag on my own breath, and my eyes are so wide that I feel the icy wind blow through the balcony and cut like daggers. My chest erupts into desperate sobbing, and I sink to my knees, feeling my tears overtake me. I can't even scream for someone to come help. My chest is caving in, and my throat is so dry that nothing but desperate heaving comes from my mouth.

I wrap my arms around my torso and let myself cry until my vision blacks out, erasing all thoughts of Kai's attempt to kill himself.

8

KAI

I gasp as I hit the water, all the air knocked out of my lungs in large bubbles that rise to the surface. I look down, the saltwater burning my eyes, and see that a large, sharp rock has gashed straight through my torso. My blood stains the gray water red.

I fight against the water to press my hand to the wound, feeling sharp agony rip through my stomach. The rock luckily missed my ribs and cut through the fleshy part of my side, but the pain is exquisite. The pain is also welcome, as is the burning sensation from the water.

The icy tides rip at my arms and legs, and I can hardly fight back through the raging pain in my side. I want to cry out because as I watch the red pour out of my side, staining my torn shirt, I can still see the blood dripping down Astrid's neck. I can still taste the way the air tasted when she came out of the bathroom.

I didn't even know what was happening to me. I was sound

asleep when I felt something come alive inside me. I thought I was dreaming, but then I opened my eyes, ravenous, and she was there, looking as radiant as ever with blood staining her skin.

Never in my life have I hated myself more than I hate myself right now. I had to physically jump out of a window to abstain from my lustful tastes. And I didn't want to leave her alone! She was obviously hurting, and who knew if Caden would see her. Or worse, what if my father found her alone and crying because I rejected her?

I want to scream at the sky. I don't even know if it was sunny or overcast. I just hurled myself over the ledge. What if I had burned up on the way down? Would that honestly be that bad?

Limp and directionless, the current hurls me toward shore, and I risk popping my head above water, gulping a large breath of fresh air. It doesn't help. The taste of her blood is still on the back of my tongue. Luckily, or perhaps not, the sun hasn't shown its face today. It's hiding like a coward behind thick billowy clouds. I curse silently at the sky, feeling that it will help to curse something other than myself. What more can I say?

I hoist myself out of the water and onto the rocky shore, pulling off my cloth shoes, dragging my body to shore with sopping wet clothes. I flop onto the ground and sit against a tree, running my tongue against my gums, feeling my teeth retract back into their sheaths. I rub my temples, trying to clear my head with the feeling of ice against my skin and salt burning my wound.

Peeling my wet shirt back, I feel a sharp stinging almost debilitate me. The gash is still fresh. The bleeding has stopped, probably because of the saltwater, but it's still an open wound on my side. I haven't fed in a few days, and now, I don't know if I am strong enough to. I might just take a sip and then sprint right back to feed on Astrid. It's incredibly tempting, knowing that she's in my bedroom waiting for me, with a giant festering wound. It's disgustingly irresistible.

I poke at the wound in my side, and pain shoots through me. I wince, sucking air through my teeth. This pain is punishment for what I am, what I'll always be. I rest my head against the tree and fight tearless sobs that threaten to tear my chest apart. The pine needles look black against the dark clouds, and slowly, softly, the clouds drip giant raindrops on the ocean.

I huff a breath. It seems as though the sky is crying right along with me. How many more times will I find myself here, on the shore of a dangerous cliff diving experience? In the distance, mist starts forming in the crevices of the mountains. The green of the forest turns grey and desaturated. The tree starts dripping on me. I hang my head by my knees and close my eyes, taking in the sounds of the droplets against the leaves and the rocks. Slowly, the salt washes off my face, the rainwater fresh and clear on my lips.

I take a deep breath, and my side shoots pangs of sharp pain through me again. I grab at the wound with my opposite arm and hoist myself up, feeling like my bones are blistering through my skin. This is too much. I can hardly handle my internal turmoil, let alone this physical pain too. I walk, or rather limp, back up to the castle.

No one blinks an eye at my appearance. I'm holding my breath as I walk past the dining hall and up the stairs to the throne room. Hopefully, my father is finished with his daily business. I push open the giant wooden doors, and I heave a sigh of relief when I see that Alheri is the only one in the room. I almost fall to my knees with a strangled sound peeling from my mouth.

She sees me, and her eyes instantly widen.

"Prince Kai! Oh my, what happened?" She rushes over to me, her hands glowing slightly. I'm thankful for the help.

I don't even have to respond because she starts looking me over, taking off my shirt and finding the large purple gash in the side of my stomach. She forcefully pushes me to the ground, where I sit, groaning and wincing at the pain. Black holes dot my sight as she works. She presses her fingers to the sides of the cut and starts saying soft words so quickly that even my advanced hearing can't decipher the words. Almost immediately, I feel the pain recede and warmth return to my body. I exhale loudly, my chest heaving with relief.

As I breathe, staring at the ceiling, I smell Alheri's blood underneath her skin.

I look at her and watch her face contort with her words. Her eyes are closed, and her face twitches ever so slightly. Her ebony skin is a stark contrast to my translucent, snow-like skin. Typically, I can pick out witch blood simply through their scent. Their blood is not the same as the average human, at least not to me. It usually smells like alcohol, even the best whiskey or ale, but not like food.

"What troubles you, Prince?" Alheri asks, her voice deep and vibrant. "Why do you come to me with a wound that should have healed on its own?"

I look away from her, towards the large wooden throne.

"You are plagued with torment. I can see it," Alheri says, her eyes still closed, searching through the darkness. I take a deep breath, tasting her aroma. It's like the darkest whiskey coated with vines and herbs. Even her appearance is almost primal. I suppose it's the destiny of every witch to be connected with the earth. "Kai," she says in hushed tones. "Where is Astrid?"

"She's in my room," I reply, my voice thick with contempt.

Alheri sighs, her face full of relief.

"I wouldn't hurt her," I promise.

"I know, my Prince. I know. I simply worry about her. She is a young soul. She must be protected." Alheri pulls her fingers away. I look down at my waist and find no trace of the gash. I lay my head down against the hard, cold stone floor. "Can you tell me what happened?"

I turn my head to look into her dark brown eyes, "I don't know how to be around her. I don't want to feed on her. I don't want to hurt her." Then, a thought occurs to me. "Actually, could you help me? She was attacked yesterday by someone in the dining hall. She hasn't healed, and the open wound is proving bad for my sanity. That's selfish, I know." I shake my head in disapproval.

Alheri closes her eyes, a small smile on her lips, and bows in agreement.

"I will help you, Kai," she says, following me up to my room to tend to Astrid.

9

ASTRID

"Astrid? Astrid, wake up"

I jolt upright, panic grabbing my heart as soon as my eyes open. Alheri is shaking my shoulders gently with a worried expression on her face.

"Al! Something terrible has happened," I stutter, quickly shuffling to my feet and jumping over all the broken glass towards the balcony.

I fling myself against the stone railing, my hands catching me as I throw my head over the side to look at the savage waters below. I heave in several tight breaths, trying to keep my chest from collapsing into another round of sobs. Kai's nowhere to be seen.

He's drowned.

He's gone.

"Oh my God, Al! He's dead! He threw himself over the edge!" I cry out, reaching back toward my friend. She curls me against her chest as I sob and blubber some explanation. "I hurt him and made him so mad. I tried to help—to fix it—and he just *jumped*!"

I'm shrieking, and she's shushing me, trying to say something, but I keep falling into a dark abyss thinking about Kai drowning in the glacial waters below.

"Astrid! Astrid! Please calm down."

"How could you ask me that?! He's *gone*! My Prince, he's just gone!"

"Astrid, please—"

"It's all my fault. If I'd just *listened*—"

Alheri grabs my shoulders and shakes me, stopping my blubbering for just a moment. Long enough for me to finally hear her.

"He's fine, Astrid. Please calm down. Kai is fine. He came to see me. He's not hurt," she says.

I feel a wave of relief so strong that it physically brings me to my knees. I grab at Alheri's skirts and cry harder, though now it's out of relief.

"He's just outside, but he wants me to heal you first," she explains.

I swallow my tears and hiccup a few deep breaths. I nod at her to proceed. She grabs my thin hands and sits me down on my bed before muttering her steady chants. After several moments, I start to feel my energy return.

"I can't believe he's okay," I whisper, though I know she can't hear me. "I thought for sure I'd driven him mad."

"I'm okay," Kai says, standing in the doorway now.

I try to turn to him, but Alheri locks my hands in place. Instead, I talk to the wall.

"Kai, I'm so sorry," I whisper, suddenly glad I can't see his face. It is easier to talk to him when I can't see him. "I've ruined everything. I'm so sorry."

"It's alright," he says in a low voice. "I'm sorry for frightening you."

I breathe and smile to myself, looking down at my hands, clenched tightly into Alheri's. The emotional whiplash is almost more intense than the physical pain. I'd been so sure he was gone, and now I'm so relieved he's okay. I don't know how to even explain how I'm feeling.

"Okay," Alheri says. "I'm finished."

"Thank you," I breathe. "Thank you for everything."

She smiles and reaches up to touch my cheek. For a moment, while I'm staring into her chocolate eyes, I feel a wash of warmth and comfort weigh heavily on me. I miss her so much. My lips twitch downward as she sighs and stands, taking her warmth with her. I choke back another round of tears and stand to embrace her tightly, feeling her hands press me to her. Without saying a word, she releases me and turns back toward Kai.

I finally look up to see him looking much better than before, but he's still upset. He's frowning, with his arms crossed, and he's leaning away from us. He thanks Alheri as she walks past him. She touches him lightly on the shoulder before turning back to me and smiling.

"Come see me when you can," she says quietly.

"Of course," I say. "As soon as I can."

She nods with a content look before leaving me alone with Kai again.

I fidget restlessly, scratching my arm and trying not to look at him. I start moving around the room again, fixing up the table and throwing the used laundry in the cloth hamper again. I start towards the balcony, thinking of ways to clean up all the glass. I can feel Kai watching me.

"Are you okay?" he finally asks.

"Yes," I say, looking up at him. "I'm just glad you are alright."

He shakes his head and smiles softly at me. "Astrid, *you* were the one that was hurt. Why are you worried about me?"

"You jumped off the balcony!" I shout, gesturing widely before shrinking back.

"That? I do that all the time," he says.

I drop my jaw and feel my eyes bug out of their sockets.

"It's not what you think," he says, shushing me with his hands. "It's not dangerous. It's just like swimming."

"But you jumped! You must have fallen four floors!"

"I'm much more resilient than you give me credit for," he says, leaning against the wall, his arms uncrossing as he slips his hands into his pockets.

I shake my head, trying to reconcile this new information. So, vampires can survive a lengthy jump. Much more, Kai seemed to enjoy it and do it frequently.

"I'm sorry I scared you," he says again.

"I just don't understand why you fled," I ask, looking away from him again. Everything feels uncomfortable and confusing again. And, after all of Alheri's meddling, I feel exhausted.

"I'm sorry," is all he says for an explanation.

I nod, pausing briefly before heading into the bathroom to grab the bristly broom and dustpan. I start sweeping up the broken glass, feeling Kai's eyes on me still as I work.

"I've made you uncomfortable," he says.

"No, no, you could never," I lie. "I'm just confused is all. And exhausted. Please don't misunderstand me. I'm glad you're okay, and I'm grateful to you for bringing Alheri. I just know that I've ruined what we had between us. I don't know if I can make it right. I mean, I don't even know how to read. How can I possibly relate to you at all when I cannot do the one thing you love?"

He steps toward me and takes the broom from my hand, brushing his fingers over mine just slightly. My heart jumps at the casual touch, at how close he is to me now. I look up into his dark crimson eyes, feeling my stomach flutter.

"Let me," he breathes. I blink and relent the broom, unconsciously breathing him in.

He smells of seawater and rain with hints of pine and something else I can't place. I've never stood so close to him before. I swallow deeply, watching him take the broom and continue my chore of tidying the glass.

"I don't want you to hurt yourself," he continues, still looking in my eyes.

I nod, wrapping my arms around my stomach to steady my fluttering.

"You should rest," he says, finally looking down at the dustpan. The glass starts tinkering against the stone floor as he sweeps.

"As you wish," I say, turning away from him and laying down, fully clothed, in my bed.

For a moment, I wonder how I could *possibly* fall asleep with my mind all jumbled up with thoughts of Kai's beautiful eyes and his primal aroma. But after only a few minutes, Alheri's lingering spell drags me under, and suddenly my thoughts swirl into beautiful dreams. My body unclenches and unwinds, healing itself with Alheri's magic.

When I open my eyes again, I feel completely new. I smile happily for the first time in days. I don't feel exhausted or overworked. I simply feel like myself.

I look around, seeing Kai fast asleep in front of the fire, his book resting lightly on his knee. His mouth is opened slightly, his face slack and peaceful. His black hair sways in the light breeze that flows in from the balcony. I wonder how long he'd been asleep. I feel my heart swell slightly, only vaguely remembering why I'd been so upset.

There's a light knocking on the door, and I arise quickly, looking ruefully at my light-yellow dress. I lace on my shoes and move to answer the door. Behind it, Caden is leaning lightly on the doorframe. At first, he seems completely taken aback that I'm answering Kai's door like he didn't expect to see me here. Then, his face brightens, and he gives me a beautiful half-smile.

I've never talked with Prince Caden before, not that I can remember, at least. Though, looking at him, I feel the ghost of a memory tickle the back of my mind. His hair is shorter than Kai's, a slightly warmer brown, and combed away from his face. His eyes are not bright red any longer, but a mellow black, trailing over my face and making me blush. His gaze feels like he is caressing me.

"My Prince," I whisper.

"Hello, Astrid," he says softly. He peers around me, finding Kai fast asleep. "I didn't expect to see you today. I was hoping to."

I begin to say something, but suddenly, Caden traps one of my stray hairs in between his fingers. He gingerly tucks the strand behind my ear, trailing his hand across my jawline.

"What can I do for you, my Prince?" I say, feeling my insides shake.

"Nothing, dear, nothing. I was told to summon you and my brother to see my father," Caden says, his voice low. "What are you doing here in Kai's room? I thought I'd find you with the other *thralls*."

"I am the Prince's *kvinne* now," I explain, though I'm not sure that's news to Caden. Surely he knew of my assignment.

"Are you now?" he says. His expression darkens for a moment, so briefly that I think I'm imagining things. Then he's smiling at me again, swaying just inches from me. It's like a switch has been turned on.

"You say the king has summoned me?" I say in a shaky voice. What would he need me for? "I will wake Kai to go see him right away."

"You know, you're very beautiful, Astrid," Caden says, swiftly blocking the door with his arm. He is very close to me now, and I can smell expensive fragrance and spices on him. I look up, and he's staring directly into my eyes. "It's a shame that you were given to my brother."

"What do you mean, my Prince?"

"You should have been considered for better care."

"My master is wonderful, your highness," I say quickly.

"Yes, Kai is fine and all. But we both know he isn't treating you properly," Caden says, his voice like butter. His eyes are trailing my face with precision.

I swallow slowly, unsure of what to say.

"I would take much better care of you," Caden whispers, reaching up to touch the back of his hand to my cheek. His hand feels like ice, burning a trail of fire across my skin. I shiver under his touch, and the corner of his mouth tugs upwards.

"I should be seeing to your father," I say, barely audible.

"Yes, yes. Don't worry, I'll wake Kai for you," Caden says, dropping his hands and gesturing for me to exit the room. "Oh, and Astrid," he says, grabbing my hand as I pass. His hands feel so soft and gentle.

"Yes?" I breathe.

"You always know you can come to me," he says, his face open and inviting. "For anything."

"Thank you, my Prince," I say, turning away from him before I say anything more.

Releasing my hand, he turns to rest gently against the doorframe, watching me as I walk away from Kai's room. I turn only once, just to see him one last time before heading quickly towards the throne room. He's still smiling a brilliant, gleaming smile at me with his seductive eyes still staring straight at me.

I turn the corner and pause, pressing my hand to my stomach to try and quell my shivering. *Oh my God.* Caden is a divinely handsome man. His eyes are like sharp knives, piercing and beautiful, especially when they are stark red against his porcelain skin. His allure is devilish and charming, with sensual gazes and debilitating caresses. I feel a wave of hysteria bubble in my chest, thinking about how he stared at me with his beautiful eyes and how he smiled so lavishly with his full lips.

And Kai…well, he is something altogether different. Where Caden has charm and wit, seduction oozing off of him, Kai is like a dark angel with jet black wings. He's the kind of hero in the stories that that takes the damsel away, flying her away from all of the evil things threatening her, all the while begging her to stay with him, to comfort him and keep him whole.

With my thoughts in a tangle, flitting between the two princes, I trudge to a stop. I have to get my head straight before seeing the king. He's summoning me specifically, so I need to be able to give him my undivided attention.

I hike in a large breath, exhaling away all my girlish thoughts about Caden. I push on the heavy wooden door, opening it to reveal the large throne room completely empty except for the king and a single servant.

As soon as he sees me, he sends away the servant, leaving the two of us alone.

"My King," I say, bowing low to the ground. I stay there, hearing him arise from the throne and walk loudly over to me.

"Rise, Astrid," he says, his voice weary and strained. I stand, keeping my hands clasped together and my eyes cast to the ground. I don't want to show him how nervous I am.

Baldassare heaves a loud breath, blowing it right past me. I feel his looming presence all around me. This is the most powerful vampire in the kingdom.

"Astrid, can you tell me why you are here?" he asks.

"You summoned me—"

"Not here at this precise instance, dear," he chastises. "Why are you here at Feilfri castle?"

I hesitate, unsure of his underlying question. Surely it was known that I was born and raised here.

"I live here at your disposal, my King," I answer humbly.

"Yes," he says, his voice grave and deep. "Yes, you live here because I *allow* you to."

I shiver, feeling the weight of his words.

"You have not proven yourself to be the woman I thought you were. Instead, I hear you have been living in tandem with my son, not allowing him to use you the way I intend—"

"That's not—" I stop suddenly when his hand flies across my cheek, striking me. Pain blossoms across my cheekbones and I flinch away, my hands covering my horror-stricken face.

"You will speak when spoken to, *thrall*," he growls at me. I feel wells of tears gather behind my eyelids. "Why have you not given yourself fully to Kai? Answer me."

I gulp back the terror and face him, keeping my eyes downward. "I have tried, my King, but he does not respond to my attempts."

"You must try something *else*," he hisses at me.

My cheek stings as a tear rolls away from my eyelashes. I blink the tears away quickly. He reaches out to me, and I force myself not to cringe away from his touch. He puts his arm around my shoulders like I was not just hit by the same hand.

"You are a smart girl, Astrid," he says softly now. "You must make Kai into a man. It is up to you. Force his hand." He pauses for a moment. "My son is not like other vampires, and we all know this. The entire kingdom will be watching his every move, and every vampire will laugh at our rule if they find out my son does not wield his abilities without remorse," Baldassare explains. "I will *not* have my family's name turned into a laughing-stock. That will incite riots and civil war between the vampires. They will seek to remove him from the throne. That cannot happen. And I won't have that brat Caden rule instead. Do you understand?"

"Yes, my King," I respond automatically.

"Tonight, you will go to him and force yourself on him. Give him your body. Give him your blood. Can you do that?" he demands, gripping my shoulder tightly.

I look him in the eyes, just for a moment, before bowing low again.

"Yes, my King."

I return to Kai's room in a haze, feeling the shock and terror turn into apathy. When I realize Kai is no longer asleep in front of the fire, my conversation with Caden fading into a dream, I tidy the room quickly, my thoughts turning towards how to "force myself" on Kai. I have no clue what I should do, so I keep working. I walk into the bathroom, cleaning the bathtub of the filthy water, turning absently to look at myself in the mirror.

I briefly take note that the spot where Baldassare hit me does not bruise or show any indication of hurt. Is that because of Alheri's healing? Is it some lingering effect? Or did I imagine the entire encounter?

At any rate, I feel my brain turn to mush, thinking of ways I could offer myself fully to Kai. I look at myself in the mirror and note how terribly dirty my yellow dress looks. I quickly strip myself of the filthy clothes, chastising myself softly for allowing the king to see me in such disarray. Once I am down to my shift, a thought occurs to me.

I step out of the bathroom, my gown in my arms. The dwindling fire still feels warm compared to my frigid skin. I throw my dress under my bed with the rest of my laundry and turn to place more logs on the fire. After the wood catches the flame, the fire warms the room nicely.

Without much more thought at all, I tug on the tie holding my shift together at my neck. Once it's loosened, I let the underwear fall to the floor, piling by my feet. I feel the fire warm my skin, feeling confident that this is the solution. No man has resisted my body before.

With renewed confidence, and also pure terror and anxiety, I sit down on Kai's bed to await his return with nothing to cover my bare skin.

10
KAI

"Kai? Are you awake?" Astrid's voice washes over me in almost dreamlike waves.

My eyelids flutter open to see Astrid's face only inches away from mine. She smiles at me, locking my heart in my chest. We've never been so close to one another. Her eyes are wide and bright, alight with an almost childlike gaze. I let my eyes trail down from her face to see that her neck is fully healed, no longer bruised or cut in any way. Though, as I stare, my vision turns a fuzzy red, and all I can see is the pulsing of her blood underneath the thin layer of skin.

"Kai? Are you alright?" Astrid asks in a breathless voice. She sounds far away, like I'm dreaming.

I don't answer her. Instead, I watch my hand reach up to touch her cheek. She closes her eyes and makes a warm sound, a vibrating hum in her throat. My eyes are fixated on the spot on her neck where I can see her quickening pulse. The voice in my head, which usually stops this kind of behavior, is silent.

I lean closer to her, reaching to touch her waist with my other hand. Her heart lurches forward, beating steady and strong underneath my touch. Pings of yellow adrenaline spike the red in my view. In an instant, I'm sitting close to her, having pulled her almost onto my lap. She's still standing, her thin nightgown touching my face as she straightens. My hand falls to meet her hip, putting my face even with the base of her navel. I brush the tip of my nose against her stomach, my lip catching on the threads of her nightgown.

"Astrid…" I whisper, feeling my entire body throb.

"Yes?"

"What's happening?" I ask, my voice sounding like it's coming from underwater.

She doesn't say anything, but I feel her quiver underneath my hands like her stomach is filled with a thousand butterflies. I watch her sigh longingly, raking my eyes up to her face. My hands press deeper into the skin on her hips. A sound of longing escapes my lips.

She opens her eyes and meets my gaze. Her eyes are hungry. Expectant. In one swift movement, I stand and lift her easily, crushing her body against mine, and press my lips to hers.

I don't stop when I notice she doesn't taste like anything. I don't stop when I notice her scent has disappeared. I continue in a blind haze, kissing her face, her eyes, her cheeks. She doesn't say anything but simply kisses me back, wrapping her arms around my neck.

Shouldn't I feel her warmth?

I can't think. My thoughts are throbbing to the tempo of her pulse. I press her closer to me, feeling her heartbeat thrum underneath her skin. Everywhere I touch her feels intoxicating, luring me deeper into her blood's siren song.

Before I can stop myself, I'm kissing down her cheek towards her jawline. If Astrid had said anything, I can't hear it. All I can hear is the pounding drum of her heart and the rush of blood behind my ears. My mouth hovers over the skin at her throat, and I pause for just one moment, feeling the phantom electricity that's pulling at every fiber of my being. Then, in a moment of pure ecstasy, my senses overtake me, and I bite into Astrid's neck, feeling her blood pour into my mouth.

No…

No, this is wrong*!*

I tear my eyes open, reality rushing at me like a gust of wind. My heart pounds in my chest. I heave in several breaths, sticky sweat pouring down my face as I look around the empty room. My shirt is drenched and glued to my skin. Shaking and quivering from head to toe, I feel my body recoil at the desire for Astrid. I look around into the parlor, seeing that she's no longer in her bed.

Instead, I hear a slight laugh come from the door.

"Caden," I growl, feeling my heart surge with rage.

"You're *too* easy, brother. Your mind is like an open book," Caden whispers, leaning against the doorframe. His eyes are black and bitter.

"What the fuck is this?"

"Oh, I just wanted you to see what you were missing," Caden says. "Astrid is delicious, isn't she?"

I gag on the bile that arises, caustic in the back of my throat.

"You tasted it, didn't you?" Caden continues. "That sweet taste of her blood in your mouth."

"Stop it," I whisper, gripping the chair underneath me. My body feels like it's a fragile clockwork piece, and Caden is winding me too tight.

"You can barely stand it," he says, astonishment clear in his voice. He kneels to bring his face level with mine. "Maybe I shouldn't have shown you what her blood tastes like. Maybe I should have kept that to myself."

"How do you even know?" I hiss.

"Oh, I've fed on Astrid before."

I roar, a vicious wave of jealousy and shame overtaking me. I grip the chair so hard the wood splinters under my fingers, stabbing into my skin.

"She's so lovely," he says, nonchalantly examining his nails. "To think she's being wasted on *you*."

"What are you talking about?"

"She was supposed to be *mine*," he snaps, his eyes fixed on mine again. His irises were pitch black, like a demon. "Yes, I've used Astrid many times. I even asked Father for her. But of course, like the manipulative dick he is, he gave her to you."

He stands and crosses his arms, clearly bored of taunting me. Instead of relieved, I feel vile, like my insides are being ripped out of my mouth and shown to me.

"And to think that plenty of other men have *tasted* her and you haven't," he cuts, insinuating more than just bloodlust.

I say nothing, but a snarl rips through my guts. I feel my body keel forwards until I'm on my hands and knees, gripping the stone floor so hard that my fingers have turned bloody and bruised. With the cutting sensation of pain in my hands, I feel my desire subside, the healed wound in my side like a haunting pain. Just the memory of the cut helps. I suck in the smell of the soot and ash from the fireplace, feeling the dry, acid taste in the back of my throat slacken from a roaring fire to a dull ache again. The desolate, jealous fire blazing inside me does not stop, however. A sinful desire to kill anyone that's touched her creeps through my body.

"It's no matter," Caden says, absently. I look up to him, feeling the sting of sweat trickle into my eyes. "Father wants to see you."

Caden grins widely, his face darkening more and more by the second. I stand and peel off my soaked shirt, replacing it with a new one. It soaks through in an instant. I choke down another gag as I try to drink some water. Caden saunters away without a word, leaving me gasping but relieved of the pressure of his presence.

I fall onto my bed, leaning my back against the wooden frame. I keep my eyes wide open, staring into the low fire, for I know that if I close them, I'll surely see Astrid's gaping neck.

I walk to the throne room, Caden beating me by a solid few minutes. He's chatting with our father, who is tapping his fingers against the wood. As soon as I walk in the room, he glares at me, his face contorted and his posture tight posture. This doesn't bode well for me. I walk across the long room, eyeing Caden who's sitting next to him.

"Father," I say, not meeting his eyes.

"What's this I hear about you and your slave? Your brother tells me that you aren't using her properly."

I glare at Caden. I should have left immediately when he did. I can't believe he *told* on me. I sigh and look back to Father.

"I don't wish to feed on her if I'm being honest with you."

"What is this nonsense, Kai? Not feeding? That's what she is. A walking blood supply. Why are you not taking advantage of her?" Father's temper threatens to billow.

"I don't think he's embracing his true nature," Caden says, sounding like a petty child.

"Silence, *boy*! You shall not speak unless spoken to," Father booms loudly, silencing Caden's conniving whispers. "Well? Answer the question, son."

"I'm sorry, Father, I have a harder time feeding on a living person," I confess.

"Is she a problem? Is there something wrong with her?"

"No, no, not at all. It's my problem."

"Then, I expect the problem to be solved by tomorrow. She's one of our greatest assets. I would hate for her blood to go wasted," Father says.

"As you wish, sir," I reply, feeling the words burn in my mouth.

"And of your manhood? Have you used her sexually?"

God, how the fuck did this conversation even start? I threw daggers at Caden with my eyes.

"No, Father, I—"

"Then why did I give her to you?!" Father stands, his face contorted with anger. "She was a gift so you could attend your coronation as a man. If you don't use her properly, I will take her away. I will give her to someone else, someone more fitting."

The threat rang out loudly. I didn't want to see Astrid in the hands of another vampire. They certainly wouldn't protect her. They would drink her dry, but not before fucking her senseless. Every bone in my body aches at the thought of someone else touching her. Even if I never touch her myself, the thought of her with someone else is almost unbearable. What is this intolerable envy brewing inside me?

"As you wish, your Highness," I say through my teeth.

"Get out of my sight," Father says, and I turn and practically sprint out, rage flowing easily off my arms. I shake my hands out, trying to stave off some of this restless anger. I walk quickly back towards my room, pausing only when I see my mother in her study. She looks up and sees me outside the room, balling my fists up at my sides.

She sets her book down and stands, her face painted with worry.

"What is it, Kai?" she asks.

"Nothing, Mother."

"Son," she chides.

"I just hate him. I *hate* him." I'm pacing back and forth. I don't care if he hears me.

"Kai, please," she whispers.

"No, Mom. No! He wants me to be someone that I'm not, that I will never be! I can't be king. I certainly won't be like him!" I'm shouting now, and in the back of my head, I know I should keep quiet, but I've been quiet for so long now that everything wants to pour out of me. "I don't want to keep humans as *pets* or fuck them or feed on them. I want to live in peace with them. We have lived amid horrible tradition for so long that most vampires have forgotten that humans offered themselves to us when we were starving. Then we just overtook them! We enslaved them. They didn't even stand a chance."

"Kai—"

"No!" I shout, shaking off her touch. "I can't just sit by when I know we could be living in a better world. There's so much wrong with this damn kingdom, and I don't want it! I don't want to be here. I don't want to be king!"

I breathe quickly, never having said all the words out loud. My mother doesn't look shocked or confused. She just looks sad, sad that I am burdened with this decision. She must have known a long time ago that I didn't want the crown.

"I don't want to be king," I say softer now, feeling the weight of a giant decision rest on my shoulders. "But if I forfeit… then Caden rules."

I look up at the ceiling and cradle my hands behind my neck. Another tearless sob threatens my sanity. It's been too much today, and I feel the entire castle push down on me.

My mother walks towards me and wraps her hands around my waist, pulling me into a long hug. I crack, and a sob hiccups through my throat, jolting my body against her grip. I drop my hands to my sides and let her motherly affection completely break me down.

"What do I do?" I ask, my voice thick with emotion.

"My son, I cannot make this choice for you," she says against my chest, and it feels like my heart is breaking again. "But Kai, you have the opportunity to do great things. If you rule, you can make great change."

"Free the humans? Father will never allow it."

"There will come a day when your father and I will be gone."

"But still, the kingdom would sooner see me dead than give up their precious *property*," I spit the words.

"You have greatness inside you, Kai. You can affect change wherever you see fit. You have the strength and will to enact reform. You simply have to answer the call and fight." She releases my torso and cups my chin with her cool fingers. "Just because your father and brother threaten you with big words and claims does not mean they have more power than you. You are kind, son. Kindness will see you through much more than greed and lust."

Looking into my mother's eyes is like watching the sunlight against the bark of a tree, and it hurts to look at for too long. I nod, and she releases my chin. I step back from her embrace and heave a breath.

"Do you have something for me to drink?" I ask, unsure about how I will respond. I'm still nervous about my earlier breakdown, but I can't go back into my room with thoughts of Astrid's blood without something to keep me going.

She nods and walks away from me to pour me a drink. I stare into the fire, noting the flickers of the flame. I wish I was like a flame, burning bright enough to affect change, then blowing away in a burst of wind, caught forever in an endless breeze. Instead, I'm a damned creature of the night.

When my mother returns, she hands me a goblet filled with cold blood, and I drink it quickly, feeling the liquid burn my insides for a moment before settling into my stomach. My gums itch, and my throat burns with lingering thirst, but I'm stronger than before. My reaction is steady, and I feel calm. My mother smiles at me, and I return the cup back to her. I wipe my mouth and bow to her, leaving the room before she can say anymore.

I know that she wants the best for me, and she really believes that I'm right for the crown, but her words just put more pressure on me to take it when I really don't want it. I don't want to rule a people that thrive on predatory traditions. I hate it, and I can't stand that I'm the one that has to choose. The only thing I want is sleep. Endless sleep.

My hands are stuffed in my pockets as I walk slowly back to my room. The castle is mostly asleep, and the hallways echo with my footsteps against the stone. The lanterns are burning down, and it looks like the walls are fighting to stay awake for me. I take a deep breath, smelling the hints of mildew and moss growing just on the other sides of the wall, the reckless ocean casting salt spray onto the stones.

When I face my bedroom door, I hang my head, my nostrils flaring from the scents of Astrid on the air. I press the palm of my hand against the grain of the wood, resting for a moment, feeling the flicker of thirst play on my tongue. Squeezing my eyelids shut, I'm tempted to just curl up against the floor and sleep here. Surely, I won't survive this challenge from my father. And now that Caden is taunting me with images and dreams of Astrid's blood? I might as well give up.

Opening my eyes, I see light play from underneath the door. The fire is lit. She is waiting for me. One thing is clear: if I fail and my father reassigns Astrid to someone else, they certainly won't treat her like I do. I will not only fail my father, my kingdom, but I will fail her. I don't know if I can live with that. Not now.

Straightening up, I yank on the metal ring to open the door, but I am not prepared for what I see behind it. Instead of finding the same young, naive girl that I had seen last, the light from the fire flickers against a woman's body. Instead of finding Astrid wearing her pastel blue dress laced up to the base of her neck, instead of her caked with soot from the fireplace, tinging her yellow skirts, I find Astrid completely naked, sitting on my bed.

My jaw drops instantly, and I am frozen still as she greets me, though I don't hear it, and starts walking up to me. My whole body stands on edge.

I was expecting that the first time I saw a woman naked, it would be another vampire. I never thought that I would see a human naked. I never thought that I would even try to fool around with a human. I'm already so tempted by their blood that I figured thirst would overcome all other senses. Seeing Astrid in the firelight, I know now that's not the case. Feelings of arousal and confusion spring to the forefront of my mind, and I barely notice the taste of Astrid's scent on my tongue.

I stare at her form. The way the flames accentuate her gentle curves, the way her waist slopes at each side to form her hips. I can't keep my eyes from trailing her up and down as she stands before me. Her legs are longer than I thought, and she is actually quite thin for such a tall woman. Her skin is so pale that it's like it has its own light.

My eyes glaze painfully over her thighs, and I begin to tremble. It feels like my entire body is having a heart attack. My eyes continue their bombardment by trailing over her bellybutton, her ribs softly protruding from underneath two breasts, curved gently. I can't help but wonder what they feel like. My hands tingle at the thought.

I gulp and force my eyes to her face. She looks just as scared as I feel. What does she have to be scared of? She's the most beautiful person I've ever seen.

Maybe I should say something. I don't even understand how this is happening. Did my father put her up to this? Caden? Annette? Who told her that she could just show up naked? Does she *want* me to hurt her? I would certainly hurt her if she pressed.

I can't have sex with a human. The thought of giving in to the arousal makes my stomach lurch. I could so easily strangle her. I could so easily run my lips over her throat. It would be easy, so easy, to bite down in a moment of bliss.

My thoughts become so unbearable that I break eye contact and walk swiftly to the balcony, breathing the fresh air as soon as I step out onto the terrace. I can feel that she follows me. Is she speaking to me? The urge to jump off the ledge is so present, but I can't just keep abandoning her. My thoughts feel mechanic like I'm completely rigid as I sense Astrid's every move next to me. The wind breezes between us, making us both shiver and sigh, billowing breaths of icy air.

She lays a hand on my shoulder, turning me away from the darkness and back to face her.

"Kai," she whispers, looking down at my body.

I swallow deeply, trying to force myself to look away from her, but the way her eyelashes brush against her cheeks, the way her freckles look against her stark pale skin, the way her bottom lip juts out makes me crazy. I feel my body change in ways I have never experienced before.

"Yes?" I breathe.

She leans closer to me, just *barely* not touching me. I grip the railing for support, feeling the stones dig into my back as I press against them.

"I couldn't stop thinking about you," she said, her voice warm and inviting. "I've been waiting for you."

Oh my God.

"I've never felt like this before," she continues. "I want to take care of you. Will you let me do that?"

Her eyes are still cast down like she doesn't really buy into what she's saying. Like the words were scripted for her.

I reach up and use my pointer finger to lift her chin up, fully dedicated to explaining to her that she doesn't need to do this. But when her bright blue eyes meet mine, I'm trapped once again in her enchanted gaze. Her skin shines like silver in the moonlight, with pools of perfect blue shadows collecting in the contours of her face. I cannot look away from her, and I feel my heart throb fervently underneath my breastbone as her crystal eyes move over my face.

The tension between us is physically jarring, palpable electricity flowing between us. I can barely handle the new sensations coursing through my blood. She is so close to me now, her heartbeat like a warm vortex calling out to me. I flick my eyes to her lips, parted just barely. I could so easily kiss her.

I shift ever so slightly next to her, and the fabric of my trousers brushes her bare skin. She makes a small gasping sound, causing her breath to brush against my face so wonderfully. Overcome, I place my hand on the small of her back and draw her close, feeling her warmth emanate against my skin. She sucks another sharp breath in through her lips. I feel every inch of her skin against me, and I can't help but sneak my other hand to her waist, feeling how smooth the skin is on her stomach. She shivers as my fingertips brush across her back, and her skin erupts in prickles of goosebumps.

She runs her tongue across her bottom lip, driving me absolutely crazy. In a hasty attempt to avoid kissing her—*God*, I want to kiss her—I put my forehead against hers, my nostrils burning from the scent coming off her. She breathes a shaky breath, and then I feel her hands on my stomach, in turn making *me* shiver from head to toe. I clench my teeth together and growl softly as she untucks my shirt from my trousers, running her fingers over my stomach muscles. Every part of my body explodes with electricity. My head slips from her forehead down to the crook of her shoulder. I can feel her heartbeat underneath her skin.

I yank back. I can see her pulse through the vein in her neck, the pump of her blood flowing beneath the thin membrane of flesh.

Her siren song is so strong that I can't help but stare at the symphony of life playing inside her body. I'm holding her so close that she's practically defenseless. Unconsciously, my head lowers toward the source of the ballad that sings to me. Her ear brushes my cheek, and my body erupts with sensation. I open my mouth, feeling my teeth unsheathe, my gums throbbing like the rest of my body. I graze her skin gently, just barely, soft enough to not break skin.

If I take a breath, I'll be able to inhale her decadent aroma, feasting only on the smell. That would be okay, right?

"Kai?" Astrid whispers, her breath hitting the skin on my neck, and a flash of heat courses across my back.

I whip my head away from her and use one of my hands to press her away, pushing at her shoulder joint. I can't live Caden's fantasy. I have to stop this.

As soon as she is no longer a threat, I remove my hand and look at her, careful not to take note of her heightened breathing or hear the thudding of her heart, careful not to look any further below her collarbone.

"Astrid, would you please cover yourself?" My voice sounds completely disconnected from my body. Am I actually speaking? It sounds at ease, the opposite of how I'm feeling.

"You don't want me?" Now *her* voice sounds more like how I'm feeling. Hurt.

"No, that's not it at all," I say, and before I can stop it, my fingers are brushing her cheek. A wealth of blood floods to her cheeks, turning her pale skin pink underneath my touch. Holy God. "I simply had a trying day," I lie. My hand trembles as I pull it back. "I wish to sleep."

Her face falls. I suppose I can't even do that right.

"Will you help me get ready for bed?"

"Yes, sir," she says dejectedly.

Once she's back inside, and I can feel the unyielding icy winds caress my body, the stiffness and throbbing start to subside. I think my chest actually caves in from relief. I take several deep breaths and try to reign in my thoughts before walking back into the room. It feels a lot more like a heated dungeon of lust now, but I have to focus on sleeping. I have to get through the night. The morning will surely be better.

In the room, Astrid is fully clothed now in a light nightgown, and when she stands between me and the fire, I can see her figure clearly through the sheer material. I sigh internally. I suppose I won't be able to escape my thoughts after all.

She folds over the blanket on my bed, and I take my leave to the bathroom to undress. I look down and notice all the changes that my body has made in the last hour. My skin is no longer pale and grey but more pink and even-toned, save for the bright red splotches across my neck and chest. The blood my mother gave me must be helping. Suddenly, I'm very glad I stopped to see her before coming back here. I don't think I would have been able to resist Astrid otherwise. My body seems to agree since I haven't fully returned to normal. I look down, taking note of my 'manhood' and roll my eyes. If this was my father's plan, it was fucking working.

God, she is beautiful. How am I supposed to live in the same room with her, having seen *everything*? My dreams will be vivid, haunting. Even worse now that I have the phantom taste of her blood in my mouth, Caden's vision taunting me.

But I'm still confused. Why did she do that? How did she know to do that?

The horrid realization hits me, and I feel my body inflate with something different now. I feel my hands clench, and my chest tightens with anger.

"Astrid," I ask, exiting the bathroom.

"Yes?" she replies, still despondent.

"Have you been with a man before?"

"Yes," she says, looking at me, her figure clearly outlined underneath the white sheet. "I figured you knew that."

"No," I hissed through my teeth. Of course, she's been with someone else. Of course, I'm now also cursed with knowing someone's hands have gripped her skin. Someone's lips have trailed her neck and kissed her lips.

Someone *else's*.

"Thank you, Astrid. That will be all. Get some sleep."

I throw myself on the bed, knowing that I will see every other man in the castle pounding Astrid's flesh in my nightmares. I curl the blankets over my shoulder and face the stone walls, the images starting even before I close my eyes.

11
ASTRID

I wake early the next morning, jostled upright by the frozen air that wafts into the room. Kai's already awake, readying himself in the bathroom when I stand to get dressed. I slip off the nightgown, cursing under my breath at the chill in the room. It feels like my toes are completely numb. I quickly pull on my blue dress and tug on my cloth shoes. I run my fingers through my hair, and by the time I'm fussing with the laundry, Kai comes back into the room.

"We have to go to court today," he says in a monotonous voice. He barely looks at me.

"Alright," I reply, standing and dusting off my apron. "Shall I attend to you?"

"Yes," he says quickly, meeting my eyes with a look of desperation. It almost seems that he wants me to be there as a backup, like he doesn't want to go alone.

"Alright. Lead the way."

I gesture to the door, feeling a little backward. Isn't he supposed to be instructing me?

"What will the court be deciding today?" I ask as we walk down the hallway.

"Who will be my wife," he says, his voice low and clipped.

"Oh."

"Tomorrow is my birthday," he continues. "I have to decide on who I'll marry by the end of my coronation so the announcement can be made."

"I didn't realize…" I let it trail off.

He gives me a sidelong glance, perhaps measuring my comfort level. It feels exquisitely awkward, going to meet Kai's potential suitor when I practically threw myself at him last night. And, what's worse, I failed in my task. If Baldassare asks me what happened, I won't be able to lie to him.

By the time we reach the throne room, I'm hanging my head in defeat, feeling all but helpless. The room is in the process of being decorated for Kai's coronation. Large iron ornaments have been added to the sconces, and banners of gold and black silk hang from the center chain chandelier. The place looks beautiful, dressed in perfect colors to match the outfits Eileen and I made for the royal family.

Kai departs from me and heads toward the throne. I know I'm not supposed to follow, so I begrudgingly take a spot in the line of servants on the back wall. Noble after noble files in, and I can't help but gawk at all the beautiful dresses that pass by. Every woman is clothed in the finest materials, from purple silks to beautifully embroidered skirts. Their dresses billow out with layers of petticoats so that each woman takes up the width of three people. I stare as all the ladies gather in cliques to talk vehemently about Kai and Caden, who strolls in looking incredibly dapper. Comparatively, Kai looks rather underdressed. I look down at the tile, thinking of all the things

I should have prepared for him.

Alheri comes to stand next to me and smiles brightly.

"Kai looks wonderful today," she says to me. I watch him, feeling invisible against the back wall.

"He does, doesn't he?"

"You sound upset," she asks, looking at me worriedly.

"You worry too much. I'm just thinking that I should have made sure he had nicer clothes to wear," I explain.

"He looks fine," she says, looking back to him.

I frown, watching girl after girl go up to him. Kai stands in a line with his mother and father on either side of him, and Caden beside his mother. I can see Caden staring towards Annette with a sly smile that she returns with a shy gaze. Her cheeks blush, and she looks away from him. My frown deepens; Kai has never looked at me like that.

As Kai lifts each candidate's hand, he kisses it and smiles warmly. My stomach clenches, and I try not to think about how just last night, he'd held me so close, how his eyes had sparkled when I touched him. I try not to think about how his fingers splayed across the small of my back, pressing me against him. I had been so certain he wanted me then.

It almost physically hurts to watch him laugh and flirt with each beautiful lady of the court. Of course, they are all stunning with their perfectly pinned hairstyles and touches of makeup on their cheeks. It doesn't help that all these beautiful women have striking red eyes set in dark lashes. They all look so mature and vibrant. Kai certainly doesn't look at me in the same way he does with these women. I'm a fool to have ever believed that last night was anything more than physical flirtation between a man and a woman.

"Come on," Alheri says after a few minutes.

"What?"

"Come on, let's get out of here," she says, smiling and pointing to the door.

"I'm not supposed to leave. Kai asked me to stay," I protest.

"We won't be gone long. I'm sure he'll be just fine for a few minutes," she says, grabbing my arm. She leads me down into the lowest level of the castle, back towards our quarters—well, her quarters. "What's going on with you and Kai?"

"What do you mean? Nothing," I insist.

"Has he fed on you?" she whispers urgently as soon as we are out of nobility earshot, her hand aiming to sweep my hair back from my neck.

As I pull away and swat at her hand, I say, "No. He doesn't want me. He hasn't fed on me. He doesn't want me to cook or clean, and he never gives me any instructions. Last night I offered my body to him, and he turned away from me."

"How ridiculous," another voice chimes in. It's Annette, looking haggard. I suppose I hadn't looked at her too closely in the throne room.

"What happened to you?" I ask, eyeing her torn clothing and the bruises along her chin and neck.

"This is what success looks like, Astrid," Annette says as she walks up to us. She turns towards Alheri and points to her body with an expectant expression. Alheri's mouth forms a tight line, but then she steps behind Annette, offering her a chair. I pull one up and sit next to her as well. Then, Alheri touches her neck, and the bruises start melting away. "Caden asked me to be his *kvinne*! Can you believe it?"

"That's wonderful!" I exclaim, taking her hands. She looks back at me with a gleeful expression at first, then turns serious.

"Look, if Kai is turning you away, it's *your* fault. Caden simply takes what he wants, and I give it to him. I never have to ask or even speak to him unless he wishes it."

A soft hum comes over us as Alheri speaks some distant

language. I watch the bruises fade, and Annette's skin returns to a normal color. I feel a swoosh of air pass over us, and I try to focus on Annette's words.

"Caden is the most wonderful man to have walked these halls," she says, her words slurring slowly. I smile warmly at her, feeling my own heart twirl. "Kai is his brother, and he needs you, Astrid. You must serve him well. Make sure he knows he can have you. He's going to become king."

"Yeah," I whisper, feeling a warm sensation flow over my stomach. I blink slowly, watching Alheri's lips move. And then, I blink, and Alheri is smiling and looking at us. "I know you're right. I have to be better," I say.

Annette looks like she's still in a trance but then slowly reaches up and touches her neck lightly, flinching when her fingers touch the skin under her ears.

"Astrid, why don't you go back to the throne room? I'm sure Kai will be missing you," Alheri instructs me. I nod, looking at Annette's hollow eyes. Alheri shoos me with her hands and then places them back onto Annette's skin, and her eyes roll back slightly as she closes them. I smile and turn away from them, putting away all my thoughts about Kai's hands on my skin.

12
KAI

I relax my face muscles as Lady Corinne moves on to talk to Caden. All the smiling and kissing has turned my face into a tense collection of sore muscles. I turn away and gingerly rub my temples and jaw for only a few moments before the next lady appears.

"Son, this is Sasha," my mother says.

Sasha extends her hand, smiling wide. I return the smile and take her hand, pressing my lips to her cool skin. She coos at me, and I release her, putting both my hands behind my back.

"So, Sasha, tell me something about yourself," I ask.

"Thank you, my Prince," she says. "Well, I work with my mother, keeping up our estate in Livsnerven. I'm sure you've heard of the Soroya Manor?"

"Oh yes. You have a lovely home."

"Thank you so much, your Highness," she says, curtsying. I roll my eyes when she's not looking.

"Well, what are your hobbies? Do you like to read?"

"Oh, no, sir. I do not waste time on fanciful stories or busying myself with pointless tasks. I simply have too much to do," she says, with a look of disgust on her face.

I pinch my lips into a tight line, trying to remain bright and civil toward a person of my court. Is it even *my* court?

"Yes, thank you for coming today," my mother says, passing Sasha over to my brother. Luckily, my father chooses then to leave me alone with my mother for a few moments.

"How are you holding up?" she asks, gently rubbing my arm.

"They're all so *boring*," I confess. "How am I supposed to pick a wife out of people I can't even relate to?"

"You don't have to love them, son. You just have to choose. Didn't you like Sasha?"

"Sure, I guess. She doesn't like reading, though. And she seems overly opinionated on 'spending time on pointless tasks.' How am I supposed to rule effectively if I have a wife that critiques my every move?" I huff in irritation.

My mother chuckles at me, and I nudge her back before the next lady approaches us. I continue the charade of smiles and questions for a few more moments before my father announces the dancing portion of the evening.

A harpist sets up in the corner alongside a lute player and what looks to be a singer. My mother ushers me onto the dance floor, where all the other eligible bachelorettes join me. Caden is on the floor as well, taking up the free ladies' attention. I'm somewhat grateful he's here. As much as I've hated being around him lately, he's so much better at all of this than I am. I can barely look at other people in the eyes.

The bard begins to sing, and I bounce up and down, following the ladies' motions as they lead me through a touchless dance of mirroring hands and swaying skirts. Everything about this feels pointless. How can Sasha be okay with *this*? How could dancing be more important than *reading*?

I dance with all the ladies of the court, hoping that one of them will catch my attention, but by the time the music stops, I simply bow and leave the dance floor. No sparks. No interest. Nothing.

Astrid is still standing against the back wall, looking frozen and rigid as I move back over to my mom. I can't help it; I just want to talk to her. She is infinitely more interesting than these women. Her golden, red hair is braided into an intricate series of knots that collect on the back of her head, leaving her pale, long neck and collarbones sneaking out just beyond the lace of her dress. In other people's eyes, they probably see a simple girl with plain wool clothes and a smudge of fireplace soot on her skirts. But to me, Astrid's hair and eyes glow. Her dress looks like an angel's garment, and her skin shines with so much life.

I sigh and force my eyes away from Astrid. I turn my attention back to my suitresses, walking amongst them to try and find even a tiny glimpse of attraction.

"And there will be a marvelous selection of the king's finest servants," I overhear someone say as I walk. I turn instantly towards the clique of women, Corinne and Sasha amongst them.

"Oh hello, Prince Kai," Sasha says. "Wonderful dancing, your Highness."

"Thank you," I reply robotically. "What were you just saying?"

"I was telling Corinne about the feast your father is planning for your coronation. I hear it's going to be *decadent*! Aren't you excited, Prince?"

"Yes, of course," I lie through clenched teeth. "If you'll excuse me."

They all curtsy, and I turn swiftly away from them, nodding goodbye to my mother before grabbing Astrid and leaving the room in a hurry. Of *course*, my father is going to serve up all our humans to the nobles to feed on. I look at Astrid, worried suddenly about what she will be doing this time tomorrow. Surely, I can't keep my eyes on her the entire night, despite how much I long to do just that.

"Kai?" she whispers, looking at my grasp on her arm.

I relent and rake my hands through my hair. As soon as we're back in my room, I quickly shut the door behind us and throw myself into the chair by the fire. The room is so cold. I look disgustedly at my broken balcony door. I'll have to get it fixed. I let out a long sigh.

Astrid kneels beside me and lays her hand on mine.

"What's wrong?"

I look at her wide, childlike eyes and just let myself bask in her presence for a moment. I turn my hand, so I'm cupping hers in mine now. I rub my thumb lightly across the back of her palm, feeling her heartbeat ever so lightly under her skin. It doesn't frighten me nearly as much as it once did, though, I'm still afraid. I think I'll always be afraid.

She looks at me and nods, urging me to answer her.

I sigh and say, "I hated that. All of *them*."

"The court ladies?"

"Yes," I say, gauging her reaction.

"Why?"

Standing, I begin to pace as I talk.

"They are all so damn *shallow*! And completely bloodthirsty, just the same as all the rest. They just have a little bit more class than Caden does," I say, tucking my hands into my pockets. "And get this: one of the girls basically said reading was a waste of time."

"That's ridiculous! Reading and education are some of the finest tools in a kingdom," she says.

"Exactly!"

"If you don't have an educated kingdom, how are you any

different than the animals of the land?"

"Sometimes, I wonder if they are any different," I mumble. "All those girls just want status or money or fame, and then they spend all their time feeding. I don't think they are different than beasts."

Astrid nods, her eyes drifting towards the balcony as another gust of wind bursts through. She wraps her arms around her waist and goes to her bed to fetch a blanket.

"Hey, give me just a minute," I say, suddenly. "I'm going to go get someone to fix the door. We'll probably have to leave the room for the evening, but we can stay in the guest quarters if we need to."

"The Prince of Feilfri Castle staying in guest quarters the night before his coronation?" Astrid asks with a mock smile.

"You have a better idea?" I smile back, nodding to her before springing downstairs to meet with the blacksmith.

By the time I return, Astrid has cleaned up the bedroom, lit the fire, and is making a pot of tea. I smile, wanting so badly for my heart not to ache at the sight of her.

"Hi," I say gruffly.

"Welcome back," she says, then gives me a winning smile. "What did Bjorn have to say?"

"You know the blacksmith?"

"I know almost everyone, Kai," she says, playful now. I'm amazed at how easy it is for me to talk to her.

"He said he'll be here after dinner. He said he already has the measurements for my door and just has to assemble it before bringing it up," he says. "Looks like we'll be perfectly fine to sleep in our own beds."

"That's wonderful," she says. "Well, I've gone ahead and replaced your bathwater, so feel free to take a bath, and I'll have the tea finished soon," she says, her voice like a bird.

"It looks like you could use a bath more than me," I say, eyeing the soot from the fireplace on her orange dress.

"Oh, does this bother you? I can change."

"No." I can't help but laugh. Why would I care about something so stupid as a little bit of dirt?

"What did I say?" She smiles, laughing with me.

"Nothing, I just find you funny."

"I'm…glad?" she says, smiling at me, and I can't help but feel a warmth inside my chest. Her smile is like a breath of fresh air after being in court all day.

"Yeah," I breathe.

"Well, would you like me to take a bath?" she asks, her smile turning slightly more into a smirk, and she looks up at me through her eyelashes. My body feels like it's going to have a heart attack again. What's that all about? She's not even naked, but she might as well with the way my blood is fluttering all throughout my body. I clear my throat before replying.

"What are you implying?" I ask, my voice unsteady.

"Well, you need a bath. I need a bath. Would you like me to take one with you?" Her voice turns to honey under the implication. My jaw pops open as she takes a step towards me, and she lays one of her hands lightly on my chest. My skin erupts in flame under her touch. I gulp and try to remain calm.

"While that's very tempting…" The twinkle in her eye diminishes slightly, but she's still smiling, so I take her hand away from my chest and continue, "I've had quite a hard day, and I'd like to be left to my thoughts."

She draws her hand away but continues to smile. "As you wish, Kai. I'll just see to the rest of my chores, and I'll find us some dinner," she chimes and practically bounces back to her tea.

"I guess I'll be in the bathroom then," I say.

"Alright," she replies, smiling widely at me. I start to walk away, but she starts humming along to a small tune, and I look back.

"What is that song?" I ask before I can help myself.

"Sorry?"

"That song you're humming. What is it?"

Her face flushes, and my thoughts revel at the blood coloring her cheeks.

"Oh, I didn't realize that I was humming. Does it bother you?"

"No!" I say too quickly. She smiles, though. "I just wondered what it is. It's lovely."

"My mother used to sing it to me as a baby," she says, a sadness looming over her face. She's never mentioned her family before this. Suddenly, I feel like an ass because I never once asked about her family or anything else about her.

"It's very nice," I say before turning into the bathroom. I eye the balcony doors. I don't want to leave yet. This is the first decent conversation I've had in days, and I make a quick decision. "Would you like to come to the roof with me?"

"Sure," she says lightly, her face like sunshine itself. I'm surprised I can look at her without my flesh burning away.

She puts away her tools and wipes off her apron before taking it off and walking up to me. She still has a large spot of soot on her face, and before I can even think about what I'm doing, I reach up with one of my hands and wipe away the dust from her cheek with my thumb. She's frozen solid, and I hear her breath catch in her throat. My own heart stops. I'm not sure what I just did.

Instead of panicking, I blink and smile at her, and she smiles widely back at me. I listen to her heart as it restarts, beating wildly. I open the door, and I can't help but smile too. That made her happy. I actually made her happy.

As I lead her up to the large rooftop terrace, she continues to hum that wonderful lullaby, and I want nothing to ruin this moment.

I walk beside her, my hands clasped behind my back. The hallways are bare, and the fading light trickles in from the small windows.

"I have to confess," she says, her voice bouncing lightly off of the stone walls. My heart does an anxious little flip flop in my chest, but I keep moving forward. "I had a hard time watching you today."

I frown. "Why's that?"

"It's just that it was…well, it was difficult for me to see you with all those other women," she says, and I glance at her as she hangs her head. "Please don't misunderstand me, Prince. I fully understand that you are going to be crowned tomorrow and that you need a Queen to rule beside you. I'm simply confessing that I didn't like seeing all those other women fawn all over you."

I'm silent, absorbing her words. Doesn't she know I hated it too?

I could easily tell her how much I wished I was dancing with her today. The thought never left my mind. How wonderful I imagine it would feel to twirl her around the floor, holding her close in my arms, feeling her heart sputter as we moved.

Instead, I pinch my lips together and don't say anything. We walk in awkward silence as I try to collect my thoughts, to say *something.* After a few minutes, we arrive at the end of the hallway. I reach up and pull down the step ladder to the roof's terrace.

I climb up to open the hatch carefully. The clouds are thick and heavy as I push aside the door. The wind instantly rushes in, and I worry for a moment that Astrid will be too cold. I bite my lip but climb out anyway and then reach my hand down to help Astrid. As our skin touches, I feel a spark pass through our fingers. She smiles breathily, and I hear her heart flop around again when I pull her up onto the terrace. That's a very pleasing sound. Almost addictive.

"Wow, this is beautiful, Kai." God, even the way she says my name is splendid.

"This is one of my favorite spots in the whole world," I admit.

"I can see why. The waves, the mountains, the view is just beautiful."

Like a goddamn sap, I can't stop staring at her. The view pales in comparison to her auburn hair and rosy cheeks. Her eyes are like frozen ocean water as she looks over at me, and I smile back at her easily. I can't help it.

I clear my throat, "I used to come here all the time as a boy. It was the only place I could get away."

"Away?"

"Well, away from the smell of blood," I say, looking at her, watching her reaction. She doesn't say anything, just looks at the distant mountains.

"Does it bother you? The smell?" she asks me, and I watch how the muscles feather in her jaw as she speaks. After a moment, she looks back at me. I don't really know what to say, so I nod.

"Not because it's bad," I clarify. "It's just…too much sometimes."

"I see," she says.

"Do you really?"

"No," she admits, smiling sheepishly at me.

I give her a half-smile and look down at my hands. I take a deep breath, the icy salt spray a welcome addition to Astrid's aroma. The distant mountains are misty with rainfall like the clouds are breathing fog in between the peaks. The overcast weather makes the colors of the world desaturate, and everything looks a shade darker. The greens of the trees are moody instead of gleaming and bright. The water below looks grey and green instead of blue.

But Astrid…her hair is still just as rosy golden, her eyes a bright blue. Looking at her, I feel things that I can't explain. Things I've not felt before.

"It's hard to be around humans," I say in a low voice. She leans in closer to hear me over the wind. "The last time I drank blood from the vein was the worst day of my life."

She's quiet but lays her hand on mine. Her warmth is welcoming. I turn my hand over to intertwine our fingers, feeling my heart skip a beat.

"What happened?" she whispers.

I give her hand a small squeeze and look back toward the mountains. Telling her my darkest secret feels too raw, too real, to look in her bright eyes.

"It was ten years ago, when I was just barely an adolescent vampire," I say. "Do you remember what I said about how vampires came to Nordøya?"

She nods.

"Well, all of those vampires fell back into their primal state, the state of every vampire that comes into the world. Thirsty and savage. Our instincts take over and cloak our vision in red until we see only the heartbeats of living beings so that we can hunt and feed quickly.

"As a vampire grows and matures, they can overcome their instincts. They learn to be more civil," I explain. "It's a balance, of course. But every vampire can succumb to their more basic instincts at any given moment."

I pause, feeling shivers caress my skin as she lightly rubs the top of my hand with her thumb. I take a deep breath, tasting her scent pleasantly. It tethers me to the moment, reminding me that I am no longer the version of myself in the story.

"The last time I fed," my voice shakes, "it was a woman, maybe just under forty years old. She was a *thrall* in the castle. Caden and I had been out hunting, feeding on a small tribe of humans that dared to camp outside of their city. When we were finished and headed back to the castle, I was still ravaged and starving. I couldn't control my thirst, and Caden and I went to the dungeons. I grabbed the first woman I saw."

Astrid is frigid beside me, her hands trembling ever so slightly.

"After only seconds of feeding, I couldn't stop myself. I kept drinking and sucking the life out of her. Caden tried to stop me, but I was insatiable. I drank every last drop of her blood."

The words hang between us.

"I killed her, Astrid," I whisper. Her face goes blank with shock.

"But…that is forbidden," she says, barely audible.

I nod, looking back to the wilderness. I can't bear to look at her face.

"I immediately was cursed with an enormous amount of pain. Our resident witch, Alheri's mother, was there. She explained my mistake, though I was already fairly aware of what I'd done. She said I would feel the woman's death seven times over. To this day, I still don't know if I felt all of it then or if I continuously feel her death. I watched her shift into my own mother's face, hallucinating that I'd killed her. It was agony," I choke, remembering the deep grief.

Astrid wraps her hands around mine, leaning her body against me for comfort. I feel my eyes stain with tears as visions of the beautiful red-haired woman I'd killed flashes across my eyes.

"It was the worst day of my life," I stutter through my thick throat. "I told Moroya that I would never kill again. I'd never feed again."

Astrid nods, and I can feel her body shake.

"So you see," I say, freeing my hands from hers to wipe away the stray tears, "I hate being around blood."

I laugh shakily, then continue, "It took me ten years, ten *years*, to realize how horribly all the *thralls* are treated here. At first, I avoided feeding because I was so afraid of the pain. Believe me when I tell you it was worse than death. But in my abstinence, I evolved. There was a clarity of mind that came over me and made me realize what a messed up place this is. Astrid, I don't feed because I am the problem. I'm a vampire. It's not just because I don't want to feel that pain again but because I *understand* now. I never want to make someone else feel that way. Even if it was just a fraction of what I felt, I wouldn't wish it on my worst enemy."

I straighten up and pull my hands through my hair.

"And being around humans, around any blood, I'm reminded of that day. I'm reminded of how easily I can fall into the temptation," I continue.

Astrid is quiet, but her face is worried, sad. I look deep into her eyes as I continue.

"You have no idea how hard this has been for me." I feel my voice reverberate in my throat. "Having you so close and for you to be so wonderful, so perfect."

Her eyebrows raise in the center like she's in pain. Her mouth opens just slightly.

"In a lot of ways, you're the perfect woman for me, Astrid," I say, feeling my heart hang on my sleeve. "But even still, whatever I feel for you…"

I step forward and grab her hands in mine again. Her hair tugs gently in the breeze as she stares up into my face.

"I can't change what I am," I whisper. "Your blood sings to me stronger than anything I could feel for you. I know I'm not strong enough to withstand my instincts, my bloodlust. Even if I never drink human blood again, I still won't be free from the lure of it. At any moment, I could turn into that version of myself, the monster inside me. And that scares me more than anything."

Her lip trembles, and small tears pool in the corner of her eyes. I want so desperately to take her in my arms, to kiss her deeply and passionately, but as soon as I even think about her skin on mine, the bile in the back of my throat flares, and suddenly I'm staring at the pulse in her neck again.

I step backward and release her hands. I clench my teeth together, feeling my chest ache at being away from her. But I can't stay here. I can't be alone with her. My vulnerability could turn to thirst in a second, and there would be no witnesses to her death, no punishment save for the pain that would curse me. And that wouldn't be enough to stop me.

"I'm sorry." As I jump down and flee back into the castle of the damned, the last thing I see is her broken expression and the tears rolling down her cheeks.

13
ASTRID

My breath billows out from numb lips. The wind ripples around my face, and small raindrops cut against my skin. I'm trembling and shaking, but not from the cold. My fingers stung where Kai had touched them. My knees shake, and my stomach jitters with a million butterflies fluttering inside of me. The cold and rain have seeped into my shoes, freezing my toes and soaking the bottom of my skirt.

I know I should get out of the frigid air. If I stay out here, I'll likely catch a cold and die. Such a human thing to do. Get sick and die, slowly and sadly. I know I should get inside and warm my hands against the fire, thaw out my rigid muscles. I know I should *move*... but I can't. My feet are melted to the stone, locking me in place.

Had Kai really said all of those things? Did I imagine it all? My thoughts swirl with endless questions. Who was the woman Kai killed? Did the curse really exist? Did Alheri know about any of this? Of course, I know that vampires are not allowed to kill humans, but

I always thought it was simply to preserve their supply of servants and blood. I never imagined there was a curse put on any vampire that killed us. How could that possibly be? I *know* people that died at the hands of vampires. They never seemed to be hurt the way Kai described.

Oh, my heart hurts for him. I can't imagine Kai suffering like that, and I certainly don't want to. It was hard enough to hear him talk about it. I clasp my hands together and press them to my chest, just over my heart. He'd been so sad, so utterly vulnerable as he confessed his greatest sin. Of course, he said he didn't care about his own pain; he simply wanted to spare others. That made it even worse to me. He was acting out of selfless intent. All these thoughts of whether I was good enough or pretty enough…Kai only pushed me away because he was afraid *for* me. He didn't want to hurt me.

I lean my head back, letting the tears fall from my eyes. I blink quickly and stare at the sky's fading light.

It doesn't matter what Kai said. It's no matter that he feels the same way about me that I do about him. Tomorrow, he will be crowned King of Livsnerven, and he'll be married to a beautiful vampire queen, someone who won't hurt him or tempt him.

I bite down on my lip to keep it from trembling. Whoever he marries, she will be able to give him everything he wants. And I can't. Even if he has feelings for me, they will quickly be washed away with his new marriage. She will whisk his attention away from me, replacing his grief and fear with laughter and comfort. He needs someone that can build a life with him. Someone to build a kingdom with.

I close my eyes tightly, willing my heart to piece itself back together as I start toward the hatch. My legs feel like numb stumps as I fumble down the narrow ladder. My legs quickly get tangled in my skirts. I curse softly as I land on the ground, my legs failing and my body sprawling across the floor.

I haul myself up and brush off the bits of debris from my dress. Frowning, my eyes trail over the dirt and soot-covered hem of my skirt, wishing only for a moment that I could be one of the court ladies, dressed in fine silk and dancing with Prince Kai forever and ever.

It doesn't matter. I can't think of him like that. I'm here to serve him, that's all. That's all I will ever be. A servant.

Locking away my thoughts, I walk back to Kai's room, pausing only when I see Prince Caden walking toward me with a devilish grin. He's alone, which strikes me as odd since Annette was assigned to him just this afternoon.

"Astrid," he says when he reaches me. "What are you doing alone on this fine evening?"

"Your Highness," I say, curtsying to him. "I was simply walking back to my quarters."

"How about instead you come with me to mine?"

"I'm not sure that is such a good—"

He stops me by gripping my jaw and forcing my eyes to his. In an instant, I'm trapped in his beautiful gaze. His red eyes swell, and my thoughts stop in their tracks. I sigh longingly, feeling nothing but a strange yearning to do as Caden wishes.

"Of course, my Prince," I whisper.

He smiles, his eyebrow cocked. His lips part as his mouth curves into a sensual smile, and I can't help but shiver at the sight of his teeth.

"Good girl," he says, stepping toward me and wrapping his arm around my waist.

He tows me only a few steps until I'm inside his bedroom. It's much larger than Kai's, and it's draped in beautiful decorations. His fireplace is raging, lighting the entire room in a warm glow. His giant bed is clothed in black silk sheets that look incredibly lavish. Never would Kai allow himself this kind of luxury.

Caden shuts the door behind us and saunters back toward me, trailing his fingertips across my collarbone as he passes me. He moves to sit on a large chair, grabbing a goblet of what looks like wine. It stains his lips a dark red. He eyes me expectantly, pointing to his shoes. I jump at the unspoken instruction and kneel to unlace and remove his shoes.

As I work, he leans forward and traces his hand over my cheek and down to my throat.

"Your pulse is intoxicating," he whispers, his breath caressing my skin. I gulp, and my heart beats quicker. He smiles loosely, closing his eyes and listening to the sputtering of my heart. "Mmm."

I look away from him, feeling my cheeks flush. I tuck away a hair behind my ear, and he quickly grabs my arm, leaning forward to brush his nose against the back of my wrist.

"Your scent is divine as well," he whispers against my skin.

"Thank you, my Prince."

"I wonder," he says, gently loosening his grip on my arm. He leans back against his chair again, holding my hand gently now. "Do you think Kai knows you're in here?"

"I'm not sure. I don't know where he went," I admit.

"So he's not in his room? He's not right next door?"

"I don't know, my Prince."

"*God*, I love the way your voice sounds," he says, his voice dripping with seductive energy. "But you're too proper, Astrid. Think of me as just another guy."

"As you wish, sir."

"Tell me something," he says, sipping on his wine. He licks his lips slowly, as though he's cherishing every drop that stains his mouth. "What do you and Kai do when you're alone together?"

"I'm not sure what you mean."

"Does he kiss you?"

I gulp and blush again.

"Does he hold you close?"

Caden leans forward, and my eyes are level with his knees. He positions his face toward the top of my head, his nose close to my hairline. His lips brush the skin that meets my hair, breathing in and out, his breath swirling into my hair. I close my eyes, and my body trembles. The fire burns the side of my face.

"Does Kai do this with you, Astrid?" he asks, rubbing his hands up my arms and back behind my neck.

"Caden," I whisper.

"Mmm. Yes," he breathes. "I want you to say my name. I want you to call me master."

I want to pull away, feeling uncomfortable and shaken with the request. Kai is my master. I know for certain that I should not be allowing Caden to ask me this. But his hands lock onto my neck, keeping me in place as he moves his nose down the side of my face, ending where my jaw meets my ear.

"Astrid," he purrs. "Give me your wrist."

When I don't respond, he pulls back and looks into my eyes again, warping my impression once again with his molten, red eyes. Before I can think clearly, I've given him my hand. He grabs it, still holding tightly to my neck. He rubs the bridge of his nose against the inside of my wrist, his nostrils flaring. I see familiar signs of thirst appear on his face. His eyes turn black, with slithering dark veins appearing on his face, shrouding his eyes in darkness. But somehow, I'm not afraid. His wine-stained lips kiss my wrist briefly before he sticks his tongue out to lick my skin. I shiver at the sight.

"Does Kai do this with you?" He turns his pitch-black eyes to me, and like a mouse caught in a predator's gaze, I gasp and flinch backward.

"Shh," he says. "Don't move."

I freeze in place, and he flashes a brilliant smile and lowers his teeth onto my wrist, breaking into the skin. He pulls on my arm as he feeds, pain radiating up my skin. I don't move or think or make a sound. He stops after just a taste of my blood.

"Delicious," he says in a low voice. He slowly drops my hand back to my side and licks his fingertips.

His eyes fade back to their normal bright red, the darkness leaving his face. He looks me over, and I follow his eyes with my own like I have no control over myself. His brown hair glows almost red in the firelight, and I watch as he combs his fingers through it, putting each strand back in place.

A few moments pass before he stands, pulling me up next to him. I move with robotic movements, stiff and aching from kneeling for so long. He stands me in front of the fire, and I watch the flames as he walks around me. He looks like he's assessing my attire, though I'm not sure why he would care.

"Astrid, dear," he says. "You should be clothed in the finest gowns."

He clicks his tongue in disapproval, looking at my dress with disgust. I follow his eyes to look down at the drab material. It has no sheen or drape to the fabric. It's just a utility dress. I want to explain this, but he stands in front of me again.

"I want you to take it off," he commands.

"What?" I breathe.

"Take it off," he snaps, grabbing my jaw again and forcing me to look into his eyes.

I unlace the front of my bodice, letting the overdress fall to the floor in a heap. When I'm in nothing but my shift, Caden smiles and runs his hands over my body, making me tremble and shake.

He moves behind me and presses his body against my back. I can feel every inch of him against my skin with only the sheer fabric between us. He brushes my hair away from my neck, exposing the skin above my collarbone. I quiver as his hands move up the front of my body, stopping just above my breasts at the opening of my dress.

His fingers play with the edge of the lace that holds my shift closed.

"Why are you doing this?" I manage to breathe.

In a flare of disapproval, his hand grabs a fistful of my hair and pulls my head to the side, providing a clear passage to my neck.

"You were supposed to be *mine*," he hisses through his teeth, and I can feel his hot breath against my skin.

With one hand in my hair and the other hand moving to press against the skin beneath my navel, he trails his nose down my throat, pausing only to brush his lips against the vein in my neck. A strangled moan escapes his lips, his breath blooming across my skin. I shake as he presses me even closer to him.

"You *will* be mine," he growls. My body floods with terror as his sharp teeth break into the skin on my neck.

14
KAI

I flee from the rooftop with irritated and fearful energy. Why did I say all of those things? How could I tell Astrid how much I feel for her when it won't matter? Tomorrow, I'll be king of the damned, and nothing will be the same.

I huff and pace endlessly before deciding not to go back to my room. If anything, I have to sort through my feelings before facing Astrid again. I have to focus now. I have to pick a wife and put on my new outfit. I have to address my Kingdom, and I can't be stuck thinking of how to fit a human into all of this chaos. The sun has set on my time as prince. It's now time for me to become a king.

I sigh, feeling completely unprepared and unwilling. Before I realize it, my feet have led me to the throne room, which is completely dark and empty. The decorations are set, with large tables around the room for the visiting nobles. Giant metal chalices line each table, waiting to be filled with wine or blood or ale. Plates and silverware are set. Ribbons of fine black and gold silk are strung from the ceiling. The large wooden beams are dressed in hanging decorations, maybe even candles that will be lit.

I walk into the middle of the room, lit now only by the passing moonlight filtering in through the tiny windows. After only a few seconds, the moon is shrouded by clouds again, darkening the room once more. I run my hands over the tables, liking the way the silk feels under my fingertips.

I wish Astrid was here.

But I can't think that.

Okay, let's think instead about who a good candidate is to be my wife.

Astrid.

Ugh! No, Kai! What about Sasha or Corinne?

God, now I wish Lilith was here. She would tell me to shape up and just pick one. Or she would make a joke about how ridiculous it all is. I kneel, raking my hands through my hair. I feel so completely alone.

I don't want to pick a wife from people I barely know. I don't want to rule a kingdom I despise. I don't want to be the center of attention, fawned over by people who disgust me. I don't want to have to be kind and courteous to those with lustful red eyes. I just want to be *alone.*

I smirk at the irony. How can someone hate feeling completely alone and then want to be alone at the same time? I suppose it's more that I feel desperately *lonely.* I don't want to be devoid of relationships like my father. I don't want to live in a friendless world.

Right now, Astrid is my closest friend and ally. She understands me, wants to learn from me. She's more than just someone I find attractive. She's the perfect friend.

I stand with renewed energy. If I had to explain my thoughts to her, this is a good place to start. Surely, she can understand why I can't be with her, but that doesn't mean I can't be friends with her.

If that's all I can get, I will take it a thousand times over. I will be the best friend she's ever had.

I move with purpose now, feeling a smile tug at my lips. I want to talk to her. I *need* to talk to her about everything. Maybe she'll be able to help me, make me see things that I've been blind to. Maybe she can direct me towards the best path. She's already made my life so much better by simply being in it.

But before I yank the metal ring on my door, I breathe in, unconsciously tasting the air for Astrid's scent. She's not in my room, but she is close. I frown, confused, before looking down the hall to the boiler room. Maybe she's fetching hot water. I walk towards the boiler, mentally preparing what I'm going to say. Surely, she's confused about everything that happened between us on the roof.

I walk into the steamy room, but Astrid's not here. My worries start to manifest in my stomach as I turn back to my room again. That's when I hear her voice.

"*Why are you doing this?*" I hear, just barely.

My head twitches to the neighboring door. Caden's door. My heart clenches in my chest, and my arms flex with rage as I stomp toward his room. Before I open the door, I notice how pungent Astrid's smell is now. He's *feeding* on her.

My body reacts quicker than my brain can. I kick the door open with such ferocity that the hinges come undone, and the door flies to the far wall, splintering into large planks of wood. Astrid screams as the sound of shredding wood rips through the room.

Standing before me is Astrid, wrapped in Caden's unbreakable grasp. His eyes are blood red when he lifts his teeth away from her skin, her blood dripping down the sides of his mouth. He smiles wildly at me, taunting me with her. I force my mouth shut but feel my teeth spring out of their sheaths. My eyes zero in on Caden's disgusting mouth, Astrid's blood coating his teeth like oil on water. Before I launch at him, I stop myself.

Caden is stronger than me in every way right now. I can't fight him. Not when I haven't fed in days, and he's high off of Astrid's blood. Everything about him is stronger than me right now.

"Good girl," Caden purrs to Astrid, nuzzling his face into her hair. To my horror, he doesn't attack her ruthlessly; he just holds her. He combs his hand through her hair, and I desperately try to see past the teeth marks, dripping with blood, on her neck. He traces his hands down her throat, touching his fingers to her blood, then licking it off with his tongue.

Her face flashes signs of fear. He has her locked in a tight grip against his body. He looks me in the eye as he holds her chest with one hand and her waist with the other. My voice, my heart, my stomach are all writhing in pain in my throat, choking me from firing any sort of warning or retort.

"Kai, so good of you to join us," he slurs, high on blood.

"Let her go," I barely make out.

"Oh, no. Why don't you come and have a taste?"

"*Caden*," I growl.

Astrid whimpers as he presses his fingers into her throat.

"You know you want to."

"I'm going to kill you," I hiss through my teeth. "Let her go before I rip you to shreds."

"Now, now, brother," he purrs. "Is that any way to treat your host? Especially in front of a lady."

He laughs, a horrid, taunting sound. He bends his head back, and Astrid's eyes close as he shakes with laughter against her.

"It's okay, Astrid," I whisper, wanting so badly to reach out for her.

"Don't test me, Kai," Caden spits. "You know you want this as much as I do."

"No," I snap. "I'm not going to engage in a fucking blood threesome with you."

"You've grown so *weak*! How can you expect to be king when you can't even do this right?!"

His eyes turn black, and his face morphs until he looks more like a demon than my brother. My body coils in furious preparation.

"Watch, and learn, Kai. This is how to be a vampire."

In a vicious blink, he bites deep into Astrid's neck, so deep that blood spurts out of the wound and trails quickly down her front, dripping into her dress, staining it red.

Before I can understand what's happening, there's an excruciating roar that rips through my throat, and I'm blind with rage.

My body swells with anger and power as I rip Astrid away and throw Caden to the ground, hearing his bones shatter against the stone floor. He hisses loudly at me, trying to get back up, but I throw my arm against his face, despite Astrid's screams, and knock him out. The red fades from my vision quickly as I look at his broken face. His legs are bent in sickening ways, and his black eyes are wide open, frozen in place. Caden's mouth is slack, and his jaw is hanging loosely from his head.

I look around, panicked, until I find Astrid passed out against the floor. Her dress is soaked through with sweat and blood. It's a blessing I'm so furious that I can't notice the acid bite of wild thirst in the back of my throat. The only thing I can feel is my broken heart as I scoop Astrid's limp body into my arms and jump out of the room and back into mine, not bothering to close the door behind me. I feel her blood seep into my clothes, but there's nothing I can do but move.

When I'm safely back inside my room, I don't know what to do. A pain-filled hiccup breaks through my lips, and I hold Astrid's limp body close to me. I don't want to put her down, but I know that I have to go get Alheri. I have to heal her. I *need* to heal her.

With a heavy heart, I lay Astrid down lightly on my bed and adjust her head gently so that she's laying just like she sleeps. And before I can take another breath, I'm sprinting down to the dungeons to get Alheri. I'm sprinting at double the speed I could with Astrid, and I'm there in under a second. Thankfully, Alheri is sitting on her cot with a small book, startled by my presence and probably my appearance.

“ Please,” is all I can say before she's up and following me back to my room. The walk is painful, but I try to muster out some sort of explanation for what she'll find. She silences me with her hand and a striking look, and suddenly she's running in front of me. She bursts through the door, and I'm so glad that our witch is the only sane person who ignores every fucking protocol in the book when there's an emergency.

“Get her in the bath,” she orders, and I pick up Astrid again easily. “No, strip her first.”

I hesitate for a moment but then lay Astrid back down, moving to unlace the front of her dress when she moans softly. My heart breaks.

“It's alright, Astrid. I have Alheri here. She's going to fix you,” I whisper to her. What am I doing? She probably can't even hear me.

I gingerly unlace the shift that she wears to bed and hesitate again when I see how much blood has stained her gown. I feel my eyes darken, and my teeth itch against my gums.

“Kai, *please*,” Alheri instructs harshly, snapping me out of my trance. I quickly pull on the gown, careful not to hurt Astrid's wounds as I pull it out from under her and over her head.

And then, she's naked before me. The sight of her limp body doesn't send the heart attack feelings through me, though, not like this. Before, she was so full of life, so full of fire and youthful joy, that she made me want to break all my rules just to have the chance to kiss her. Now, her arms are bent in strange ways, and I know she can't be comfortable. Her hair and skin are stained with blood and dirt and sweat, and her entire chest has rivulets of blood running down it.

I can't help it; another sound of emotion bursts through my lungs, and I close my eyes, clenching my body to contain myself. Alheri lays her hand on my shoulder lightly, and I stifle my tears quickly and scoop up Astrid, her skin smooth and wet underneath my touch. I kick open the bathroom door, and I suddenly remembered that Astrid changed the bathwater just this morning. I stifle a sigh of gratitude and slowly lay Astrid into the tepid water. Alheri suddenly hovers around me with candles and salt, already speaking in a different tongue.

When I know that I'm no longer needed, I retreat backward, watching Alheri through tunneled vision. I feel like my chest is on the cusp of collapsing, and I feel like I can't breathe.

"Kai," Alheri snaps at me, giving me an intense look as she tumbles the salt into the bath, and Astrid moans slightly. "Pull yourself together. I cannot fix two problems at the same time."

"I'm sorry, I'm so sorry," the words begin to tumble out of my mouth. "It wasn't me, Al, it wasn't. I don't even know how it happened. We were having such a wonderful time," I say, the room sucking the air straight out of my lungs, leaving me gasping. "I can't breathe."

I walk out onto the balcony, barely noticing the brand-new door. Moonlight trickles past the heavy cloud cover. I force a deep breath, tasting the salt spray like its caustic. The stark tinge of thirst at the back of my throat makes itself known, and I scream out into the ocean.

I rip off my shirt and throw it onto the floor, hating that I know Astrid will lecture me about cleanliness later on. I half-laugh in my hysteria, then pick up the shirt and toss it into the laundry basket, the weight on my chest even heavier as I spy all the chores she will insist on doing later.

"What kind of fucked up place is this? That she has to clean every damn thing!" I know I am bordering on insanity, but the tirade of words keeps pouring out of me. "What kind of place is this, where she doesn't fear us, she doesn't protect her own frail human life? Why the hell did she let him feed on her?!"

"Kai, please!" Alheri yells. But I don't stop. I can't.

"I can't live here. I can't fucking rule this piece of shit kingdom! I hate them! I *hate* all of them! I just want to see this place burn to the ground. They treat humans like goddamned puppets, existing to do their bidding. That's messed up! How can she not see that?" I rake my hands through my wet hair, panicking, and throw on a new shirt. I tuck it into my belt and lace up my leather boots tightly before gathering up Astrid's belongings.

"What are you doing?" Alheri asks, her hands red with blood as she exits the bathroom.

"Is she going to be okay?" I drop Astrid's chest and walk up to Alheri, smelling spice and blood on her skin. I grab her arms and hold her in front of me.

"Yes, her wound is closed, and she's resting. You can pull her out of the tub if you'd like, but she's fine to soak as well—"

I interrupt her by stepping around her and into the bathroom. The smell of Astrid's blood is tainted and smells horribly of spice and fire and salt. I cringe away from the scent as I pull Astrid out of black water that used to be clear. I look over her body and see that her wound is completely healed, and her skin is clear of any blood. I press my forehead to her shoulder for a moment, my relief almost palpable.

After I lay her on my bed again, I turn to Alheri and say, "Dry her and get her dressed."

"What are you doing?" Alheri repeats.

"I'm leaving," I hiss as I return to continue packing up Astrid's belongings. "*We're* leaving."

"What?! You can't!"

"I can't stay here, Alheri, I can't. I can barely protect her even though I'm going to be king. I can't just fucking let them tear her to shreds," I know that most of my words don't make sense, but I say them anyway. Alheri stands there gaping at me, so I stand and snap, "Dry her and get her dressed!"

My words are so loud and strong that they shake the room, and Alheri looks genuinely afraid for a moment. Whether that fear is of me or the circumstance, I'm not sure.

"I can't rule, I can't forfeit the crown, I can't do anything here. If I rule and don't act properly, my father will take her. If I forfeit the crown to Caden…" I hiss through my teeth. "They will take her. She'll have no protection, and they'll rip her apart just to get at me."

"She didn't have protection before," Alheri says quietly.

"She didn't mean anything before," I admit, hating myself for even thinking the words.

"What are you saying?"

"None of you *mean* anything to them! They'll use you, abuse you, rape you, and kill you, Alheri." I face her with an expression meant to cut.

She flinches at my words, but I don't back down.

"Astrid means something now, which puts a bigger target on her back. Caden knows my feelings now." I choke on the last words. He knows, and there's no way he will just let me out of that. He will torment me until the end of my days. I turn back to my work, swallowing tears, and Alheri finishes dressing Astrid. "Where's her cloak?"

"She doesn't have one," Alheri replies.

"What? Fine, put this on her," I say, throwing a cloak at her. I pull on a long coat. I also toss Astrid's shoes at her, and she stands still just long enough to make me angry.

"Alheri are you *listening* to me?! They won't just kill her. They'll torture her just to spite me!"

"You think I don't know what goes on it this place?" she fires back at me. "You think I don't see the horrible things that happen? I heal everyone here! I know *everything* that happens, Kai."

The comment brings me up short. It's not like I was blind to that fact, but it wasn't something I lingered on.

"Then you know why I have to leave," I say.

"You can't," Alheri whispers, defeated.

"I must."

"You don't know what's going to happen outside these walls," Alheri says.

"I don't care."

"You don't know what Astrid wants!"

"I don't *care*," I repeat.

"Kai, listen, you don't know what I've done for Astrid. For her entire life! I've… helped her," Alheri says, rubbing her arm like a nervous habit. "My mother and my grandmother, they both told me to protect her. To keep her safe. She's special, Kai."

"What do you mean?"

"I'm just…I don't…I don't know," she huffs in frustration.

"Spit it out!"

"If you take her now, where I can't help her, she might not be the same person when she wakes up," Alheri says delicately.

"Whatever, I don't care. Whoever she is, she deserves freedom," I say, feeling the weight of every human I am leaving behind on my shoulders. "I have to go, Al. I'm sorry."

She nods, tears welling in her eyes. I sling on a large rucksack filled with Astrid's belongings and some provisions. I'll have to stop by the kitchens for food.

God, what am I thinking? This isn't going to work.

Looking down at Astrid's unconscious body moves me. I

can't leave her here, and I can't stay here. Everything I had told Alheri was true. Only now, I don't know what to expect, and fear is a very real part of the process for me. I give Alheri one last meaningful look before bending down and scooping up Astrid into a tight ball against my chest. She is light, and I know I am strong enough. The hour is late, so leaving won't be difficult.

I move quickly and quietly through the halls towards the kitchens. Once inside, I sit Astrid down on a chair and pull up her hood. Alheri was thorough in her dressing. Not only is she dressed, but she's overdressed, bundled up for warmth. I smile softly. Alheri had pulled up Astrid's hair into a long braid that runs down her back and keeps her hair inside the cloak. That will make movement easier.

I scrounge around the kitchen for several moments, taking dried jerky, fruits and vegetables, and loaves of bread. I stuff as much food as I can into my bag before giving up and picking Astrid up once more. She snuggles against my chest this time, and I hold onto her more tightly. My heart is racing as I moved past the dungeons and towards the sewers, where I know I won't be traced.

When I face the final door, I feel a heaviness weigh on my steps that has nothing to do with the small woman I'm carrying.
My mother.

I am leaving my entire life without a backward glance because of something awful Caden did. I'm leaving without saying goodbye to my mother, the only person who ever understood me or loved me unconditionally. Will she applaud my choices tomorrow? Will she be disappointed that I didn't stay and rule the way she wanted me to?

"She'll understand," I whisper to myself, feeling the wet stones soak up my words. With a sad smile and a short glance at the woman I'm fleeing with, I open the large oak doors and step into the darkness.

15

Astrid

My heart races as I stand in the frigid air next to Kai. My body flutters with warm butterflies as he looks at me, smiling.

He looks back out onto the water, and I let my eyes linger a little longer, taking in his features. He looks relaxed, calm as his dark hair rustles in the wind, brushing against his cheekbones and eyelids. He doesn't realize that he flinches just slightly as the tips of his hair tickle his eyelashes. It's something that I've noticed over the past few days, noting that he doesn't mind the length of his hair. It's much longer than other men in the castle, and it gleams with the candlelight shining against the smooth texture of it. I find myself thinking about his hair in my idle moments. I wonder if he's ever had a woman brush his hair before.

"Well, well, well." Caden's voice billows through the wind, like a whistle on the breeze. I turn to face him, but part of me notices that Kai does not turn. It feels like all movement is slow and exaggerated. Something about the air feels different, like it's not cold, though I know I should be freezing.

Kai freezes in place. As Caden climbs out onto the roof, I see why Kai must be bothered. Annette follows behind him, and she's obviously feint with bloodless. Her gown is stained with blood, and she's clutching at her neck.

I feel Kai's stillness beside me as I speak with Caden. I look up and smile at the young prince, noting that his fangs are out, and his eyes are bloodshot. Black veins protrude from his eyelids. I feel Caden's stare on my skin like wet fingers, trailing over my bare skin. Kai says something, but his voice gets caught in the wind. I glance at him for a moment, but he's not looking at any of us. He looks trapped.

"Caden," I hear Kai growl, his voice rumbling alongside the ocean.

Caden is gesturing with his hand for me to come close. I start towards him, feeling a sudden compulsion to be near him.

"No, Astrid, please," Kai says, alarmed and pressing a firm hand against my waist. My breath catches at the touch. I smile at him, and his face contorts into a tortured expression as I push away his hand and step around him. I focus on Caden, who seems incredibly pleased.

I feel a thrill go through me as he brushes my hair behind my ear. I smile at him, ignoring the hateful stares coming from Annette. His eyes are wildly red, a sign of a satisfied vampire.

Everything feels right as Caden bows his head toward my neck. I bite down on my lip, expecting the sting of my skin puncturing, but instead, his lips meet my ear, brushing against my skin lightly, sending shivers down my spine.

"You will be mine," he whispers so quietly that I'm not sure Kai can hear. His words send shock and the faintest fear into my heart, and suddenly he's spun me around so fast that it has me dizzy as I face Kai. His words ring like echos against the distant mountains. I feel I must be dreaming.

Caden wraps his arms around me, pressing his entire body against my backside, so close that I can feel every inch of him. His hands hold me firmly but tickle my skin, playing with my dress as he holds me. My heart pounds.

Fast, so fast, I feel his teeth bite strongly into my neck, and I can't help but scream out from the pain. Usually, feeding is a peaceful process, but this feels more like revenge. Caden's teeth are so sharp, and quickly the stinging turns into a dull, deeper pain as he seeps the blood out of me. I feel my muscles tense, and my eyes close. A loud rushing sound plays over my ears, but not loudly enough that I can't hear Kai roar.

He closes the distance between us and rips me away from Caden's grip. Caden's teeth rip out a hole in my neck, and my eyes blur as I stumble to the edge of the terrace. I barely see Kai move upon Caden like a wave of black death. His hair whips recklessly in the wind.

In the briefest of moments, I catch a glimpse of Kai's deadly expression as he rips into Caden, who looks weak in comparison. My heart caves at the sight, and I feel like the world is shattering beneath my feet. Kai's black, blood-shot eyes scream of death and punishment.

Annette is screaming at them, screaming at Kai to stop, but he doesn't listen to her. She's yelling at me that this is all my fault. She's pulling at Kai's clothing, but he doesn't even notice her. He's acting on blind fury, and somewhere in the back of my mind, I feel happy about this, but I can't process it. I can hardly think about anything.

I look down at the ground, my vision blurring, and the stones seem to fall out from under me. Suddenly I'm feeling cold brick against my skin, and the world shifts to the side.

I try to call out, but I can't find my voice.

Did I do something wrong? I was just trying to serve. I just want to be a good kvinne. I feel tears break through my eyelashes. My side feels numb now. I can't feel anything. I can just barely make out the warping shapes of Kai and Caden as they fight. I want to tell them to stop, but then my eyes turn black, and I realize it was a dream.

Somewhere in the darkness, I can hear Kai's voice shouting and in pain. Alheri is there too, and she's chanting and yelling back at him. I'm so confused; I don't know why they would be mad at one another. Caden's words are still ringing through my ears as Kai and Alheri shout gibberish back and forth. Did Kai bring me to Alheri for healing? That's probably what I would have done. I hope that they aren't mad because of me.

Something cold surrounds my legs then. And my waist. And my arms. What is this? It's unyielding, like cold water instead of a brush of air. Am I underwater? And what smells so bad?

I cough and try to open my eyes, but everything is dark. I feel my breathing accelerate, and I try to stave off panic, but it's really cold now, and I'm not sure what's happening. I try to speak, but it feels like I'm pressed tightly against something.

"Astrid. Astrid," Kai's voice whispers above me.

"Kai?" I choke out. "What's happening?!"

"It's okay, you're alright. We are underneath the castle right now," he says. That explains the darkness. And I guess that smell is dead fish then. I try not to gag.

"Okay…why?"

"I'm leaving the castle, and I want you to come with me. Please don't panic," he says, and there's a waver in his voice that isn't usually there. Is he afraid that I will say no? I smile, beside myself, glad that he can't see how pleased I am. I'm sure he can hear my heart racing at the thought of running away with him, but still. I take a breath, my chest still tight.

"Why is it so hard to breathe? What are we doing right now?"

"Oh, sorry. I am carrying you."

"What?" I ask, genuinely surprised. He's carrying me away? My smile widens.

"You were still asleep when I decided to leave, so I thought I'd carry you," he says, and his voice sounds like he's chastising himself. "Oh, here," he says, releasing the hold on me, and I begin to sink deeper into the water.

"Kai!"

He surprises me by laughing. "You're fine, Astrid. It's not that deep. I'm just taller than you."

"Oh my," I say, flustered and scared and still gripping tightly to Kai's arm. He doesn't say anything, so I don't let go. "Yes, to answer your question. I'll go with you."

"Good," he says breathily.

"It smells absolutely terrible in here."

"Yeah, we have to cross the Feilfri River to get far enough away. It's going to be treacherous. Are you sure you don't want me to carry you across?"

The thought of his arms wrapped tightly around me thrills me. I want to jump at the opportunity and say yes, but I decide to be practical. "No no, I'll be fine. Just lead the way."

"Okay. We're almost there. Just past this – uhn!" He grunts, and then there's a loud snapping noise, making my heart jump nearly out of my chest. I hear splashing and cracking next to me, spiking adrenaline throughout my body. I jump out of the way and crash into Kai when light starts pouring into the tunnel, and I can see how close our faces are to one another. My heart hammers in my chest.

"Sorry," I whisper through chattering teeth.

"No, it's uh…it's okay," he says, stumbling over his words. He steps out of the sewer and into the moonlight, pulling me along with him by the hand.

The moon-shine gleams against his midnight black hair, and his pale skin shines brightly. After awakening to darkness, everything seems so bright, even though it's nighttime. I smile at him.

"Um," I start, not wanting to offend him. "Why did you decide to take the path of dead fish and ice-cold water? Couldn't you leave through the front door?"

"Well, seeing as I'm running away from being king and basically abandoning my people, I thought it would be best to avoid the sentries my father has posted," Kai explains, pulling on my hand as I wade through knee-high water now. It's not as deep as before, but the tide is restless against my limbs, pulling at me. "Since the coronation is in just a few days, Father posted extra guards. There's extra nobility in the castle now, so it makes sense. Just inconvenient for a midnight getaway."

"I've never heard you talk like this," I say without thinking.

He gives me a glance and a somewhat wild smile that sends my heart fluttering away.

"Well, anyway. Good thinking," I say, trying to avoid any awkward silences.

"The river is just ahead, and it's a rough one. It's feeding directly into the ocean, so there's a lot of movement," Kai warns.

"I'm ready."

"We'll have to duck underneath the drawbridge and hopefully avoid any keen guard's view."

"Okay," I say, still holding tightly to his hand. I know that now isn't precisely the right moment to have a girly moment, but I'm flying that we are touching. That he carried me, that he *wants* me. I smile widely at him, watching him duck into the shadows.

Vampires are creatures of shadow and moving night. Kai is no exception. Stealth and poise wrap around Kai as he moves quickly across from boulder to boulder, twirling me across the river, completely obscuring our path by moonlight and gleaming streams of water.

In the past, I would have described myself as clumsy and left-footed, but with Kai leading, it feels like we are dancing across the river as opposed to sneaking away. He hoists me up when I need, holding my waist and lifting me up with ease. He pulls me close in the darkness, so close that I can feel his accelerated breath brush against my face. Even with the freezing water and ice, it feels more like a tango than an escape. Everything is made better by Kai's presence.

I smile so wide that my cheeks hurt. He wants me. He really wants me. He wants to have a life with me, run away with me. He's putting his entire life in the past because he wants me. I can't believe it. There won't be any more rules or confusion. Just the two of us, and we can do whatever we want! I stifle the giddiness in my heart, focusing on just Kai's hands as he leads me to dry land.

ØDEMARK

16
ASTRID

"Okay, up ahead is Livsnerven," Kai says, ducking into the shadows of the tree line as soon as we cross the river. My eyes follow where he is pointing, and I see walls and several small buildings.

"Okay," I say, not picking up on his meaning. "So, are we staying there? Why are you hiding? Surely they can't see you now."

"No, we're not staying in Livsnerven. That place is home to vampires that aren't nobility. They are ruled by my father, but he despises them, and they hate him. I don't think they would take too kindly to my presence."

"I see. So, where are we going then?"

"I'm not sure. Let's just make it past the town. We'll have to disguise your smell somehow. I don't want to have to fight off a hundred thirsty vampires," Kai says, looking around for something. "Luckily, you already smell mostly of fish."

"Hey! Not my fault," I tease, but he's not laughing. I close my mouth but still smile.

"Okay, here." He grabs a sharp rock and stabs his palm. I jolt and gasp, but he says, "Quickly, before I heal."

He offers his hand, and I take it, looking very confused, I'm sure. Then, he sticks his hand on my face and rubs it on my skin despite me gasping again and protesting the actions. His blood is sticky and cold, but he keeps rubbing his hand on my face, neck, and dress.

"It's to disguise your smell," he clarifies.

"Surely, there could have been another solution?"

"Nope. Plus, this is a good look for you," he says, his eyes alight with amusement.

"Alright, now what?"

"Let's go. Keep your hood up, and don't stop walking. Here, take my hand," He holds out his bloodied hand, but the cut is nowhere to be found. I blink in surprise but grab it regardless.

In a whirl, we are walking quickly through the town. It's mostly empty, but there are some people out in their gardens and near their doorways. Some of them are deep in conversation, some are laughing and drinking, and some of them glance at us. Kai ducks behind his hair and holds onto my hand like it's a lifeline. He doesn't pull me or walk too fast, which is shocking because I feel like I move so slowly.

As we walk, more people start to come out of the little huts and stone houses that line the shallow street. Kai is completely silent, but their stares prickle my skin like they can see right through me. When three or four men start towards us, Kai hisses several profanities under his breath, still holding onto my hand, his grip like iron. I shiver as the vampires call out to us, drawing more attention to us as we move along, more quickly now.

When a line of bodies cuts us off from the path, Kai finally releases my hand and throws me forward, kicking swiftly at the furthest man, breaking their line in two. I see a small gap in the people, and I start towards it, looking behind me.

"Astrid, run!" Kai shouts at me, and I break into a sprint. My legs tangle in my long, wet skirts, but I press onward. After several moments, I notice that I'm not the one the vampires are interested in. They seem to shroud Kai in darkness, calling him names and swearing at him. I watch Kai's face scrunch into a dark grimace before he's closed off from my view.

I keep running, but I don't watch my footing, and suddenly, I'm falling down. I throw my hands in front of me, trying to brace myself for impact. I feel a sharp slice against my palm as I land on a jagged rock. I struggle to sit up, seeing black blood drip from a long gash in my hand.

All at once, I'm surrounded by multiple pairs of black and red eyes, including Kai's. I scream as they grab at me, viciously tugging at my skin and dresses, but it's only for a moment until I'm yanked out of the circle and thrown over Kai's back. Then he's sprinting at high speed away from the angry crowd of hungry vampires.

I grapple with locking my arms around Kai's neck, but he hisses at me, cringing away from my cut hand. I place my hurt hand in the folds of my skirts while still hanging on for dear life as we continue onward.

"Are they still coming?" Kai asks, his voice barely strained, as though running so quickly has no effect on him at all.

I peer behind us, but there's nothing but darkness winding through the black trees.

"No, I think we must have lost them," I say. Kai slows to a walk before dropping me and moving quickly away from me. His eyes are still pitch black against his snowy skin, the darkness coating even the whites of his eyes. Black veins slither around his face.

"We didn't lose them. They simply didn't want to follow us," Kai says, his voice sounding like a blade against stone. He rubs his hands over his eyes and hair.

I swallow a few breaths, trying to calm the adrenaline hammering through me. "What do you mean? They seemed hellbent on catching us."

"We're in the wastelands now," Kai says, his voice struggling to remain calm. "Bind your hand, Astrid. Please."

Quickly, I rip a section of my shift and wrap it tightly around the wound. The bleeding had stopped, but I'm sure that's not enough to help Kai. Once my skin is bound and no longer showing any blood, I see Kai visibly exhale.

"Thank you," he breathes. After a moment, he looks back up at me with a small smile on his lips. "I thought for sure I was a goner."

"They seemed to really want to get at you," I say, unsure of my words.

"I'm a popular target," Kai says bitterly. "The men specifically. Baldassare made sure they knew their place, but all the women want to get with me and my brother. So, it makes them even more restless and angry at us."

"That's not fair to take it out on you, though."

"Isn't it? No, I suppose I didn't ask for this," Kai says, pushing his dark hair away from his face and tucking the strands behind his ears. "We should keep moving. Are you okay?"

"Yes, fine, thank you," I say, standing to face him.

He nods, breathing heavily, though I'm not sure it's all the running that's exhausting him. After a minute, he looks at me curiously.

"What?"

"You seem fine," he says.

"I am," I repeat. "Why wouldn't I be?"

"Because of everything that just happened? You've been through extreme trauma tonight, Astrid."

"Falling down and cutting my hand does not count as trauma," I say with a laugh, brushing my hands on my skirts before starting to walk. Kai matches my stride.

"I'm not talking about that," he says, giving me a sidelong glance.

"I'm not afraid of those vampires if that's what you're thinking. I feel perfectly safe with you," I say with confidence.

Kai furrows his brows but doesn't say anything else.

Traveling at night is a must for vampires, I suppose. That's why we haven't stopped to make camp or a plan. Kai just keeps walking, and I suppose I'm fine with that, but my feet are starting to give way. My body is not meant for long journeys, and I'm certainly not in shape to withstand them. I don't want to ask him to carry me, though, since my hand is still freshly hurt.

"Can we stop?" I ask after a moment's hesitation.

"Why, what's wrong?" Kai asks, worry thick in his voice. It reminds me of Alheri and the way she would flit about me when she worried.

"No, nothing, I'm just tired. I apologize, Prince, but I'm not built like you are. I must rest," I say, hanging my head and breathing heavily. My eyelids droop, and I frown at my lack of strength.

"Oh, I didn't realize. Of course, let me build a fire," he offers.

I take a seat, rubbing my sore feet with my good hand. Kai stumbles around, and I smirk, recognizing the problem. "Kai…have you ever made a fire yourself?"

"What? Of course, I have," he says.

I raise my eyes brows at him, and I know he can see me.

"No, not really," he admits finally.

"Let me help you," I say, standing to help. It only takes me a few minutes to gather the proper materials, and then another few to get a brush fire started and heat moving. Slowly, the wood catches fire, and I huddle around it, Kai taking a seat next to me.

"Oh here," he says, pulling around his satchel. "I have food and your things."

"You brought all this for me?" I ask, snatching a piece of dried lamb.

"I grabbed as much as I could. Your small pillow, your dresses. Well, everything except your nightgown," Kai says, thumbing through the bag.

"Oh…you didn't get my nightgown?" I ask, my heart thudding low.

"No, but it was practically ruined anyway. There was a lot of blood on it," he says, staring into the fire.

"No, that's fine. Thank you for everything else," I say, and I can't help the sadness from leeching into my voice.

"That was a special nightgown, wasn't it?" he whispers after a moment.

"Yes, but that's okay," I assure him. "My mother gave it to me."

"Tough day to be a mom," Kai mumbles.

"What do you mean?"

"I left without saying goodbye to my mom," Kai says, using a stick to poke the flames.

I nod slowly and nibble on the jerky.

"I'm sorry about the nightgown."

"No, that's okay. You didn't know," I say. Truthfully, I'm not that sad. It was just the only thing that remained from her. Her simple nightgown, the one she would wear when she sang me to sleep, stroking my hair as I rested against her lap. All that remains now is the memory.

"Tell me about her."

"My mother? I don't remember much, honestly. Her name was Hanna, and she died when I was still very young," I say, trying to remember what her face looked like. "I think she had red hair like mine."

"She must have been beautiful," Kai says, looking at me through his hair.

"What makes you say that?"

"Um…" He looks away, and if I didn't know better, I'd swear he blushes.

"Oh," is all I can think to say. I smile at him, though, and my heart flutters when he returns my smile.

"How are you feeling?" he asks, obviously trying to change the subject.

"Better, thank you." I settle closer to him, enjoying his smell of pine and salt in the breeze.

"No problem," he says, poking absently at the fire with a thin stick.

A silence settles between us, and I'm not sure what to say. The forest surrounds us like a blanket, and the fire creates a protective bubble of warm air, despite the chill.

"Thank you," I whisper as I fiddle with my pillow.

"For what?"

"Everything. Thank you for saving me back there."

Kai gives me another curious look like he's trying to figure something out.

"You could have easily outrun those vampires and left me alone, but you didn't. You made sure I was safe."
He squints his eyes down at me like he's confused about something.

"And more than that…I want to find some way to express my gratitude for trusting me to come with you."

"Your safety is all I want," he says slowly. "And you're okay from before? From what happened in the castle?"

I half-frown, not really understanding his question. "I'm grateful that you're taking me with you, that you saved me from the vampires," I say again. "I'm not sure what you mean."

He stares at me for a long time before clearing his throat and saying, "It's my pleasure, Astrid. Really. I enjoy your company."

I smile, my heart fluttering in my chest. I can't help but notice how close we've become in such a short amount of time. It's like we jumped over several steps. The last conversation we had was the night before Baldassare reprimanded me. But none of that matters now. Now, Kai's all but admitted he wants me all to himself. Why else would he have stolen me away in my sleep?

Before I can convince myself otherwise, my hand stretches out and touches his cheek. I feel him freeze underneath my touch, but I continue anyway. I trail my fingers over his ear and into his hair, which is much softer than I imagined, even with its tangles and wildness. He closes his eyes, and his mouth opens ever so slightly, and suddenly my heart is racing, bounding away out of my chest. I'm close enough that I could lean in and kiss him, but part of me is still so afraid. I just want to please him, and if he doesn't want me, I shouldn't force myself on him. Even though I know he needs me.

I reach out my other hand and wrap it around his neck, forcing him to face me. I see in his eyes that he's trying not to wince at my bandaged hand. I smile softly and lower it back down into my lap. His eyes search my face, and they are warm, the red fading slowly from his irises. There's something in his expression that warns me to be careful but also begs me not to stop. I watch his face as I twirl my fingers in his hair and rub the back of his neck. I feel him sigh, and he closes his eyes again when I lean in.

My lips lightly brush the skin on his cheek, just above his jawbone. I hear his breath catch, but he doesn't pull away. My heart is threatening to explode, but I keep going. I'm not very well versed with seduction, but I'm certain that after a kiss comes the undress. Granted, I usually don't have to try this hard. Usually, the man sort of steps in and takes over.

But with Kai…His breathing is uneven, his skin is warm to the touch, and he's so still that you could argue he's a statue. Save for the small breaths he's taking, he doesn't move an inch. I move my lips cautiously and slowly, afraid my passion could burst through at any moment.

Softly, I graze his jawbone, his earlobe, and then the skin by his neck. His hair tickles my nose, so I lean into the movement, trailing my nose into the depths of his hair, breathing in his wintery scent. I never noticed how strong the smell of pine and salt spray lingers on his skin.

Slowly, I take my hand away from his hair, but I keep kissing his neck as I move to untie the cloak and the laces on my dress. My breaths are ragged, and my heart is beating so loudly that I can feel the rush of blood in my ears.

I undo the top lace before I feel Kai's hand on my hands, his head pulling away from mine to meet my eyes. I brace myself for him to kiss me, but instead, his eyes are tortured, and he tries to feign a smile.

No, no, please.

"Don't," he whispers. He doesn't break eye contact as my heart drops.

"I'm sorry," I say, pulling away and looking back into the fire. "I didn't mean to—"

"No, it's fine. I'm not upset or unhappy," he clarifies.

"Then what?"

"You just…don't have to do that," he says, his voice breaking and rough.

I furrow my brows and wait for him to continue, feeling the fire lick heat onto the bare skin on my chest now. Kai doesn't say anything else for a while. We just sit in awkward, tense silence for what feels like ages.

"Get some sleep, Astrid. I'd like to put some distance between us and Livsnerven tomorrow," Kai says. Then he stands and walks into the darkness.

After a moment of staring into the forest where Kai disappeared, I grab the pillow from his satchel and lie down, still staring deeply into the fire.

17
KAI

My entire frame shakes, and my body feels like it's going to burst, my heart threatening to break and explode at the same time. The darkness of the forest beckons me away from the fire's heat, away from Astrid's heat. I shiver, and a tingling sensation ripples up and down my body.

God, I want to kiss her. I want to race back to her and lie her down underneath me and rip that dress right off of her body. It doesn't help that I know what she looks like underneath all those layers. The way that her waist curves from her breasts to her hips, the gentle slope of the small of her back. Her lips brushing against my skin lit me completely ablaze.

With a deep, primal grunt, I push further and further into the darkness, the damp air whipping past my face until I can no longer smell Astrid's wonderful peachy scent, like spring honeysuckles. I crouch down, feeling tension stretch over my knees and ankles, and heave in several deep breaths. The air has a pungent, almost rancid smell to it. I try to tap into the red vision, into my basic instincts, but part of me is afraid I'll just run straight back to her. Instead, I take a deep breath, pushing past the dank, stale air to feel around for any animal I can find.

I've never been this far from the castle, so I don't know what to expect. I know the forests go on until the other side of the island, where the humans reside. Maybe that's where I'll take Astrid. Menneskelig. The giant castle that my father warred against so many years ago. Maybe there, Astrid could live without fear of torture. She could learn that humans aren't meant to be blind blood bags.

Why did she feel the need to take her clothes off tonight? It sickens me to know that she grew up thinking that giving over her body was just some average day for a human. It's entirely preposterous she could be so okay after everything. I'm not even the one who was hurt, and I'm still reeling. How could she just forget that Caden attacked her?

Something in a tree flickers in the darkness, my ears twitching. I throw myself into hunting, knowing that it's the only thing that will truly keep Astrid safe on this journey. Safe from me.

My jaw aches as my teeth extend. My vision tunnels, and suddenly the darkness isn't so dark anymore. I hunch down, quiet as a mouse, and touch the ground with my hand. I close my eyes and inhale deeply, still as stone. Notes of rotted flesh, dead animals, dirt, and rain waft through my nose and seeps into my skin.

But then, there it is. My eye flick open, and before I even register the urge, I've lurched forward and caught the animal in my hands. I rip through the fur and skin through to the blood. Animal blood is something no vampire ever covets. Though it satiates the thirst temporarily, it's nothing like human blood. It tastes like dirt. This animal, a small white fox, squirms just briefly before it no longer has any life left.

I drop the carcass and stifle a gag as I wipe my mouth with the back of my hand. The blood looks black in the darkness, but my stomach feels less tight. I run further into the forest, hoping to find another animal, but the stench of death coats each tree so strongly that I have to turn around quickly. I'm not sure where I am after a few moments. I'm not worried about finding my way back, though. Astrid's smell still lingers in the air; the trail back to her is almost like a lit path.

The air seems to clear as I run. My jaw doesn't ache anymore, and I'm glad to know that I still have functioning vampire instincts. I haven't hunted traditionally since I was a boy, hunting for sport with Caden. I suppose it's written in my DNA. Hunting is a basic instinct for a vampire. I can't just forget how to do it. No matter how hard I try.

Before I know it, I've cut through the tree line and reached the far west of the island. I slow to a walk and look left and right, seeing no trace of either human or vampire, just the coast up ahead. The air tastes fresh, and breathing in the salty air is a reprieve from the last twenty-four hours. The night is black, and the clouds hang low and daunting. I stroll up the slight path until I reach a cliff of sorts. The tide sounds against the rocks below, softly, almost like the water is petting the stones instead of crashing against them.

I sit, letting my feet hang over the edge, and contemplate what I've done. I take a deep breath of the fresh air and rub my hands over my face, feeling the blood of the fox crusted against my skin.

How could I have been so stupid? Run away with Astrid? When I'm a mental case vampire? I can't feed right. I can't abstain right. The only thing I've accomplished here is simply taking her away from even worse vampires. Surely, there had to have been a better way of saving her. Maybe I should have sent her away with Alheri. Would they have survived? I know Alheri is versed with healing magic, but could she have protected Astrid from the wild?

Maybe I should have just brought Alheri, too. Would she be able to protect Astrid against me?

Images, horrible images, flood past my eyes for the briefest moment. Astrid's limp body in my arms. Her blood on my lips and teeth. My body strong and stable for the first time since I was a boy. I grip the edge of the cliff and let the rocks cut into my knuckles.

No, I don't think Alheri could stop me. I should just leave now. Let Astrid go on her own. I smile and shake my head. I can't do that either. Ødemark is called a wasteland for good reason. There's no telling what kind of monsters live in that forest. Rabid vampires and animals for sure; the stench was proof of that. Not to mention the wild halvblods as you get closer to the human capital.

I sigh. The only thing I can do now is to find my way back to her and figure out how to get her to Menneskelig safely. I will just have to fight every instinct in my body. Once I get her to the city walls, I will be free. I can go anywhere I want, and I'll never have to hurt another human ever again.

Something cracks inside me as I think the words.

I'll never get to see her again either.

God, this fucking dichotomy of a problem. Why can't you just get over it and move on? I rake my now bloodied hands through my hair. I won't let myself put her in further danger just to be with her. No, I'll drop her at the gates, see that she's safe, and I'll go. I'll leave her and live a life of solidarity, enjoying the fresh air and solitude for the rest of my life. Eventually, I'll forget her. I'll have to.

I look at my hands, darkened with dirt and blood. I know my mouth is crusted with it, too. I should clean myself up before returning. I had hoped to find another animal to feed on, but I'll let that be tomorrow's problem.

Shirking off my clothes, I peer over the edge of the cliff, planning a jump. It doesn't look too treacherous below. The cliff is cleanly cut all the way down. But I don't know how deep the water is below, and I don't know if there are any rocks beneath the surface.

I ponder the odds for a moment before huffing out a loud sigh, and then I launch myself off the side of the cliff. The icy wind slices past my skin, and a huge smile pops onto my face as my heart lurches with adrenaline. The freefall is always my favorite part of every jump.

I contort my body into a dive and hold my breath as I break through the surface of the water. Luckily for me, there are no rocks under the surface, and the water is plenty deep, so I can swim easily without touching anything. I feel the water tug at me softly, considerably gentler than the water outside of Feilfri Castle. It's almost calming. I can't tell if it's colder or warmer than the wintry air; it just feels nice. I quickly scrub my skin and hair with the water and then hop out and retrieve my clothes.

I start running back to Astrid, wondering briefly if the cliffside is on the way to Menneskelig. It would be nice to show her something beautiful.

The clouds begin to lighten as I find my way back to our small camp. Astrid is already awake, peering up at me briefly when I walk up. She looks rested, though her dress is ruined by dirt and the sewage from last night. She's nibbling on some jerky as I take a seat next to her, the warmth of the fire soothing against my freshly bathed skin.

"How did you sleep?" I ask awkwardly.

"Fine," she replies curtly.

I frown for a moment, noting that she's still upset about last night. I look at her for a moment, but she's actively avoiding my gaze. Well, fine. That's perfect. That means that even though the journey will most likely be terrible, and it will be easier to part from her at the end.

"We should get going. I scouted the area last night, and it's a long way to get through the forest," I say, making mental notes of where we will turn. I also briefly hope we will pass a sign pointing us in the right direction. "If we head straight North, we should hit Menneskelig in a few days."

"What?" Astrid perks up and stares at me with an indecipherable expression.

"What?" I echo, confused.

"You're taking me to Menneskelig?"

Whoops. I suppose I hadn't told her that yet. Is that bad news to her?

"Um, yes," I say, watching her face contort bitterly. "Is that a problem?"

She looks me dead in the eye for a few moments before blinking hard and staring back into the fire.

"No," she replies, then stuffs the last of the jerky in her mouth. She packs her pillow and food back in the satchel.

"Okay," I say, more confused than before. "Well, as I said, we could just go straight north, but that's directly through the forest and wastelands, which I want to avoid at all costs. I can't protect you against everything. So, we'll stick to the tree line on the west side and hopefully just trail the coast until we get there."

"Fine," she says with a cutting tone. I frown again, not knowing where I went wrong. How could things have gotten so sour between us so quickly?

"Okay then," I reply, standing when she stands.

She starts walking away from me, and I find myself running and grabbing her arm, to which she gasps and turns into my body, looking up at me through her eyelashes. My heart catches in my throat, and it takes me a moment to regain my senses.

"Um…" I whisper, her breath brushing past the skin on my neck. "We have to go this way." Her hip touches mine. I gulp down a breath and turn towards the north. Her face falls ever so slightly before she shrugs off my hand and starts walking again, leaving me breathless and watching after her.

I take a moment to breathe and blink at the sudden change in tone before stamping out the coals and following after her.

We walk in silence for what feels like forever. When I'm not watching her walk slowly in front of me, I'm trailing the forest with my eyes, trying to find anything that could be threatening. Astrid asks to stop and rest at steady intervals. I ply her with food, and she accepts, not meeting my eye.

The forest is coated with thick, dense fog, which is good for me while the sun is out, but it doesn't help make the journey any less creepy. Fog makes it difficult to see anything past a few paces. It looks like the forest is green and grey, with white clouds fitting in between every branch, filling the negative space with its mist. The ground feels like mush with damp leaves, moss, and mildew covering everything. The moisture in the air is so thick that beads of water begin to dribble down my arms and legs, making my hair stick to my forehead and the back of my neck.

As we walk, I notice the color of the leaves leeching away, leaving us in a black and white forest. The only source of color is the bright strands of golden-red hair from the woman walking in front of me.

Astrid walks like she's in a trance, paying me absolutely no mind. She barely deviates from the straight path she is taking. Tree branches come close to touching her, and she hardly ducks out of the way. It's strange to see her like this. Whether she is just mad at me or something else, I can't tell.

The ground begins to give way underneath my feet, and I quickly hop to steadier ground, looking at what I stood on to make the dirt cave in. I notice the flesh of a rotting corpse underneath the dirt and leaves, leaving me gasping from the strong urge to vomit. I turned to see if Astrid had seen the body, but she just continues walking, caught in her trance.

Ignoring the body and holding my breath to stave off the stench, I hop back into step behind her, watching her curiously. How is she not be bothered by this? The smell, the creepiness of the forest? Has she just seen worse? Surely, her life in the dungeons of Feilfri hadn't been pleasant either, but had it been worse than this? I shake my head, completely humbled by her perseverance.

But then, Astrid whirls on me, her face red and distressed. I halt in place, taken aback by her sudden movement.

"What is this, Kai?" she demands, her voice strange, different than before. "What are we doing?"

I gulp.

"Your father gives me to you as a gift, and yeah, I get it. You're not like your brother or father. But what *is* this? I did everything I was told. Everything!"

"Astrid—"

"No, Kai. I did exactly what I was told. Your father gave me to you to make you a great king. Do you not want me?"

"What? No, Astrid, you've got the wrong idea—"

"Then what?" She pauses. "What am I to you?"

The silence that stretches between her words war inside me, illuminating the contrast of my desires.

"I…" I can't find the words.

"Why don't you want me?" Astrid whispers, her anger subsiding into something worse.

My body tries everything to combat her words, knowing how much I truly do want her. But no words come forth.

"You don't drink from me, you don't want my body," she says, matter-of-factly. "Why did you take me with you just to banish me to Menneskelig?"

I gape at her. I know she can't understand why I would run away from my home, but how can she not understand this? The fact that I'm *rescuing* her should be perfectly clear.

"I took you away from the castle to *protect* you. You were hurt, and I couldn't bear to see you like that," I say, my voice cracking.

She blinks at me, evidently stunned by my response.

"I just wanted to make sure you were safe," I continue. "But I'm no better than my brother. I'm still not sure if I'm doing the right thing."

"Better than Caden?" she says like she's caught in that trance again.

"I know he's more outspoken about his desires, but I feel the same things. Underneath all of this hard work, I'm still a vampire. I want to protect you, but I'm frightened that I'll hurt you."

She looks down at her feet but doesn't say anything. I grab the bag she dropped and extend my hand toward her. She stares at it for a few moments, then looks up at me with a blank expression. I sigh and drop my hand.

We walk in silence, the air tense around us. Everything about this feels wrong, like we've gone back to square one again. It's like she doesn't remember anything that's happened between us – the conversation on the rooftop, the night I held her in my arms, how I stupidly admitted how I felt about her… Could she have forgotten? In the craziness of Caden's attack and fleeing the castle, could she have just forgotten everything we said to one another?

Astrid gasps suddenly, and in a flash, I'm there, holding her elbow as she slips on a frozen leaf. I feel her shiver next to me, and I take note of the chill in the air. Most of the time, ice and snow don't phase me, but Astrid is human. She's more susceptible to the cold.

But before I can say anything, I realize the fog had dispersed, giving way to big, fat snowflakes falling all around us. I watch Astrid's eyes grow wide, and I can't help but feel like a child. Her innocent gaze is intoxicating as she watches the snow flurry between us.

Several flakes get caught in her hair and eyelashes, making her look frosty, like a winter angel.

When she looks up at me with those big, blue eyes, I reach out to brush off a stray snowflake from her cheek. Instead of the tension returning, she simply smiles at me. My mind is reeling from her wild mood swings, but I can't help but feel joy, watching her pure, child-like reaction to something as simple as snowfall.

18
ASTRID

"I'm sorry, Kai," I whisper into the silence, still distracted by the big, fat snowflakes. My heart has been through a swell of emotional whiplash, bouncing back and forth from fascination to anger to joy in matters of minutes. We've been walking for ages now, and my confusion has turned into fierce head pains.

"For what?"

"For lashing out at you. It was rude, and I'm sorry," I say. I look up at him, expecting him to say something else, but he doesn't. He's quiet now. "It's just that…lately, I haven't felt like myself," I explain, trying to put my feelings into words. "My head feels strange, like all my memories are hazy."

I see him give me a sideways look from the corner of my eye. I self-consciously pull my cloak around myself, feeling the chill set in around me.

"I don't know what to think or what to feel," I finish lamely, my voice dwindling as a gust of wind carries away my voice.

"Are you okay?" he asks simply.

"I don't know," I admit, rubbing the sides of my head. "I'm just sorry for yelling at you. You must know that I'm grateful for your protection."

He nods.

"I'm not sure what else to say," I confess.

"You don't need to say anything, Astrid."

He steps toward me and grabs my good hand, giving me a small smile as he continues forward. The snow starts falling quickly now, shrouding the path ahead in pillows of white. My heart lightens, seeing all the fluttering snowflakes. They billow in the breeze, catching on tree branches or floating into the distance. It's easy to think here, now, with my hand tucked into Kai's. It's easy to breathe with the beautiful, crisp air as it flushes out my lungs. I can almost forget how much trouble we've already gone through since leaving the castle.

The daytime fades, giving way to the darkness, and I try to push past my anxiety. This time of day would usually bring a sad nostalgia to my brain, but today, everything's different. Today, I got to see snow. Real snow! Something my mother told me stories of. Stories of Christmas and presents and snow angels. It was something I didn't miss since I hadn't experienced it before, but *now*...I feel lighter.

The snow settles in, covering the black leaves of the forest with a beautiful layer of white powder, swirling ever so slightly in the breeze. Even now, as the sun sets behind the clouds, I watch little tornados of snow flurries play in the wind. I had always imagined snow to be heavier, pulled down by gravity like raindrops, but it's the opposite. The snow has a weightless quality, the ability to dance on the breeze instead of being forced down towards the ground. Slowly, the snowflakes choose their resting place, free to float down towards their small slopes of powder on the ground.

I try to remember the smile that plastered itself on my face upon seeing the first bit of snow, the memory of the golden snow-flakes tugging my mouth into a smile. After a while, Kai pulls me towards a fire, insisting we light the wood while it's still dry. I sit, rubbing my hands together and warming myself against the firelight. I had never realized how *cold* snow was.

"I'm freezing!" I stutter through my chattering teeth.

Kai chuckles softly with a hint of worry in his eyes. "You need to tuck your cloak around you, Astrid."

"I can't believe I saw snow," I say, still amazed.

"You'll see more tomorrow as well."

"It's nothing like I thought. I had always pictured ice and frozen water. I didn't realize the snow on top of the mountains was so light."

"Well, snow is nice and powdery only on the first day, really. Then it melts a bit and re-freezes into harder ice," Kai explains.

"But still, it's so beautiful, so purely white," I say. "I thought the whitest thing I would have seen was your skin."

"What? I'm not *that* pale," Kai teases, obviously trying to keep the mood light.

"You have absolutely beautiful skin, Kai. But the *snow*…" I trail off, running my hands in the snow by my cloak.

"You're going to freeze your hands off if you keep doing that," Kai laughs quietly.

"I don't even care!"

"Astrid, please. Save your hands for me," he says, reaching over to grab my hands in his, his skin warm compared to the frozen snow. I marvel at how his skin feels against mine. So soft.

In an instant, Kai freezes solid, his expression cautious as he stares into the distance. I halt all my movements, feeling the icy grip of fear on my chest.

Kai rises to his feet quickly, not releasing my hands but instead grabbing me close to his chest. In the distance, I can see a small golden light peering at us through the black trees. The fresh snow is brighter between the trees. The light flickers like fire.

"What is that?" I whisper, so softly I almost didn't speak at all.

I feel Kai's breath accelerate, and I quickly look up at his face, expecting him to look fearful or battle-ready, but instead, he looks as though he's watching a ghost in the distance.

"Kai?" I speak up more loudly than before.

"*Sankta Lucia*," Kai breathes, with a look of astonishment.

"St. Lucia?" I whisper back, the name striking up hazy memories in the back of my mind.

"Let's get closer," Kai says and starts walking forward, lifting me easily and cradling my arms against his chest as he moves us towards the light.

While he expertly weaves through the darkness and away from our fire, I feel the chill grapple at my limbs, and I lightly lift my legs so that I'm curled against Kai's chest. He doesn't seem to notice, focused on the distant light. In the back of my mind, I try to trace the name, St. Lucia. Saint Lucy? The words are similar to my family's native tongue, but just slightly different. The name only reminds me of a Christmas story that my mother used to tell me of a woman dressed in candlelight.

Kai leads us right up to the path of firelight, setting my feet on top of a large boulder and pointing ahead. His hands linger around me, making me shiver in his embrace, despite the actual chill. I see many marvelous candles lining a small pathway. In the distance, I hear soft footsteps. I peer out from Kai's grasp to see a woman walking straight towards us. I look at Kai with wide eyes and find he's smiling at the woman, then looking down at me with an infectious expression of glee.

As the woman walks or rather *floats*, towards us, my eyes adjust to the flickering candles to see that the woman is dressed only in a pure white gown, draping down to the floor and pooling against the snow. I would have expected her to trip on her long skirt, but she continues walking effortlessly in between the candles. She has a thick red sash tied around her waist that would have accentuated her curves had the rest of her dress not blended in so perfectly with the snow. She walks, carrying only a large candle in front of her face, showing her perfectly coiled blonde hair billowing down past her waist. The wind tugs at her beautiful hair, tangling it softly, making her look like a golden angel.

On the top of the woman's head, she's crowned in five tall candles, illuminating the snow on the tree branches around her. Her face is plain but alight with joy as she walks through the snow. I remember my mother's voice describing the woman dressed in candlelight. She was not wrong. This woman is bright with glistening light, which reminds me of how the sunlight glints off the ocean at sunrise.

As she passes us, her mouth opens in a piercing, high-pitched song, like the *kulning* you would hear at the edge of a pasture. She turns her face directly to me, her soft eyes bright and gleaming as she sings. Shivers roam over my skin from the ends of my hair to the tips of my toes. I feel my chest hitch as she smiles at me. Magically, she seems invulnerable to the freezing snow because she keeps walking and singing. In the candlelight, her breath billows out in front of her as though her melody is caught on an invisible musical staff in the air. When I look up at Kai, his black hair has fallen in front of his face, and he's mesmerized just as I am with the faery that's floating along with the glistening snow.

The woman walks slowly, softly, away from us until we can no longer see any trace of the light, nor the candles she had walked in between. I close my gaping jaw and look up at Kai, who has glassy eyes. He smiles softly down at me, and I'm still huddled gently against his chest.

The stillness in the forest is a perfect frame for the woman's beauty, the darkness encasing the candlelight just as the silence surrounds her hypnotic melody.

"Who was that?" I whisper.

Kai closes his eyes, the edges of his lips pulling up into a warm smile like he's cherishing the moment. "*Sankta Lucia*," he replies, his voice like low wind chimes. He slowly rises and carries me back towards our campfire, a soft glowing light in the distance, completely void of the magic the woman's candles had. "I had read stories and heard tales of St. Lucia. I never thought they were real."

"I've heard the name before," I say softly, bobbing quietly against Kai's chest as he walks.

"They say on the longest night of the year, a fairy-like woman appears across Scandinavia, bringing food and drink to those who hold onto the faith of Christ," Kai says, with obvious wonder in his voice.

"I did not think you to be a religious person," I whisper, feeling inadequate in my knowledge of different cultures and religions.

"I'm not, really," Kai admits. "I've just heard the stories. Some say she was a saint only three hundred years ago who was martyred after bringing food to Christians hiding from persecution. Some say she is a faerie, symbolizing the celebration of Christ's birth at Christmas time. There are others, especially in the witch and vampire communities, who believe she is simply a messenger of Freyja, showing them that they have suffered through the worst of winter and longer days are approaching."

I nod, trying to reconcile his words to the magical woman we just saw walk across the snow and leave without a trace.

"My mother loved the story of *Sankta Lucia*," Kai says, bringing me out of my reverie. "She would always sing to us as children…"

His voice trails off as we walk, the sound of his footsteps like the beat of a drum. Then Kai opens his mouth and starts to sing. I never thought I would hear such a beautiful sound as this man's voice, but as he starts singing of St. Lucia, I feel gooseflesh prickle the skin all over my body.

"*Natten går tunga fjät runt gård och stuva.*
Kring jord som sol'n förlät, skuggorna ruva.
Drömmar med vingesus under oss sia,
tänd dina vita ljus, Sankta Lucia."

My heart swells at the words and melody, an incredible wave of nostalgia rolling over me at the sound of my mother's voice singing the same song. I open my mouth, not wanting to spoil the sound of Kai's singing, but unable to hold back my own voice either.

"*Trollsejd och mörkermakt ljust du betvingar,*
signade lågors vakt skydd åt oss bringar"

Kai's face is alight with joy and incredulity at the intermingling of our voices. I break off into a harmony that my mother taught me so many years ago.

"*Drömmar med vingesus, under oss sia,*
tänd dina vita ljus, Sankta Lucia.

Stjärnor som leda oss, vägen att finna,
bli dina klara bloss, fagra prästinna.

Drömmar med vingesus, under oss sia,
tänd dina vita ljus, Sankta Luci."

We finish together, breathing steadily as the song echoes endlessly in the trees.

Kai swallows visibly, having stopped walking, and holds me tightly against his chest. I gaze into his eyes, feeling something bubble inside of me. Before I can blink, I feel a wet tear roll down my cheek. Kai smiles warmly at me, using his free hand to wipe the tear away with the back of his thumb.

"You're Swedish is quite good," he whispers. I laugh, feeling emotion thickly line my throat and mouth.

"It's only the song that I know," I admit. "My mother sang that to me as well."

"Something we have in common, I suppose," Kai says.

"Thank you for singing, Kai. You have a lovely voice."

"My voice pales in comparison to yours, *kjære*," Kai says, and my heart throbs. Does he truly mean that I am dear to him? Or is it simply the magic of the snow and the music?

I gaze up into his glassy eyes, my heart thumping beneath my ribs as he tightens his grip on me just slightly. I stifle a gasp when he cups my cheek in his hand. He presses his lips to my forehead, lingering for a moment before pulling away. My stomach flutters, and my body longs for more as he moves to put me down. Inside my chest, feelings stir in me, stronger than I've felt before. More than simple physical yearnings. Something powerful.

"Thank you, my prince," is all I can think to say before he lays me down next to our dwindling fire, leaving me to my thoughts of magic and candles and fairies and golden women dressed in firelight. The last image behind my tired eyes is of a red-haired woman, dressed in a plain wool gown, humming softly as she works, a bright smile on her face.

19
KAI

Over the next several days, we finally reach the edge of the tree line, the west part of the island. We depleted our food supply days ago, and we're living off of the land. I hunt at night while Astrid sleeps, and in the morning, I bring her food I've found – sometimes bird's eggs, sometimes rabbits. The first time I brought her a rabbit, Astrid protested killing such an innocent creature. I responded by breaking the rabbit's neck and slicing it open to provide her with meat.

But then, something changed. Now, Astrid finds food for herself, skinning and stripping different animals of their fur. She seems stronger than before, somehow more comfortable in her own skin. Like she is more herself. As we walk, I wonder if she left the old Astrid behind, abandoning her somewhere in the snow.

She is different from the woman I knew at Feilfri. This Astrid was stronger, more aware of her surroundings. She resembles the version of Astrid that I confessed my deepest feelings to on the top of the castle, but somehow, I prefer her company even more now. It's wonderful to talk to someone who treats me as an equal. Everyone I ever met before her treated me as a prince, as a noble. It's nice to be treated just as a person. By now, we are completely accustomed to one another.

We have pleasant conversations about things we like, things we dislike. I've learned she really likes the way ale tastes; it's one of the things she misses most from the castle. I tell her I really loved the chef; his food was always stellar. She smiles while telling me stories of the castle's chef. She had somewhat of a father-daughter relationship with the man. My smiles come easily, listening to her stories of the basement. It's all like a dream, though, the memory of Feilfri fading away with each day we lived off of the land.

There are even moments where I think she's not confused anymore. She looks at me, and somehow her eyes change. Not in color or any tangible way, but in the way she doesn't shy away from my gaze. Even after watching the snow faerie, she seemed distant and confused, like she didn't know how to be around me. She seemed tormented with some internal discussion that she wouldn't let me be a part of. Now, she is more confident, as though there was a haze on her that has lifted. Her smiles and laughter are more…mature.

Maybe it's just the effect of hard travel, but somehow, she seems to have aged. Like she is truly a woman now, not just in age. Of course, this newfound confidence in her has sparked something horrid inside me. I find a deep attachment growing towards her. I don't want to stop talking at the end of each night, and it seems she felt the same. We talk easily into the darkness of the night without feeling tired of one another. There were even moments right at the end of the firelight where we gaze into one another's eyes, and my whole body comes alive like each limb has its own heartbeat. My breathing becomes unstable in these moments, and I have to tear my eyes away from her just to regain some normalcy.

"I miss Alheri," Astrid says, breaking my thoughts.

I clear my throat and ask, "You were close to her?"

"Yes," she says, giving me a sad smile. "She was my best friend. My only friend really, except you."

I hide a smile.

"Does she even know that I'm gone?"

"Yes," I say. "She helped me get you ready to leave. She was in the process of…healing you when I decided to run."

I sigh in my head. I don't like covering up my own decisions, but I have to stay on the positive side of the story instead of remembering how horrible it was. If I remember how badly she was hurt…

"Do you know much about her family?" she asks.

"Not really. Why?"

"I'm just thinking," she says. "I don't really know much about her either. I never met anyone like her."

I nod, smiling to myself. Neither have I.

"My mother told me stories about Alheri's mother and grandmother," I start. "My mother and the witch Moroya, Alheri's mother, were very close. She was one of the original witches as Feilfri Castle."

"One of the witches that were found with the indigenous people? The ones that saved the vampires from starvation?"

"You remember," I say, smiling. "Moroya would have been probably two generations under those people, but yes. They are from the same bloodline."

"How interesting," Astrid whispers.

"Alheri, like her mother and grandmother, has an incredible amount of power," I say, with clear awe in my voice. I shuddered to think about Alheri in that castle by herself. "But she's all alone."

"What do you mean?"

"She told me about her family once, not too long ago actually. She said her brother died. He lost his power in the harsh winter, and because of that, his skin bleached to a sickly pale, and her father took him into the woods and killed him to keep him from going mad."

"Oh my God," Astrid breathes, her hand pressing against her chest.

"She never mentioned what happened to her mother and father, but I can only imagine. Alheri does well because she knows how to take care of herself."

"I wonder if there are other witches," Astrid says.

"Of course," I reply. "In Menneskelig, there are covens of witches, much more than in Livsnerven. They can practice freely; they provide the city with all sorts of magic."

"That's incredible. How do you think they manage it?"

"My guess is there is power in numbers. Alheri is by herself; she can only sustain her own magic. But if she were part of a larger coven, they could sustain one another, building up each other's magic in an endless loop of energy feedback."

"It sounds like you are envious," she says, eyeing me with a smile.

"I am," I confess. "I think Alheri is one of the most incredible people, and not just because of her magic."

We continue in silence, stewing over thoughts of witches with rich black skin and magic seeping in and out of their fingertips like rainbows streaking across the sky.

After a few minutes, we pass through the tree line and onto a rocky, grassy area that looks over the Norwegian Sea. I pause to stand at the edge of the tree line. I know that the cliffside I found on our very first night is only a few paces away. I smile at the thick golden clouds hanging low in the sky. The wind is warmer now, tickling my neck as it throws my hair around. I breathe in easily, completely accustomed to the smell of dirt and sweat and *Astrid.* I peer sideways at the woman, knowing she isn't looking at me.

Astrid sets down her belongings with an unspoken agreement that this is where we will stop for the night. I know she's looking for things to start building a fire, but suddenly I get the compulsion to grab her hand. She looks up at me with wide eyes. Her heart flops, just like it did on the top of the castle before everything went to shit. It is the only sign I get when I make her happy. I smile at her and give her a wink before slinging her easily onto my back, hearing her yelp as I start to run.

I run at the speed of light towards the cliffside, not quite sure if I'm going to stop. A swell of excitement and hysteria sweeps through me, and I burst out laughing. I can feel Astrid laughing with me, but as she sees the cliffside, she starts to panic. But I'm not afraid. I know that she's strong enough for the cold water. I make the decision to keep running, full speed ahead, before jumping.

"Kai! Oh, my God!" Astrid screams, pushing against my back, but I'm holding her close to my body as I leap, feeling the wind whip past us, warmer than before, and Astrid is screaming, now clutching to my neck. My stomach feels like it's still at the top of the cliff, my heart screaming at the confusion. A guttural laugh escapes my lips, and then we're underwater.

The tide rips Astrid away from my back. The water is warm, somehow, but the tide is strong. I kick up to the surface, looking frantically for Astrid as panic grips at my throat. I didn't even stop to consider if she knew how to swim or not. Alarmed, my heart does somersaults until I see her darkened red hair pop up out of the water. Her eyes are wide, and her face is red, but she's smiling as she starts screaming at me.

"What the *hell*, Kai?!" she yells, trying to stay above water. I laugh at her, seeing that she definitely enjoyed herself, despite her protests. I nod towards the shore and watch her swim with grace, impressed yet again at her abilities.

I climb onto a rock and shake my hair, feeling it stick to my forehead and the back of my neck. It must be longer than my face at this point. Using the back of my hand, I push the hair out of my eyes and behind my ear, watching Astrid ring out her own hair. I catch her eye, and she smiles at me before walking over to punch my upper arm.

"Ow," I laugh.

"You could have killed us," she says, her eyes alight. "How did you even know what was down there? Where are we?"

"This is Ingunn Cliff, I think," I say, trying to remember my mother's maps. "I came here on our first night away from the castle," I admit. Her eyebrows shoot up in surprise.

"You came all the way out here on your own?" Her face droops. "Am I really that slow?"

I smirk. "I could have made it all the way to Menneskelig and back several times by this point."

I think the comment about our destination is going to make her sad, but instead, she takes the insult with another punch at me and a half-laugh, half-scoff.

"Well I'm sorry, your Highness, but I'm not superhuman nor a vampire, so," she jilts, shaking out her hair. I inhale, unthinking, as the wind carries her now-familiar scent to me. Rose petals and honeysuckle. I smile sadly to myself.

"Let's go back up to the top and make camp," I say, weighed down and not just because of my salt water-soaked clothes.

I sprint to grab the rest of our dropped belongings, including our dinner and Astrid's well-dirtied satchel and cloak, before making it back to the top of the cliff. The sun is still above the horizon, catching the clouds with beautiful yellow light. It would be a perfect sunset if the clouds didn't obscure it so fully.

"What do we need for a fire? I'll grab it," I ask, listening to Astrid's instructions before sprinting to back to the forest to gather the bits of brush and wood for the fire. By the time I've returned, Astrid has stripped down, wrapped only in her thin shift, with her dress laid out on the ground to dry. Her hair is plaited behind her head, a common style she has taken to wearing during days of long journeying. My heart stops seeing her bare shoulders and knowing she is completed naked beneath the sheer fabric.

I take a jagged breath before stepping into her view. She stands, reaching for the wood for the fire, smiling breezily at me. Seeing her move so naturally makes me itch all over, but I stifle the urges by looking out at the water and listening to the gentle rustling of leaves by the cool breeze.

"Tell me something," Astrid says after she's eaten a few bites of her dinner.

"Like what?"

"I don't know. Any stories or tales that your mother used to tell you? I enjoyed hearing you talk about St. Lucia and Alheri's family."

I'm lying on my back when she asks, so I sit up and face her, thinking about different stories from my childhood. Most were scary stories that Father would tell us, but I remember the story about the witches. I decide to go with that one.

"Have you heard of Sollys?" I ask.

"Mmm, I think…maybe?" she responds with a mouthful.

"Well, it's a faraway land, where the witches are born. I'm pretty sure Alheri was from Sollys, or at least her ancestors were. They are born with gifts that connect them to the earth."
Astrid watches me intently.

"It's said that Freyja herself touched down in Sollys, granting powers to the native people there and that any practitioner of seiðr is considered a *heks*, or *Aje* in the common tongue, and can command elements of the earth to serve her."

"Her? Can men not be these nature's servants?"

"As far as I know, I don't think so," I reply. "I've never met anyone from Sollys other than possibly Alheri."

"Tell me more," Astrid pushes.

"Well, it's said that the women from Sollys can perform all kinds of magic," I tell her, reciting one of the books my mother had given me. It was a deeply illustrated and fantastical look at the witches from Sollys. "These women of deeply colored skin have magic that can heal any wound," I say, standing and enacting the rituals illustrated in the book. "They speak in unintelligible languages, calling on Freyja for Her sovereignty to reign over the lands they walked on. They ask Her to perform miracles. It's said that no one could even touch a *heks* because they are protected by the goddesses that watch over them."

I swirl my hands around, picking up dirt and grass and throwing it into the fire, watching blue-green flame spark from the salt.

"These women can call upon demons, angels, and servants of the earth to perform rituals and spells. You've even seen this. Any time Alheri healed you or Annette or anyone else."

I pause, trying desperately not to remember Astrid's broken body after Caden's attack.

"They say that these women are the most powerful lovers you'll ever meet," I say, not really sure why only to steer the conversation away from bleeding bodies. "They have the power of heaven and earth within their grasp and can take down any foe if their magic is peaked. I've seen in books how they cast different spells with colored light springing from their hands. I bet they can make you feel anything they want you to feel," I say, tickling Astrid's neck, and she laughs, enraptured in my storytelling. I smile at her laughter.

I plop down next to her and extend my hands towards the fire. The sun has gone past the horizon, and the clouds are turning purple rather than orange. I turn to see Astrid's hair ablaze with the firelight, and suddenly the talk of magic and power hushes over both of us. I'm stuck in Astrid's gaze, just like I am every night…although something's different tonight. Cliff diving broke down the last barrier between us, and I am almost painfully conscious of her arm brushing against mine, the electric current that sparks between our skin. Suddenly, I'm very aware that we are both already half-naked.

I don't turn away from her, though. Her face is nothing like it was the night she first offered herself to me. She doesn't look terrified of me or obligated to do anything. But for a brief moment, her eyes flick down to my lips, and I'm overcome with the desire to kiss her. I start unconsciously leaning towards her, a magic that only she can possess. I blink rapidly, feeling my heartbeat throb throughout my entire body again. Her eyes close slightly, her long eyelashes brush the tops of her round, red cheeks, and her braid falls over her shoulder.

Her eyes open, a vortex with tides stronger than the ocean. They melt into my soul, and my chest aches to reach out and grab her. She leans in, closing the distance between us, and I brace myself for her soft lips to ever so slightly brush mine. And for the briefest of moments, my head swims with emotion, and I push through just enough to kiss her back. For a moment, I hold my breath and clench my hands to my thighs, warning the rest of my body to behave. A somewhat guttural sound escapes my lungs, but her lips are on mine, like soft feathers with the gentlest of touches.

I start to loosen up as she leans into me, her body shifting so her shoulder touches mine. I relax my hands and brush the backs of my fingers against her cheeks before cupping her head. She sighs against my lips and runs her hands up my back and into my hair. My body shivers in delight as she traces my lips with hers, pulling away just enough to drive me crazy. As she kisses up and down my cheekbones, I briefly open my eyes to see the fire light up her hair in a blaze of golden-red.

Her lips meet my ear, and I bite down the urge to sigh her name. I simply bury my lips into her neck, forgetting for just a moment what I am.

The heat turns to fire in an instant as I feel her rapid heartbeat throb against me. I close my eyes and press my lips to her throat, reveling in the feeling of her blood rushing throughout her body. It would be so easy…

My hands automatically grip her neck, and her body shudders against mine. Feeling the delicious thud of her heart against the palms of my hands, I pull her mouth back to mine, kissing her fiercely. She gasps, and her breath flows past my lips and sighs against my teeth, turning my mouth into a chasm of dark pleasure. I can feel my body shift and press against hers, meeting every inch of her skin against mine. My eyes roll back as I feel her pulse throb underneath the thin fabric of her shift, and I automatically lean my mouth down her neck and trace my tongue against the largest artery in her neck before letting out a delicate groan of pure restraint.

Memories of biting down and feeding on her spring to the forefront of my brain, taunting me through Caden's nightmare vision. I remember how he implanted my thoughts with desire for her, feeding upon my innate lustful tastes. The memory turns to ash as my brain fasts forward to holding her limp body in my arms after Caden ruthlessly used and attacked her.

I can't be like him. I *can't.*

My brain regains control after a moment longer, and I turn away, ripping my lips away from her. My entire body groans with restraint.

"Kai," she whispers my name like a spell, and my heart forces me to look at her again. She reaches out to me, but I grab her hand before her fingers can brush my cheek. Her eyes fly wide open.

"I can't, Astrid." I release her arm, and it remains aloft for a moment before she drops it to her lap. "I can't do this."

She's breathing heavily, and I have to force myself not to think about her pounding heartbeat, singing to me like a siren's song.

"I can't just *kiss* you like it's nothing, Astrid. You think it's easy for me? If I give myself over to my body…" I stop, my breath catching in my throat. "If I give myself over to that part of me, the part that *wants* so deeply…"

She stares at me with wide eyes, reflecting the darkness and flickering flames.

"If I hurt you," I choke, "if I killed you… I could never live with myself."

"Kai," she breathes.

"You're precious to me. You always have been," I continue. "If I tried and failed and lost you forever… You forget, but I fed on a red-haired woman once before. She's dead because of me."

I drop my head into my hands but keep my eyes wide open, hoping not to see the horrific images of a dead woman who looked like Astrid. Phantom pain radiates under my skin, and I shake.

She reaches out to touch my face again. My hand catches her wrist, and she gasps softly as my gaze cuts through the fog of the non-existent spell. My fangs spring forth, and I bare my teeth at her as a warning, kissing her wrist softly, so softly. She freezes solid. I look deeply into her face, which is stark white against the darkness. She has never seen this side of me. And now she is just my prey. She is perfectly still, waiting for me to kill her.

I take a deep breath and feel the darkness leave my eyes, my teeth returning back into their sheathes.

"I don't ever want to hurt you, Astrid," I tell her quickly, scooping her hands into mine again. She's stone-cold with shock. And with good intentions, I say, "I'll never hurt you, Astrid."

I look into her eyes and smile, and after a few moments, she moves, meeting my gaze.

"That's why you've stayed away from me?" Astrid says, her

voice soft like silk.

I nod, lifting her hands to my lips again.

"How can you be like this then?" she asks, looking at her hand, my mouth.

"Because I know I'm in control," I say, trying to make sense of this myself. These feelings, so strong and so feral, are still brand new to me. When all I want to do is kiss her, hold her, *love* her, the other part of me, the animal part of me, wants to revel in her blood. It's dangerous to even be alone with her. I sigh.

"And before?"

"I didn't," I admit.

"I don't understand. What changed?"

"My desire for you is so strong sometimes that it scares me," I say, cutting my heart open just to show it to her. "It comes upon me so quickly that I can't prepare for it. I don't know how to be that way with you, with anyone. I've never done it before. What if the feeling is so strong that I can't control myself?"

"Kai." She slowly reaches out to touch my face again. This time I let her. "I know you're afraid. I know you're unsure of what to do, but I'm not. I've been with a man before, and I know what it all entails."

Every warm feeling in my body turns cold, and my heart stops. I grind my teeth together and rip my hands and face away from her. In the back of my head, I know she only means she's familiar with the process, that she can help me through it, but that's not what I'm thinking of. Suddenly the nightmares of every castle vampire fucking her blinds my eyes.

She's not been with a man before. She's been raped by her masters.

I stand up, enraged and blind with fury. The same irrational, possessive instincts from before come flooding back, with a stronger grip now. I can't keep going forward as if everything back at Feilfri didn't happen. It *happened*, and Astrid needs to remember.

"You've had sex as a *slave*, Astrid," I say, my voice sounding like it's a million paces away. It sounds strangled with every emotion that's coursing through my body. My hands shake, and I clamp my fingers into tight fists.

"What?"

"You were a slave! Don't you understand that?" I shout at her. "Don't you understand how badly you were treated? How fucking messed up that whole place was?"

I look at her, but she just looks confused.

"Of course, you don't. For some ungodly reason, you never realized how wrong you were treated. For some reason, you've *forgotten* how you were used, raped, and attacked. Even after you came to me, you were still sought after and hurt because you're human!"

"I don't understand," Astrid says, looking up at me. "Why are you saying this?"

"My father used you. When you were a *thrall*? As a servant or slave or whatever word you want to use to describe it, you were seen and treated like dirt. Not just with the cooking and cleaning, but the feeding and the fucking." I spit the words, and she flinches at every syllable. "It's messed up, Astrid! And you can't see that, and I don't know why."

I'm yelling and angry, and I know I should stop, but the words keep flowing out of me.

"Every *thrall* acted like they were brainwashed, even though I could still tell they understood that they were inferior to us. They hated us, though they served us happily. It's sick! But you…you never saw it. You *wanted* to serve. You were happy serving. And you made me feel pressured to use you. Do you know how *wrong* that is?!

"And my *brother*? You never saw or seemed to recognize how messed up Annette was because of what Caden was doing to her, the horrible trail of bruised and broken people he left behind him. You don't even remember how he attacked and almost killed *you*!"

I grip my hands together, and my fingernails break through the skin on my palms. I welcome the biting sensation of pain.

"You don't know what it was like for me to see you bloodied and half-dead. The night we left, he hurt you. Alheri was quick to seal your wound and heal your body, but it left scars in your mind that you don't even know of. I can still remember how the bathwater turned black with her magic as it leeched the putrid venom from Caden out of you. So, no, I can't do that to you. I can't let myself get close to that. I'd sooner die than hold your broken body in my arms again."

I fall to my knees and drop my head, feeling heavy and weak. Everything that I had bottled up since that night had come out all at once. And I'm tired. Even weeks away from that horrible place, it still haunts me.

I look up at the silent Astrid and find her staring into the fire, tears streaming down her face. Every fiber of my being wants to take it all back, to reverse time to find the day she was born and flee with her, far away from the nightmares and vile creatures that haunted her.

She cries quietly. My heart throbs sadly in my chest, making my ribs ache. I take a deep breath, and for a moment, I use all my strength to try to peer into her mind. I haven't used my powers in such a long time, but as soon as I try to push past the threshold, her mind opens wide to me, speaking one word over and over again. Shame. Shame. I've made her feel ashamed for acting poorly against me.

I clench my fists tighter, swallowing my vicious retort. This is what I mean. She's been so corrupted that she can't even see this isn't her fault. Vampires are a plague. I said that to her once. For however many times she was fed on, an equal number of vampires played with her mind. Even Caden admitted he'd compelled her into subservience.

But I can't yell at her anymore. I can't even say anything else. Her mind is fragile, and her body is broken and abused. If I press her anymore tonight, she'll fall apart, and I don't know if I could help her.

God, I wish Alheri was here. Or Lilith. Even my mother. They would know what to say. They would know how to comfort her.

I know I can't fix what I said, or at least how I said it. But now she knows, even if she doesn't remember it herself. Now, she understands she can't push a vampire. She should stay away from us forever. She has to stay away from me.

"I'm sorry, Astrid. I shouldn't have lashed out at you. Please know that none of this is your fault," I say, my voice hoarse and my throat parched. "Go to sleep. I'll be back by morning."

Without another glance back to the weeping woman on the cliffside, I launch back into the forest and become everything I despise just so I can eat.

20
ASTRID

I open my eyes, greeted by a pale, white sky and the sound of crashing waves. My back aches, and my stomach growls, but I don't move. I stare at the white, cloudy sky for a moment, actively clearing my mind from the dreams that plagued my mind all night. Images of a beautiful, raven-haired man dancing around a fire in tandem with pictures of his sharp teeth and black eyes.

In the back of my mind, I know I have no reason to be afraid of Kai. And yet, the forefront of my brain that begs for logic and reason tells me to be careful. I am a human that walks closely with a vampire, trusting him almost completely with my safety.

The light bouncing off the misty, low hanging clouds is almost blinding, but I welcome it. It blasts away the darkness that lingers from dreams where I watched Kai rip into my wrist with his overgrown teeth. But even the blinding light can't turn off my thoughts.

Shivering, I pull my cloak over my eyes, smelling the grass stains on the deep brown leather. The light can't penetrate through the material, and I question whether I should close my eyes a moment longer. Exhaustion pulls at every fiber of my being. Instead of finding peace and sleep in the stillness, my brain keeps trudging through.

Kai's words from the night before bounce around in my head. What did he mean when he said I had been mistreated? Was it just so horrible for him to imagine himself in my shoes? And if that was the case, shouldn't I think the same?

Thinking back on my time at the castle, I can't remember anything but happiness. I had friends, a purpose, shelter. I didn't want anything other than to serve. I remember that much. I remember being frustrated when Kai didn't have instructions for me. Was that why he was angry? He wanted me to fend for myself? No, that couldn't be right. Why would a prince like Kai have ever thought about my life? I'm a nobody. Even now, Kai made it his mission to guide me to safety, even though I never asked.

But he was so *angry*. Why was he so angry?

I can't think about asking him without picturing his horrific fangs and black eyes. Even though the Kai from my dreams was so pleasant at first. A quiver runs down my spine.

"Astrid?" his voice calls from only paces away. My heart is pounding, but I peek outside my cloak, finding him sitting by a fire, looking right at me.

He doesn't look strange or angry now. He smiles and waves me over, and I can't help but go to him. My heart still pounding with fear, I push myself up, brushing the dirt off of my salty dress.

"I can hear your heart," he says with a low voice. "You don't need to be afraid."

I freeze midstep, unsure about how to respond to him. He just looks up at me, his eyes a deep grey, his face is relaxed. There's nothing physically scary about the Kai that's sitting in front of me now. So, I take a seat opposite him across the fire.

He holds out a giant leaf with several berries and cooked meat from some animal he must have found.

"Eat quickly. I want to get moving," Kai says, standing to pack up our belongings.

I watch him for a moment and notice something different. Not with Kai, but with me. I don't know when it happened, but for some reason, I don't feel the need to get up and help him. I don't feel the desire to serve him. Is this a new feeling? Because of what he said last night? Or had I felt this way since leaving Livsnerven?

While we lived in Feilfri Castle, I distinctly remember wanting to meet his every need. Fetch his bathwater, clean his fireplace, wash his clothes. Now, all of that sounds rather boring and unnecessary. Kai is a grown man and can do his own work. Except maybe make a fire, I think, looking at his poorly made campfire.

No, now I feel like I only have to watch out for myself. Is that a by-product of being away from so many servants? Had I just convinced myself that all that work was necessary just because it was what everyone else was doing? Even that sounds too complicated. There should have been a reason I would stoop to such a low level, beyond humility, to a longing to serve. Right?

Right?

My thoughts are trapped, reeling from all of the confusion, even after we've been walking for an hour. Was Kai right about my treatment?

I shake my head. No, he couldn't be right. I remember being happy. How could that be? Was my sense of right and wrong that messed up? Had I been tricked or confused?

"Kai—" I try to say, but my voice is lost. I swallow hard against the grainy feeling of dehydration. The salty water and ocean air have done a number on my throat. I unconsciously put a hand up to my throat, feeling dry and sick suddenly. I stop walking, and Kai takes notice of my appearance.

Without a sound, he nods at me and takes off in a sprint, leaving me all alone with the ocean on my left and the thick, dark forest on my right. I quickly get off my feet and sit in the rocky sand.

Alone with my torturous thoughts…

My skin feels like it's burning, even though the air is icy cold. I whip my cloak off and unlace the front of my dress, allowing the wind to chill the skin on my chest. I take a deep breath, ignoring the soreness in my throat, and try to sort through my pain.

Before, I was confused and hurt by Kai's neglect. I thought he didn't want me. I remember feeling overjoyed when he talked to me, so lucky to be speaking with royalty. Now, I'm questioning my position. I don't feel that I'm below Kai. Not out here in the wild. I find him serving me in the kindest ways. He finds and cooks my meals, helps me trudge through the forest. How can I be the same person that I was before? Am I even the same Astrid? Or has another woman taken her place completely?

In the blink of an eye, Kai whips back to my side, holding a leather canteen out to me, not even breaking a sweat from the run. I grab it and start guzzling the water, feeling the cold seep back into my system, the water quelling the anxieties and heat that was scorching my skin.

"Are you okay?" Kai asks, kneeling to meet my gaze. Looking into his dark grey eyes, like stormy seas, I can't help but question his motives.

"The water tastes amazing. Thank you," I say.

Kai smiles and takes a seat next to me, allowing me to rest while I drink. I fidget, slightly uncomfortably next to him, feeling that same electric current play between our un-touching arms.

"Kai," I say, finding my voice once more. He looks at me, expressionless, with his long hair falling in front of his eyes. "What did you mean last night? About how I was treated back at Feilfri? I only remember being happy while I worked for your father."

Kai scoffs softly, but I continue.

"How can our recollections of that time be so different? You seem so angry at my treatment, but I never saw anything wrong with it. How can that be?" I ask, sincerely curious.

He must see the confusion in my eyes because his response is nothing like it was the night previous. "I don't know. I just know that *I* hated living there. Every second. I never wanted to hurt anyone, and that's the entire culture there. My family preyed upon anyone whose title was lower than them. Everyone in that godforsaken castle was bloodthirsty."

"Except you," I correct.

"Right." He pauses. "Except it's not true. I still killed. I still allowed my brother to hurt others, like Annette, right in front of me. I still allowed my father to treat lesser vampires and humans like garbage. I didn't do anything to stop it. I just ran away."

I hesitate with my response, but after a moment, take a breath and ask, "Do you feel guilty for leaving?"

"Yes? No?" Kai says, looking out towards the ocean.

The cliffside has leveled with the surface at some point in our walk, and now it's mostly beach that connects us with the water. I stare at the tide, rolling up and down the rocky sand.

"No, I don't feel guilty. I'm doing the right thing by bringing you to Menneskelig," he says like he's trying to convince me. Maybe he's trying to convince himself.

I bob my head up and down. What could I say to that? Thank you?

"I'm sorry if this wasn't what you wanted," Kai says, "but I couldn't just leave you there. Not in that disgusting place."

I sip on the water, feeling a renewed sense of memory recall. On some level, I can still hear the waves and birds in the air. I can still hear Kai's voice and soft breathing next to me, but I don't feel it. Instead, images of my castle life pass over my eyes like flashes of a dream.

I remember the man that called upon me that night Alheri and I had eaten in the kitchens. The baker tried to tell me to say goodnight to the man, but I hadn't listened. I remember telling the baker it was fine. I went with the man that night. The vampire. He hadn't even introduced himself. I remembered the way he looked at me, but something is changed in the memory. The image of Kai's fangs and black eyes replaced my memory of the man. He had looked at me with a hunger in his eyes I hadn't seen before.

I shiver, remembering the man close to my neck and smelling behind my ear. I scratch nervously, trying to shake off the memory. I remember not being afraid as he led me back to his room. Why wasn't I afraid? Why hadn't I been more prudent? That man had obviously wanted one thing from me. My body. And I had given it to him easily, just like countless before him.

The memory flashes and I feel pain spark in my neck as the vision of the man pierces the skin under my jaw. I gasp audibly and try to fight against him, but he's not there. The vision disappears, and I'm still staring at the ocean. My heart is racing, and tears are streaming down my face. When did I start crying?

I see his fangs retreat from my neck, but it's not that strange man anymore. The sharp teeth belong to Caden with lustful red eyes as he licks his blood-stained lips. I feel his hands press me against him as he tears into my skin over and over again, ripping away at my flesh. I jerk away, trying to fight him, but I can't seem to shake him off of me.

"Astrid? Astrid," Kai whispers, watching me curiously. His face is distressed, but not with his own pain or disgust. He's looking at me with fear, not for himself, but fear for me. I swallow hard and look away into the ocean.

And like a battering of strong wind and rain, encounters with every vampire at the castle barrage my eyes, and I yelp in pain at every pierce of their teeth, remembering the tingling sensation in my fingertips. Why had I liked that feeling? They each looked at me with unsympathetic hunger, only minutes from draining my entire body of blood. Alheri had been *right* to worry.

The images kept up, like punches in the stomach. I scream, unsure of my own reality. I know I must be still sitting with Kai, but I can't see him. I can only see images of evil battering my brain with renewed vision and purpose. My brain is deconstructing my carefully designed prison of memories. It is revealing the madness that kept me shrouded in innocence. My brain is showing me the truth in Kai's words.

Kai saved me from that evil place. But that isn't all.

In his *kindness*, Kai robbed me of happiness.

"Astrid! Astrid!" Kai shakes my shoulders, shouting at me. Between the assault of images, I find myself fighting against Kai's grip.

"Let go of me!" I scream. "Let go of me!"

"You're having a panic attack, Astrid! Calm down!"

"Calm down? *Calm down*?!" I yell. "How can I calm down?"

I somehow hit him, and as he recoils away from me, I jolt upright, running as quickly as I can away from him.

"You ruined my fucking life! Did you do this to me? Did you plant these memories? Why am I seeing these awful things?" I scream behind me, and Kai sprints up to me, grabbing my wrists in his hands again.

"I didn't do this to you, Astrid! It was all my father! He ruined both of us! I'm just trying to save you. I'm just trying to bring you to safety," Kai says. He's trying to calm me down, but his words just rip holes into my heart.

"Save me!? You've *ruined* me! I was happy! You've stolen

away all of my happiness and replaced it with the disgust you have for yourself! I was an innocent bystander, and you stole me away!"

Kai says nothing but keeps his grip tight on my arms. I struggle, pulling restlessly on my arms to try and get free.

"Astrid, stop! I'm not trying to hurt you!"

"You are! How could you do this to me?" I ask, my strength diminishing into a crippling sadness, and I drop to my knees, Kai's grip still strong as he holds my arms up. I let my head dangle loosely as tears stream down my face and sobs wrack my body. "How could you do this? You took me away from everything that made me happy."

"You're just seeing the truth, Astrid—"

"Well, I don't want it!" I scream at him. He lets go of my wrists, and my face drops right into the sand.

Hatred and misery writhe in my limbs, and I taste sand on my lips, mixing with the tears that probably will never stop. The unwanted memories return behind my eyes.

"I don't want this," I mumble into the dirt. I raise my head to look Kai straight in the eye. "Yes, you've opened my eyes, Kai. You've shown me what fucking *monsters* vampires are. All I see is teeth and black eyes," I say, a hollow horror filling the void in my chest. "They keep tearing into my skin, and I remember it all. I remember everything."

I'm shaking and cold suddenly, the tears replaced with chattering teeth and wide eyes. The sand flakes into my mouth and eyes, making my flinch with real and imagined pain.

"I can't bear it, Kai!" I scream, and he's there, shushing me and wrapping his arms around me, but I can't even feel it. All I feel, all I see, is his black eyes and sharp teeth close to my neck.

Panic-stricken, I jolt away from him, but it's a visceral reaction of self-preservation.

"Astrid, stop! Please!"

"No, you're one of *them*! You only want my blood! You're going to kill me!" I shriek into the open sky. There's no one here, no one around for miles. My prince has trapped me all alone with him. "Was this your plan all along? String me along with a web of lies just to get me alone? Just to kill me in peace?!"

"What?! No! I would never hurt you! You have to believe me! Astrid," he says, sprinting to me again and wrapping me up in his arms.

My entire body screams at his touch, but he holds me fast, simply staring at me. He's not attacking me. Even though my heart is racing, I stop struggling against his solid embrace. My breathing is heightened, and all I see is his teeth, but I tell myself I have to play this smart if I'm going to get away from him.

I look to the horizon and notice the sky is darkening. I say a silent prayer to all the gods, thanking them for short winter days. All I have to do now is wait for him to leave to get food or to go hunting, and I'll slip away.

The thought of his fangs sends a shiver down my spine, but I will myself to look him straight in the eye. I meet his gaze, his eyebrows raised in question. I take a deep breath and nod, trying to reign in my heart and lungs, but he seems content and lets me go.

"I'm not going to hurt you, Astrid," Kai says in a pleading voice. "I'd never intentionally do that. Please believe me when I say I'm *trying*. I'm trying so hard to be better. You make me want to be better."

He pauses and looks me straight in the eye, and I can't help but question his sincerity. In his stormy eyes, I see the pure intentions in his words. But after everything, he's done everything he could possibly do to make me disbelieve even the truth. Vampires are plagues. That's what he *wants* me to believe.

"Everything you're feeling, everything you're remembering," he continues, "that was all my father. He did this to you. He ruled a kingdom that treats humans like dirt, and you were caught up in it. And for that, I'm truly sorry. The only thing I can do for you now is to get you to Menneskelig, where you'll be safe."

I take a breath, relief washing over me. In the chaos, I had forgotten we are headed towards the human capital, where it's rumored there is an anti-vampire border around the whole city. Surely, I'll be safe there. I nod at Kai, hoping to sell my calmness even though I still feel my heartbeat thudding in my ears.

Shivering, I watch Kai, and he looks around, probably coming to the same conclusion I had about stopping for the night. He sighs and sprints back to where our belongings were dropped before returning to me, making me flinch and gasp in fear. He holds up his hands in peace.

"Are you going to be okay if I run and get you some food?" he asks, and I sigh in relief, nodding. "Okay, stay here and see about building a fire. There's probably some driftwood around somewhere. I'll be right back."

As soon as he's behind the tree line and shrouded in darkness, I gather my dress in my hands, and I'm running. I move forward, in the same direction we had been traveling, my lungs already on fire with the effort. I stifle a cry because I know it won't help. I must keep quiet and move quickly.

I have to get away from Kai.

What had he said about disguising my smell? My mind reels back to when we were moving through Livsnerven and a chill runs through my veins. I had been surrounded by vampires before, and I still got away, I remind myself. But Kai had been right before when he had smeared his own blood on my face. I need to disguise myself.

I look into the forest and quickly decide to step blindly into the darkness. The stench of rotting flesh burns my nostrils. Was the forest this awful before? How did I not realize how horrible the smell was before?

God. My memories are like a burning shipwreck.

But I can't think of that now. As soon as I'm free, I can stop and sort through everything. Try and find the truth.

I grab onto a tree and shirk off all the clothing I can without freezing to death. I dig up dirt and grass from the base of the tree and start rubbing it over my skin and hair, hoping that the earthy smell will disguise my scent. I move away from my discarded clothing quickly, hoping it won't draw Kai to me. I look around, finding the light quickly diminishing from the forest. The green-grey leaves turn ink-black all around me.

Dammit. Which way is north?

I search around for the opening of the tree line, hoping to find the shore again, but it's no use. I can't see anything. I'm alone in the darkness, and suddenly a very different, very guttural fear creeps into my heart. The forest is quiet in the darkness, and I can hear my breathing like thunder. I close my lips and kneel down to the ground, trying to become as small as possible. I know that I'm not even close to far enough from Kai. He could easily track me here. I have to keep moving.

Shutting my eyes tightly, I will myself to see the tree line. I fling my eyes open wide, letting in as much light as I can, and barely make out a soft grey light filtering in through the leaves. I hoist myself up and quickly run towards the edge of the trees, just far enough so I can walk inside the forest but keep an eye on the ocean as well.

After a while, my legs turn useless underneath my dress, and though I try to push on, my body decides it's otherwise inclined. I slowly sit down on a fallen tree. The sun is almost gone. Nighttime will be around me quickly. If I don't make a fire now, I will be trapped in the wasteland's trees in the dark.

I look all around, trying to be as quiet as possible. I listen and look for any sign that Kai is following me. I hear the distant cries of birds, the crashing of the waves against the rocks, and a slight drizzle of raindrops on the trees. But no sign of Kai.

I heave in a jagged breath and start to build a fire. I just hope that I have enough strength to stay awake.

21

KAI

I sprint around Ødemark's god-awful forest for several minutes, searching for any kind of food that I can bring back to Astrid. I gather several eggs, which are no bigger than my thumb, but it is better than nothing. I catalog my knowledge of the wastelands in my mind. The lands closest to Livsnerven are completely desolate, with only the stench of death all around. Vampires have hunted the place dry; nothing lives in that section of the forest anymore. As you move north, though, the forest starts growing life again. Birds and other forest animals had built nests closer to Menneskelig.

I stand in the section of Ødemark that is thriving. But where there is life, there is also death. I know that the section closest to the city runs rampant with wild halvblods, crazed vampires that feed on anything living. They are the product of humans and dhampyrs that weren't given the proper amount of blood during their adolescence and thus were driven mad with thirst. Even if they did drink from a human or large animal, their thirst would not be quenched.

I shiver, thinking of the demons lurking in the forest, worry gripping my heart for Astrid. I swallow my fear, knowing that she is safe along the coast. Most halvblods don't venture from the forest. They aren't smart enough to know the sun is hidden.

But instead of feeling relief, I feel more anxious to get back to her. She had been so scared, so out of her own mind... Why had her memories come back now? After days and days of forgetting everything that happened at Feilfri, why was she remembering *now*?

I throw myself into a sprint again, angry that I haven't been able to feed in days, and now I only have a handful of eggs for Astrid. It's bad enough that I am starving; I don't want her to starve too.

Of course, it's bad enough that she forgot what happened between us at the castle – how I told her my feelings, how we held one another, her own admission of jealousy toward the vampire suitresses. Now that she's remembering, it's like she's only seeing the bad things. The putrid, disgusting monsters that preyed on her innocence and beauty. I hang my head as I run, feeling pitiful. It makes perfect sense. When a striking memory is pitted against a less vivid one, the latter pales in comparison and gets brushed aside. Astrid's mind is filled with dark, graphic memories, and they are overtaking all the small, insignificant moments that happened between us. I'll be surprised if she ever remembers how we once were.

As I emerge from the forest, I see Astrid's bag in the distance, tucked in the sand. Past the dirty, empty bag, I see footsteps, and my heart lurches forward. Astrid is gone. She ran away from me.

In a haze, I move forward, following her steps easily, seeing that she had fled into the forest. I sniff the air, sensing that she tried to disguise her smell. Part of me wants to laugh at the memory of seeing her face covered in my blood while we fled through Livsnerven. She had been so happy then.

But I don't laugh. I can't even smile.

Is she right? Have I robbed her of happiness?

I can't resolve myself to thinking that way. I know that taking her away from Feilfri castle was the right thing to do. I *know* it was.

I shake my head quickly, forcing myself back onto her trail. I follow it into the darkness of the forest, seeing different bits of her clothing strewn over different tree branches. I snatch them up and stuff them into the bag, which I have slung over my shoulder. I sigh loudly.

It feels somewhat like I am taking care of a young child. Astrid was throwing tantrums even before we left Livsnerven. She had been angry with me for not feeding on her, irritated that I didn't sleep with her. She'd been inclined to do anything and everything for me, angry when I told her to rest. I shake my head, stepping slowly in the direction of Astrid's lingering smell.

Then, in the distance, I notice the soft smell of smoke in the air. I focus my eyes to see Astrid warming her hands against a small fire just inside the tree line. I stop and sit down on a damp rock, letting the bag hit the ground. I watch her cook something very small against the flames. A bird? She killed it, skinned it, and was cooking it completely by herself.

Does she even need me?

I think back to the first day I saw her skin an animal. She had watched me do it, and then the next night, she did it herself, flawlessly. It was like she just needed to see someone do it once to learn it. Then she could imitate the chore perfectly. She protested the killing of animals so strongly the first time. Now, she's providing for herself. She is stronger. She seems complete. She doesn't need anything.

I feel my heart sink into the heels of my feet. My intestines twist up and choke off my throat.

Maybe I need to let her go. Maybe I am the one holding her back. I've been so afraid to see her go, but is that fear justified? Am

I afraid for her wellbeing…or am I afraid to be alone again?

I sigh shakily. I *don't* want to be alone. But I can't make that Astrid's problem.

For a brief moment, I think back to Lilith and Alheri, talking about boys underneath the sunlit sky. I wonder if Lilith had taken the chance to get close to her human – William, I think his name was. Did she stay away from him because she knew she could hurt him? Or did she succumb to the loneliness at last?

It wasn't a secret that vampires lived a torturous life. If we didn't befriend our own kind, we were destined to live alone. Sure, there are some like my mother who fall in love with humans, living off of small doses of their blood. But humans age. They *die*. Venn died of old age, leaving my mother alone again.

Maybe I should leave Astrid and go find Lilith like I'd always planned. Maybe I should spend the rest of my life with my best friend. Sure, I won't have the exciting fire that exists between Astrid and me. But isn't it better to save Astrid from the pain of death at my hands?

Won't it be better for *me* if I save myself the pain of losing her?

My thoughts continue relentlessly as the evening draws on. At some point, I watch Astrid's eyelids droop and her back lean lightly against the back of the fallen tree she has been sitting on. I watch her breathe in and out slowly as she sleeps. It's a peaceful sight.

Eventually, I have to make a decision. I suppose I will leave Astrid and let her find her own way. I will stand and walk away. Menneskelig is only another few days away at Astrid's pace. She can make it there on her own.

I watch the bright moonlight peer over the edge of the ocean's horizon, gleaming onto the waters for a moment before the thick clouds cover it. I sigh, knowing that I am weak. If I allow myself another moment with Astrid, I'll never be able to leave her.

She doesn't need me. She doesn't *want* me. Not now, not anymore.

I turn to look at the beautiful, red-haired woman I adore so much. I inhale the scent of her flowers-and-honey blood before turning away, heading south, walking at a desperate snail's pace.

If I could cry, I would shed a million tears over the thoughts of what might have been. What I wouldn't give to be loved by Astrid. To sire her children and watch her sleep peacefully every night. I would give away my immortality for a simple life, a *whole* life, with my Astrid.

Instead, I will settle for half a life, living forever amongst the trees and ocean, learning to survive on only animal blood, and letting my eyes turn silver. Maybe Lilith will join me if she grows tired of the humans, but I know in my heart that even Lilith will die eventually. She's still half-human. Someday, she'll wither away, just like all the rest.

I'll have to learn to be alone. I can find some way to live happily. It seems like an incredibly difficult task at this point, but I can do it. I have to.

As I round the island, finding Ingunn Cliff again, I stop for a moment, reliving beautiful memories with Astrid. What I would give to kiss her without the urge to tear out her throat…

I close my eyes, and for a moment, I can hear Astrid's screams, remembering how we launched into the air off the side of the cliff and into the salty waves below.

Then, a moment later, I hear her scream again. I whip my eyes open, realizing I hadn't dreamt it that time. In an instant, I'm sprinting again, hurtling towards her voice. I cry out, smiling so widely as my heart throbs with fear. Never in my life have I felt such joy and pain at the same time.

22
ASTRID

I awake with a start, feeling groggy and sore. The visions and nightmares were incessant all night, seeping terror into my veins. But I was still alive. I gather up my skirts, grabbing my cloak around me tightly, and start north again.

I blink and rub my hands over my face as I walk. My eyes are bleary from seeing so many horrible memories, but somewhere in the haze of my mind, I start to remember things. Not just the horrible memories of ravaged vampires and sharp teeth, but also the mundane tasks I was asked to do. The endless cleaning and cooking on top of hauling water back and forth from the boiler room. I remember talking into the night with Alheri about different gossip and what spells she was working on. I remember meeting Kai and wondering if he liked me or even thought of me as more than a servant.

In the barrage of horrible images, I saw simple things, like how orange peel made my skin feel soft when I died fabric with it, or how I enjoyed embroidering with silk thread. I remember Queen Eileen's conversations and beautiful craftsmanship with her bolts of fabric and how she had praised my work.

I remember Kai.

Not the vampire that frightened me just yesterday. Not the vampire master that I served as *kvinne*. I remember Kai as he was when we talked in his bedroom when we weren't bound to the rules of the court. I remember how passionately he spoke about the vampire's migration to Norway. I remember our conversation on the rooftop and how he had so soulfully admitted his greatest sin, how even though he felt deeply for me, he would never act on it because he was afraid. He didn't want to hurt me.

In all my crazed thinking and panic-stricken choices, I somehow remembered how I felt about him all those weeks ago. I know now, through somewhat clear eyes, that I loved him.

How could that possibly be? How could I love someone who had *killed* another person?

But it's true. I loved him, and part of me loves him still. When I'd watched him dance with all of his potential mates, my heart was sore and sad. When he spoke of his friend Lilith, even though he claimed they were simply friends, I'd been overcome with jealousy. I don't know if I even know what love is or how to properly feel it, but deep down, I know that I loved Kai.

I step sadly over tree branches with uneasy steps and blind eyes. I walk slowly, catching brambles and twigs on my fabric shoes. With every snap of a branch, I curse internally, hoping I'm not drawing any attention to myself.

My mind reels from the newfound realization. If I could love a vampire, even under some sort of compulsion, does that mean they aren't that bad? Even now that the spell on my mind has broken, I never remember *Kai* hurting me. If anything, he hurt himself trying to stave off his own thirst. I remember how he hurled himself off the balcony and how he'd pushed me away so many times now.

How could I think that he was bad? What if he wasn't bad at all? What if everything he had said was true? Even if he's a vampire, and I know I can't stay with him forever, wouldn't it be better to let him escort me to Menneskelig?

I shake my head, feeling my braid stick to the skin on my back. I grimace at how filthy I feel.

I can't simply run back to Kai because I'm afraid to be alone. He is a vampire, and he's been trying to tell me that all along. I shouldn't go back.

In the distance, I hear a small movement, and I automatically gasp and freeze, searching the dimness for any indication that I'm not alone. My heart lumbers around in my chest, making my breaths erratic and loud.

A twig snaps, and fear penetrates my limbs. That was definitely not me.

I'm frozen solid and holding my breath, hoping to any god that will listen that it's only a fox or rabbit. I close my eyes and feel myself tremble. My arms start to ache with the weight of my dress and the fact that I've been clenching every muscle for what feels like a lifetime.

The forest is dark around me. I hadn't realized how far I'd drifted. There's no hope of sunlight coming through the trees now. Whatever is around me, it has me pinned in place by fear. I can't move. I can't breathe. And, after a few moments of complete silence, I feel it coming closer.

It moves slowly, and I can hear it breathing, like it's almost choking as it draws breath. The sound is pain-inducing, like sharp razors shooting out of its mouth and hurtling towards me. I close my eyes, and a single tear rolls down my cheek.

And suddenly, several things happen at once.

I hear the creature's breath coming from one direction, and

I take a chance and bolt the other way. Adrenaline pumping through my entire body, I move quickly through the forest, toward a small light coming from outside the trees. I know the creature is right behind me, but if I can just get to shore, I can see what it is.

Sticks and rocks cut at my feet to the point where I feel my skin break, and I know I'm bleeding. The creature howls behind me, and I can feel it gaining on me. I push ahead. Faster. *Faster.* And then, I'm through the tree line, and the shore is in front of me. I smile but keep running. I look to my left and right and suddenly see Kai in the distance, but just briefly before turning on my attacker and finding a dark demon in the shape of a disfigured human. Its eyes are red like fire, and in an instant, I trip on my skirt, and the earth falls away as I land squarely on my back, watching it lunge towards me. I shriek, and the creature doesn't hesitate to rip into my neck.

"Kai!" I scream, struggling as I feel the disgusting demon writhe in joy upon feeding. But before I can start to feel the numbing sensation of blood loss, Kai is on top of us, ripping the creature away like a blaze of black fire burning away the disease. I grab at my neck, feeling blood gush between my fingers. I stagger away from the two vampires dueling it out for my blood and briefly see Kai's rage in his face before he blurs into action again.

I crawl, unsuccessfully, towards the north, the innate desire for self-protection pumping adrenaline through me. I keep moving when I hear the tearing of flesh and bones behind me. Someone was victorious. I brace myself for the winner to retrieve their prize — my blood.

But instead, I get flipped around and meet Kai face to face. His white skin is splattered with black blood, and his eyes are black as night. He sees my wound, and for a brief moment, he flashes his teeth and black eyes at me. I clench down on my tongue to keep from screaming again. I close my eyes and wait for him to kill me.

After a few moments, though, I open my eyes, and Kai is still standing there, his own eyes closed. He's visibly holding his breath, but he rips a piece of cloth from his shirt and moves my hand to bind my wound, writhing pain shooting through my neck at his touch. Then he puts his own wrist to his lips and bites into his arm. I grimace in shock at the sight of his bright red blood dripping down his arm.

"Drink," he commands, thrusting his arm at me. His black eyes are violent as the dark veins slither across his pale skin. I hesitate and stare at him. He screams, "*Drink*, Astrid!"

I'm shaking when I touch my lips to his wrist and slowly drink the blood that's pulsing out of it. It tastes like rust and salt and iron, and I gag as I swallow. He rips his arm away, and I cough, wanting to vomit. I feel spit and blood dribble down my chin as my teeth chatter.

"Why did I do that?" I ask, surprised that I can still find my voice.

"My blood will heal you," Kai snaps.

He doesn't look at me again before stripping down and running into the ocean water to wash off the blood of the demon that attacked me. I shake as I watch him. I take a deep, shuddering breath, feeling helpless, tired, and utterly afeared.

I drop my head into the sand, feeling the sting of my skin knitting back together. I cry openly, my chest heaving with fear and relief that I'm still alive.

Kai appears in the corner of my eye, shaking off the water and uttering profanities left and right. I suck in a breath, trying to steady my sobbing.

"What—what was that?" I stutter over my jagged breathing.

"A wild halvblod," Kai says flatly. His eyes are back to normal, looking particularly light grey now. Have his eyes always been grey? "They are vampires driven mad by their thirst. They will drink the blood of any living thing that crosses their path."

I force myself up into a sitting position, wincing at the lingering pain in my neck.

"Why didn't it feed on you?"

"It *tried*," Kai said, smirking. "I'm a Pureblood vampire, Astrid. I will always be stronger than halvblods."

His words came out bitter and harsh, and I flinch slightly at his tone. He stands and steps towards me, holding out the leather water canteen. I take it, looking up at him, but he's looking into the distance.

"Thank you," I whisper. Sipping on the water, I feel more than just gratitude for Kai.

There's a moment of silence as I drink, but then he whirls on me, his face fuming. "How could you do that?!"

"What?"

"Run away from me like that? You could have been killed!"

"I almost was!" I shout at him, a shocking amount of red-hot rage bursting through my chest. I push myself up to face him. "You think I was *looking* for that? That I wanted that?"

"Then why did you run? Why did you leave?"

"Because I was afraid!"

"Afraid of what?" he asks, his hands in the air and his face tightened with anger.

"I was afraid of *you*! How could you expect me to just believe that you are what you say you are? That you won't hurt me? After I'd seen all those images of hideous creatures coming at me again and again?!"

"Oh my God, Astrid, how can you ask me that? I've been running away from my thirst, *proving* myself good enough just to stand next to you, and you don't even care to notice!"

"Don't pin this on me! This isn't my fault!"

"Well, it's not mine either. Do you think I like being like this? That I like thirsting after your blood? I don't! And it's the hardest thing I've ever had to do to refrain from my basic fucking instinct!" he shouts, emphasizing each word strongly.

"Well you're doing a damn fine job pushing me away! All you've said since we've met is how disgusting vampires are. What do you expect me to do?"

"I don't expect you to think you can survive on your own!"

"How would you even know!?" I scream at him as adrenaline, fear, and anger boil together into my words. "You think you know what's best for me? What I even *want*?!"

I breathe heavily, and fire rages through my veins. His posture mimics mine, but he's taken completely aback like he'd never expected me to lash back out at him. He's standing with his body loose and heaving with deep breaths. His brows are furrowed like he's in pain, and he's half-turned toward me like he's torn between wanting to stay and wanting to run away.

In an instant, we both take quick, long steps toward one another, closing the space between us in a deep embrace, holding each other as closely as we can. I grab onto the back of his shirt, tugging him close to me as I bury my face in his chest. I sob against his shirt, staining it with salty, wet tears. His hands press against my lower back and my hair before pulling back and cupping my face in his hands, looking me all over to see if I'm alright before grabbing me against him again.

"Are you okay, are you okay?" he whispers over and over again.

I nod, unable to speak through my tears.

"I thought I'd lost you forever," he chokes. "I saw that thing attack you, and my heart jumped out of my chest."

"I'm okay," I manage.

"I'm so glad. Astrid, Astrid," he says, cupping my neck with his long fingers. I'm trembling as he runs his hands over my body, pressing every part of me against him.

"I'm so sorry, Kai," I wail. "I shouldn't have left. As soon as I woke up, I knew I had to come back to you. I remember, Kai. I remember."

"No, no," he sputters. "I shouldn't have pushed you so far away. I'm sorry, Astrid. I'm sorry."

He grips me tighter for a moment, then pulls back and tucks my face into his hands again. His eyes are glassy as they search my face.

"I remember everything. How you protected me, healed me. I remember you jumping out of the window just to keep yourself from feeding on me," I whisper quickly, the words flooding out of me. "I remember our conversation on the rooftop when you told me how you felt about me."

"I did," he says. "I *do*. Astrid, I feel so strongly for you. I care so much about you."

"I do too, Kai. I never said it back then because it didn't matter. But I'm telling you now."

"Astrid," he whispers, then pulls my face close to his, pressing his lips just briefly to mine.

"I'm sorry I left," I weep, unable to hold back my tears.

"I'm sorry I didn't chase after you. I stayed just long enough to see you were okay without me."

"But I'm not. I'm not okay without you," I cry.

"Then, I won't leave. I'll stay with you for as long as you need me," he declares.

I nod, feeling his hands on my neck drape back down onto my back.

"I'll walk with you and protect you. I'll make sure you're safe," he vows. "I won't let anything hurt you again."

I grab him and kiss him quickly, tasting dirt and ocean water on his lips. He hugs me against him, splaying his long fingers across my back. I move my mouth against his with reckless abandon, still feeling hysteria and adrenaline course through my veins. Tears pour from eyes, but not from fear. I'm overwhelmed and so grateful for Kai's vow of protection that I grip his shirt into my fists and pull him close to me as we kiss. Our lips lock in a silent expression and declaration of love to one another.

After a moment, he breaks off, leaving me breathless. He presses his forehead to mine as we breathe heavily in tandem.

"We should keep moving. There may be more than just the one," he whispers.

I nod, feeling lightheaded and electric from his touch. He loosens his grip on me, moving his body away, but grabbing my hand in his. I follow as he leads me forward once again. But this time, I'm not afraid.

23
KAI

I wipe my mouth with the back of my hand, feeling sticky black blood from the small fox I killed. The night is pitch black in the forest, and even though my eyes can't really see in the dark anymore, my nose and ears let me see everything. The wind breathes through the trees like a light guiding my every step, and Astrid's scent carries with it a path that I can follow back to her.

It's not a secret that she has changed. After she was attacked by the halvblod, she's barely said a word to me. She simply stuck to my arm as we walked. Every once and a while, I feel her shivering, even though it was noticeably warmer out. She twitches as she sleeps, shouting for help as the nightmares wrack her brain. It's pain-inducing, seeing her so helpless.

I've finally figured out what happened. I had been wracking my brain for why she had suddenly regained all her memories. She had blamed me for taking her happiness away, for making her see the truth, but I didn't know how that was possible. How could things have changed so suddenly?

Until I remembered what Alheri had told me before we escaped. She said that she "helped" her, that Astrid might not be the same woman when she awoke. When she said those words, I thought she meant when Astrid woke up from being healed that night, the night Caden had attacked her when she slept so silently until she woke when we were in the sewers. I had written off Alheri's words as nonsense. Astrid seemed fine to me.

Until now.

She *is* different. I just couldn't place the reason before. Whatever Alheri had done, it wore off, and the compulsion to serve withered away. Maybe it was the distance that we put between her and Alheri, I don't know. But how can I tell her the truth now? She was so mad at me for taking away her happiness, and now, things are okay between us. She's finally starting to see things clearly. How can I blame this all on her best friend, ripping away any sense of happiness and trust she might have left?

I pause. Astrid is several steps behind me, breathing loudly, and I know she needs rest, but that's not what stops me.

In the distance, just beyond the tree line, I see a small mountain range, with a plateau at the edge and a bright castle sitting just atop it. A dome surrounds the entire castle and bridge, gleaming like the sun, so bright that I have to shield my eyes.

Menneskelig.

It's breathtakingly beautiful, but I can't help but feel disappointed. This is the end of the line. We will reach the castle by the end of tomorrow night if we press on, and I'll have to say goodbye to Astrid.

My heart aches, and I turn to face her, just to see her notice the castle. A brief smile flashes across her face before she turns to me, and I can see my heartache mirrored in her eyes.

What will happen at the gates? Will they arrest me? Take me away and have me killed? It isn't a secret that I'm the crowned prince of their enemy. It also isn't a secret that my father attacked Menneskelig countless times when I was just a boy, up until the point where they had their witches put up the anti-vampire border. I've wondered time and time again whether it works or if it's simply a ruse.

But looking at it now, I can see that even if it isn't anti-magic or anti-vampire, some power of the sun is held there. I doubt I can pass through the border unscathed. It radiates even here, stinging my eyes if I look too long. That fact alone brings a slew of unanswered questions.

Should I leave Astrid outside the border to fend for herself? Should I say goodbye outside the city, hoping she can get in? Should I try and see her safely inside the gates? Will I be killed if I enter the city?

Astrid sits at my feet, obviously sick and unsteady, her eyes still fixed on the beautiful little domed castle. I watch her heave her breaths, ragged and tired. Her lips are chapped, and her eyes are drooping. There are long, deep shadows bruising the skin around her blue eyes, making her pale skin look stark and lifeless. She bends over to scratch the skin on her shins, and I can see her feet are covered in blisters. The veins on her legs are bruised a deep purple. She pulls on her braid, and I can see her hair has matted, looking all but impossible to untangle. As she leans limply against a tree, she struggles to keep herself upright, exhaustion pulling deeply at her eyes. The effects of prolonged travel are clear on her body.

No, I can't just leave her. I have to make sure she arrives safely inside the city.

"Astrid," I whisper, though I know she can hear me. "We have to keep moving. It's too early to rest. I could carry you if you'd like."

She looks up at me with her wide eyes. I once thought she had child-like eyes.

"That's okay, Kai. I can make it," she says, giving me a drooping smile.

Though it hurts to see her so weak, I'm glad she doesn't fight with me. Maybe she's just too weak to protest walking further. I'm too selfish to end the trip early. I want to spend as much time as I possibly can with her.

I hold out my hand for her, and she takes it, leaning heavily on me, her face only inches from mine. I'm surprised at my resilience, thirsty as I am. I note that her blood still sings to me, but my strength is peaked. I don't have the slightest urge to feed on her. Not since the attack.

So, we walk.

As the sun behind the clouds fades away. The castle remains a bright spot, illuminating everything surrounding it. It looks almost like the sunset I'd seen with Lilith and Alheri, so long ago now. It's hard to stare straight at the dome, with its shining iridescence, shimmering like oil on water. Even as we close the distance and the sun goes down completely, the city remains lit. That answers my most obvious question: the city is protected from vampires because they somehow remain under sunlight for the entire day.

Astrid whimpers slightly and leans heavily on me. I peer sideways at her, noting that her eyes are half-closed as she lets me guide her forward. I feel my lips twitch. It would be so much easier if she let me carry her. When we were just outside Livsnerven, I had considered just carrying her overnight to Menneskelig. The only thing that stopped me was the gash on her hand. I hadn't trusted my strength not to hurt her, but now, it would be easy to resist her. Almost like her blood is too weak to truly tempt me. That's when a thought crosses my mind.

With a frown, I sit Astrid down on the damp, sandy ground.

I hold my breath for good measure and look underneath the fabric binding on her neck. It's been days since she was attacked, and surely my blood should have healed her.

But instead of finding smooth pale skin, I find a shallow black wound on her neck, looking sticky with pus. I hiss softly.

It should have been healed for days now. I just hadn't taken the binding off.

In the distance, I hear a strangled howl, and my heart leaps into panic mode.

"Astrid, get up, now," I say quickly.

In an instant, she's wide-eyed and staring at me with pure fear in her eyes. I grab her up in my arms, curling her into a ball, and I launch into a full-on sprint. I feel the fire in my throat sting as my muscles work themselves into fatigue. I'm nowhere near as strong as I should be. I haven't fed properly in weeks.

Out of nowhere, I smack straight into a dark being, howling loudly. My body crashes into the halvblod in a sickening crunch, sending Astrid flying out of my arms. I hear her yelp, and the vampire turns away from me to Astrid with a vicious snap, unflinching and unhesitating.

"Astrid, run!" I scream, moving as quickly as I can to position myself in between the demon and her. I feel razor-sharp teeth sink deep into my shoulder, and I curse wildly.

I cringe away as the vampire draws my blood, kicking the heel of my foot into his gut. I feel him tear a hole into my arm as he whirls backward. I press my hand into the sticky, bloodied wound and jump hastily onto the demon, grabbing a fistful of his hair. I lock my hand on his head, and I tear into his neck with my own teeth. I kick his back to the ground and pull upwards on his hair as I rip his throat to shreds, tasting bitter, black blood in my mouth. In several seconds, I feel the head pull free from the body with a disgusting rip.

I spit out the bile and blood in my mouth like its poison

when I hear Astrid's strangled screams. I spin as fast as lightning. Two more vampires are on top of her. I shriek profanities into the sky as I charge towards them, seeing a brief streak of silver lightning beside me.

Ripping one of the demons off of Astrid, I hear her fall limply to the ground with a small thud. Before I can tear into the vampire, I see another man with wild silver hair shouting harsh Norwegian and ripping into the other halvblod. I lift my leg high and thrust my heel into the shoulder of my victim, slightly impressed at my own flexibility. Hearing bones crunch, I stomp onto the vampire's back, snapping his spine into two. I quickly tear the head off, using my foot to hold him down.

I don't wait to thank the silver-haired vampire for his help before rushing in a flash to Astrid, whose body is limp and lifeless underneath my arms. I quickly rip into my arm and press my blood to her unmoving lips, leaning my head down to hear her faint heartbeat grow weaker and weaker with each passing second.

"Get off her!" the silver-haired vampire yells, ripping me away from Astrid easily like I'm nothing more than just a twig.

I land on my feet, several steps away. I can see his body leaning over Astrid easily like his silver hair gives off its own light. I stop just long enough to feel my heart constrict wildly, remembering my rage when Caden fed on her.

"If you don't back away now, I will kill you," I growl, crouched low and already planning my attack.

"I will *not* leave her to be a pawn for you to feed on, *Prince*," the vampire hisses back.

He turns away from Astrid, and upon seeing my crouch, he curses in Norwegian and mimics my stance. His eyes are bloodshot but still bright and silver, not black. This is not a vampire looking for blood.

"*Faen*!" the silver-blood shouts.

My brain is split in half, listening intently to Astrid's dwindling heartbeat and circling with the vampire who has just proven to be equally strong or stronger than me.

"Who are you? How do you know who I am?" I yell. I can't keep myself from exploding.

"I watched you grow, Kai. Before I left the capital. You were raised by demons and—"

"What the fuck do you think I'm doing? I *left*," I scream. It's outrageous that I have to explain myself to anyone. "Look in my eyes and tell me what I am!"

In a flash, I'm held absolutely still in the strong grasp of the vampire, whose eyes are staring deep into mine. I'm met with a mirror image, except all color has been bleached away. Instead of raven black hair, he has bright, pearlescent locks, and his silver eyes search mine for the exact answer we are both looking for.

Neither of us has fed on a human in weeks, matching silver eyes as proof.

He lets me go in a huff, relaxing his stance just enough for me to sprint over to Astrid. Her breathing is low and wheezy, and she has gaping wounds pouring blood from her arms and neck. The demon halvblods were ruthless in their attack. But Astrid's original wound is still the worst looking by far.

I scream out profanities, cursing everything around me before the silver-blood is standing beside me.

"She needs to be healed, Prince," he says.

"I *tried*! I can't heal her. I don't know what's wrong. She's dying!" I shout at him, curling Astrid's head in my arms and pulling her into my chest.

My throat burns at the smell of her blood, but it's so weak that I know she'll be gone in a matter of moments. I drop my head and press my forehead into her dirty hair.

"I just wanted her to be safe! All I've accomplished is *killing* her! She's filthy and bleeding, and there's nothing I can do," I cry.

The silver-blood kneels and surveys the two of us, looking at Astrid's wounds with deep curiosity. I watch his eyes grow dark, and I pull Astrid away from him. Black, demon eyes, with pulsating veins throughout his face, darkening his pale skin. It's the sign of every hungry vampire.

"I see you've already tried to heal her," he says in a low voice, his pitch-black eyes fixed on me. He swallows quickly, and I watch the blackness fade away, peeling away from the silver irises below. I watch in awe as he sidesteps his thirst almost instantly. "You are weak, Kai. You should not have tried to heal her when your own blood is dying."

I shake, feeling Astrid grow cold in my arms.

"Please," I whisper. "If I cannot heal her, you must."

The vampire looks at me deeply; his expression is caustic and grim. His eyes blacken in a flash as he tears a hole into his wrist, red blood spurting forward. He presses his arm to Astrid's lips. For a moment, we simply sit there, the vampire's blood dripping into her mouth. Then, she simply exhales loudly. I hear her heart sputter, then stop.

I meet the vampire's gaze and watch him close his eyes and drop his head.

"No," I breathe. "No, no, no…"

"Come, Prince Kai. Take her in your arms and follow me. Quickly," he says.

I sit in stunned silence, Astrid's still body in my arms.

"*Now*!"

The silver-blood hoists me upright, and I spring into action, awkwardly curling Astrid's body into a ball against my chest. Her head lolls back and forth as we run. I follow the man closely, noting how dark and oppressive the forest is around us. We run for several minutes at top speed before I see two dim lights ahead, one much brighter than the other.

"That's Menneskelig up ahead," the vampire shouts back. "And next to it, Gamvik Tavern. We'll be going there."

I can't think. I can't even breathe. I simply follow the man with blind instincts. If Astrid is gone…

I can feel how rigid and cold Astrid's body is becoming. Is that simply due to the frozen air all around us…or is it something else? My breath catches into my throat in a hysterical cry. I quickly press forward, hot on the tails of the silver-haired vampire ahead of me.

"Stop, please," I cry. "I can't go on. She's dead. She's dead."

I fall, hearing my knees thud against the ground instead of feeling the impact. Astrid sprawls out from my arms, her head rolling to the side before her chest hits the dirt. In the darkness, I see her limp body, her arms bent in horrific ways. Her braid lays tangled in the brush, leaves and twigs in the matted strands. Her eyes are bruised, and her nose looks broken, dried blood streaking her chin. Her lips are stained with the silver vampire's blood, a clearly failed attempt at healing her.

"You can't be dead!" I scream to the air, gripping tightly to her shoulders.

Her skin looks stark white, as though her life has completely left her body. She's cold under my touch. I hiccup and cry, squeezing Astrid's shoulders and moving my hands to cup her head. I press my forehead to hers, feeling my tears drip down my nose to stain her cheeks.

"Please, wake up," I whisper desperately.

I look at her for a long time, seeing nothing but still flesh.

"Wake *up*!" I scream to the sky and slam my fists onto her chest.

The jolt spreads through Astrid's body, and she jerks awake with a giant, screeching breath. I scramble forward, screaming and crying and laughing hysterically, pulling her close to my chest. Sounds of strangled joy and horror escape my lips, and I can feel the other vampire watching us from a distance.

I can hear her heart thudding out of sync in her chest, but it's loud and strong. Her eyes are blind and wide, searching the darkness. I don't understand how this is possible, but I'm too hysterical to speak. This silver vampire's blood must have saved her.

"Prince, we must bring her to safety. They are still all around us. She is not safe," the silver-blood says.

I scoop the wild and confused Astrid into my arms and press onward with renewed energy. Not only has Astrid essentially come back from the dead, but she's also brought me back with her. I feel my chest explode with happiness, fear, and anxiety all at the same time.

She is gasping and crying and shivering in my arms as we run, but she's alive. She's *alive.* I breathe easy, wiping away the stream of tears from my face.

I sigh gratefully when I see the tavern at the bottom of the cliffside, lit up by the castle's dome but still dark in the night. Astrid is curled against my chest, breathing jaggedly.

"Astrid, look ahead," I say, breathing and knowing that she's able to respond to me.

I nod towards the tavern that seems only a few paces away now. Her eyes are woozy, but she sees the little hut with smoke coming from the chimney and a tear escapes her eyes. Her lips are chapped, and as she smiles, blood seeps through the cracks. I wipe away the bead of blood, and she meets my eyes briefly, and though she can barely move, her eyes say a million things. My heart swells.

As we step up to the tavern, I notice it's larger than I expected. As I guessed from the silver-blood's description, the place is crawling with both vampires and humans, chatting away over campfires. There is a stable with horses and large feeding troughs. Chickens and pheasants peck at the ground, and there's a handful of other wildlife grazing the thin grass beside the building. Workers roam in and out of the tavern, holding rakes and pales, chatting idly with one another. My jaw drops when I notice that they are not just human workers. Silver-eyed vampires walk amongst them, looking almost indistinguishable from the humans, working right alongside them. I smile wistfully, feeling at peace in this place. It looks like it's a breeding ground for equality between humans and vampires.

As I approach the door of the tavern, Astrid whimpers weakly in my arms.

"Hey!" A few large men approach us. "No feeding allowed on the premises. Take your human and leave."

The silver-blood steps in-between the guard and I defensively and says, "*De har det bra, venn.*"

"*Han er en pureblod. Hvordan kan du stole på ham?*" the guard hisses. His eyes flick between the silver-haired vampire, Astrid, and me.

"*Stol på meg, da.*"

The guard eyes the silver-blood warily.

"I'm not here to feed," I say with conviction. "This is Astrid. She's not *my* human. She's just a girl in need of food and water and rest. We've traveled very far."

The biggest of the group looks me up and down, squinting at our ragged and bloodied appearance, but after a moment, he grunts loudly and nods for his group to let us through.

"Thank you," I say softly, meeting the eye of the gatekeeper. I nod to the silver-blood, pushing past him into the warm room. Astrid moans softly next to me as we enter the fire-lit building, smelling smoke and food. I could cry. It looks absolutely perfect.

I move with Astrid over to the main bar, and the host eyes me suspiciously. I explain to him the same as with the guards outside. His eyes widen at my story, but he quickly grabs a pale of water and runs to the kitchens to grab her some food.

When he returns, he has meats and bread and water for Astrid and a cup of blood for me. I look at him curiously.

"We serve both human and vampire. Don't worry," the man says. He points at Astrid's plate. "The blood is from the animal her meat came from."

I nod at him and down the blood, tasting notes of lamb and wood and feeling insanely grateful for this place. I feel my body shiver as the drink hits my stomach. I grumble pleasantly. I start helping Astrid with her food and water, and after a few moments, I find her struggling so hard with her food that I look around for something else. She can barely open her eyes. The bartender watches me struggle and then appears with a glass of milk, nodding at me. Astrid sips gingerly on the milk, moaning gratefully. I smile at the bartender, searching my pockets for money, but the man grabs my hand.

"We don't accept money here. You eat, drink, sleep, but you gotta work for it," he says in a gruff, low voice. "When you're done here, we have jobs for you in the back."

"Let me do her work for her. She's too weak for labor," I ask. The man squints back and forth between us but nods before returning to his work. I sigh graciously. I watch the silver-blood sit on my other side, but my attention is quickly pulled back to Astrid.

When she's finished her milk and drank all of her water, she leans limply against the wall. I throw her arm over mine and half-drag her to the empty bedroom that the bartender points us to. I lie her down on the bed, peeling off her cloak and tattered fabric shoes before returning my eyes to her face. She's instantly relaxed and slack as she falls deeply asleep. I sigh heavily, sitting down on the chair adjacent to the bed.

We are safe.

24

ASTRID

Nightmares swirl together, and I can see only darkness. My skin pinches and stings as I feel ghosts of teeth tear through me. My bones feel heavy like lead, breaking under the weight that keeps pulling me under. I try to open my eyes, to wake up because surely, I must be dreaming. All this pain and suffering can't be real.

My ribs are sore, and it hurts to breathe too deeply, almost like I've been hit squarely in the chest by a large boulder. I try and blink, realizing that my eyes are open, but I can't see anything. I'm frozen. I can't move my arms or legs, and it feels like an invisible force is holding me down. I open my mouth and try to speak, but only wisps and breathy air comes out. My heart races as panic sets in.

Where am I? I can't remember anything. The last thing I remember was walking with Kai and stopping to get some water. I remember feeling tired and sore, but nothing afterward. Had I passed out and was taken away from Kai? Could we have been separated somehow? I wrack my brain trying to remember something, *anything*, that might remind me of what had happened.

I open my mouth again and try to scream for Kai, but my voice is trapped in my throat, leaving my helpless in the dark. I blink, feeling wetness seep into my eyelashes. I have to be awake, right?

"Astrid?" a voice calls in the darkness. I try to say something, but I'm stuck. "Astrid, it's okay, I'm here."

Kai. That must be Kai.

Suddenly, Kai strikes a match, lighting the whole room, blinding me momentarily. He lights two candlesticks at each end of the small room, dousing the walls in a warm, flickering light.

I turn my head, and magically, the paralysis fades away. I sit up quickly, rubbing my sore arms and legs, sighing gratefully that I can move again.

"What happened? I could barely breathe," I whisper, parched from my slumber.

I look around, noticing that we're in an actual room, a *furnished* room, and I'm sitting on a comfortable yet economic bed. The room is plain, with stone walls and a simple clay brick flooring. I run my hands along the mattress, feeling familiar wool bedding.

"We were attacked," Kai says, sitting next to me on the bed. "You were badly hurt, but luckily we had help. A Silver-Blood came and healed you. Then, he brought us here."

"Where are we?" I murmur, still feeling lightheaded.

"Gamvik Tavern, I think he called it. It's right outside of Menneskelig," he says.

I nod, my hand pressing against my chest. I feel sick and stale and dirty, sweat starting to bead across my forehead.

"Don't worry. We're perfectly safe here," he clarifies.

"How do you know?"

"Well, for one, there are about twenty people outside this room," he says with a soft smile. "There are both humans and vampires, but no feeding is allowed on the premise. It's the perfect place for us."

I bob my head up and down, not knowing what to say.

"We're safe, Astrid," he says, reaching for my hands. I let him cup my cold hands in his. I meet his gaze, seeing that he's relaxed and unconcerned. His silver eyes are wide, and he looks much less haggard.

"We're safe?" I ask breathily.

"Yes. We made it," he says, smiling wider.

I hiccup a small breath and fall into his arms, feeling my chest heave with joy. I feel him wrap his arms around me, pulling me into his chest. All my anxiety and fear is washed away almost instantly. No longer will we have to wade through thick snow or bathe in streams. We won't have to starve through most of the day, exhausted from the constant walking. We're finally here. Menneskelig.

The thought both thrills me and makes me slightly nauseous. I don't want to think about what happens next. Not if we are going to part from one another.

"I can't believe it," I say instead. "I can't believe we walked across the entire island."

"I know. I can barely believe it myself. And this place is wonderful. They have food and rooms and ale, just like you like."

"And for you?" I ask hesitantly.

"Animal blood," he says with a relieved smile as he lays his cheek on my head. He's so happy, it's infectious.

"Wow," I breathe.

"And you're safe. We're safe."

"You said we were attacked? What happened?" I ask, pulling away to look at him squarely.

"We had stopped for a moment when I heard a halvblod howl. I picked you up and started to run, but they were too quick and caught up to us. Three vampires. They were hellbent on getting to you. I fought one off on my own, but I couldn't fight off all three. Thankfully, a silver-blood came and fought off the rest with me. He was the one who healed you."

"You didn't heal me?" I ask with a furrowed expression.

"No," he says, his face tightening in a small grimace. "My blood can't heal you. Not anymore."

"Why?"

He looks away from me with a thoughtful expression. "I don't know. The silver-blood said something about my blood dying."

"Dying?!"

He surprises me by laughing. "Don't worry about me, Astrid. It would take a lot for me to be killed."

"What do you mean?"

"Someone would have to get close enough to sever my head from my body. And, as a pureblood, I'm stronger than almost any animal. Except maybe the wolves."

"What did he mean by your blood, though?" I ask, grabbing for his hands. I can't lose Kai, not after everything we've been through.

"I'm not sure." He brushes a stray hair from my face. "Look at you, all worried."

"Of course, I'm worried!"

He pauses for a moment, his eyes trailing over my face. His skin is golden in the firelight, and his black hair curls around his jawline and ears. I can't help but squeeze his hand, feeling an uncontrollable desire to never be parted from him.

"After the silver-blood first healed you, your heart stopped beating," Kai says, looking down at our hands. "We ran to try to get you some help, but it was too late. You died."

"What?" I breathe.

"I thought I'd lost you," he chokes. "You weren't moving,

you weren't breathing. But somehow, you pulled through. I swear, I've never been so happy in my life."

"Oh, Kai," I wail, throwing my arms around him.

I feel him shake as he pulls me close again. I pet his hair and rub my hands across his back, feeling him do the same. One of his hands cups the back of my neck, and the other presses against the small of my back. His breaths are jagged as he nuzzles his forehead into the crook of my neck. I feel more tears spill over my cheeks as we embrace one another, elated that we're together, safe and sound.

I pull away, wanting to see his face. His eyes and the smile on his lips are soft. I reach out to touch his face, and he grabs my hand, pressing his lips to my palm. His eyes are glassy, and a small tear breaks out of the side of his eye. He closes his eyes and takes a deep breath through his nose. My heart throbs as I feel his chest expand. My own lungs feel like fluttering butterflies.

I trace the side of his face with my fingertips, noting how different he looks than when I first met him. This Kai is more rugged, stronger even, and his lanky body shows stronger muscle through his shirt. My fingers brush over his jaw and down his long neck, stopping just above the opening of his shirt.

When I look back to his eyes, I see him staring at my lips. My eyes flick down to his, finding that his mouth is open just slightly, and I can feel his breath on the skin of my arm. I lean forward, almost unconsciously, driven by a strong desire to kiss him. When he notices my movement, he looks back into my eyes, searching my face for something.

"What are you thinking?" I whisper and can almost feel his sharp intake of breath.

"How badly I want to kiss you right now," he sighs longingly.

"Then, kiss me, Kai."

With a winning half-smile, he leans forward, closing his eyes as he brushes his lips against mine. I slowly twist my hands into his hair, feeling my heart race underneath my ribs. I breathe easily as Kai pulls me closer and closer to him, kissing me softly all over my entire face. This kiss, unlike the others, is unrestrained. It's joyful. Ecstatic. We're drinking in one another's presence, moving against each other with abandon. We've never been allowed to be this close to one another before.

I untie the lace at his neck, seeing his collarbone peek through. I trace my fingers across his chest and feel him shiver with pleasure. His hands sit at the tops of my hips, and I can feel his grip tighten on me, just slightly. I search his face, memorizing the lines underneath his silver eyes. I watch as his hair tangles across his forehead and curls behind his ears in gentle waves.

His neck muscles tighten as he reaches his lips up to mine again, pressing against my chin, my cheeks, and my nose. He trails the bridge of his nose across my jaw, making my body ache to be against his. Unable to help myself, I lean down and catch his lips with mine again, running the tip of my tongue tenderly across his bottom lip. He slides his hands up my back and opens his palms, laying them flat against my shoulder blades. I make a warm sound in my throat. He moves his mouth in sync with mine, and I watch as his long, black eyelashes spread out across his high cheekbones.

After a few moments, I shift my legs to the side, and gravity pulls us down toward the bed. Our lips part, but our bodies stay pressed against one another as I face away from him. He lays beside me, stroking my arm, my hair, my cheeks. Before I realize, Kai starts humming softly, lulling me back into a deep sleep, safe and warm within Kai's strong arms.

25
KAI

I could lay here for hours.

Astrid's heart thrums between my arms, and though my arousal has long faded, I'm left with a reassuring feeling of completeness as she sleeps peacefully in my arms. Her face is soft and serene as she lightly snores, her breath playing gently on my chest. The candles are slowly fading into darkness, but light starts to trickle in through the foggy glass window near the ceiling. Grey light seeps into the room, awakening the colors again. I watch as the orange light from the candle fades away, leaving only Astrid's hair a warm golden-red.

I inhale, closing my eyes and smiling at the beautiful scent of Astrid's honeysuckle smell. After so long, I expected the scent to fade or for me to become desensitized, but since she was attacked and I almost lost her forever, my search for her aroma has been unquenchable. Nothing is more enticing to me than Astrid's strong and vibrantly colored fragrance.

After weeks of only the tiniest portions of blood, last night's meal was intoxicating. My powers have come back almost fully, and I can hear the main room come to life outside. Even though I could lie here and soak in these precious moments with Astrid forever, I feel duty call. I pull my arm gingerly away from underneath her head. She shifts away from me, curling into a small ball. I lay the blanket over her and hear her hum softly as she stretches back out. I smile, petting her braid back behind her neck again before re-lacing my shirt and walking out of the room.

After several moments, I find myself starving. I look around the room, seeing yawning faces and tired eyes. There's a large hearth in the middle of the room with cast iron pots and kettles lined across it on a solid iron rod. The place smells of cedar and the musky scents of ale and smoked meats. I grin as I warm my hands against the fire.

My eyes meet roam around the room for a moment before I see the Silver-blood from the night before sitting quietly at the bar. I sit next to him, grabbing some water on my way. The host greets me and hands me a mug filled with blood.

"Thank you," I say. The bartender nods gruffly before turning away to continue his sweeping. "What is your name, *sølvblod*? I'm grateful for your help last night," I say, turning to the bright silver-haired vampire. "We wouldn't have survived without you."

"*Sølvblod*? Only one other has called me that," he says, smiling widely. "My name is Brynjar."

"Well, thank you. I am forever indebted to you."

"Nonsense. I would kill those demons regardless. You hold no debt to me, *Nikolaj*."

I freeze at the sound of my full name.

"You know an awful lot about me, Brynjar," I whisper. "How is it that you know all my secrets, and I've only just met you?"

"I know many things," he says quietly. "A name is a powerful tool. Say the wrong thing, and you might have a stampede on your hands."

"Aren't you Kai? Crowned Prince of Livsnerven?" someone asks from behind us. I quickly duck behind my hair, letting it shroud my face in darkness.

"My point exactly," Brynjar says, a smile in his voice.

"Kai?" another voice, a woman's, says weakly. "Kai?!" she says again, and this time I recognize it. I look up, trying to find the voice, and spot a vampire with long brown hair and damp, brown eyes hurtling towards me.

"Lilith?" I ask incredulously. She's sobbing and hugging me so tightly that I can hardly breathe, but I know it's her. I pry her off of me and notice the glassiness of her eyes and the redness in her cheeks. She's been crying. "Lilith, hey, what is it?"

"Oh God, Kai, oh God!" she wails again, gripping tightly onto my shoulders. She looks like she's going to collapse.

"What's going on?" I ask, more urgently now. What is this about? "Hey, hey," I coo.

"God, I'm sorry. I can't hold myself together for even a second," she says, her brown hair tangling in her neck and clothes. "It's good to see you."

"Yeah," I breathed. "You too, *Liljen*."

Lilith makes a whimpering sound as she grabs onto my arm, regaining her balance.

"What's going on?"

"Oh, you know," her voice cracks, and she utterly avoids the question. "What are you doing here? Wasn't your coronation like two weeks ago?"

I give her an expression, and realization shows plainly on her face.

"Oh," she whispers. "You ran."

I nod, remembering a conversation with her that feels like a million lifetimes ago when we were still children. She had told me she was running away, and I cried for hours on end, begging her to stay. She wanted to live free from human killing. I remember telling her that I would leave the first chance I had because I couldn't imagine my life without my best friend. My only friend.

"Well then," she says, sniffling.

"I grabbed Astrid the first chance I got and left," I explain, biting down from expelling the whole story. There are still people watching us. If I had any hope of keeping my identity a secret, that's completely ruined now.

"Astrid is here?"

I nod, pointing to our room. Lilith's expression is a mix of shock and disbelief. "I'm taking her to Menneskelig," I explain.
She considers this before someone calls her name. She looks back, and I can see an abandoned broom and dustpan on the floor.

"*Pureblod*," a harsh voice calls to me. "Time to work."

I nod at the guard before turning back to Lilith. Before I can say anything, she waves me off with a smile.

"Go," she says. "I'm paying off my own debt. I'll be here when you get back."

I nod at her, pulling her in tightly for a hug before she huffs a short laugh and pushes me off. I smile and walk off with the man who called me.

The large man leads me out into the stables, handing me a large rake and trowel, indicating that I should clean the soiled hay from the stalls and shovel coals into the large fire. There are several large dutch ovens hoisted above the flames, with various soups and meals being prepared. I smell loaves of bread inside the cast iron. That's an inventive way to bake when you don't have an oven.

Lilith. I smile, shaking my head. I can't believe that I've run into her here, of all places. She was a sight for sore eyes. I grab my tools and look around, still shaking my head in astonishment. This place is a godsend.

I start shoveling and raking, listening to the gentle breathing of the large horses inside the stalls. They face me with deep, intelligent eyes, contained by a simple wooden gate. The larger horse is a deep russet brown with a long, black mane, wild-looking and tangled. I reach out to touch the animal's long nose, and at first, he rears backward with a low grunt. I look into his eyes for a moment, hoping he will see and understand that I mean him no harm. Then, he presses his muzzle to my fingers. His nose is soft and warm, with little whiskers poking out. I smile briefly, feeling the breath of the animal blow through my fingertips.

With a heavy reverence, I take my hand away from the horse and work on my chores, listening closely to the heartbeats of the two horses, like a drum-song accompanying my work. I've never had to do chores like this in my entire life. I never even thought about the work that went into food preparation and travel accommodations. Back at Feilfri, I had my choice of food, clothes, bedding, books, anything and everything. My mother was a gracious host and provided everything for me. I only realize now that not only did my family use humans for their blood but also for their labor as well.

"You certainly know how to wield a pitchfork," Brynjar calls from the opening with a low laugh in his voice.

I huff a laugh, eyeing him before awkwardly shoveling another set of coals onto the low fire. Despite the chore, it feels good to have the warm fire against my skin.

"I suppose this is my first time doing chores," I admit.

"No matter. You're doing your duty, and that's what matters."

"It's the thought that counts? That's good enough?" I reply, setting down the trowel and picking up the rake.

"Precisely. Though I figured you might use some company.

And this," he says, handing me a large mug of ale. I smile, taking it and nodding to him.

"I could, thank you."

I swish the drink in between my gums, savoring the taste before returning to rake the soiled hay.

"I wanted to thank you again," I continue awkwardly, watching Brynjar sit next to the fire, peeking into the pots. "For saving Astrid and me. We would not have made it without your help."

"Don't mention it," he says. "It was a pleasure to rip the halvbod in half."

"You've fought before," I say.

"Yes. Many times. You might say I was raised fighting," he says.

I look over him. His arms are covered in thick, braw muscle. His skin is light, though tainted with dirt and blood.

"Were you in the war? Fighting with my father?" I ask tentatively. Conversing about the war between humans and vampires, some fifty-odd years ago, is always a touchy topic.

Brynjar surprises me by laughing.

"No, my prince. I did not fight alongside your father," he says, combing through his silver hair with his fingers. "I did not live in Livsnerven at that point in my life."

"How old are you then?"

"I think I'm probably nineteen or twenty," he says. I nod, thinking briefly that he has only been alive for maybe eight human years longer than I have. Though, that didn't really matter to vampires. We only "aged" every four years. One vampire year to four human years. I had once complained about the complexity, but as I grew to see the maturation of humans alongside, say, my brother, I understood clearly.

Humans matured every year. Vampires only learned and matured every four years. I slowly figured out that humans grew at a faster rate than vampires because they feared for their life. Evolution had conditioned humans to mature quickly, so they could survive. I had often wondered what would happen if vampires didn't exist.

"You think? You don't know your age?" I ask, ignoring my unkempt thoughts.

"Not precisely. I didn't grow up in the traditional sense. I don't know my mother or father," he says. My eyebrows shoot up in surprise, and he laughs softly. "I did not grow up in the kingdom."

"Then where? Surely you didn't grow up here."

"No, not here," he says, considering. I wonder if he's questioning whether he can trust me. "Eighty years ago, this place did not exist. Gamvik Tavern was created by several abstinent vampires, seeking to bind themselves together after fleeing from *your* father."

"I can understand that," I say sourly.

"I grew up across the river, in the mainlands," he says, ignoring my comment. "Though, I was not raised among vampires."

We're sitting now, speaking softly and drinking our ale. I can't place why, but I feel at ease next to Brynjar.

"I was cast out of Feilfri castle as a fledgling. I was barely a child when Baldassare found out my mother had slept with a lesser vampire, my father. Being of noble blood, she completely denied any knowledge of his heritage. She claimed he lied to her, impersonating a noble. Baldassare allowed her to start again if she severed all ties to me and my father."

Sour bile stings the back of my throat. I know I'm not thirsty, but the bitterness in my mouth feels like acid.

"So, she did. Baldassare killed my father and threw me into the forest. Of course, I didn't know what was happening at all. At that stage in my growth, all I could see was a red throbbing everywhere, simply following my instincts. Where there was a pulse of blood, I ran to it."

"How did you end up in the mainland?" I ask, my tone flat.

"I swam there," he says, eyeing me, his silvers eyes like daggers. "I heard singing across the water, so pure that I could not help but follow. When I arrived back on land, I realized that I was hearing the blood song of a fierce group. The *ulver*. The wolves."

I feel my face go slack at the words. The blood leaves my cheeks.

Brynjar laughs at my not-so-subtle response.

"Don't worry. As you can see, I am still alive," Brynjar says. "Of course, at the time, I didn't know what they were. I simply saw the blood pumping in their veins, and I was severely malnourished. I hadn't fed in days while swimming across the ocean. I attacked as soon as I saw them. Their large arteries looked like rivers of blood, just waiting for me."

He pauses to drink his ale. Whether to keep me in suspense or for dramatics, either way, I have to conceal my huff of irritation.

"Upon sinking my teeth into one of the animals, the rest had pinned me down, instantly clamping their snouts onto my legs and arms. They didn't kill me, though. They just wounded me enough to see them in their real forms as opposed to simple blood bags. They were *massive*. The largest wolves—the largest *animals* I'd ever seen. The largest was pure white, a stunning creature. He became my father."

I choke on my ale.

"What?!"

"Yes, Kai, it is as you hear it. I was raised to maturity by the pack of wolves known as the *Hvit Ulver*. The White Wolves," he says.

The thought of the silver-haired vampire fighting alongside a pack of enormous white wolves is an image I can hardly process. Braw muscle clothed in silver hair, sprinting across a snowy cliffside. I let my eyes search his scarred face for a moment, trying to unwrap my thoughts.

"I can see you have many questions," he says, calmly. "Be

advised, Prince. I do not share this information with just anyone."

"Why me?"

"I have a sixth sense, if you will, that I developed in my time with the wolves. I can sense…*things* about others. Whether they are a threat, whether they are in need, or whether they are lost. In your case, Prince, I can sense many things about you. Most notably, you are someone I can trust. I feel comfortable sitting here with you. I don't feel that way around most people."

So, it hadn't just been me.

"Interesting indeed," I say, my thoughts spinning out of control.

Brynjar chuckles.

"I suppose there's really only one question that sticks out amongst the rest," I say. "Why did you leave the pack?"

"There wasn't any particular reason. I simply grew to understand that I was different than my wolf brothers. I realized that when we tore into other animals, my brothers longed for the flesh and meat. I drank the blood. When my brothers fought, they fought with skills other than my own. And when it came to my maturation, my brothers went to mate with other wolves, where I could not.

"So, I left. I found my way back to Livsnerven and tried to live there for a time. It is where I watched you grow with your brother, Caden. I tried to live in the city for almost a full year before I realized I was too different from the other vampires. I struggled, realizing that I could not find a home with my wolf family, nor could I find a home between members of my own race," Brynjar says quietly. "That's when I found your friend Lilith."

"You know her?"

"Yes," he says with a sly smile. "She visited Livsnerven once, meeting several of her friends. I knew she was different instantly. She did not smell like a vampire. I questioned her, and she introduced me to other vampires who sought to live like me - only feeding on animals for sustenance. We all left Livsnerven together one day and came here."

I nod slowly, putting the pieces of Lilith's journey together. After she left me, she wandered, and somewhere along the way, she had found a group of people to confide in. Somehow, she had thrived.

"Continue your work, Kai. We can talk more of the kingdoms of blood another time," Brynjar says, standing tall. His hair swishing around him like silver silk as he turns towards the bar.

I sigh and continue working throughout the rest of the day, my mind on thoughts of wild wolves and fearless vampires.

When I walk back into the tavern, Lilith is already sitting at a long table with a horn of ale. She's chatting lightly with Brynjar before I see her notice me. Brynjar nods to me, then leaves, grabbing a mop from the corner. I watch him with new eyes as he performs the simple task of bussing and cleaning tables before wiping them down with soap and water.

"There you are," Lilith says, as I sit next to her. She offers me a mug filled with a warm, bubbly liquid. I tap my mug against hers before sipping on the bitter drink. "I was wondering what was taking you so long."

"I didn't really know how to feed the horses," I confess. "Apparently, there's some sort of feeding trough?"

She huffs a short laugh before downing her ale.

"Why are you here, Lilith?" I ask, getting straight to the point. She looks distraught and uncomfortable, even though last I spoke with her, she was so excited about getting back to Menneskelig. "I thought you were trying to live amongst the humans."

"I was," she says, tucking a long straight of her brown hair behind her eyes. "I left."

"What happened?"

"Oh, you know," she says, with a break in her voice. She looks down at her hands, twiddling her thumbs for a few moments before I reach across the table and grab her fingers.

Lilith's face contorts into anguish in front of my eyes, and her cheeks and eyes turn red with pain. She keels over, a sound of sadness pushing through her lips. She hoists herself up to face me, looking me dead in the eye.

"I killed him," she says before falling, sobbing, into my arms.

"What do you mean? Killed who?" I ask fervently, stroking the top of her hand with my thumb. I see Brynjar give me a meaningful look, but he goes back to mopping the stone floor. I know he can probably still hear her, but he turns away regardless.

"I killed William, Kai. I killed him. I couldn't help myself."

"*What*?" I exhale but stop myself from making a retort when I see Lilith all but keel over. She's hyperventilating. "You need to take a breath," I tell her, feeling the hysteria rolling off of her. She's clutching the table like it's the only thing tethering herself to this world. She looks past me like I'm not even there. "Lilith, hey, tell me what happened."

Her eyes flick to mine, and I can see she's haunted. Not in the same way that Astrid had been after the first halvblod attack. She had looked like a victim. Lilith looks haunted in a wholly different way. I already know the outcome of this story.

Lilith was the predator.

"It's not what you think," Lilith breathes, probably guessing at my assumptions.

"Tell me," I press, softly.

"Oh boy." She takes a shaky breath. "You know William was human." She pauses, tears rolling past her eyelashes. "God. *Was*."

"It's okay, Lilith. It's okay," I try to help.

"It's not. It's not okay." She huffs a loud sigh before continuing, "Will was, well, he was my true love. I'm convinced of that."

The shock must be apparent on my face because she smiles sadly at me.

"He was human, and I made the mistake of falling in love with him," she continues. "It's like the cardinal rule not to, but I did anyway."

"How did you meet? How did you even get that close?"

"We went to school together," she admits. A look of realization washes over my face. "Yeah, you remember our last conversation? With Alheri? William was the guy I was talking about." She pauses, drinking a large swig of ale as the bartender brought us more. "You know, I lived inside the city walls for a long time. Of course, I couldn't go out in the daylight without protection, but the shade from the buildings and passageways were plenty of protection. The border is *like* the sun, but not as strong."

She's rambling, but I don't say anything.

"I don't know how it happened, but Will somehow made his way under my skin, and eventually, I couldn't resist him. His blood called to me, his voice, his eyes. I couldn't stay away. Of course, it wasn't surprising that he fell for me. *Faen.*" She hikes a deep breath. "Like the goddamn predator I am, everything about me pulled him in. My looks, my eyes, my gracefulness. Ugh! Eventually, I gave in. Our lives intertwined, and he found out what I am. I thought that would be the end of it. I thought he would turn me in, and I'd never see him again. Now, I honestly wish that would have happened."

She drops her head into her hands, stamping her feet under the table. My heart aches for her.

"He wanted me to change him, Kai. He wanted to turn," she says through her teeth.

I fall back into my chair, understanding now the implications of her words. Changing a human to a vampire is extremely difficult, and that's why most vampires seek to keep their bloodline pure through natural conception. The process of changing a human entails replacing every drop of human blood with vampire blood. The human has to drink a vampire's blood at the same time as the vampire drains away the human blood. The process has to be slow so that the vampire blood can transform the body and blood it replaces. Most vampires can't go that slow. I assume that's where Lilith failed.

"I killed him," she chokes the words. "I couldn't do it. He wanted to change so badly, and how could I refuse him? I wanted to be with him forever too. I foolishly agreed to the change. We planned everything out. I even set up countermeasures to protect him, but it didn't work. My strength failed me the minute I tasted his blood."

"I can understand," I say huskily, eyeing Astrid's room momentarily.

"I should have left. I should have never stayed with him. I had so many opportunities to leave, Kai. My strength failed me the minute he said hello." Her face is buried in a million emotions as she says the words. Her eyes are hollow like her life has been sucked away.

In the distance, I see Astrid sneak out of the room, searching the space for me. I wave to her, and she smiles brightly, leaving my heart writhing inside me. She starts to make her way over to us, and Lilith quickly hikes in a deep breath and brushes away her tears.

As I watch Astrid approach us, I can't help but mirror Lilith's experience to my own. How many times have I had ample opportunity to leave Astrid? To say my goodbyes. Even now, I could walk away from her, and she would be safe. My head drops, and I'm staring at the floor, feeling like dirt because I know I can't leave her. Not now. Not after everything we've just endured. One day, maybe soon, I'll be able to walk away. I have to.

"Astrid," I breathe, my heart inflating as she lays her hand on my shoulder. I gesture toward Lilith. "You remember my friend, from back at Feilfri? This is Lilith."

"Yes," she says, nodding politely. "I didn't expect we'd see you here."

"Neither did I," Lilith says with a fake smile. I see her façade quickly start to fade, so I turn Astrid toward me, giving Lilith room to pull herself together.

"Why don't you find some food? I'm sure the bartender will scrounge something up for you. The ale is delicious, by the way," I say, holding her attention.

"Okay, that sounds good. What will you be doing?"

"I just finished cleaning to pay for our room. I'm almost done here with Lilith. I'll come to join you in just a moment," I say.

Astrid nods, then turns her eyes once more to Lilith, then back to me. I nod to her, and she walks away, back toward the bar, where I watch the host pour her a drink and ladle some sort of soup into a bowl for her. I let out a sigh before swiveling back toward Lilith.

"What's your story, then?" she asks, eyes darting back and forth between Astrid and me.

I pause. Lilith knew about Astrid before, and I can see in her eyes that she's already guessed plenty about my reason for abandoning my kingdom.

"Why did you leave Feilfri?" she asks, pressing lightly. I glance at her, watching her grip the table. She's looking for a distraction, and I can't say I blame her.

"Honestly? Caden attacked Astrid. Ripped a hole in her throat right in front of me, and I just about killed him," I admit, watching her eyes widen.

"You bested Caden? But you don't drink from humans?" she asks, surprised.

"No, I don't. By all means, he was stronger than me in every way. But something came over me, and I went blind with rage. It overtook every sense. Even with her blood everywhere, I couldn't do anything but attack him."

I look over to Astrid, peering back at me from her stool. My heart lurches for her, to go to her.

"That's what love does, though. I think," I continue.

"It's a dangerous game, Kai. Loving a human," she says, her voice vacant of sympathy. "Don't make the same mistake I did."

"How could I leave her, though?" I finally admit aloud.

"I know. Believe me, I know," she replies.

"But she's changed now. She's so strong and resilient. Before we got here, I thought I lost her. She was *dead.* Even if it was only for only a few minutes," I say, hearing my voice crack and the breath get trapped in my chest. "But she came back to me. Somehow she's alive. I can't leave her. Not now. Not yet."

I hang my head, feeling so lost.

"But...she's been so hurt by vampires. I think that maybe..." I pause. "Maybe she loves me. Maybe she wants to be with me. But how could she overlook what I am? What I've done? I can't stay with her. Maybe for a little while, but certainly not forever."

"I'm sorry," Lilith says, reaching for my hand. I squeeze it tightly, feeling grateful that someone knows my struggle. It feels like a glimmer of peace amongst the torture and torment.

"It's for the best." I clear my throat. "I'll say goodbye in a few days, and then I don't know. We'll both be free, I guess."

"Yeah," she sighs, nodding.

"You know the castle then?" I ask after a moment. "Can you help me get her to safety?"

She nods, not meeting my eyes. "Yes. William showed me a break in the dome where you can enter safely. I don't know how you'll react to the border, though. Your blood is more vampiric than mine."

"I don't think that matters, honestly," I say. "I haven't fed on human blood in weeks. Probably months now."

"I noticed, silver-eyes," she says, half-smiling.

"My powers have all but faded completely," I continue. "The only thing I've retained is my ability to hunt. I can't influence others or read minds or anything anymore. I can barely see in the dark."

"Hmm. Maybe you'll be fine then. I'm not sure how the border works. It's witch work."

"Well, here's to hoping," I say. "I just can't say goodbye yet."

"Where will you take her?"

"I don't know. I just want to get her past the border and into the city. After that, I don't know."

"How do you know she'll be better off there?"

"I don't," I admit. "I have no idea. I left the castle with barely even any change of clothes. I couldn't think about anything but leaving. I just had to get out."

"Do you think your father will track you?" she asks, pointing out a topic I've avoided thinking about.

"I honestly don't know. If he catches word that I'm in Menneskelig, it would be cause enough for him to attack again. And the nobles have multiplied since the last attack. I don't know if the city would survive."

She nods, and I notice that though she's still in shock and haunted, she's no longer crying. Maybe we could help each other, I think to myself. I smile softly, looking at her long brown hair, pin-straight and wildly tangled. I remember admiring her beauty as a child even though my father chastised me for mingling with a lesser vampire. But I had loved her once upon a time.

Of course, she didn't hold the slightest attraction that Astrid does. But maybe, just maybe, I could find my way back to loving Lilith. At least to have a partner in this life. I had to hold onto the hope that I wouldn't live out my days completely alone.

26
ASTRID

I jolt awake with a soft yelp at the tickling against my feet.

"My apologies, miss!" a small grey-haired woman says, jumping away from me.

"You gave me a start," I say.

"I did not mean to wake you. I was just adjusting the mattress and dusting the room," she says. I note the feather duster in her hands.

"No, no. I'm sorry. Please continue."

"Would you like some food, miss? You've slept most of the day away," she asks, opening the door. The seductive scents of charred bread and boiled eggs waft in. Or maybe I'm still dreaming. I stand, wobbling slightly, and move towards the door, noting that I'm still wearing my full dress. I see Lilith and Kai sitting at a small table, so I smile and start toward them.

"Astrid," Kai says, looking up with a warm expression. He

curls his hand around mine. "You remember my friend, Lilith, from back at Feilfri?"

"Yes," I reply, feeling awkward and confused as Kai reintroduces the friend that took him away from me for several days. Of course, Kai said they were just friends, but I don't know what friendship even looks like to Kai. Had they been more than friends before?

He sends me away to get some food, leaving my thoughts reeling as I take a seat at the long bar. The host leaves me with food and drink, and I search through the pockets in my dress for a form of payment.

"They don't accept money here, *frue*," a silver-haired man says, leaning against the bar next to me.

"Who are you?"

"Brynjar. I helped Kai bring you here last night," he says, looking over to Kai and Lilith with the same expression I feel on my face. Is this Brynjar attached to Lilith in some way?

"Thank you, sir. I am grateful for your assistance. Kai says it was your blood that saved me," I say, looking down at the bowl of clear broth.

"It is nothing, *kjære*," he says, nodding and turning back to his chores. I watch him for a moment before sipping on the hot soup. My stomach grumbles with pleasure.

The tavern is warm and bustling with life. I nibble gingerly on the cured meats and bread that the host brought, feeling more alive with each bite. I guzzle down as much water and an unknown warm juice that I can stomach, feeling the moisture return to my chapped lips and dried skin. What I would give to take a proper bath, I think, as I shift uncomfortably in my stale dress.

The place is built of large wood beams and carpeted with thick wool rugs, completely unlike the cold stone Feilfri Castle is made of. Wood is warm. Wood is comforting. Even with the tall ceilings and large wooden beams running the length of the place, it feels cozy. Not in a way that makes you feel claustrophobic, but that encourages restful sleep.

I sneak a look at Kai and Lilith in the corner. She's crying softly, but I can't make out what they are saying to one another. Every so often, I see his silver eyes look up from the conversation to check on me. I turn my gaze away, trying not to feel confused or jealous of the vampires.

I ponder the difference between Kai and Lilith. He has beautiful grey eyes, like the clouds in the sky. She had muddied brown eyes, different than any vampire I've ever seen. Neither of them looks all that dangerous. Certainly not like Caden with his bright red eyes.

That's the only difference I can see between the different vampires. Kai's eyes never turn from silver or black lately. They're always earthy colors. But Caden's eyes had always been red. Red from bloodlust and murder. I don't know why the other colors are important. Brown, silver, red, black, and Brynjar has the brightest silver eyes I've ever seen. Almost pearlescent. None of it really makes sense, and it makes me wonder what else I don't know about vampires.

In fact, the vampires that roam in the tavern all have similar shades of eye color to one another. In the dim light, they could easily pass as blue-eyed humans. The only thing that truly gives them away is their grace and pale skin. They are also all beautiful, like paintings instead of real people.

"You doin' okay, sweet?" the host asks, approaching quietly.

"Yes, thank you," I say, my voice hoarse and low. I clear my throat loudly. "Thank you for the food. It's delicious."

"Where ya from?" he asks with an accent that's similar to the vampires back at Feilfri, but just different enough to make me wonder.

"Um…" I hesitate. I don't know what I should say. "South, I guess. It's been a really long journey."

"Did I hear that you're here with Prince Kai?" he asks softly like it's a secret.

I close my eyes and sigh. I guess there's no point in hiding.

"Yes, he's bringing me to Menneskelig," I tell the man. His eyes widen at my words, and he stops cleaning the bar to look at me meaningfully.

"You know vampires are not allowed in the city?"

"Yes, we both know that. He's simply taking me to safety." I take a swift drink of the ale. It's bitter and burns my poor throat. My mind reels from the shock of remembering my journey with Kai. This is supposed to be the end of the road for us. How am I supposed to leave him now? After everything we've gone through together?

The man nods, his eyebrows knitting together in worry.

"I see," he simply says, still staring at me. I shift uncomfortably under his scrutiny. "Ya know, you look an awful lot like the Great King."

"What?"

"Do ya not know of Great King Haakon? The greatest ruler to have governed the proud city of Menneskelig! May he rest in peace," he says, and the room chants, "Rest in peace," loudly behind me. I swivel around to see the others at the bar taking a drink together, both vampires and humans alike. After a moment of silence, the host continues, "Haakon was the last great king of Menneskelig. We are blessed to have his portrait hanging here so that he may watch over us during this time of war."

I stare in the direction that he's pointing and see a large painting of a man wearing simple clothing. His face is hard and stoic. But…he looks so familiar. I wonder if I've seen his face before. His hair is strawberry blonde like mine, and though his masculine features are striking, the portrait reminds me of my mother.

"What do you mean time of war? Is the city at war?" I ask, my curiosity stirring.

"Where ya been living, lass? Under a rock? The war with the vampires! Those bloody bastards at Livsnerven," he spits the words, then takes a long drink from his own ale before continuing to wipe down the polished bar.

I blink at him. There's a war?

Remembering back to the last few days at Feilfri, it hadn't seemed like anyone was upset or tense. Baldassare and the rest of the castle had just been planning the coronation for Kai.

"Those filthy savages at Feilfri castle dared to steal away our beautiful Inger Johana," the man continues, and my heart stops at the words. They're familiar, too.

"Um…who was Inger Johana?"

"His wife, of course! The goddamn vampire king stole Inger and her daughter away in the middle of the night about 50 years ago as an act of war. King Haakon was so distraught by the kidnapping that he sent all of Menneskelig's warriors to war against the vampires, raiding through Ødemark's wastelands and reaching all the way to Livsnerven just to see Baldassare holding Inger in his arms. He fed on her right in front of Haakon, killed her in cold blood," the man said through his teeth. I gasp audibly.

"Do you have a picture of her? Do you have a painting or portrait? I'd like to see her," I manage. "Please, let me see her."

He looks around and sighs before walking back to the back of the kitchen and returning with a small cloth. He holds the folded painting in his hand, his own eyes turning glassy.

"I don't hang her portrait because it brings sorrow to everyone who looks upon her face. She was an angel, our beautiful Inger Johana, and her death brought many others at the hands of vampires. Look with care, lass," he says quietly, placing the thick grey fabric in my hands.

My breath catches in my throat, and I can't help tears as I begin to unfold the painting, revealing an astoundingly beautiful woman. Her skin is pale, even with the cracks of the yellowing, aged paint, and her eyes are icy blue. And her hair is long and strawberry blonde, plaited to the sides of her head. Just like mine.

I choke back a sob, wallowing in the gravity of his words. The pieces of the puzzle fall right into place.

"Lass," the man breaths, watching me struggle to keep my composure. I hiccup a breath and take a long drink from the ale, welcoming the bitterness.

"What was their daughter's name? Please," I stutter the words, knowing the truth before he can even speak.

Tears roll down the man's face, but he replies, "Hanna. Her name was Hanna."

Hearing the word, that wretched word, my heart cracks wide open. I place the painting on the bar and wrap my arms tightly around my torso, trying to keep my frame from falling to pieces. My eyes flick over to Kai, chatting away with Brynjar and Lilith. Confusion and fear stir in my brain as my eyes trace over Kai's black hair and porcelain skin. Does he know? Has he known all along?

"Lass, how did ya not know? Who are you, lass?"

Who am I? It's not a bad question.

I take a deep breath, trying to keep it together as I think the words to myself. My name is Astrid. My mother's name was Hanna. I was born in Feilfri Castle, born to serve the man that kidnapped my mother and killed my grandmother.

I am the granddaughter of King Haakon and Queen Inger Johana.

I stare at the cracked face of the beautiful woman pictured in the faded painting, my thoughts turning to the hazy memories of my mother. This woman shared her beautiful golden hair and the same long pointed nose. This face is more angular and striking, whereas my mother had a rounder face, marred only by the ever-present blush that lingered on her cheeks.

She died when I was not even a teenager. I remember her death vividly. One second she was sitting in the cells of Feilfri's dungeon, brushing my long hair, and in the next, she was taken violently and quickly by a vampire who fed on her right in front of me. The vampire killed her. She never woke up, leaving me alone, her parentage replaced by the baker and a teenaged Alheri. I don't remember missing my mother, not until recently, and now I know why. Whatever brainwashed me into believing everything was alright at the castle has unraveled, and I now know the horrors that linger in that place.

But I'm free now. I'm just outside the city…or is it *my* city? Do they still have rulers, as Livsnerven does? If I'm the last king's granddaughter, does that mean I am the heir? Does it work the same way that the vampire kingdom does?

I shake my head. No, I cannot rule. I can barely keep myself alive and well.

I close my tired eyes, trying to focus on remembering my mother. It's easier now that I've seen Inger Johana. She was simply older in this picture. My mother had never really grown into her adulthood; she was still a girl when she died. When she was killed, I correct myself.

I swallow hard on the pressure in my chest. Disbelief radiates through me as I stroke my thumb across the grey canvas. How could Kai not tell me? If he knew about my mother, why would he hide it from me?

I fold the painting gently, holding it lightly in my hand. Walking with my arms wrapped around my torso, I leave the bar towards my room. Maybe sleep will bring clarity and assurance. Maybe my subconscious mind will be able to come up with the right path.

Gingerly, I look at Inger's painting once more, feeling my heart thud. This face is so like my mother's.

Overwhelmed and shocked, I sit on the bed, looking up at the ceiling. I try to calm my heartbeat back to a normal rhythm, but the onslaught of emotions just keeps pulling at my attention. I sit up and sigh with irritation. How could things have changed so much in only a matter of moments?

This morning, I'd slept so soundly, so peacefully, without any nightmares or fears. I felt so secure in Kai's arms like nothing else in the world mattered. And now…

I stand up and begin pacing. Maybe nothing else does matter. Even if I am the granddaughter of the last great king, what does that mean for me now? Surely, Menneskelig has a different ruling government now. I can't just waltz in and expect them to recognize me as some lost princess.

It *doesn't* matter. I'm Astrid. That's all. I don't need to know my heritage to be comfortable in my own skin. I grew up with Alheri, my best friend. And now, I'm here with the only man I've ever cared about. That's more important.

Kai. He is important. He's sacrificed almost everything in his life because he cared enough about me to get me to safety.

So, why don't I just stay with him?

I pause, thinking over that last thought again. What if I stay with him? Would he want to live out his days with me? Would he be willing and able to coexist comfortably with me?

My thoughts muddle with memories of last night, how he kissed me and held me so close. If I had to guess, I would say he feels for me in the same way I feel for him.

If I ask him to stay with me, here, in this tiny little tavern for the rest of our lives, will he say yes?

By the time Kai retires to our room again, he seems shocked to see me curled up in a ball on the bed.

"Astrid? Are you okay?" he asks, sitting next to me. He lays his hand gently on my waist. "What's wrong? What happened?"

"Nothing, I'm just sad," I say, sitting up. I wipe away my nervous tears.

"Why?"

"All of this has been so wonderful," I start weakly, then pause. I really haven't thought any of this through.

"And that's a bad thing?"

He smiles gently at me, and I grab his hands, afraid to look in his eyes.

"No, of course not. This is the happiest I've ever been in my whole life."

I feel him shift closer to me.

"I'm just sad that you want to end it tomorrow."

He sighs, and I can't help but look up at him. His face is full of understanding as he contemplates my words.

"Please say something," I whisper.

"I don't know what to say," he says. "This is the happiest I've ever been, too."

My heart sings.

"But I can't… We shouldn't be together."

"I don't know how you can say that. We've traveled so far, gone through so much. Doesn't that make you think any differently?"

"Of course it does!" he says, standing now and gesturing toward the ceiling. "I can't *stop* thinking about it. But what am I supposed to say? I can't be what you need me to be."

"What do you mean? You're everything I want. Right now," I explain.

"Astrid…" He sighs in defeat.

"Kai, what is it you fear? Why do you push yourself away from this?"

"I'm a vampire, Astrid."

"So? That means nothing to me."

"You can't mean that," he says, his silver eyes like daggers. "I'm dangerous. I could hurt you. The conversation hasn't changed. I'm not good for you."

"Kai," I start, feeling my heart pound. "We've traveled for weeks with one another. You never hurt me then. Why are you so convinced that you'll hurt me now?"

He pauses for a moment.

"I don't want to live without you," I whisper, hoping to drive the point home.

His eyes soften as they meet mine once more. He kneels and cups my hands in his. My heart is thundering in my chest as I watch his eyes look between mine.

"We could run," I whisper. "We could live far away from here, where there are plenty of animals for you to feed on. Or we could stay here! I know I sound mad, but you said yourself how much you liked this place. You even have friends here. We could live forever here, together."

His eyes dart back and forth between mine, his thumb tracing the back of my hand.

"I could hurt you," he offers weakly. "I could kill you."

"So could any man," I argue. "That does not change how I feel. I want to stay with you, Kai. Please, let me stay with you."

He shakes his head with a half-smile. "It's madness, absolute insanity."

"I know." I smile, and my chest tightens as a smile breaks across my face.

"I can't believe I'd ever agree to this…but I want this as much as you do."

"Then, say it's so. Say we'll be together, *please.* And if something happens between us, I promise, I'll leave. I will walk away to the city and live amongst my own people. I won't cause you harm just because of my feelings."

"I'm the one putting *you* in danger, Astrid. Please understand that," he says, squeezing my hands tightly.

"I know, but I believe you're different now. You're amongst vampires who don't feed on humans. You're in the place you've always wanted to be. I just want to be here with you," I press, trying to encapsulate my feelings into words.

"Okay," he says, barely a whisper.

"Okay?" I breathe.

"Yes," he says, smiling so widely.

He looks so genuinely happy that I wail out a cry of joy before wrapping my arms tightly around his neck. He lifts me easily, touching his lips to mine as he spins me around the room. I can feel his laughter and delight shaking from deep within his chest like his heart is dancing right alongside mine. I kiss him deeply, a warm sound resonating in my throat as we embrace.

This is home.

27
KAI

Astrid… She cups my neck with her hand, kisses me, and laughs happily. My arms are wrapped tightly around her waist, lifting her off the ground. She's so happy. *I'm* so happy.

I didn't think this would ever happen for me. It feels like all my dreams are coming true. And, the voice inside me is quiet. When I feel weak or too thirsty, the voice in my head warns me to stay away. Run. Hide. Now, the voice is silent. It doesn't tell me that I'm too weak. It doesn't tell me to leave her be.

Instead, I'm left with a feeling of warmth and wholeness, Astrid's heart thumping loudly in my ears. Instead, I feel *strong.*

Logically, I know I am stronger. I'm well-fed, well-rested, and even desensitized. I've surrounded by Astrid's scent for weeks, maybe even months, with no other food in sight. I haven't touched her blood.

And…she died. She was *dead* in the forest. I felt excruciating pain in my chest, like all my internal organs had been ripped out. Even now, even when she's breathing heavily and steadily in front of me, I still feel the ghost of the hole in my chest. I will never let myself feel like that again. I will never put Astrid in danger like that again.

With my internal debate raging inside me, I push past my fears to lay Astrid down on the bed and kiss her. I wrap my arm around her torso and press her down toward the blankets, feeling her warmth surround me. Our lips break, and she opens her bright blue eyes, looking wild and surprised as I climb on top of her, pressing my body down along the length of hers.

When my lips are only an inch away, she reaches her arms around my neck, pulling me hastily down to lock our lips together in a dance that synchronizes with the beating of our hearts. I take a deep breath, tasting her on my tongue.

When Astrid surprised me back at Feilfri Castle, the night she waited for me, naked and fearful, I had imagined inhaling her scent, like smelling the aroma of a large bounty I could never touch. I laugh now, feeling Astrid's chest against mine, smiling against her mouth. It seems so silly now.

I lower my lips to her ear, inhaling the rich scent of her hair and blood just beneath the surface of her neck. I kiss her softly, feeling her release a slow breath. Like honeysuckle and rose, just like always. Of course, there are many other scents now too: the saltwater from the Ingunn Cliffside, the brackish taste of demon blood, the smell of dirt and rust, leaves on her skin. But she still smells like Astrid. My Astrid.

I groan, a swell of heartache pulsing throughout my body. Before, every limb had felt like it was having a heart attack. Now, it feels like a surge of strength through my entire frame. I sit up straight, ripping my lips away from hers. Her hand flies up to her chest in surprise, her blue eyes are like a wild ocean as I tear away my shirt off, and she makes a sound that sends a pleasurable jolt through my body. She runs her hands and fingers all over my torso. My muscles ache, and I grab her arms, pulling her up to meet my lips again.

I kneel gingerly on top of her, kissing her fully on the mouth. She wraps her arms tightly around my stomach, pulling me to her chest. I run my hands over her hair, and as with hunting, my instincts clearly take over. I pull on her hair, pressing my body to hers, encouraging her in every way.

After a moment, the tension is too thick. She pulls away, leaving me feeling empty and devoid of her warmth. My lips trail after hers, but she presses me back with her hands, smiling wildly at me.

"Kai," she whispers. I look at her lips hungrily, pushing my hair out of my eyes with the back of my hand.

I feel my torso erupt in gooseflesh as she pulls my hands towards the laces on her outer dress. She has to move my hands, with a small laugh, because I'm frozen in desire. When she's taken off the dress, like peeling off a jacket with no sleeves, she sits facing me, wearing only her light shift. I blink longingly at her before pushing her back down onto the bed with a loud grunt of approval.

Though, now, she feels so *soft* underneath me that I'm nervous to put my full weight down on her. She meets my lips again, raking her fingers down my back, pulling me onto her. I suppose that means *she* isn't worried about it. I exhale loudly, feeling her breath tickle my neck as my hair falls around our faces.

In a breeze, she's rolled me over and sits on the bed next to me, her hair in disarray around her face. Her cheeks are splotched with red flakes. She looks at me with yearning desire, and I find myself reaching out for her again. I stroke the side of her face, letting my hand trail down her neck where her pulse thuds lusciously, then down the full length of her body until it rests lightly on her thigh. I lay my palm flat against her leg, only the thin fabric between our skin.

I stare into her face, memorizing the thin lines in her skin, how the bridge of her nose sits between her blue eyes. I float my eyes over her golden hair. Even though it's still tangled and matted in some places, it frizzes around her face like a halo, glowing golden in the flickering candlelight.

I give her a small smile before leaning in again, this time brushing my lips just barely against hers. She lets out a soft gasp, her breath wafting over my face like feathers. There's a tightness in my chest that aches when she's this close. I move my hand to her neck, my fingers twisting into her hair and my thumb resting on her cheek. She runs the tip of her tongue over my bottom lip, and I have to stifle a moan.

She rubs her hands against the fabric of my pants, encouraging me to take the next step, the *final* step, but I'm mesmerized with how her lips feel and how thunderously her heart is beating against the palm of my hand. I move my hand away from her neck and dip my head to kiss her where her jaw meets her earlobe. She sighs and lets her head fall backward, and I nuzzle my nose against her skin, nibbling and kissing her ear.

I close my eyes, and all I can see is the flickering of red candles behind my eyelids. Still, Astrid is clear as day, like all my other senses are guiding me. I trace my hand up her thigh and stop at the curve of her hip. My other hand runs down her spine, and I can feel her shiver against me. I press my lips against her neck, running my tongue against her skin. She tastes like dirt and salt, but I can almost taste her blood underneath her skin. Her scent swims around in my head, drowning out almost every other sense.

Astrid gasps and jerks away, her hand reaching for her neck.

My lips feel cold and numb as they long for her warmth, but I see shock and confusion and disbelief flash over her face in a matter of seconds. Her eyes widen as she searches my face. I frown at her, confused.

But then I realize what happened.

I touch my hand to my mouth, feeling the sting of sharp teeth against my fingers. I jolt backward, leaping quickly to the other side of the room. It's only then that I see the red tint of thirst coating my vision. My heart starts pounding, and fear and anxiety grip my body in a wave of nausea. I keel over and feel my body contract. The palms of my hands slam to the floor as I heave from the burning thirst in my throat.

I heave in several breaths, noting that there isn't any actual blood in the room. Just my imagination.

After a monstrous display of sickening sounds and disgusting gagging, I feel my teeth retract, and my body relaxes enough that I almost sink completely to the floor.

"What happened?" I whisper to the floor.

"You bit me," Astrid says, her voice like tremors on a still lake. She sounds resigned. Defeated.

I slam my fist against the floor, the wood splintering and cracking underneath the force of it. I cry out, feeling no shame in my weakness. After all, I knew it was only a matter of time.

"I'm sorry, Astrid," I groan. "Are you okay?"

"Yes," she whispers.

"I didn't mean to hurt you…"

"I know," she says. I look up at her, and she has tears in her eyes. She looks so completely alone. So betrayed.

"I will take you to Menneskelig tomorrow," I say, standing and facing toward the door.

I reach for the handle as she says, "I know that too."

My heart is broken. My chest is heavy. I grab my shirt, reach for the door, and leave without another word.

Defeat resounds inside me. I feel shocked and confused, but mostly just horrified. The look on Astrid's face…

I rub my hands over my face, feeling my chest shake as a

small sob breaks me. I lean my head against the doorframe, my nostrils flaring at the wealth of new scents. I should be noticing how strong the hearth smells, or the sourness of the ale, or the smells of all the people in the room. Instead, I just smell Astrid.

How close did I get to hurting her? I didn't even notice I'd bitten her until she jumped away. Would I have even known what I was doing if I started feeding on her?

I rake my hand through my hair and sling on my shirt. I go to the bar, where the host leaves me with a cup of blood and a cup of ale. I nod toward him, drinking the blood instantly, on pure instinct. It tastes like sludge and dirt comparatively. I frown and wash the taste of it away with the ale.

I look to my right as Brynjar sits beside me. We look at one another, and he frowns at me. He claps me on the back, gripping my shoulder with a nod of understanding. He doesn't say a word, but I can feel he knows what's happened. I look away from his silver hair and gulp down the rest of the ale, feeling nothing quench the thirst in my throat.

"*Nikolaj.* Drink this. It will not cure you of your ails, but it will make you forget you have them," he says, offering me a leather canteen.

I take a sip, and sure enough, the liquor is strong and warm, scorching away the bloodlust in my throat, if just for a moment. The *akvavit* settles in my stomach like a fire burning through my chest and gut. I nod and hand him back the satchel. We sit in silence for a long stretch of time, feeling the night wane away, giving a wide berth to the morning that comes through the windows.

"I suppose this is farewell," he says.

I nod.

"You know you are welcome back here at any time," Brynjar says. "Come back when you can."

I nod in resolution, looking into his silver eyes. It's something. When Astrid is gone, I will have a place, a home. It's not good news, but it's something.

I sigh and push off the stool.

Astrid sits on the edge of the bed, fully dressed once again, when I enter the room again. I give her a meaningful look, seeing tears in her eyes, but she smiles sadly at me. It hurts to see the clear understanding and forgiveness in her eyes even though I've hurt her more than any other man could. I look away from her.

"Astrid…" I start, my voice breaking. I clear my throat.

She breathes out a shaky breath.

"*Jeg elsker deg*," I say, feeling the weight of the words in my chest. I stare at the floor. Astrid's told me before that she doesn't understand the language, so this is the only way I can tell her what I feel. I know she understands the heaviness in the phrase.

She's silent, so I look up and find her eyes, her face shadowed with curiosity. She nervously tries to untangle her hair with her fingertips. I meet her gaze, longing to lose myself in the depths of her crystalline blue eyes.

"I never want to hurt you, Astrid."

Her lips pinch into a tight line as she looks away from me. There's a bead of a tear that pools in her eyes and her chin quivers as she tries not to cry, but when she returns her eyes to mine, I know she understands what I mean.

This is goodbye. Tomorrow, we will be parted forever.

Menneskelig

28

KAI

We walk in silence. It's grey and misty out, despite the glowing city, as we trail the east edge of the castle. I look at Lilith as we walk the perimeter of the city. I eye the treacherous rock formations in our path, but she doesn't hesitate. The walls of Menneskelig are tall, too tall for us to scale, and I begin to question Lilith's route, but I don't say anything. If she really lived here, she must know secret ways around the walls. There's no way she would have survived going in and out of the main entrance.

The wind is cold and strong, carrying the thick mist as we walk, but the sky lightens further each minute, signaling daytime. Soon, the city will be bustling with life. Lilith seems to mirror my thinking and picks up the pace.

It's disconcerting, though. To my right, there are rocks, water, and trees, just like Feilfri Castle, but to my left, the city that stands before me is nothing like the vampire fortress. This city has sunlight surrounding it like thick, shining glass. I wonder if I touch the border if it will feel cool like the glass from my balcony door.

I keep up the pace, feeling Astrid struggle to keep up with Lilith. She pulls on my hand constantly, gasping for air as I help her over large gaps between the rocks. A vague discomfort and confusion roll off her in waves, and I can't help but hate myself for ruining our perfect chance at happiness.

Once before, part of me considered living in the city, as Lilith had, to keep an eye on her. To be there for her if she needs it. It's sickening and much like a sob story, but I thought about it. Looking at the bright city now…there's no way for me to live in a city that hates vampires and does everything to keep them out. Lilith probably got away with it because she doesn't look so different. But I look completely different than the average human. They have tan, beautifully worn skin. I'll never look like anything other than a pale sculpture. Not to mention the darkness in my face, under my eyes and neck. Humans have life in their skin; I have nothing but death in mine. My eyes scream monster with their ever-shifting coloring. And God forbid I do feed on a human. My eyes would turn an ungodly shade of red that would immediately expose me.

Though, part of me wonders if I could maybe force myself to become desensitized to the smell of blood. Maybe I could fix myself and try to be the right kind of man for Astrid. My thoughts relive the nightmare of hurting her, like a repeating loop of bad memories. Everything had been so good, and I'd ruined it so fast. I didn't even know what was happening. And that was when I thought I *had* been desensitized. How much better could I prepare? There's no possible course of action I can think of.

No, I don't think Menneskelig would be good for me. Even if I somehow avoided bloodshed or feeding, I still couldn't avoid prying eyes. I would be hunted and possibly killed. The only chance I have is to live outside the city.

I huff, and Lilith peers back at me with questions in her eyes. I shake my head at her. There's nothing I can say to make this any better. She frowns but continues on.

Astrid grunts as she lifts her skirts and pushes up. I'm impressed by her strength and resilience. She made the entire journey across the wastelands, almost without injury. She's scarcely even the same girl that left the castle. I daydream about her soft, glowing skin that I kissed and held last night. She's more chiseled now, her muscles growing in strength, even though she still had many bruises, and her skin is discolored from improper nourishment and rest. She will heal quickly in the city.

And being away from Livsnerven isn't just good for her; it's good for me too. I can already feel myself turning into the man I want to be. Simply from being away from the toxic atmosphere of my father's kingdom.

But I'm still a vampire. I'm still a monster.

Lilith is proof of that. She is one of the kindest vampires I know, and yet she couldn't save her William. She couldn't walk away from him when she had the chance. And that got him killed. For as much as I understand and relate to her plight, I can't help but hate her as I hate myself. It was her nature, my nature, that got her love killed.

Everything around me seems to be full of death, and I don't see any other way past it than running. Maybe it's cowardly, but what else can I do? I will see Astrid to safety, then I'll run. Somewhere I can be free of the smell of blood. Maybe I'll find a coven that will accept me as I am. Maybe Lilith and Brynjar and I could run together. *Here's to hoping.*

Pushing up the last rock, Lilith holds out her hand for Astrid, who grabs on quickly, pushing herself up on the final ledge. We cuddle close, the wind whipping past us quickly and frostily.

"This is it. We have to climb this small section, and you'll pass the border. Once you're on the ledge of the wall, you can sit on the edge without being burned," she says, something catching in her throat. She swallows, and with a hard expression, continues, "Once fully inside the border, you'll be exposed to the sun. You'll have to rush under the roof of the castle quickly. There's an opening to a covered pathway leading to the entrance of the castle. You'll get burned," she eyes me meaningfully. This is going to hurt, and there's not a guarantee that I'll live if I get trapped in the light. I nod, expressionless. "I think you'll be okay, though. Astrid will be fine inside. Once we are all safe, I'll show you the back route to the main courtyard, where Astrid can go and find help. That's where we'll part."

It's a solid plan. I listen carefully, trying my very hardest to hear past the treacherous ocean below us and the wind whipping past us. I listen across the great wall to see if there are humans about yet. I hear simple chimes and some movement, but not much chatter. If there are humans on the other side of the wall, there aren't many.

"Can you do this?" Lilith asks, grabbing my arm. She doesn't need to say the exact words for me to understand what she means. I haven't been around this many humans before. She's asking me if I'm strong enough not to ruin everything by going into a feeding frenzy. I gulp but nod again. She seems content enough.

"Okay, Astrid. I'll go up first. Kai will give you a boost, and I'll pull you up," she says. Astrid's face is blank, but she nods.

In a flash, Lilith leaps gracefully, reaching the top of the wall easily. Her skin is illuminated by the border, but she doesn't flinch. I hear Astrid gasp, mirroring my own astonishment. She looks beautiful with the light backlighting her brown hair like a halo. I swallow hard, automatically imagining Astrid in that sort of light.

Lilith locks her legs around the wall railing and reaches down. I turn to Astrid, and she gives me a torn look for a moment. I smile sadly at her. I'm certain that she knows that goodbye is coming. For a brief second, I believe that she wants to say something. That she doesn't want to go. But then her expression vanishes into a smooth mask of apathy. I stifle my own frown and reach down to offer her a boost. Locking my fingers together, I create a step for her, and she steps up, reaching Lilith's arms easily. I watch as Lilith pulls her effortlessly up and over the ledge.

I take a breath, mentally preparing for pain. I concentrate on my eyes and my legs, trying to channel my strength and imagine myself with quicker reflexes. If what Lilith said is correct, I can leap where she is now without injury and visualize my path to the shaded section.

I look up and see that Lilith has moved. She's made room for me. I push off the ground, easily leaping up to the wall ledge. I thought I would have a moment to gather my bearings, but the instant my skin touches the border, a tearing sensation rips across my skin. I snarl low and look around, spotting Lilith and Astrid looking at me with wide eyes. I sprint off the ledge to join them under the shade, but as I move, even though I'm moving as quickly as I possibly can, the light of the dome reflects off my skin, blinding my eyes and burning every inch of flesh on my body. I push harder, feeling like I've slowed down, like I'm walking through quicksand.

In a moment that feels like a lifetime, I make it to the shade, warm all over but still alive. The burning has stopped, but my eyes still feel bloodshot and hot, boiling inside my lids. With my hand, I shield my eyes from the surrounding brightness, and even in the shade, I can barely open them.

"Wow, so that answers that question," Lilith says, a chuckle in her voice.

"Fucking hell," I spit, feeling my body all over to see if I've been hurt. My entire body throbs, aching. I keep my eyes closed as I run my hands over my face and neck. My skin feels smooth and fine, though the warmth remains.

"What's happened to him?" Astrid's voice chirps, short and toneless. I try to look at her through my pained eyes.

"He's a pureblood vampire. That means he's extremely vulnerable inside the dome. I hadn't thought it would really be that big of a deal, but apparently, he takes damage a lot worse than me," Lilith explains, almost haughtily, like she's proud.

"Pureblood? You're not a pure vampire?"

"Nah," she answers breezily. "I'm a Dhampyr — half-human. My father was a pureblood, but my mother was human."

"Oh," is all Astrid says in return.

"What now?" I growl, not bothering to hide the anger in my voice. Being a pureblood has never given me anything but pain.

"Well we can try to get down to the common area, but I don't think you'll make it—"

"HALT!" a strong, commanding voice booms. I whip my head around, opening my eyes. Brightness blinds me, but I can make out Lilith and Astrid in front of me. I can barely see through my eyelashes that two large men are heading our way.

"Shit," Lilith breathes.

I grunt loudly and shift Astrid behind me, pulling at her waist. If this is to end in a fight, I just pray I have the strength to resist the bloodshed. I can hear their heartbeats as they pound towards us. They are shrouded in metal armor, and I resist the urge to curse. I notice two other figures, women, trailing behind the guards. They are all moving towards us.

"*Lilith*," I hiss through my teeth. She's crouched beside me, both of us protecting Astrid. She eyes me with a scowl on her face, and the brightness is almost too much again. I squeeze my eyes shut briefly, then open them quickly, feeling Astrid push me aside to face her fellow humans. My heart almost bursts through my chest as she steps away from me. I reach out to grab her hand, brushing her fingers ever so slightly with mine.

Is this finally goodbye? Will we be captured and Astrid freed? My thoughts turn quickly, but I can't stop her. Lilith straightens up, and Astrid starts to speak.

"Please, stop," she commands in a solid voice.

We all turn our attention to Astrid, and she shifts uncomfortably under the scrutiny. The guards are quiet but still point large spears toward us. Lilith and I are crouched, and my eyes flick between the guards, robed women, and Astrid. She clears her throat and continues.

"My name is Astrid. I'm the daughter of Hanna and granddaughter of King Haakon the Great."

I feel Lilith stiffen beside me, and my jaw drops, recognizing the names of the last known human rulers. Haakon was the king my father warred against maybe fifty years ago when I was just a boy. I peer through the slits in my eyelids to see the guards hesitate, and the women step around them. The guards look shocked, but the women do not.

They are shrouded in leather robes with skin as dark as night, reminding me of only one person: Alheri. My breath catches in my throat, realizing that we have come face to face with two witches. I sniff softly, catching their earthy scent, just like Alheri's. I straighten up, suddenly scared. I know how strong witches can be.

The witch on the left, who has a blue cowl wrapped around her neck, smiles warmly. The expression looks harmless, but something inside me twists at the sight.

"Yes, yes, stand down," the witch said, her alto voice low and deep but with a clear assurance. The two guards stand at ease, still watching us in shock. "Nyarai, didn't I tell you that today was the day?"

My heart throbs and my eyes strain to see them clearly. The silent witch remains still, her watchful eyes probing us.

Astrid stands tall and strong, facing the witch as she approaches with an outstretched arm. Involuntarily, a snarl rips through my teeth. The witch snaps her head towards me and smiles.

"Yes, your protectors were very thorough in returning you, Princess," the witch says.

Lilith is still frozen beside me, but the two guards gasp audibly. Astrid remains calm and collected. Shock courses through my arms and legs with a startling effect. I no longer feel the heat of the sunlight on my skin. Instead, I feel cold with surprise and confusion. Did she know all along?

"Guards," the witch commands, cutting me out of my thoughts. "This is Astrid, our Lost Princess. The prophecy said she would return at the hands of the enemy."

Her words pour fear over my heart. We are the enemy then.

"The prophecy also says we must not hurt them," the other witch, Nyarai, speaks aloud for the first time.

The first witch scoffs and rolls her eyes.

"Yes, yes, Nyarai. You've made your point," she says, answering as though they are continuing a previous conversation. "Guards, please escort the princess's…*guests* to the guest quarters. Please be careful with this one," she says, pointing at me. "He is a pure vampire."

I expect her to say that I am dangerous, that I could kill them, but instead, she continues, "We must keep him out of the light. For the time being, he is extremely vulnerable."

Her lips twist into a smile that sends chills down my back again.

Nyarai approaches Lilith and me with a less creepy expression. Nothing about this witch scares me. She reaches out to touch my hand, and I'm compelled to let her.

She grabs my hand in a handshake, and my vision clears, the brightness dissolving, letting me see clearly again. The burning from before clears, and I can see my skin has been hurt. With the witch's touch, the redness fades.

"Thank you," I say. She meets my eyes, expressionless, but bows. I turn to the other witch. "Where are you taking us?"

"The guest quarters are for our honored guests," Nyarai answers for her counterpart, who is still smiling, glaring at me.

I try to shake off the uneasy feeling from her glare and say, "Can't we leave? Go back home?"

"Is that what you want?" Nyarai asks, her dark eyes searching for something in mine. I gulp, not knowing what to say.

After a few minutes, the other witch's gaze becomes unbearably uncomfortably, and I shift in my own skin.

Nyarai whips her eyes to the other witch, "Thema, would you please?"

Thema breaks her eye contact with me and returns her attention to Astrid.

"What about Astrid?" I ask softly.

"She will be taken before the council. But first, we will show her to her room. She looks like she needs some rest and relaxation," Thema responds easily, touching Astrid's hair.

To my surprise, as Astrid walks away, escorted by the witch Thema, she looks back at me with a soft, sheepish smile. I watch her briefly, my heart feeling as though it's been torn in half. When she's out of sight, I look at Lilith, who is wearing a half-shocked, half-confused expression. But then the guards move, and Nyarai leads us into the castle and down into the guest rooms, feeling more like a leashed animal than an honored guest.

29
Astrid

The witch called Thema leads me down a luxurious hallway, bright with natural light that filters through the large windows. Rather, they are large holes in the thick stone walls. There isn't a bare slab of brick in the entire place. Every inch of stone is covered with wall tapestries, hangings, or other various sigils and plaques. It's so colorful, I constantly have to close my dropped jaw.

I assumed, as soon as I said the words—that I was Haakon the Great's granddaughter—I would have some resistance, either from the guards or from the vampires that escorted me. I hadn't dreamed that it would be so easy. Almost too easy. I gape at the portraits of my family. Here I am, surrounded by my legacy, my heritage. Should I feel more at home now?

Thema walks briskly, chattering about the castle and royalty, though I stopped listening once we'd entered the building. It's a large building, with high ceilings, completely unlike the castle I lived in previously. This castle makes the memories of Feilfri feel claustrophobic. Although it's *still* cold. I rub my arms unthinkingly, wondering how the outside could be so bright and vivid, but somehow the heat remains elsewhere. The chill reminds me of how the boiler room felt when Alheri was working. Somehow she could divert all the heat into the water, leaving the air in the room frigid and dry.

"And this is where you'll be staying," she says, stopping outside a set of tall, wooden double doors. Two guards are stationed outside the room, though I can't see why. Haven't I just arrived? Are they protecting someone else inside?

The guard's bow, then turn to open the thick doors, revealing a large bedroom, or rather *wing* of the castle. I step inside cautiously, peeking around the doors to see if anyone is hiding inside. The room is incredible. The ceilings are somehow even higher here, pointing straight up. I think this must be one of the turrets of the castle, towering over the city. Stairs hug the curve of the room, leading to an upstairs balcony with a breathtaking view, no doubt.

But I'm still in the parlor. I step into the room further and see that this is the front room to an even grander bedroom, with a giant canopy bed, topped with a bright blue duvet and fluffy pillows. More than anything, my joints ache to jump on the bed and fall asleep for the next few days. I snap my mouth closed, my teeth clicking together as I try to stop myself from gaping at the beauty of the place.

I have seen royalty before. The bedrooms at Feilfri castle were lavish, but only when compared to the rest of the castle. This room, this *palace*, is luxurious in a completely different, almost materialistic way. How can I accept such beauty and extravagance? Does the rest of the city have it this good?

Footsteps sound behind me, pulling me out of my trance. I watch Thema stride over to a large vanity and bronze ornate mirror that I had missed upon first glance of the room. I walk over to meet her, seeing new water in the basin and sighing loudly with relief. The urge to bathe and change my clothes is strong. Thema looks at me and gestures towards the vanity.

"Please," she says. "I made sure that warm water was brought before I went to retrieve you. There are fresh linens in the cupboard and dresses in the armoire. I shall make a pot of fresh tea."

I watch her gesture towards the various cupboards and dressers, all filled with clothing, beautiful clothing. I imagine for a moment, looking at one of the pale pink dresses, how much work was put into making such fine clothing.

"Our dressmaker here is quite an artist," Thema answers my unspoken thought. "He made all of your dresses and has been working for the castle for almost twenty years."

I nod and pause to watch her pour the boiling water over the tea. I make a face, knowing that she probably burnt the leaves with such hot water, but I don't say anything. She walks back towards me, handing me the decorative teacup and saucer. I sip gingerly on the tea, finding the flavor untarnished by the hot water. I wonder idly if she can affect temperatures like Alheri can.

"You must have a million questions for me," Thema says, sitting gracefully at the breakfast table, which is made of dark wood and embellished with intricate carvings.

"Yes," I say, my voice just above a whisper. Where do I start? "How did you know I was coming?"

"That's a wonderful place to start," she replies. I shift, uncomfortable with her knowing my unspoken thoughts again. "Well, I knew you were coming today because your friend, Alheri, contacted me."

I turn to look in her eyes at the unexpected use of my former best friend's name.

"Alheri? How?"

"We have ways of communicating across long distances,"

Thema says, smiling nonchalantly. She sips her tea. "She contacted me several weeks ago, presumably when you left Feilfri Castle. She told me to be wary that you would be traveling with vampires. Specifically, the crowned prince."

I swallow against the uneasiness in my throat.

"But that's not the only reason I knew of your impending arrival." She pauses, taking note of my expression. I try to smooth my face into an unreadable mask. "You see, this kingdom has been void of royalty since your grandfather's death fifty years ago. It's been quite a long time since anyone sat on the throne. Our kingdom has been broken, devastated really, for so long. There's only one thing that has kept us together.

"Instead of devolving into anarchy, we relied upon a vision the witches had. There was a prophecy seen at the point of King Haakon's death, you see. I was not alive when the prophecy was first seen. The *heks* preceding Nyarai and I had the initial vision. Since then, every year, we see the same one. 'A girl dressed in rags to appear with help from the enemy. She will claim to be the lost princess, and she must pass through with no harm coming to her or her companions.'"

Thema smiles at me, finishing her tea in a soft gulp. I realize I had been still as she spoke.

I clear my throat before saying, "Every year?"

Thema laughs a throaty laugh. "Yes, Princess. Today was the day I had the vision. Combined with Alheri's message, it didn't take us long to realize you had returned. Hanna, your mother, was taken care of by Alheri's mother, Moroya. She contacted us when Hanna gave birth to a young girl. So, you see, all the puzzle pieces came together this morning. And now you are here."

I nod, unsure of how to respond. So many questions flood my mind. How did it all work? I only know a little about Alheri's magic, and these witches sound even more complicated. Are there more women than the two I met? Are there groups of witches here? I remember something Kai had said once, about the practitioners of seiðr... My brain feels fuzzy as I try to remember back to our night on Ingunn Cliff.

"So, tell me, Princess. How was your journey across Ødemark? The wastelands?"

"We stayed mostly to the west, trailing the coast," I say, my voice somewhat hoarse. I sip on my tea. "The journey was…long." I don't know how to verbalize everything that has happened to me in the past few weeks. "To be completely honest, most of it was a blur. I had some…trouble, with my thoughts as we traveled."

"And your companions?" she prods.

"Kai was the only one with me from the castle. I only met the other, Lilith, last night. Or this morning," I correct, feeling disjointed. I don't know how much time has passed since we were in the tavern. My head feels swirly and confused, similar to how I'd felt so many days while we traveled. I expect a jolt of memories to reach the surface again, and I bite down on my lip in preparation, but nothing happens.

"And Kai is the vampire who was to take the crown from Baldassare?"

I swallow hard. "Yes, initially. He forfeited his rule when he escaped with me."

"You don't like him?"

This takes me off guard, and my heart aches. "Kai? No, he's…well, he rescued me."

"Hm," is all the witch says, and I can tell this was not what she wanted to hear.

"Baldassare is the true monster," I continue. "He kept me under some sort of spell while I was at Feilfri Castle. Brainwashed into submission. I suppose he had every *thrall* compelled to obey him. If it weren't for Kai's clear vision, I would still be there," I admit.

"I wonder if Kai is as blameless as you make him out to be," Thema replies, standing up and holding her hand out to me. I take her hand, and she leads me back over to the vanity, sitting me down in front of the mirror.

I look at my reflection, shocked at my own face. I resemble the woman in the crinkled painting, not like the girl I last saw in a mirror. There's no doubt that I am her descendant now.

"What now?" I ask aloud, trying to change the subject. I don't particularly want to talk about Kai. Especially since I don't even know how I feel. A small flash of heat blooms across my chest.

I shake off the thoughts and turn to meet Thema's dark gaze. She smiles at me warmly, her dark, textured hair almost perfectly straight, draping down the sides of her face. She looks so different from Alheri, but her warm eyes are so close that I can almost pretend she and Alheri are sisters. How I wish I could see her again…

"Let's get you cleaned and dressed," she says, grabbing a tray of beautification instruments. "Then we will see about addressing the council."

30
KAI

"Please do not leave this room until given permission. I cannot protect you outside of the castle," Nyarai explains, standing at the threshold of a giant room. Her words feel like a prison sentence.

I can't help but gawk at the decorations and palace-like bedrooms. I've only seen castles like this in drawings and books. I nod once, and Nyarai bows, closing the door loudly behind her.

Once Lilith and I are alone, I heave in a gasping breath, unsure of the anxiety that washes over me now. I shouldn't have come here. I keel over, my hands clutching my knees, trying to remain upright. I hadn't realized I was holding my breath, but now I can smell it. It penetrates through my exterior. The smell of blood, life, and growth everywhere is like a punch to the stomach. Whatever Nyarai did to heal me was doing little to protect me now from the assault of everything I had been running from.

I clench my jaw shut, my gums aching and itching with a

desire to feed. I let out a strangled sound, feeling my stomach turn to lead. Every muscle in my body is constricted like my blood has stopped flowing. I feel my eyes burn with unshed tears, the ache of loss radiate through me.

I hate myself for losing control with Astrid. I *hate* it. And now, I'm imprisoned in this room of luxury, taunting me.

Lilith silently walks over to me and wraps her arms around my torso, like she's trying to hold me together, to keep me from exploding into tiny little pieces. I feel tearless sobs wrack my frame, and I'm grateful for her support as I draw in a breath, holding it inside again, knowing I shouldn't be breathing the scent of so many humans. The smell is sure to drive me insane, like a caged hawk smelling a mouse right outside the door.

"Kai, you're okay," Lilith speaks softly, stroking my hair. I realize then that I'm still shaking.

I shudder and grab her hand, giving her a small smile as I pull myself together. I squeeze her hand briefly before she lets me go.

"Did you know? About Astrid?" Lilith asks in a cold voice. I try not to meet her eyes, focusing on the intricate designs in the wood table.

"No," I say, truthfully. "I knew that my father killed King Haakon. I heard rumors that he had stolen the princess, Hanna. But I didn't know that she had been pregnant at the time."

"How did Astrid find out?"

"I honestly don't know," I say, raking my hand through my slick hair. "I would guess that someone told her, maybe before we left? Maybe Alheri." I shake my head. "No, that wouldn't make any sense. Alheri tried to help her."

"What do you mean?" Lilith asks, peaking out the large window.

"About a week ago, Astrid started changing, remembering things that had happened to her. It was weird, like she was waking up from a dream only to remember that her life had been a nightmare. She told me that before then, she didn't remember being fed on or that it wasn't a bad thing."

"What? How's that possible?"

"My first thought was that the vampires using her had compelled her not to remember, or not to scream or think it was bad. But that didn't make sense either. Why would they treat a *thrall* with care? The vampires at Feilfri fed often and carelessly. They wouldn't have bothered covering their tracks. Not when the humans were enslaved like that."

"So how—"

"I combed through my memories," I continue. "Before I left, Alheri told me that she had 'helped' Astrid. That if I took her away, she might not be the same. I thought she just meant she would change with the travel. I only put it together later, when Astrid started waking up, that Alheri had *changed* her memories. It was almost like Alheri had brainwashed her into thinking that she was having a good time with all the terror around her."

"That's *sick*," Lilith says, her mouth forming a disgusted grimace.

I shake my head. "No, I don't think she wasn't doing it maliciously. I thought so at first too, but Astrid kept having these nightmares. I used all my strength one night and tried to peak into Astrid's mind. The things she went through..." My hands grip the table, trying to steady me from an outburst of rage. "It was horrible. Her memories were like the pits of hell. Picture any bad thing you could go through, and Astrid went through it. Rape, feeding, torture, physical and emotional abuse..." My voice broke speaking the words. "No, Alheri wasn't the bad guy. She was just trying to help. In her eyes, Astrid had no way of escaping the castle, so she changed her memories, just trying to help her live happily. Of course, there's no way she could have known that I would decide to leave. So, she tried warning me. At the time, I didn't think anything of it. I just had to get her out of there."

Lilith shakes her head, gripping the windowsill. I know she's equally disgusted with how humans were treated. That's the reason she left so long ago. I've argued with myself many times, wondering if I should have left with her back then. I sigh. Even though I could have saved myself a lot of grief, I wouldn't have saved Astrid. This seemed better and worse.

"What do you think will happen to us now?" Lilith asks, bringing me back to the present.

"I don't know," I admit. "You know this place better than I do."

Shaking her head slowly, she says, "I don't know that I do. I lived here most of the time for the past few years. I've studied the humans, and honestly, they seem just as ruthless as the nobles back at Livsnerven. The hatred they have here is staggering. I thought I would be able to bridge the gap between humans and Dhampyrs. I was wrong."

"That's not true," I say, unsure about pressing my point. I don't want to upset her. "You did better than anyone I've known. You found someone that believed in you. That loved you."

She freezes, her eyes seeing something far away.

I wish I hadn't said anything.

"Lilith," I whisper, but she cuts me off with her hand and a shockingly angry face.

"I'll be fine, Kai. I have to be."

I nod, not understanding fully but not wanting to press it either. I fiddle with my fingers on the table, my mind whirling from all the new information, all the realizations, all the deception from my father. In all the meetings we had about being king, why hadn't he mentioned anything about warring with the humans? Surely, he would have expected me to continue.

In a moment of despair, I realize how much I miss talking to Astrid. I wish I could talk about all this with her. I have so many questions about her heritage, how she found out, about the war. And what's worse, I don't know that I'll ever be able to talk to her ever again. The thought makes my chest ache. I quickly turn my mind away, back to my father and the war.

Maybe Baldassare thought they had finished the war, that the vampires had won. Maybe he didn't know how much resentment the humans hold. If he did, he definitely didn't care. Obviously, things are different now. Astrid has returned to Menneskelig, filling the monarchy's void. The humans will rally under their new queen, and then the war will continue. I swallow. Maybe Astrid will be a peaceful ruler. She had always been so childlike, so innocent.

Behind my eyelids, I watch her clean out my fireplace, humming that sweet melody, not a care in the world. I see her beautiful ocean eyes wide with glee when I speak to her. I see her effortlessly make a fire on our first night out of the castle. She was so strong and confident, becoming more lucid as we ventured out into the wilderness. I see her smile as we leap from the side of the cliff into the water. Did I make a mistake in leaving?

Will she forget what we went through to get here? Will she cast me out into the wild human mob? Or will she welcome us into her new kingdom? Will she bridge the gap between vampires and humans, like Lilith tried to do?

The memories of Astrid's innocent face change, shifting to the new Astrid that has taken her place. She's not innocent anymore. She's completely *aware* now. She knows how badly humans are treated at Feilfri castle. She knows that there's a disparity between the royalty in Livsnerven. She knows how easy it is for a vampire to lose control.

No, I don't think Astrid will go peacefully. Even as she entered the city, she turned her back on Lilith and me. I had my answer in that. It doesn't matter what she feels for me. She will cast us out, back out into the cold. She won't want us to stay. For the good of the human kingdom, she will want us gone.

With that thought, a tear drops past my eyelashes, splashing softly onto my hand like a small, glistening diamond, shattering into a million pieces as it touches my skin.

31

ASTRID

My knee bounces up and down as I sit alone in my room. It's been a few days now, and I'm restless. I feel completely isolated, alone with my endless barrage of questions.

I exhale sharply and start pacing around the room. I feel almost too clean after the multiple baths and dressings from all the servants. It felt too surreal watching someone clean my fireplace in the same fashion I had once done for Kai. I found myself critiquing her; I wanted to tell her how to do her job. It was ridiculous and silly.

I trail my hand around the wall, staring at the same paintings and wall hangings that I've been looking at every day since we'd arrived. It's maddening, sitting here just waiting for Thema to return with more instructions. I've eaten every meal by myself, and though I'm incredibly happy to be eating something more than wild meat and eggs, I'm sick of being in this room!

I'm going to be the queen, I think suddenly. I should be allowed to go anywhere I want.

With that thought and a few hysterical motives, I move toward the door, yanking it open easily. There are two guards outside my room, standing tall in beautiful leather armor. I pay them no attention as I stalk out of the room. If I walk with confidence, no one will stop me.

The hallways are bigger than I remember, and I have to keep myself from gawking at the new landscape. I turn in the opposite direction we came from on our first day and continue past two corridors before taking a quick right at the end of the hallway.

The windows are large and beautiful, with intricate stained designs depicting different stories and legends. I look at them as I walk, finding an image familiar from Feilfri Castle. There's an image of a woman floating above a lake, touching the water with a bare leg. Kai had told me once about Freya, granting magic to the *heks* who worshipped her. I wonder if this is the image of Freya. Was she a beautiful woman, a goddess, that touched down somewhere on the earth?

As I walk, I trail my hand across the stone, feeling the polished brick. It isn't blackened stone, aged with mildew and slime. It's new, like the castle has only recently been built. Kai said that Feilfri Castle was centuries old. Could Menneskelig be newer than Livsnerven? How little I know about my future kingdom…

At the end of the hallway, there's an ornate red door, unlike any of the other castle rooms. Curiosity peaks my attention, and I can't help but creak open this new door. Instead of finding a new room, with the same decorations and furniture as before, it's completely different.

Immediately, I'm hit with warm, humid air. It smells wonderfully of flowers and earth. I open the door wider, my jaw gaping as I take in the unknown sights. Behind the door, there's a wealth of gleaming plants, all shapes and sizes, growing *inside* the castle.

I step inside the room, looking up to the ceiling, and find glass above me. I can see the dome of light shimmering down on the room, sending bright rays through the windows. The light shines down in misty beams onto massive growths of trees and flowers and grasses and succulents growing with abandon across almost every surface of the room. I walk further in and take a closer look to see that there are pots and beds of soil the plants are growing in.

I touch my fingers to the large, green leaves, feeling their waxy surface. I smile widely, enjoying how warm the room is. It smells fresh, the same way a freshwater river smells in springtime. It reminds me of a small creek Alheri had taken me to once, just outside Feilfri castle. That was so long ago now.

My amazement and joy push me further in the room, touching and smelling the various plants. There are fruit trees, just barely budding with small flowers. There are grasses I've never seen before. There are beautiful flowers of red, yellow, purple, and white. How I would have loved to have a room like this back at Feilfri Castle. I could have used all of these plants to make dyes.

"Who are you?" a voice says.

I jolt up, my eyes searching for the voice that called out to me. I find a thin young man carrying a small watering jug. His eyes are curious and wide, and I can see that he has the same beautiful pearlescent eyes that Kai and Brynjar have. He must be a vampire. But how can he be here? In the sunlight? Inside the castle?

My heart jumps, sending cool waves of panic through my system. In an instant, the man drops his watering can with a horrible clanging and splashing sound. I watch in fear as his eyes turn black, his face darkening in a very familiar look of thirst. I start to walk backward, and the vampire follows me. His face is shrouded in darkness, and I can see his sharp teeth behind his lips. He snarls at me, sending shivers across my skin.

My heel catches a pot, and I start to fall backward when

someone grips my elbow. I turn around to see the witch, Nyarai, behind me. She looks at me with a frightened and fierce gaze before turning her attention to the vampire.

"Calm yourself, Elias," she says.

Suddenly and quickly, the vampire's face returns to normal, his eyes widening in shock and shame. I'm frozen solid, seeing the transition from thirsty back to normal happen quicker than I'd ever seen. Even Kai, with as much restraint as he had, could never return to normal that quickly. Who is this strange vampire that can walk in the sunlight and spends his time alongside a witch?

"I'm so sorry, mistress," he says before turning away from us.

"It's alright," Nyarai says. "It's been a while since you've been near a human. I should have prepared you."

"How did you know I was here?" I manage to choke out.

"The wards alerted me to your presence. I apologize for Elias. Please, Princess, you should not be here."

She pulls me quickly out of the room with a tight grasp on my elbow. I want to protest, but I'm still speechless. I turn my head one more time to see the pale man with wispy blonde hair return slowly to watering the plants before the red door shuts behind me.

"What was that room?" is all I can say.

"It is an *Orangerie*, princess. A greenhouse."

"Greenhouse?"

"Yes. It allows me to grow plants even in the longest winter. As long as our dome stays lit, the long nights cannot harm us," she says, her voice much lighter and soothing than Thema's. "I use it as a place of experimentation and innovation for our farmers. I would ask you that you do not return to the greenhouse without me, Princess. It is not safe for you to be around such magic."

I nod, not fully understanding.

"Thank you. Now, please, you should return to your room.

There is much to prepare for," she says, turning back the way we came. I watch as she walks back into the room with the red door. The greenhouse. I chew on my lip as my brain reels through all the new questions that have emerged in my mind.

Instead of pursuing the answers, I turn back toward my room.

I hesitate outside my door, feeling the guards' eyes on me. I don't want to go back into my room, trapped there alone.

I turn around without any idea of where I'm going when suddenly, I find myself outside the guest quarters. Kai's room. Without any second thoughts, I knock on the door.

Kai opens it easily, his face turning from apathy to surprise in an instant.

"Astrid, what are you doing here?" he asks, looking past me.

"I'm alone." I shake my head and clarify, "I was sick of staying alone in my room, so I wanted to come say hello."

He smiles winningly, sending my heart into frantic beats. I smile back at him, and he gestures inside.

"Are you sure this is allowed?" he asks.

"Well, if I'm to be queen, I don't see why not!"

He laughs. I look around and see Lilith asleep on the bed. I chew the inside of my cheek.

"Come in here, where we can talk," he says, pointing to the foyer. I follow him into the adjoined room. "How are you?"

"I'm fine, thank you," I say politely. "And you?"

"I've been better," he says, twiddling his thumbs. He takes a seat at the small table, and I follow suit. "I haven't left the room in days."

"Well, at least you have someone to talk to," I say, eyeing Lilith.

"I suppose. I've wanted to talk with you, though."

I smile, nodding along softly. After a moment of silence, Kai starts, looking uncomfortable.

"Astrid…how did you know about your mother? Did you know back at Feilfri?" Kai asks awkwardly.

"Did you?" I ask, watching his reaction.

"No, of course not. I had no idea. I never met your mother," he says, and his expression is genuine. I exhale in relief. "I heard rumors about my father and the kidnapping, but I didn't believe it to be true. My father never spoke about the war. Even when he talked to be about politics and what I needed to know about being king. He never mentioned the war. I thought it was over fifty years ago."

"When he killed my grandmother," I whisper.

"I guess," he says, fidgeting in his chair.

I give him a sad smile. "It's okay, Kai. I didn't know either. I found out when the bartender at Gamvik tavern mentioned I looked like King Haakon. I asked him about the story, and when things looked like they matched up with my mother's story, I took a chance. Thema explained there's a prophecy they've seen in visions every year about my return."

"Wow," he breathes. "I had no clue. I wonder if Alheri knew."

"I do too," I reply. "I don't think she did, though. Thema said she only heard from Alheri that we were coming and to look for us."

Kai nods, his eyes darting back and forth as he thinks everything through. I smile warmly and grab his hands, comforted by the familiarity of his touch. He looks up and returns my smile, stroking the back of my hand with his thumb.

"I also…well…" I take a breath. "I wanted to thank you."

"For what?" he whispers.

"For everything, really. You sacrificed your whole life to bring me here. You gave up your crown. And you protected me. You served me and brought joy to my life when I thought everything was hopeless. You saved me."

He smiles, dropping his eyes to the floor. He does this when he's embarrassed or shy. It's a trait I find quite endearing. I take one of my hands out from our grasp to touch my fingers to his cheeks, and he makes a warm sound.

"I'm sorry I couldn't give you what you wanted," he whispers.

"I know," I say, understanding his words. "I'm sorry, too."

"I really wanted to…"

"I know that, too. It's alright, Kai. It doesn't change the way I feel," I say, but then quickly amend, "I'm forever grateful to you."

He looks up at me, and I let my eyes roam across his face, cherishing the way his silver eyes glint in the light. His black hair is washed and clean now, almost fluffy as it drapes around his face. His skin is pale, and his eyelashes are stark black against it. This is the Kai I remember most fondly – next to the wild, cliff-diving Kai. This is the way he was when I first met him. When he was awkward and confused, unsure of his place in the kingdom. He would sleep so peacefully and talk with me so easily, like no other in the entire castle except maybe Alheri. He made me feel so special.

When my eyes meet his again, I see him mirroring me, looking over my face with a light smile on his lips. I wonder what he's thinking. Does he see me differently, now that he knows my background, my history? Or does he still think of me as the small, simple servant from the dark hallways of Feilfri Castle? The girl obsessed with embroidery and dyeing fabric, who only wanted to serve him in every way possible?

Ironically, I feel closer to him now than ever before. And I can never let him know how much I want him. Because he feels so strongly that he will hurt me, I can't ask that of him. I won't hurt him like that.

A knock on the door sounds and a guard opens the door.

"Princess," he says loudly, rousing Lilith from her sleep.

"I should go," I whisper, not looking away from his face. I wish I could stay forever with him.

"Okay," Kai says, swallowing hard as his face tightens slightly.

"I'll come back," I say quickly, standing to leave.

"Astrid." He grabs my hand. "When I leave, I will find a way to become that man. The man you need me to be."

My eyes are wide, and I feel my smile fade into something different.

"You know where I'll be," is all I can manage out before my throat closes up.

"I promise," he whispers.

I nod and turn away, making it out the door before breaking into a strangled cry.

After several more days of waiting, Thema finally comes and whisks me quickly into a large chamber hall. Several people are gathered around a long table, talking amongst themselves. My chest is tight, both from the corseted dress and from the nerves of meeting my new kingdom's ruling council. My heart beats uncertainly as Thema speeds us up, placing me at the head of the table, where everyone can see me.

Suddenly, the room is quiet, and all eyes are on me. I gulp down a staggering breath that feels like it doesn't even make it all the way to my lungs.

"Thema, who is this?" someone speaks up. I realize I have my eyes closed. I pop them open, taking in each face around the table. It's an older woman asking. I watch Nyarai take a seat in the back of the room, keeping her eyes on me.

"Ladies and gentlemen," Thema announces, and I swallow

against the nervous bile creeping up my throat. "This is Astrid Haakondatter. Yes, you heard me correctly. This is the granddaughter of Haakon the Great and Inger Johana."

Gasps and wide eyes plague the faces surrounding the large meeting table. I try to smile, but my face feels like ice as I meet the eyes of the people gawking at me. Before Thema has the chance to say anything else, the room bursts into loud exclamations of joy, of confusion, and, most importantly, of relief. I'm clearly who she claimed me to be since I look so much like my grandparents. These people also clearly know the story about my mother and grandmother's kidnapping. Murmurs ripple through the crowd. Though the confusion rests now in who my father is – a question I haven't even considered until now.

Thema holds up her hand, seeing my expression turn more and more overwhelmed. The room quiets quickly, and I sigh softly with relief.

"Astrid, dear, please tell us your story," Thema asks pleasantly, taking a seat. The rest of the group follows her lead and sits, still staring widely at me.

"Um," I start, gulping down a nervous breath. "I honestly don't remember everything properly. My memories have been tampered with…" I hesitate, waiting for questions, but no one speaks. So, I continue, "I was born and raised in Feilfri Castle. My mother was Hanna, but I didn't know her very well. My memories of her are very limited. I don't know who my father was. My guess is that my mother was pregnant when she was taken." My voice breaks on the last word, but I keep going.

"I was mostly raised by the castle witch Alheri, and I served Baldassare as a castle *thrall*." I will not acknowledge that he was king. Not anymore. "Upon my seventeenth year, I was assigned to be Prince Kai's personal *kvinne*…um, as his servant," I clarify. "I was only in service of the prince for a few days before he left the castle, taking me with him. He brought me across the Ødemark wastelands until we reached Menneskelig."

I stop, feeling like it's enough. Nyarai's eyes fixate on me with a different expression than the rest of the congress. She looks confused, perturbed, like something doesn't match up. I try looking elsewhere, at the rest of the faces in the room, but they all seem like a blur.

No one says anything, so I look at Thema with pleading eyes.

"Fascinating," she says quickly, seeing my discomfort. "So, Prince Kai gave up his own reign to escort you to the capital. Does he expect he'll be able to return to Livsnerven?"

Her words confuse me. Like she is convinced he won't be *able* to return.

"No, no," I answer. "He disliked the kingdom very much. He wanted to leave."

"Surely he wishes to return and take up his crown?" she prods.

"I don't think so." My voice is distorted with some unseen strangling force. Thema eyes me eagerly, and for a moment, I see Nyarai's eyes flick from my face to her twin witch's face. I close my mouth with a small popping sound, unable to say more. Whether by choice or lack of words, I don't know.

Then, Thema claps her hands loudly together, and the congregation snaps out of their silence. "Well! This has all been very interesting, indeed. But it's no matter! You are here now," she purrs, her alto voice like black silk. "We shall certainly celebrate your return. Menneskelig shall have a ball!"

The rest of the audience agrees with her happily. Their faces no longer show any concern or questions. I blink at the sudden change in the atmosphere but smile sheepishly at the excitement.

In a whirlwind, I'm being whisked back towards my room with a handful of commotion around me. There are members of the council running around, shouting orders at various servants about decorations, food preparation, and "getting the word out." It seems as though the entire city will know I've returned by the end of the day.

"This all seems so easy," I confide in Thema.

"What do you mean, Princess?"

"Shouldn't they have had more questions? Weren't they curious about me at all?" I ask, unable to help myself. It seems like everything has been a dream since arriving here. Like time is moving in a blur around me.

She chuckles deeply, a hearty chest-laugh. "As I told you, Astrid, our city has been desolate and hopeless for many years. We've kept them in suspense about your return, but now that you are here, with my commendation, they will accept you as you are."

With her commendation? What does that mean? If Thema had rejected me the day we arrived, would we have been cast aside? Or *killed*?

I gulp.

Sitting at my vanity once more, Thema takes position behind me, and a low hum buzzes in my ears. My eyes lock with my face in the mirror, and I notice my vision unfocus and refocus several times as she speaks.

"Kai is the crowned prince to a kingdom of monsters. He has worked with Baldassare for decades, plotting his kingdom's rise to power. Baldassare kidnapped your mother and killed your grandparents, which Kai was privy to. He knew everything and *kept* it from you."

The low hum digs deeper into my head, shaking my vision as I listen. My heart throbs against the words, and I try to push past the stupor that the hum tries to envelop me in. I can't fight it. I close my eyes, welcoming the sleepiness that threatens to pull me under.

Nightmares play behind my eyelids. Kai's face is twisted into a monstrous gaze as he rips into my throat, feeding on me countless times over the past week. And before, in the castle, I see myself cowering in his room, waiting for him to return and use me for his selfish desires. I feel his compulsion confuse my thoughts and turn my willpower into dust with a simple command. I remember how he stole me away, convincing me that he wanted me to be "free." I remember Alheri healing me time and time again, prying my hands off of the massive wounds in my neck, speaking quickly and quietly, trying to knit my skin back together.

No, this can't be right. Kai would never—

But then, the hum fights and takes back over. I can vaguely hear Thema whisper in my ear, and the memories continue to flash, haunting me. I remember Baldassare and Queen Eileen hosting feasts and feeding frenzies, hunting captured humans and massacring them in front of us, their servants. We are forced to stay there, helpless as we watched our friends and family die.

I remember my mother's beautiful hair, the same as mine. I see her brushing through my hair, humming that ever-familiar tune when I see Kai and Caden enter the room. Kai, as beautiful and graceful as ever, ignoring my screams as he rips into my mother's neck, feeding until she's dry. His eyes glow crimson red, and his mouth is stained with her blood. I remember Caden and Alheri's mother shouting, yelling at him to stop. Feeding on a human is forbidden, I try to say! But I can't stop it. I watch as Kai drains my mother, dropping her to the floor with a sickening thud, her skin grey and lifeless. I cry out, watching the memory over and over again. I can't stop it from rooting into my brain.

I open my eyes, brushing soundless tears from my eyes. I can't meet the eyes of my reflection any longer, afraid of what I might see. All my thoughts of ceremonies and glamorous balls fade quickly from my mind. All thoughts of Kai's gentle tenderness have been whisked away in an instant. I want to crawl into bed and sleep away the pain.

"What is this?" I cry, feeling my chest ache as I sob.

"I'm just showing you the *truth*, Princess. These are your memories. Hidden from you for a long time. I'm simply unlocking them and showing them to you," Thema whispers, laying her hand on my shoulder.

"Why?" I choke.

"To show you what monsters vampires are. To show you the truth," she says.

I sob and wrap my hands around my chest, black spots appearing as I cry so hard, I feel I might vomit. After a while, Thema leaves me in peace, and my tears turn to anger.

I stand and start toward Kai's room, slamming my door behind me.

32
KAI

The castle is alive with commotion for Astrid's crowning ceremony and gala. People from all over Menneskelig bustle through the doors, carrying various decorations, cakes, presents. I've never seen people move around so much. It's the third day now that I've been holding my breath, whether consciously or not. I have no room to feel thirsty in a place like this.

Nyarai and Thema's grip on the council and rulers of the city has me worried and confused at the same time. The fact that they are sisters is shockingly confusing. They look similar, I suppose, but the way they hold themselves, the way they speak, differs completely. Remembering back to Thema's glare, I can't help but think she's dangerous. I admit I'm terrified of leaving Astrid alone. And now Thema is to be her personal *heks*. What does that mean for Astrid's wellbeing? Will this witch try to influence her the way Alheri had? For my sanity's sake, I have to believe that this is a better place for Astrid. Going off pure instinct, I know for a fact that Thema is not the same caring and loving person that Alheri had been. I have to believe that being amongst her own kind, safe from the obvious predators in the world, is surely better.

Lilith stirs on the bed, lightly snoring before settling back into a deep sleep. I peek at her relaxed face, void of any of the stress of the previous day. She had obviously worried that Nyarai could sense her pain of losing William. I scratch idly at the stone windowsill. She is going through, arguably, the worst kind of pain a vampire could endure. But she isn't bound to immortality like I am, so someday she will be released from this life. Maybe she will meet her William in the next one.

I sigh. Immortality is something I often stray away from. I don't want to accept the fact that I might be wandering this earth alone, wreaking havoc whenever I'm hungry enough.

There's a light tapping on the door. I sprint to it quickly, hoping not to wake Lilith from her peaceful slumber.

I wrench the large wooden door open to find Nyarai again, with a much more relaxed smile than I'd seen before.

"Yes?"

"I'd hoped I could speak privately with you, Prince," she addresses me formally, though she should know that I'm certainly no longer a prince.

"Sure," I reply casually, stepping out of the room quietly.

She leads me silently to the front of the castle, then to the side, where there's a large door leading to an outdoor garden. She steps into the light, looking back at me.

"Um," I ask, unsure of going out into the faux sunlight.

"You will be safe, Kai. There's no need to fear," she says, reaching her hand out, beckoning me outside. I take a deep breath, stepping into the light.

I expect to feel some kind of pain in the sunlight. Being burnt by the sun is something I will never forget. I had played too close to the door as a child when the weather had turned unusually sunny. When I stumbled out into the sunlight, both curious and scared, I experienced a ripping sensation across every pore. I shiver, thinking about how the sun had erupted my skin into invisible flames. It was the kind of pain that stuns, so if my mother hadn't been so close by, I would have perished in the fire.

Standing in the light now, I don't feel fire, no pain at all. My vision is clear, and I can see through the sunlit dome. Menneskelig sits on a large mountain, so I feel like I can see over the walls and through to the woods. I unthinkingly gasp in awe of the beauty of the city, it's people hustling to and fro, alight with the new information that their lost princess has returned. Not only that, but the architecture and ingenuity of the city's design are incredible. Not to mention the vibrant colors that are cast across the various shades of stone from the crystal sun dome.

"Do you like my city?" Nyarai asks nonchalantly, strolling ahead of me. She lightly touches the plants in the garden, and whether I'm imagining things or not, it seems like the plants respond. A flower blooms, eager for her touch. It takes me a moment to find my voice again.

"Yes," I breathe. "I never knew Menneskelig was so beautiful."

"Hmm," she hums, moving towards a weeping willow tree. It's leaves bend down to touch her cheek. She seems completely vulnerable with her trees and flowers. It's almost too intimate to watch. "Tell me something, Kai."

"Yes?"

"Why did you leave? Why did you come here?"

"You mean, why did I give up my crown?" I ask, not avoiding the real question.

"Yes, you did give up your crown," she says, a statement

rather than a question.

"How did you know I was the prince of Livsnerven?"

"I've been in contact with Alheri this morning. We've been talking for a while now. She reached out to us after you and Astrid first left Feilfri Castle."

I nod.

"So, I don't understand," Nyarai starts, sitting down on a wrought iron bench. "If you were to be crowned, to take Baldassare's place as king, why did you leave?"

"Would you be surprised if I told you it wasn't planned?" I debate internally how much information I want to share with the witch. Her mouth twitches, but she doesn't respond. I clear my throat, eyeing her closely, then sit gingerly on a stone flower bed, placing my elbows on my knees. I sigh loudly, deciding to trust this witch.

I tell her of my repulsion of my father's lifestyle, how I would abstain for days, weeks, before feeding again. I tell her of my first moment seeing Astrid's golden-red hair, how her blood sang to me louder than any other human in the castle. I tell her how my father mistook my obsession with Astrid's wellbeing for greed.

"He made her my personal servant, my *kvinne.* At first, I was angry. How could I abstain properly if I had a living person in my room, in my *mind* at all times?" I huff, still angry. "But then my mother told me how she lived peacefully with her own servant. How she loved him..."

Nyarai's face remains smooth and composed, but I can see a flicker of understanding in her eyes.

"So, I tried to live with myself. I tried to keep her safe. But she was *relentless.* I'm sure you know about Alheri's 'help.'"

Nyarai nods once, her eyes sliding closed, and her hands visibly more stressed.

"Well, Astrid threw herself at me time and again, both body

and blood. But I lived through it. I was surprised to find her scent more reassuring rather than tempting. I knew I had to help her. I couldn't see her harmed, I —"

I pause for what feels like a long time to me.

"I love her," I breathe.

At this, Nyarai's face softens, a light smile on her lips, her eyes still closed. Like the tension slipped away from her body.

I gulp down the sudden choking of tears and breathless lungs and continue, "So, when my brother attacked her, I fled. I took her away from the pain and suffering. I had thought of running before, but I thought I should stay and try to help the kingdom. I thought maybe if I was king, I could affect change to help the humans and other vampires in Livsnerven."

"Power can change people," Nyarai responds, her voice solid.

"Yes," I whisper, thinking of Caden. He wasn't always so evil. "At Feilfri, resisting blood is a prison sentence, both physically and mentally. I could barely stand it, and I spent all my time in my bedroom."

She muses on my words for a moment before continuing her line of questioning.

"Tell me," she starts. "Why are you still here? Why have you not asked to leave again?"

I blink, taken aback. It's not like I hadn't wondered why Lilith and I hadn't been released. We were basically caged inside that room, without any instructions or questions about Astrid or the upcoming plans.

"Truthfully, I don't want to leave," I say, selfishly. "I don't want to leave her."

"I see the purity in your heart, Prince," Nyarai says, nodding and humming low in her throat. "But you've entered a dangerous place. Being the crowned prince of Livsnerven, Menneskelig might not welcome you."

My heart tightens at the words, and I slant my eyes at her. Her gaze is stoic and unflinchingly hard. Is she warning me or threatening me? Is she talking about the city's residents or *Astrid*?

Before I can respond, she stands, her leather robes dragging behind her as she walks back towards the castle. I follow, afraid of being in the light without her.

"I advise you to get dressed for the ball, Kai," she says, not turning back to face me. "You're a guest of honor. You should look the part."

I swallow hard, trying to imagine myself in a room with thousands of humans, pretending to be one of them. The thought of trying to fool them leaves me wondering if the humans will see right through us. Is that the meaning of Nyarai's warning? Will tonight be a turning point? Will Lilith and I perish in an angry mob? Or will we truly be treated as honored guests?

I reach the doors to the castle, not pausing to look back at Nyarai's retreating figure before heading back to my room, walking rigidly as I consider the meaning behind Nyarai's questions.

I look around at the bright walls of the castle as I think. It's unsettling, feeling like it should be dark outside. There hasn't been a proper night in days, and I feel the strange sense that it's summer instead of winter outside. The ever-present golden-bright dome illuminates the castle every second, a prison of daylight.

When I turn the corner, I see Astrid outside my door. My face brightens in an instant, thinking she's come back for another visit, like last night. But when I open my mouth to greet her, she finds me, and her face is a strange mix of horror, fear, and grief. Her eyes are bloodshot, and her cheeks are splotchy red.

"Astrid? What's wrong?" I say, rushing to her side, but when I reach out to touch her, she flinches away from me. Her eyes search my face for something. "Astrid?"

She doesn't say anything but opens her palm to unfold a piece of thick grey fabric. I watch her in panicked curiosity. When she holds up the canvas toward me, I recognize it as a painting. It's cracked and faded, but still clearly a picture of a woman. A very beautiful woman.

"Who is this?" I ask, reaching out to take the painting from her. I study it closer, seeing hints of Astrid in the woman. "Is this your mother?"

"Don't you recognize her?" Astrid says with a cracked, haunted voice.

"Not more than seeing how you bear her resemblance," I say with a questioning tone.

"That is my grandmother. Inger Johana. She was my mother's mother and carries the same traits that flow through me."

"I can see—"

"Don't you *recognize* her, Kai?" Her tone is biting.

I shake my head quickly, waiting for her to explain. She bites down on her lip like she's trying to keep herself together.

"My mother, Kai. Who killed my mother?"

"Astrid, please," I say, pulling her inside my room. Luckily, Lilith is not in the main room. "How would I know that? You know I was just a boy when your mother died."

"Yes," she says, ripping her arm away from me. "Listen to me, Kai, and *please* tell me if I'm mistaken. This can't be right…"

"Explain, Astrid, please. I want to help."

"You said that every vampire is born into the world, screeching and searching for blood, that if they don't feed correctly when they are young, they turn into wild halvblods."

"Yes, much like the ones that attacked us outside the city."

"You told me that as every vampire grows, they change and mature, finding a balance between civility and instinct," she explains, her tone desperate.

"Yes, that's all correct."

Her face shrivels up, and tears start flowing from her eyes.

"Please tell me I'm wrong," she whispers through her choked throat.

"About what? Please tell me, Astrid!"

"Did you…" A cry cuts her off. "Did you kill my mother?"

I frown and rear away from her. How could she think such a thing?

"How can you ask me that? You know I haven't fed on a living human in over a decade."

"Then tell me, because I can't bear this, Kai. Who killed her? Who killed my mother?"

"I don't know! I couldn't possibly…" I trail off, finally seeing the meaning in her words. Her mother died at the time I was still maturing. When I was still ruled by my senses. I wrack my brain for memories, anything that might help. I try to remember a woman that looks like the painting. Could I have known Hanna?

"You told me the last person you fed on was a woman, a red-haired woman," she says weakly.

"I couldn't have," I whisper. Shock courses icily through my veins, making me shiver.

She shoves the painting into my face with malice.

"Look, Kai! Really look! And tell me you didn't kill her because I remember! I remember watching you drain her blood to the point of her death. I remember your black hair and red eyes. I remember Caden was there and Alheri's mother," she shouts.

I look closely at the painting, trying to remember what that woman had looked like, but my mind is blank. All I remember is the taste of her blood and the excruciating pain that followed.

"Oh, my God," Astrid whispers, her face a wreck of emotion.

"I don't know, Astrid. I can't remember her face," I admit

painfully. Shamefully. "She did have red hair, and there were two girls in the room with us. I remember feeding, then the horrible curse of killing her."

"I can't breathe," she says, heaving in large breaths.

I reach out to her, but she pulls away with a savage glare.

"Don't touch me," she snaps.

"Astrid, please!"

"I remember it," she breathes. "I remember you killing her. I remember how you fell to the floor afterward and suffered like she suffered. I remember feeling sorry for you!"

"Astrid! I didn't know!"

"Get away from me, Kai. You are *nothing* to me now! I can't believe I ever trusted you! And cared for you! You made me care so much for you, and now everything is ruined. I can't even look at you," she curses, starting toward the door.

I grab her arm and pull her back to me, unwilling to let her go.

"Let me go!"

"Astrid, you have to believe me. That was the worst day of my life. I still think about it and how awful I felt. Please, say you believe me. I would never have done this if I thought I would hurt you—"

"But it would have been okay if it was someone else's mother?" she snaps. "Just as long as it didn't interfere with *our* love story?"

She rips away her arm, leaving my hand feeling like it's been shocked with lightning.

"Astrid, I didn't mean to hurt you," I cry.

"I know, Kai," she admits. "But that's what makes this infinitely worse. You're a vampire. You just can't help it."

With that, she turns on her heel and storms out the door, leaving me breathless and broken, watching after her with tearstained eyes.

33
Astrid

I stare into the bronze mirror, stunned at my appearance. They dressed me in a pale pink silk robe with a wildly embellished stomacher and petticoats that extend the gown out several paces from my actual body. My hair is done up in tight curls piled on the top of my head. They had tried to place feathers and beads in my hair, but suddenly it was too much, and I ordered them away, feeling lightheaded and smushed in my corset. I look like a complete stranger.

I feel the large pleats of my robe lie flat against the back of my neck and shoulders, hanging effortlessly down all the way to the floor. The smooth silk does nothing to hide the sweat that's breaking out in small wet beads on my skin. I take a few deep breaths and try to wipe my forehead, but it's too late.

I'm being whisked out of my bedroom, walking briskly toward the throne room. People bow as we pass, and one of the maids is still trying to paint makeup onto my pale face. I shift my eyes back and forth nervously, trying to find a familiar face, anything familiar, but come up short. Thema had told me she would meet me at the throne room, but she didn't warn me about the throng of people that would surround me until then.

Claustrophobia claws at my chest, and I feel sick with so many people bustling around me. I've never been around this many people at once in my entire life.

Luckily, I'm distracted by the decor of the throne room as soon as we burst through the massive double doors. The place has been completely transformed, with gold and silver banners, bouquets of flowers on every flat surface, and food being carried from the kitchens in heaps. My stomach gurgles hungrily, seeing the large roast of lamb. I look away, my eyes straying to the head of the room.

The throne.

It's a large, golden chair with a deep red velvet covering the cushioned sections, tufted against the back of the chair. Sitting on a pedestal next to the throne is a large, glistening crystal crown and a staff made of metal and rubies. My heart sputters caustically as I zero in on the suddenness of this moment.

I will be crowned Queen of Menneskelig today. How did that happen? Hadn't I just wanted to be free of the vampires?

My face contorts into an uncomfortable grimace thinking of them. My brain flickers from confusion to anger to fear as I consider my life over the past few months. How did I come from being a servant of Baldassare to the queen of his enemies so quickly?

"Astrid, dear," Thema approaches, out of nowhere, grabbing my hand and smiling warmly at me. "Please don't be afraid. I know this is a lot and very sudden, but you have nothing to fear. You'll be a wonderful queen."

I try to smile at her, to let her know I appreciate her reassurance, but I can't respond because she pulls me to her side, careful not to disturb my gown. I watch wordlessly as the members of the council enter the room, all dressed very formally. I see the servants and attendants finish setting up quickly. For a moment, I'm wondering why we're simply standing in the middle of the throne room, but then I hear them.

Nyarai stands at a different set of doors, leading outside, on the opposite end of the room as the throne. I hear a low rumble of shouting and singing outside and swallow hard against my fear. Thema begins to walk me toward the doors, and two guards open them, stepping outside to protect me as I take my place on the small balcony.

I walk until I'm shrouded in blinding sunlight. A high-pitched ringing sounds in my ears, drowning out the cheers of the massive crowd below me. My legs are numb, and my lips feel like they are buzzing. I look around and realize that Thema is no longer at my side. I'm alone, standing on the terrace, in front of my new kingdom. I reach out and grab the railing of the balcony to steady myself.

I can't hear anything but the sound of my own breathing and the ringing in my ears, but before I can blink, someone is placing something on my head. I freeze, assuming I'm now wearing the crystal crown I saw next to the throne. The man that placed the crown on me meets my eyes with a sympathetic expression. I try to smile, figuring it looks more like a grimace. He hands me the ruby staff, and with an announcement, the crowd goes berserk.

"Queen Astrid the Triumphant!" they all shout in unison, cheering and screaming and singing my name.

I feel weak. Had I ever accepted my rule as queen? I can't remember even *asking* to be queen.

But before I can even think about it, I'm whirled off the balcony and back into the throne room. Someone takes the crown off my head, replacing it with a small, more manageable silver band that sits lightly on my forehead. I sigh, relieved that I won't have to wear the heavy one all night.

The staff is a welcome addition to my ensemble because as I walk, I use it to steady myself from the onslaught of emotions that course through me. And suddenly, I come face to face with the throne. My throne. Nyarai and Thema and standing on either side, watching me with opposite expressions as I gawk at the gold and red chair.

Behind me, the room sounds with guests arriving, taking their places at the large decorated tables. I turn to face them, and some of the guests come straight towards me, placing flowers and presents at the base of the small stairs. I look down on them with speechless confusion. Why are they bowing? Don't they know I'm one of them? They shower me with words that I still can't hear over the anxiety ringing in my head. I look around, feeling rude for not thanking each of them for their gifts. I can't stand it; the overwhelming urge to run away is too strong. I look at Thema with a meaningful expression before turning away from her towards the kitchen.

Or, at least I *think* that's where I'm going, but I open the side door only to find another hallway. At least there doesn't seem to be anyone here, outside the ballroom.

I heave my breaths in and out, trying to grasp at the air, but it doesn't seem to reach my lungs. I feel lightheaded and overwhelmed, the lights are a little too bright, the smells of the food and flowers a little too strong.

"Astrid?" a familiar voice cuts through the ringing in my ears, and my gaze shoots up.

In the middle of the empty hallway stands Kai, looking incredibly handsome. He's dressed to perfection, his black hair slicked back into a low ponytail with a few strands framing his face. He's wearing a loose-fitting white shirt with navy satin pants that hug his legs. Over his shirt, he's wearing a dark overcoat that looks closer to black than navy in the flickering hallway lanterns. His boots are laced up to his kneecaps, and he wears a decorative scarf around his neck.

It seems he didn't bother to lace his shirt up all the way because a hint of skin peeks through a small opening by his neck.

My heart, already beating chaotically, starts pulsing at a million beats a minute as I look him up and down again and again. I've never seen him look so striking. I pause on the small opening in his shirt, not wanting to meet his eyes. My brain is screaming *danger* at me, but my heart can't convince my body to move. I'm frozen in place as he slowly walks towards me, his hands reaching out towards me almost in surrender.

I meet his eyes unwillingly, and my heart almost jumps out of my throat onto the floor for him. His eyes are warm charcoal, like hot chocolate in winter, but that means he's close to thirst. His expression is relief and confusion and pain all washed together over his sheepish smile. I want to run into his arms and have him take me far away, back to our cliff, away from all this nonsense.

It's been days since I found out about my mother, and I've done everything to convince myself that my feelings for Kai are a product of his compulsion or Baldassare's brainwashing, but I can't. I can't shake the feeling of betrayal and pain that came from severing ties with Kai. I've been plagued with a constant recollection of all the *good* we've been through. How he sang with me in the middle of the snow, or how he'd recklessly jumped us off a cliff. I can't stop remembering how much I love hearing him talk about history or how I felt when his lips touched mine.

Amid the panic and realizations of everything that has happened to me, Kai was a constant. He was steady. The only time I felt remotely afraid of him was our last night in the tavern and when I learned about my mother.

Panicked at my horrible line of thinking, I turn swiftly away from him. I've seen what a true monster he is in my memories. I can *not* afford to be fantasizing about running away with him. I am a queen now. I won't think about Kai again.

"Astrid, please," he whispers, his voice strained, breaking my heart, but I keep walking. I turn the corner, finally finding the kitchens.

I walk in, and the whole staff stops working, watching me with wide eyes.

"What?" I ask, suddenly furious at their response. "Keep working!" I order, and they move again, not looking in my direction anymore. I realize I'm not angry at the staff. If anything, I feel helpless that I'm not working amongst them.

No. I'm outraged at that *monster* outside. Kai and his family have taken everything from me. His family is the entire reason I wasn't raised as a princess, the reason I don't have any family left.

He is the reason my mother is dead. He's the reason I am utterly alone in this castle.

"My Queen," Nyarai's low voice speaks from behind me. I whirl on her, my flare of anger not diminishing as I face her peaceful expression. "I must remind you that Prince Kai gave up his own throne to see you safely returned to your rightful place."

What the hell is with all these witches reading my mind?!

"He means nothing to me," I bark at her, pushing past two servants, knocking them aside with my large dress, before exiting back to my throne room.

34
KAI

"You look good," I say to Lilith when she appears in the doorframe of the washroom. She's dressed in a pale blue gown, reminding me of Astrid's favorite dress. Her hair is piled up in uncharacteristic curls on the top of her head, and it takes me a moment to realize that she's painted her face with some sort of makeup. Her lips are a shade darker than usual, and her cheeks look rosy, something that most vampires go without.

"Thanks," she says mechanically, looking me over with a surprised expression. "You ready for this?"

I give her a calm shrug, unsure.

"Are we supposed to wait for Nyarai?" Lilith asks, sliding on a pair of white silk gloves.

"I don't think so. I assumed she'd be with Astrid for the rest of the evening," I say. In the same breath, I take a step and peak outside the doors, meeting the gaze of one of the guards outside. "Are we free to attend the celebration, or do we wait?"

The guard says nothing but opens the door fully, cringing slightly away from me before extending out his arm towards the throne room. I take this to mean we're on our own.

I grab Lilith's arm, pulling her with me. I feel her tense with anxiety and check her face. That same haunted expression she's worn since the tavern returns. I expect this will be a difficult evening for her. I place my other hand on hers, holding her arm tightly in mine.

My ears catch the whiff of celebration before my nose does, and I clutch my last remaining breath inside. Being surrounded by humans will be difficult. Lilith must feel my tension because she turns and looks at me with an understanding expression.

"Just don't breathe. You'll be fine," she whispers to me, looking straight ahead again.

We walk slowly, in exaggerated movements, attempting to look casual and human-like. Lilith looks calm, and I realize that it won't be difficult for her. She's been living with humans. For her, this is just another day. I wonder if being around this many humans again makes her miss William more, though.

"Lilith?" a weak voice calls.

Lilith freezes at the sound, and I turn to see two older humans, maybe middle-aged, looking straight at us with horrified expressions. I look at Lilith's face, and the haunted expression turns caustic. She looks like she's about to be sick and burst into tears all at the same time.

"Lilith, is that you?"

I feel her gulp, but she finally turns to face the two humans. One is an older woman, clutching tightly to the man next to her. The woman looks dreadfully exhausted and red-eyed. The man seems no better, but he holds his composure as Lilith meets their eyes. The woman starts wailing in agony, tears streaming down her cheeks like she's already been crying. The man clutches at the woman, trying to keep her upright.

"Lilith, what *happened*? Willi—"

"Please," Lilith interrupts in a small voice. Tears slowly pour from her eyes.

My gaze darts back and forth from her to the couple. My brain feels fried, watching the complete agony rip between the two women.

"Lilith," I ask her quietly, knowing they can't hear me, "who are these people?"

She starts to reply, but something chokes off her words and a strangled sound whimpers from her chest. I've only seen her this upset once before.

Oh.

"William's parents," I breathe.

Sounds of complete despair pass through my ears, and I'm at a loss for words. I know the pain of loss, but only to an extent. Never have I lost a *child.*

Their expressions turn deadly as they face one another, Lilith's face in agony, Will's parents' full of vengeance.

In a flash, Lilith meets my gaze for just a moment, her glassy eyes piercing as she whispers, "I'm so sorry."

Then she is gone. She doesn't move at vampiric speeds but instead slowly runs away, William's parents mobilizing after her. I stand stark still, watching the scene unfold around them. I fidget, not sure what to do.

I hear movement inside the throne room, guests taking their seats. The coronation is finished. Astrid has been crowned Queen of Menneskelig, and I missed it.

I gulp, trying to steady my own emotions. I can't afford to be emotional while surrounded by so many fleshy humans.

Behind me, the door opens, and I turn towards it, intending to walk inside and take my assigned seat as the 'honored guest.'

When I look up, I catch the gaze of the woman I love the most.

"Astrid," I breathed, the air knocked out of my system at seeing her.

To say she looks beautiful is an embarrassing understatement. She looks *divine*. Her golden hair glows red under the flickering lantern light, and her eyes have never looked so blue before. Her face is painted with makeup, but her cheeks flush a light red as she takes my appearance in, and suddenly she's the most beautiful being on the planet. Aside from the perfect curve of her lips or her strong jawline, she looks older. Her face holds new lines — laughter lines and frown lines, crow's feet at her eyes, and a furrowed brow.

But the childish glint I've grown so accustomed to gleams in her bright blue eyes, the same as always. In a moment of innocence, I feel that her gaze is reminiscent of how she looked at me on our cliffside. After we jumped into the water when nothing surrounded us but the wilderness, she had looked at me with eyes that were... pure. Unashamed, unfiltered, and untamed. I remember thinking she looked the most real that night.

And, as I stand watching a million emotions pass over her expression, I think maybe she's thinking the same thing. Could she ever want to return to that state of our relationship? Will she ever want me that way again? I feel my heart pound, forcing my eyes away from her face so I can see the rest of her.

In a similar fashion as Lilith, Astrid is dressed in a tasteful pale pink gown, billowing out from the waist. She wears her hair in curls pinned to the top of her head, topped lightly with a simple silver crown that seems to twist in and out of her hair perfectly. She straightens as she watches me. She looks *better*. Her hair shines more. Her skin glows brighter. Her back is straighter, and she holds herself with more confidence.

On some level, I'm happy to see her thrive, but at the forefront of my brain, I can't help but note how she needs me less and less. I watch her face contort with some new feeling, and my heart feels like it's filled with tiny wooden splinters. She glares, shooting knives into my skin with her eyes, and I feel devastation tear through my chest as I read her plans in her face.

"Astrid," I try again, my voice cracking.

She swiftly turns and throws open the door to what looks like a kitchen.

Stunned silent, I have to force my body to move. I have to get inside and sit quietly, knowing that my carefully crafted exterior could shatter at any moment, and I will ravage the kingdom. As I push open the door that Astrid exited from just moments earlier, I feel the swell of heartbeats pulse all around me, like I'm underwater, and the heartbeats are currents pushing and pulling at me.

Red haze coats my vision in the same way it had so many years ago when I tore away the life from Astrid's mother. I gulp, aching while I hold my breath. The urge to bare my fangs and breathe in their scents is almost overwhelming. The dull ache in the back of my throat turns to exposed flame instantaneously.

I move to my predetermined place in the room, facing the throne from the far side of the room. I try to look around, to see the humans as more than just bodies, to see their faces as they laugh and talk with their neighbors, but I can't see anything. Their faces are invisible, and all I see is red where their blood pulses. I try to hear anything else—the distant ocean waves crashing against the mountain, the sizzle of the magical dome around the castle, the clicking of silverware on porcelain plates—but I can't. I only hear the pulsing of arteries, the clicking of teeth behind lips, the movement of fabric against skin. I close my eyes fiercely, willing my body to behave, knowing it was fool's hope I'd be able to function normally today, as thirsty as I already am.

Then, sounds of movement pull me out of my trance, and I realize that Astrid has taken her seat on the throne. Her expression is passive, smoothed to the point of apathy. A pit sits quietly in my stomach as I watch the audience call for her to speak. She holds a golden staff with rubies on the tip that she leans on heavily as she moves. She holds up a hand, silencing the audience.

Everyone in the room quiets in anticipation of their new queen's speech. All but a few voices remain. Astrid's attention is drawn towards the loud yells happening in the corner of the ballroom. I follow her gaze to see that she's staring at Lilith, who's still sobbing. William's parents are shouting at her, talking over one another, berating Lilith with an endless supply of confusing questions and angry expletives.

I shiver with anticipation. I know Astrid understands when her expression turns deadly. But only for an instant before it smooths back out again.

No, I think. *Please.*

"My people," she speaks, royalty ringing so surely in her voice that it startles me. I've never heard her speak so confidently. "I am so thankful that you've welcomed me home. To say that I'm happy would be a lie. I am exuberant. I am ecstatic. I am thrilled to be serving you as your queen." The last word rings with a thrilling sensation that the entire audience seems to feel.

Astrid stands, her dress billowing out, glowing pearlescent against the deep gold throne.

"I have traveled a long way," she says. The audience shuffles, intrigued by the mystery that brought Astrid back home. "I would like to say it was a happy journey, a safe journey. But it was not."

I swallow hard, bile biting at the back of my throat.

"I was *enslaved* by Baldassare for eighteen years. I've been raped." the audience gasps. "Fed on!" Another gasp and growl from the audience. "I've been abused by so many of the so-called nobles at Livsnerven and Feilfri Castle that I cannot recount every moment."

The crowd murmurs, the atmosphere tense with suspension.

"My memories have been tampered with, my body plagued with diseases, my blood turned against me," she says. "I had no way of escaping, save for Prince Kai."

She gestures toward me. Suddenly, every eye is on me. Of course, I can see all their faces *now*. Every face looks different. Some suspicious, some curious, some plain hateful.

"The crowned Prince of Livsnerven escorted me back to my rightful place, and he sits here as an honored guest," she explains lightly. Most of the eyes turn away from me, back to their queen. Several remain watching me, the most hateful of the eyes. "But his intentions were *not* pure."

The words flash heat into my body, and I flick my eyes back to Astrid's face. She looks angry, almost furious now.

"No, Prince Kai has used me in the worst ways. Now, with clarity of mind, I remember that he has fed on me, used me, raped me, and almost killed me, both at Feilfri Castle and on our journey to Menneskelig."

What?!

"He used his vampiric powers to erase my memories, replacing them with happy ones so I would stay with him. So I would *trust* him! How easily my mind was tampered with!" Astrid yells through her teeth. Her eyes dig into me like they are drilling into my brain, trying to kill me.

The audience is frenzied, the atmosphere turning against me. I can't look at them, though. I'm frozen solid, fixated on Astrid's hateful glare, pleading with her silently. *Don't do this.*

"Kai and his accomplice," she finishes, more calmly now and pointing straight to Lilith, and the eyes in the room flick away from me to her. I see all the color bleed from Lilith's face as she stands accused. "She murdered an innocent human being then confided in Kai as they attempted to lure me into the city. But Kai? He's the worst of all. He killed my mother, Hanna! *Your* lost princess! He fed on her right in front of me until she died in his arms, completely helpless to fight him off!"

Her words don't make any sense, but it doesn't matter. They serve their purpose.

The audience turns vile, gathering themselves for a fight. I realize I'm standing along with them, unsure of whether I should grab Lilith and run or if I even can. I peer out the double doors and see that the light still shines brightly outside. Even if I could run, there's no way I could get out of the city without burning to a crisp. In any case, my feet are molded to the ground. There's no getting out.

I meet Lilith's gaze for just a moment and see my horrified expression mirrored in her tear-streaked face.

"As your queen," Astrid continues on, the crowd growing wilder, "I call for the arrest of Prince Kai and his accomplice, Lilith, for crimes against the crown."

"MURDERER!" William's parents' screech.

Two guards appear from nowhere and pin my hands behind my back. I can see that Lilith has been taken as well, and I watch as someone throws their food at her face, staining her dress.

The audience is in chaos, swarming Lilith and I as I watch Astrid's face grow astonishingly smug. Rage flows off her in waves. Her face is twisted into a smile that isn't her own.

The men wrench me backward, and I gasp in pain. I know I can take these guards and try and make a run for it, but Astrid's gaze is still pinning me in place.

Please, I mouth to her, and her smug smile contorts into a deep grimace.

"Take them away!" she screams. "Tomorrow, we will begin our preparations!"

The guards start wheeling me away as I fight against their grip. I can hear Lilith screaming and the crowd shouting. They're still throwing food and debris at us.

"At dawn, we will rally our allies and begin our strategies. I *know* the enemy! I have seen all of his plans!" Astrid continues shouting, fueling the chaos, firing up the crowd even more.

The guards are wrenching me out of the room, struggling against my weak flailing. I hadn't realized I was screaming until we exit the room. I can still see Astrid through the double doors.

"I declare war on the vampires! Every human will fight. Every man and woman will help!" she screams. "We will *rid* this earth of the parasites and emerge victorious! I DECLARE WAR ON BALDASSARE!"

No, I yell helplessly in my head.

My body goes limp as I meet the gaze of Thema, smiling wickedly at me. My eyes briefly meet Nyarai's worried expression. Then, my sight gives out with some magic, and all I can hear is the slamming of the doors behind us before the darkness overwhelms me.

***

www.ingramcontent.com/pod-product-compliance
Lightning Source LLC
Chambersburg PA
CBHW020248030826
48979CB00030B/2660/J

* 9 7 8 1 7 3 5 1 4 4 7 0 2 *